ALSO BY J.L. HUGHES

R.A.Y. A Step Too Far
Dark Justice

PRAISE FOR DARK JUSTICE

Think homicide detectives don't take their work home-think again. Unravelling this criminal entanglement will leave you breathless.

HEATHER GRAHAM, *NEW YORK TIMES*
BEST SELLING THRILLER AUTHOR OF
THE *KREW OF HUNTERS* SERIES

To paraphrase Brad Pitt's character in the hit movie *Seven*, Ladies and Gentleman we have a Serial Killer!

JON LAND, *NEW YORK TIMES*
BEST SELLING THRILLER AUTHOR OF
THE *CAITLIN STRONG* SERIES

In DARK JUSTICE, a prolific serial killer's methods echo the murder of homicide detective Jade Carmichael's mother, launching her into a relentless pursuit. This story will keep you on edge, up late, and haunt you long after the final dark twist.

D.P .LYLE, AWARD-WINNING AUTHOR
OF THE *JAKE LONGLY* AND
CAIN/HARPER THRILLER SERIES AND
CO-CREATOR OF THE OUTLIERS
WRITING UNIVERSITY

DARK DIVIDE

DARK DIVIDE

BROKEN JADE
BOOK 2

J.L. HUGHES

ROUGH
EDGES
PRESS

Dark Divide
Paperback Edition
Copyright © 2025 by J.L. Hughes

Rough Edges Press
An Imprint of Wolfpack Publishing
1707 E. Diana Street
Tampa, FL 33610

www.roughedgespress.com

Editing by My Brother's Editor

Paperback ISBN 978-1-68549-369-1
eBook ISBN 978-1-68549-368-4
LCCN 2025939610

For my daughters, your strength shines so brightly it lights the world.

DARK DIVIDE

PROLOGUE

E xacting a method of killing didn't make it easier to execute. The stranglehold on Magdalene's neck, perfectly placed in the crook of his elbow, guaranteed pressure would result in her demise. Sensing the end, his tears snaked down his face, raw and unrestrained, dripping onto hers, cross contaminating. If detectives ever discovered the kill site, they would possess everything required to convict him of the crime and, being it was his third homicide, the death penalty was all but certain.

They'd never find it in time. He'd clean it and never face their version of justice.

The enemy they sought fit a profile he never could. He was so far off the radar he may as well have been on Mars. Untouchable. He watched every aspect of the case from afar and then, oh so near. It wasn't difficult to identify his victim pool. They swam freely in plain view, never fearing being recognized for the sharks they were. But he saw them. Caught their scent, targeted and eliminated each one, swiping them from their lives as cleanly as an eraser on a chalk-board but with less residue trailing. By the time police recognized a pattern, if ever, he'd be finished his mission and disappear. Not that any of them knew he existed in the first place.

What plagued him through his youth and into his adult life sheltered him now, the cloak of invisibility. He never stood out, never the quarterback or point guard though he could've crushed any on the team. Lace was the only one who didn't dismiss him, whose eyes lingered long enough to absorb. She was his for a time until...

He pushed her from his mind and held his grip.

Feeling the fight slip away and Magdalene's muscles go slack beneath his embrace, waves of grief, guilt, and horror served another brand of justice. One cutting an untraversable divide into the core of everything he once was.

What he was now was a killer...but he had good reason.

That fact didn't matter to Magdalene any more than it had her sister. Those who weren't privy to their whole story would say he was in no position to speak for either woman.

They'd be wrong.

ONE

T he gate was off its hinges and with every footfall, Jade knew it would never hang quite the same. Errie was gone. When Amy called, panic broke her voice the way only homicide detectives recognize as the herald of bad news. The kind you don't come back from, at least not the same. Jade paused before entering the home's inner yard, surveying the walkway with the eyes of a seasoned detective approaching a crime scene, though none had been officially determined. Pulling gloves from inside her jacket, she stretched them on. The Nitrile barrier, a new impenetrable layer of skin, dense and protective, smoothed over her hand but the need of them sent a sickening awakening down her throat, churning her guts and reverberating back up leaving an ache along its path. All of it telling her what she already feared.

Errie was taken, added to the collection.

From Shadow Hook's major crime division, Jade followed the case up the coastline as victims, stolen from their vacation homes, drew nearer to her beloved New York lake country. Crossing the porch, striding within view of the door to Errie's lake house, left ajar, she didn't want to admit the nightmare finally hit home.

Her phone vibrated in her back pocket. Amy, too terrified to wait for a response. Desperate to hear Jade give her shit for jumping to conclusions, egging her fiancée to bust her balls while the opportunity presented. Jade imagined Errie laughing at Amy's expense while brewing organic coffee, the beans brought from her family's farm in Colombia, a mix their cop shop had fallen in love with along with the trash-mouth ballerina one of their own was set to wed. But no coffee brewed in the open kitchen beyond the door. Inside, the dark roast aroma of home was under shadowed by a scent more sinister, blood.

Heel scrapes and drag marks smudged into scattered grains, stole center stage cutting from the butcher block to a couple feet inside the doorway. The path the Collector used to steal Errie from her home against her will. The mess of the floor said she'd put up a fight before being subdued and plucked off the mosaic tile to disappear into thin air. Jade stood frozen, absorbing every detail, knowing the next call she made would change everything and bring an onslaught of FBI involvement adding her to their already heated investigation.

The media played up every disturbing aspect of the case's previous abduction scenes leaving vulnerable woman ages twenty to thirty-five arming themselves and their homes. The victim pool thus far spanned from athlete to nurse, lawyer to unemployed, and now a ballerina. The crime scenes were identified by a calling card left behind. Varying ninth cards of a tarot deck, each one different, tailored to the victim's lifestyle, all signifying strength. Their captor studied his targets and came prepared. Jade held no illusions of the likelihood of Errie's safe return. All indications pointed to a seasoned, well-honed adversary capable of remaining hidden and lethal.

A recipe she was all too familiar with and one that nearly killed her. The year previous she fought for justice through a string of murders with the team and not one of them was spared deep penetrating scars. Those she wore were vivid and ran, literally, in her blood. This past case, that defined her, left many doubting her reinstatement and, worse, fearing her. The serial killer they unearthed ended up shot and comatose, survived an attack on his life while in hospital. The attempted murder case was ongoing, lacking evidence and a suspect.

This new aberration was of a different breed, none of the victims were discovered dead. So far, all were listed as abducted, taken by force, evident in the scenes left behind, like the one she stood in today.

On top of the wooden surface of the prep counter, smeared in spilled and splayed coffee grounds, sat a tarot card depicting a beautiful ballerina dancing surrounded by nine orbs of light. Jade didn't touch the card to inspect it further, she snapped photos with her phone of every aspect she could pull from the scene, zooming in on those most telling, like the odd smudge alongside the trail of blood from what appeared to be the area of initial confrontation.

Errie had smeared her left hand through coffee grinds and blood. At a glance, the mark was a desperate ploy to prevent forward motion, but to Jade's trained eyes it spoke of something more. Capturing every angle, she was caught off guard when Amy's third call sounded off in her hand.

She texted: Give me 3 mins. And kept working the scene.

Amy deserved the truth, but not until Jade was confident she could deliver it accurately. Skirting to the opposite side of the island, where Errie may have been confronted, Jade's eyes scanned from floor to ceiling and back. A splatter pattern from castoff stained a faint track over white boards, leading Jade's gaze to a discarded carving knife. Left strewn in a mess of torn burlap, the broken remnants of a grinder, and glass fragments, the knife appeared to have been dropped from a height. It bounced on impact, clear from impressions left behind. The blood may be the abductor's and not Errie's. If she cut him, she'd left crucial evidence. And he hadn't retaliated to the extent of ending her life, at least not here.

Jade placed a gloved hand gently on the steel kettle sitting on an extinguished gas burner. Warm.

Her first call wasn't to Amy. After initiating an All Points Bulletin before the federal boys got wind and stepped in to orchestrate the pursuit, she summoned their investigative wing to flood Amy and Errie's property. Better their own then a distant team with no emotional connection. Captain Grey muddied her thoughts. She wasn't certain he'd agree with her approach but he was never one for sharing and they had first rights to the scene until it was confirmed as part of the federal case and not a copycat kidnapping. Jade knew better; this was no imitator, and so would he. Before expanding her search to the heritage two-story's other rooms she stepped back outside and dialed.

"It's me, kid." Jade's eyes fought for something calm to focus on but all she envisioned reminded her of what was at risk. "I need you to sit down and stay calm." She heard Amy shuddered out a breath. "Errie is not here. He's got her. I'd say taken within the last hour. I need access to your security system and a grid search of CTV footage from every conceivable access point off this property. Can you do that?"

Jade waited. Knowing how she would respond, better to work it and stay privy to every step than go insane waiting on news.

"I'm here, I'll pull footage, send out—"

"It's done. Focus on access. We need a make, model, anything we can start running down. Okay?"

"Okay. Jade, I need you to find her. I need you to find her alive. Promise me you will not stop until you have her." Amy's voice dropped an octave and her tone carried the depth of her demand in ways words could not.

"Amy, I will not stop until I bring her home." Jade hung up, switched her phone back into camera mode, backed out of the property all the way to where her new rival entered their lives, and started gathering the pieces to bring him down.

The road accessing the area, recently swept clean by rain, offered little in the way of possible tire tracks to identify tread or vehicle model. Located on the far end of an isolated, heavily treed district, the parking allowance couldn't be viewed from neighboring properties. Unless an area resident, slightly paranoid, aimed their security camera beyond their drive to the roadway, set their system to record all movement, and the suspect crossed slowly enough to be recognizable, there'd be little to glean from personal security footage. Still, Jade made note of all possible addresses and aimed to be first questioning each.

Before retracing her steps back into the home, Jade stood before the broken gate intending to see what her adversary did. Distance and thick foliage dampened sound and distorted visual access weighing in his favor. No secondary vehicles crowded the street ensuring with relative accuracy Errie had been alone inside. At this time of day Amy would typically be at the shop. Did he know? Was he aware he broke into the home of a detective? Junior, yes, but a damn fine detective, nonetheless. This fact may have been missed with his focus on his prey and no other.

The one fact Jade didn't question, he picked the wrong victim.

When Jade's phone sounded the next time, she couldn't ignore the caller.

"Amy's a mess. Are you certain it's him, the one running the coast?" Grey's voice held no disdain. She was right to activate.

"It's him. I didn't tell Amy; he left his calling card on the counter. I could be wrong but it looks like she got him with a knife during the struggle. We may have his DNA. I called in our team so we could safeguard the scene."

"I figured. The federal boys will take it over. There's no way to stop them but I'll do everything I can to keep you involved. Find me something to steer this our way."

He hung up and Jade moved methodically and quickly through the scene. The conflict didn't extend past the kitchen and entry. Upstairs, nothing was disturbed. She maneuvered from room to room, detail to detail, catlike and laser focused on possible clues. Her sweep of the interior landed her back in the kitchen when the crime scene crew pulled in. Backing out of their incoming unit, she sidestepped the blood smear and froze hovering over it from a new angle. Something about it initially plagued her; at this vantage point she recognized the brave brilliance of Errie in her fight for survival. Her abductor must have said where he was taking her, a place so remote no one would ever venture there. No one except a homicide detective that hiked its unforgiving terrain the previous fall with Amy and Errie on a dare. There was no mistaking it.

The blood smear was a map of The Divide. An overgrown valley region located miles into the forest with no marked trails and dangerous sudden drop offs that kept would-be visitors away. Jade snapped a zoomed in picture and slithered through scene investigators. Stepping off the porch she caught their lead midstride.

"Mitch?" Jade's violent green eyes held his muted brown ones for a beat.

"I got this," he promised.

Heading for her car, a wave of exhaustion hit reminding her the last few hours, stretched like a bad week, were a rough start to a journey with no easy end. Out of earshot to those converging on the property she called Grey back.

"I've got it," she whispered. "I know where he's taking her, maybe where he has the others too."

"Not over the phone. Come in. We have hours to show just cause for your involvement." Grey's breathing labored under the stress of defending one of his own.

"I'm on my way. Wait until you see this. Amy should be proud. If anyone can outwit this bastard, it's Errie."

"Takes one to know one," he said. Then ended the call.

Jade drove the winding roads back to town as if competing in a motorsport safari race, scenery a blur, dust erupting beyond the reach of the rearview, and a singular focus ahead.

TWO

The roof above wasn't secure; broken rock, dirt, and vegetation threatened to release through cracks time left between aged wooden support beams. It soared high above, not like a building, more attune to a cavern or bunker. Was that where he'd taken her? A bunker abandoned by time? A place he could violate her without fear of discovery.

Errie's head ached from the impact of whatever weapon he used to knock her out after she sliced his arm with the turkey carver. Before reaching to inspect the damage, she listened carefully for movement in close proximity. Was he right there, watching, waiting for her to fully come to so he could attack again? She refused to make it easy. Hearing nothing save a distant white noise, her pounding head struggled to identify, she risked a further peek at her surroundings.

Lifting off whatever she laid on came with an instant price; a wave of dizziness incited nausea difficult to contain. She forced control over her body's reaction to analyze her state. Oddly, there was little in the way of restraints. Her hands were free to massage the goose egg on the back right of her skull. Her feet weren't tied though she had no shoes, nor was there any rope, chain, or cuffs. An old-time lantern hanging from a hook sunk into the rock wall cast a dim light across the stone cavern. Sitting prone on the elevated tray-shaped iron table she peered into the darkness beyond, recognizing it seemed to have no end. Turning the opposite direction, a large tractor-like machine with a ladder long front end housing two ominous extensions easily mistaken for monster-sized automatic rifles impeded her view. Errie had never seen anything like it and found its presence less than comforting.

Studying her bare feet, she scanned left and right for a source of material, something to fashion makeshift slippers from to cover her soles. Her feet ushered in success and opportunity as a dancer and she hoped they wouldn't let her down now. When your only means of escape is on foot and you have no clue how far you'll travel to reach safety, it's wise to keep your feet protected. Errie was wise. Amy always said, "Wise to a fault." Here, locked away literally in a criminal's lair, she prayed wisdom could save her if Amy couldn't.

Sliding off the table, she headed first to the machine. More intimidating on closer inspection, its purpose didn't become any clearer. Searching the driver's compartment, she stumbled on no means to operate it but did find two sets of thick men's leather gloves. Taking the ones shoved behind the operator's chair, she left the other set where she discovered them in clear view on the dash. Sliding her tiny, size six foot comfortably inside a glove, she then removed it and scoured the area for a hiding place for the leather sheaths. Closer to what must be the exit side, she shoved a rock away, dug a shallow hole, placed the gloves inside, rolled the rock back, and threw dirt and pebbles to conceal her approach.

Avoiding sharp stones and branches; she walked to the lantern but couldn't reach to retrieve it from its hook. The cavern wall, smooth though uneven, provided no grips to climb up. Without light, she ventured well passed the machine in all its shadowy violence. The cavern didn't lose width but boulders stacked on either side closed in to a door-sized opening. And it was guarded by a metal frame and door, cemented into the rock, sealing any hope of easy exit.

There had to be another way out, but by all evidence if one existed, it was deep in the belly of a mountain. Amy's face again flashed in memory, but this time she was trekking alongside Jade, warning of unstable ground, halting them all before a dangerous drop off ledge in the heart of The Divide. "Three more steps," she warned. "And there'll be no one to marry at our wedding."

The wedding. Errie pushed the thought down.

That's where her abductor threatened to house her. That was where she was, but without the soaring trees, pronounced valleys, and raging rivers. If she was there at all, she was deep inside the rock terrain and no matter how she tried no one would hear her screams. This reality hit and pain, fear, and fury shuttered up from within carrying a wave of tears she fought back. Not now. Now she must fight.

Her movements were fast and fluid, a dancer's drift, with greater purpose. She didn't know how long she had before her captor returned, if he had eyes on her now, or if this place he brought her to was so impenetrable and remote he feared nothing.

She glanced into the darkness, then back at where she stored the gloves.

"Fuck it," she whispered, retrieving them, dusting off her feet and slipping into them. "Come find me, you prick."

Errie glanced back at the lantern, its flickering light dancing against imagined patterns in the rock wall, knowing she'd miss the light but that befriending the darkness was her only way out. In her sweep of the space she came across nothing of use save the gloves, a tin bucket she clutched in her left hand, a length of discarded rope twisted inside the pail, and a sharp metal rod with a triangle end on one side and a straight edge on the other. Without food, water, or light her chances of survival were scarce so seeking those were all that mattered. Finding them before he found her, finding a way out, a way back to her life, this is what drove her as she disappeared into the blackness.

Edging close to the wall left of her, brushing her hand along its gutted edges as a guide, she moved as quickly as safe footing would allow. The gloves protecting her feet included an adjustable strap and snap meant to tighten around the wrist to secure. She refashioned these to a snug fit on her ankles, grateful for every small measure of means. With no way to determine distance visually she used a song from memory to map how far she moved when in the light and replayed the lyrics now counting one for every estimated twenty-foot marker. A football field later the tunnel curved, she paused, feeling around until determining two possible avenues of access. The ground below was unlevel and she tripped catching herself short of face planting in the dirt. Her hands examined what her eyes were blind to. Railway tracks, too close to be used for any train but perfect in size for a coal rail. Her captor brought her to an abandoned mine and mines had more than one way out. Choosing to remain left she continued for a short distance before her hand slid against something wet. Following the moisture to a crack in the rocks, she smelled the liquid before tasting the first drops of water. Removing the contents of the pail, she used it to catch the runoff and save for future, drinking from the trickle snaking down the rock. A sound echoing from a distance startled her back into motion. If she could hear him, chances were he could hear her.

Placing her footing carefully, she traveled forward to a second bend, pausing at its edge to listen for movement. A fleeting light cast from the entrance to her tunnel. She waited, expecting it to brighten on his approach, knowing there was no means of escape at her disadvantage. With her heartbeat drumming hard in her chest, pounding in her ears, her breath trembled in small gulps. Then the light vanished. Sounds faded. He broke right, the path most followed.

A newfound urgency drove her, blackness enveloped, but she had learned where the tracks lay, allowance on each side, and the curvature of the rock wall. She viewed her path in mind's eye and all but ran it. Expanding the distance between her and her captor, shortening the distance to escape. Her gloved feet found momentum until running full force into a jut out of granite catapulting her over its top into a battered heap of bruises. Accustomed to enduring the physical pain of performance, she sprang up in full ballerina *ballon* fashion then froze. Had the sound of the impact been carried down the rock walls? Nothing. She brushed herself off, secured her slippers, and tested her limbs for damage unable to check visually. Evading serious injury, she felt the surrounding area, her hands making sense of the obstacle that she'd collided with.

Searching on hand and knee her head pounded from the near concussion he inflicted, her left leg throbbed from taking the worst of the clash with the heap of boulders, and any water she collected was most certainly splashed across the unforgiving ground. Locating the pail she was shocked to find water mostly spared as it sat balanced on the rocks where her hand released it. Retrieving the length of rope, she felt around for the tool she absconded from near the tray where she woke. Before making contact with it, she slid her hand across something of heavy metal, on inspection a mining pick. She gripped it fiercely, found her place along the rock wall and continued down the tunnel, a little slower, a little sorer, but no less determined.

Not far ahead, a sliver of light cut the darkness. Oddly, it erupted from the ground, not above or alongside the pathway. Apprehensive she approached with caution, not willing to near it for fear of being seen in the sharp contrast of its gleam. Clinging to the wall, she inched across from it, close enough to recognize the ground below her feet could not be trusted. In this passage, rock gave way to punch an opening between the tunnel she treaded and a cross section of one running directly beneath. Gingerly she laid her tools away from the light's reach and inched her body across the left track to squint below. She spotted a cord first and her eyes traced it to a bulb hanging from a hook. Her view was limited to a few feet surrounding the opening but she glimpsed the framed edge and a few inches inward of a door. There were rooms underneath her and someone left a light on. Caught up in searching for insight, the sound of shuffling feet shocked her back from the edge and against the stone wall.

"Where are you, my tiny dancer?" He spoke into the hallway of the area below. "I will find you. There is no way out, I'm afraid."

He laughed; a full chest, bellowing laugh, and she caught a whisper beneath his sickening joy as she ran again, with tools and heart in hand. He wasn't alone down there. The other sound was the voice of a woman, a plea even, She could, in sheer panic, be mistaken, but she thought the woman said, "Run."

THREE

"She stays on the case until the end." Captain Grey's voice carried from his office to where Jade exited the elevator. "Oh but you do." She heard him threaten as she rounded the corner. "Try pulling that with me and you'll get no cooperation from anyone local and I'll guarantee the media depicts you as an asshat," he continued, smiling and directing her to take a seat while he finished the call. "Yeah, yeah. Fine. Get it done in writing and we'll talk." He hung up and dropped into his chair, assuming a relaxed stance despite the dissipating tension in the room.

"So they're real team players and can't wait to work with me?" Jade kicked her heavy combat boots up on his desk. He stared them down and she readjusted her position using the footstool he brought in for moments such as this.

"Yeah, you're heading into a dragon's den and I haven't found you an ally in the lot." Grey wrung his hands contemplating. "It gets worse."

"Great. I promised Amy—"

"I heard. Yeah, the second in command is related to one of the Redeemer victims." He chewed on his lower lip, which he only did when the next words he delivered would hurt.

"Which victim? How is he related? Wait, who is he?" Jade ran the list of Redeemer victims down in her head, not really hearing Grey answer. "I got to know most of the families. Was it the first victim, we didn't have much background on her, her addiction made it—"

"Wenzel," Grey barked, bringing her focus back to center. "I said he's a cousin of the late and far from great detective Wenzel. You know, the one you and Kane wanted tossed off the force, the one who was stalking you to gather evidence to end Kane's career. The asshole that upended my best and brightest. That victim."

"Oh shit." Jade's expression froze with this realization. Her partners on their most devastating case, Kane and Tex, hell everyone involved, suffered setbacks and unwarranted scrutiny until Wenzel met his end with his head blown through at the behest of the Redeemer.

"Oh yeah. How his cousin made it to the bureau I'll never know but he demanded you not be involved before confirming the abduction fell under their jurisdiction. I have the distinct suspicion Wenzel shared his opinions and none of them accolades."

"So...?"

"So, what do you have? Whatever it is, it better be good."

"I'm certain Errie knew if anything happened to her Amy would be on it. And, when she couldn't be she'd call me in. Knowing that, and Kane and I being such good friends with them, she left me directions." Jade leaned into the desk. Closing the distance between them, she whispered, "She drew a map of The Divide, the place we hiked last fall."

"Where Amy ran into the poison ivy?" Grey had brought Amy to his naturopath for ointment so she wouldn't scar and heard a rundown of their trip along the way.

"Exactly. Here, check this out." Jade brought up her phone and scrolled to a split screen of the bloody smear from Errie's crime scene and a map she drew for Jade a year earlier of The Divide. There was no mistaking the similarity. Errie joked about the shape of the river breaking the two sections of mountain terrain apart.

Pointing out it mimicked a silhouette of the perfect breast, the curve, undeniable. The smear matched.

"Jesus. There's no chance anyone unfamiliar would pick up on this. That woman will not go down without a fight." Grey stood, pacing the expanse of his office. "Okay. Leave this out. They'll have access to the same scene you did. We won't release this as a link. Work the neighborhood. With any luck, residents won't be comfortable being questioned by feds. If they are forced to use you to access local support, they'll be inclined to keep you on." Grey stopped walking and stared down at her, regret clouded his eyes. "This won't be pleasant."

"I know, but I promised Amy."

"What did you promise?" he asked, his tone a warning.

"I'd bring her home." Jade stood, glancing back as she made for the door. "I never said alive. I learned not to offer that the hard way."

Grey shook his head and circled his desk. Leaving him to contemplate what they'd all been dropped back into, Jade paused at the threshold. "I'm working this one alone."

"I figured you'd say that. You are but you're not. The feds will be all over every move you make. Be smart and careful. You may not have considered it, but you're in the victim pool."

"The profile of abductees?"

"Yeah. And I can't lose you again."

Their eyes met, and Jade broke the stare first, leaning out into the hallway then back inside. "Does he know?" she asked.

"I don't think so or they would've used it already," Grey said, staring at his hands folded over paperwork on his desk. "Doesn't mean they can't find out."

"Yeah." Jade stood motionless for a few seconds. "And when they do?"

"I hope by then we have enough, you've done enough, to make yourself indispensable. But, Jade?"

"Yeah, Chief."

"Find her first."

There was no denying, in light of the mountain of distrust

stacked against her, to bring Errie home safe Jade would need more than luck and determination. She'd need an act of God.

The Redeemer case cast darkness over the town of Shadow Hook but more than that it created a spotlight on Jade. The truth of a past she couldn't have known about growing up arrived with the power to steal her future in law enforcement. Grey, being more of a father than captain to her, did everything legal to bury the most damning details about her connection to the killer they caught, shot, and almost ended. With every day that passed as he recovered in a private medical facility, sporting a name change justified as a means to keep him safe from a second attempt on his life, his existence loomed as an ever-present risk. The Redeemer held secrets capable of hurting many but none as much as Jade. So far, he was unable to vocalize them but if the day came? She wondered often if sparing his life was the wrong call and a curse. She didn't know but feared one day she may find out.

Walking the halls, she recalled a time when they didn't close in so tightly, when the scent of stale donuts and bad coffee comforted. Home was where you were comfortable existing and for her the shop provided that. Not so much today. Fellow cops averted their eyes, made busy, and ceased speaking when she rounded the corners.

She ducked behind the metal door leading to the parking garage and opted to take the stairs. No elevator music. No awkward silence. No one wondering if she was as damaged as they'd been told.

The truth far worse than imagined.

FOUR

ir tunnels. Errie identified the staggered whispers of light filtering in from above as air tunnels cored through the rock to provide oxygen for miners far beneath. Only there were no miners now only her, the beast that abducted her, and the haunting female voice she heard before running blind down whatever subterranean passage she navigated. In utter darkness with rock above, below, and beside her, the mine became a maze and she its runner. Panic interfered with her intent to mark and gauge distance and time. She was lost many turns away from where she started. So many she allowed herself to collapse on a heap of what, to the touch, felt like burlap bags.

The smell of sand confirmed her assumption they were meant to hold back falling rock, stockpiled but serving no use. She arranged them to conceal her while serving as a nest, a mini fortress to collapse within. She was so very tired though she couldn't be certain of time. The last shaft of light reflected muted moonlight. Even killers and kidnappers had to sleep. She nestled in, cold but grateful for a modicum of comfort and protection. Rearranging a lesser bag as a pillow she heard a ting, ting, the sound of thin metal or glass. Searching with careful but desperate hands, her fingertips connected with an old miner's lamp. Feeling knobs and switches she pushed and clicked until it sprang to life dispelling darkness from her hovel.

Light.

Inspecting the aged lantern, she noticed it was near full of oil. Exhaling breath she hadn't realized lay trapped in her chest she searched her immediate surroundings. With the care of a surgeon, she placed the lantern on the flat surface of the outer ring of sandbags so its light had optimal effect. On hands and knees, she gathered rocks, scattering them on the pathway a significant distance from her safe space as an early detection system. Anxious to continue down the passage and out to safety, her body betrayed her intention, too exhausted to continue. She desperately needed sleep.

One pass through the furthest side revealed nothing but the same rock cage she had run through for hours. Crawling up and over to the safe side of her makeshift bunker she drew the lantern close, eyes fixed on the bags around her. After resting she would rip one open and give her makeshift shoes much needed support.

That was if he didn't find her first.

Clenching the iron bar she saved at the outset of the journey in her hands, she curled around it and, fighting back dark thoughts with an inner light of her own, succumbed to the drain of energy survival thus far cost her. Somewhere within the meshing of her outer and inner nightmares she captured the vision of a familiar face, Amy's.

Her life with Amy was worth fighting for, a life of unconditional love and acceptance. They discovered in each other everything they hoped existed but never fully experienced. Their last conversation puzzled her, even under the shroud of exhaustion buried beneath a mountain of rock and playing hide and seek with a maniac, she couldn't shake it. During the finalization of last-minute wedding details she caught Amy in another of her deep contemplations. Errie came to understand being a homicide detective separated Amy from the pack. She witnessed depravity in a way most only experienced in the twisted plot of a horror movie. Sometimes, especially lately, Amy held it too close. Errie knew something extra plagued her, but she hadn't pried it loose before being ripped from their life. It resurfaced; seeping in from the darkness beyond the rock walls as something sinister taking hold with a grip Errie was too far removed to loosen.

In panicked dreams she fought for air, the darkness closing in so tight it crushed her throat and made it impossible to breathe. Or, had he found her. Was she being punished for a failed escape attempt? Errie's eyes snapped open, blinking and searching the darkness but seeing no one. She'd simply collapsed so weary that her head slipped off the pillow sandbag to be lodged between two others restricting air. She readjusted to ensure a safe return to slumber at least within her nest but images of Amy's face, fraught with worry, didn't fade. She could only imagine how her current situation was adding to that state.

She needed the hell out of this mess and to return to Amy in one piece. She strained listening for the slightest noise to echo down the tunnel. Hearing only her own labored breathing she curled up and drifted back into the darkness praying she'd wake long before her captor did.

Amy found Errie, shattered like a china doll and abandoned in a heap to a cold forest floor. Nothing pretty remained save her favorite necklace housing a delicately carved rose quartz crystal at its center. Though abstract it mimicked a ballerina in full pirouette. Amy bought it for her the night of their first date in the city to commemorate her outstanding performance on stage. New York was tough. Errie proved tougher and won over the crowd effortlessly. But here she lay in pieces.

A high-pitched streaming beep penetrated Amy's thoughts and she startled awake. Confused, devastated, and dog-tired, she'd fallen asleep at her desk. The search engine for CCTV footage in the districts surrounding their home, the home Errie was kidnapped from and the same one Amy refused to return to, left a listing of feeds blinking on her open screen. She hit Print and shook free of the amassed paper turned pillow on the table's hard surface.

She retrieved the printed information, packed up her bag, shut down her computer, and grabbed her coat. Stopping midway to the exit, she realized she had no destination. Prying her phone from her back pocket, she hit recent calls, tapped a number, and waited.

"Hey Kane. You guys wouldn't mind a visitor would—"

"You on your way? I'll heat up the chili and make up the guest bed." Kane Kolton never left time for her to argue. He did what brothers on the force did best. Welcome the broken parts and help heal them. He knew all about broken and was still mending from his last brush with evil. He and Jade had been fortunate to survive and while he was on sabbatical, researching and recovering, he wasn't distant to everything happening back at the shop. In fact, he may be more aware than when working a case laser focused on evidence. She needed outside eyes and no better set existed.

Arriving half asleep from the lull of the highway, she stammered in the unlocked door dropping her bag at the shoulder of the foyer. She realized, eyes locked on the leather satchel too weary to lift, she had brought exactly nothing useful with her.

"Hey, you made it in good time. Jade left a welcome kit in your room." Kane's smile warmed her heart. In sweatpants low on his hips and revealing the ugly edge of past scars and a tan T-shirt highlighting his blond curls, he scooped her bag and her from the floor, in the literal sense, escorting her up the back stairs and down a wide plank hall to a waiting sanctuary. "She said to tell you clothes are in the drawers of the bureau, towels in the lower bathroom cabinet, and chocolate and snacks on your nightstand. Oh, yeah. Toothbrush and toiletries in the basket by the tub."

"Damn, you guys are better than a five-star hotel," she managed to voice.

"Jade is. If left to me, you'd be wearing the same outfit for a week and stealing my toothbrush or using your finger." His smile held.

"Nasty. Thank her for—"

"Not necessary." Kane slid to the threshold. "Chili is on. Come down when you're settled in. I have something to show you."

His voice caught that wisdom deep edge on the last sentence. He'd been working the case. She suspected as much but was glad it didn't require coaxing. She was too bone tired to muster. After assessing the room, changing into pajamas bottoms and a T-shirt Jade left for her, she made her way back to the kitchen never testing the comfort of the bed fearing she'd be out cold. The security of friends that were family initiated the crumble of her outer shell, there wasn't much left.

"Eat," Kane commanded, pointing to a place at their large refectory table. Jade was thrilled to acquire the heavy wooden antique piece from a monastery until they all strained muscles moving it in. "It's piping hot. Buns to your left."

"Okay. I'll eat if you tell me what you know." Amy locked eyes and held; her way of confirming she could handle what came next.

Kane slid up an end chair and sat back to front, leaving shallow distance between them, space for Amy to breathe. "I tracked all known abductions up the coast and called in to the locals actively working cases. No bodies. Those taken could all potentially be alive. There isn't a clear victomology. They don't look similar, varying hair color and heights, no matching occupations, or family backgrounds on first glance so we'll be digging deeper. And when I say we I mean—"

"You better mean you and I cause I damn sure aren't sitting this one out."

"I did and I know." Kane's eye softened. She was glad when a timer sounded summoning him back to the counter. Too much kindness was as crippling as none at all amid tragedy.

"Were you ever into Ouija boards when your were a kid?" he asked with his large back to her, pulling warmed buns from the oven. "Tarot card readings?"

"I dabbled a little," she said between mouthfuls of hot chili. "I had an aunt who went full occultist after losing my cousin in a shooting. He wasn't the intended target so she needed connection or justification, I suppose. Honestly, I found it and her pretty cool. Why? You want me to interpret the cards left at the scenes?"

With a tray full of buns to dump into a basket left of her, Kane's expression glowed mischievous. "I already have." He spun his chair and sat normally, grabbing a bun, tossing it between hands until it quit burning. "The cards left all referenced the victim's life—ballerina at Errie's abduction scene—but the tell is in the number—"

"Nine? I don't remember its significance, so couldn't say how each was relative." Amy kept eating, the food and the conversation felt good and nothing had since Errie was confirmed taken.

"A point of culmination." Kane announced, like he solved a key aspect of the case though none was penetrating her brain. He read her confusion.

"If this guy is seeing the kidnapping, possession of the victims and Errie as a culminating act then we have a history leading up to it. I'll show you where I am with it after dinner." He bit into the roll, devouring it in a couple bites then stole another and started tossing again.

"They can't still be that hot?" Amy asked.

"Oh, no. Dexterity. My hands aren't yet where they once were, so every chance I get, I test them." He set the bun aside and dug into his bowl of chili.

"How is all that? I'd like to put in a daily check on you and Jackson but I know I'd only serve as an annoyance or bad reminder. I see Jade so it's different. I know when a bad day hits."

Kane's head dropped lower by the slightest bit. Not enough for most to register, but enough for Amy to feel in her already aching heart. "Yeah. She has them less and less now but...Jackson is as tough as the dusty trail as he puts it and we're all healing. Time, you know."

Standing to clear her near empty bowl, though his sat half consumed, his pants dragged down a little. The angry scar so close she could touch it.

"I know, right? It's a beast. They weren't real concerned with appearances." He joked, revealing more of the sliced area emergency services tore open a second time in twenty-four hours to save his life. "I told Jade I was set on getting a fierce tattoo around it. She said if I did, she'd give me a matching one on the other side."

Amy almost laughed but couldn't find it. "Where is she? Shouldn't she be here by now?"

"That's a whole other discussion. Let's leave the dishes. I have to show you my mapping and get your input before you crash."

"That obvious, huh?" Amy dragged her frame from the chair to standing position, every cell involved screamed in protest.

"Here." Kane shoved a hot, clear glass at her, complete with bamboo lid and glass straw. A green liquid swirled inside it over a handful of ice cubes.

"What the hell?"

"It's great for exhaustion and it'll help you sleep so you're ready to fight for our girl tomorrow." He laughed and shoved it toward her mouth. "It's actually really good."

"Seriously? What the fuck happened to you and where is the old Kane?"

"Dead and buried, I'm afraid. And what didn't happen to me? Can't come out of shit like that the same. You still love me." He sauntered down the wide plank hall in front of her, leading the way.

Avoiding the green liquid, she instead drank in the layering of strength and beauty in their well-executed and formidable home. Both aspects were necessary for Jade to relinquish her former house and dive into their coexistence without reservation. From the reclaimed hardwood and ceiling beams to the maneuverable and adaptable furniture, each contribution spoke to who they were as individuals and as a couple. But entering the den left of the hall and the last room before the great room, Amy was surrounded by everything Kane. Even his signature drafting table, or a restored original from a hundred years back, that Jade gifted him as a welcome home present, all reflecting the man and his passions. Amy sank into one of his worn and battered leather wingbacks, astonished at the decorative mural ahead. No Van Gogh or Vermeer, instead a collage of evidence, victims, criminals, and possible holding sites crawled out from a center point like a newsprint spider reaching for hard edges. Below, across the bottom and at eye level from her seated position, were pasted copies of tarot cards.

"Are those from the scenes? You got all of them?" She didn't conceal the shock in her voice.

"I did. And I'll do you one better." He strode up close to the crime board and tapped two open areas. "There are two missing. And I think finding them will be key to knowing how our guy ticks. We find them..." He turned back to face her, promise in his eyes. "And we find him and bring Errie home."

Amy trusted Kane, had since the day she joined his homicide team, and while the feeling was mutual, so much had happened. Too much. Her heart ached to confide in him, release the unspoken terror locked behind her rib cage, but there were no words.

"I know," he reasoned. "Your heart won't let you be at peace in any way until she's back. I understand. You know I do. But I'm telling you I've come at this from every angle; Jade and I were following this one long before he ventured into our neck of the woods, and everything is saying she's alive. In fact, I think they all are."

"I want to believe you. I want to cling to that."

"Then do. It's late and you're exhausted. I'll get you something to help you sleep so I have your undivided attention to work this in the morning." Kane headed for the doorway, pausing on the threshold. "He didn't take them to kill them, Amy. Not like the Redeemer. This one..." He waved back at the wall of evidence. "He's a collector."

Amy said nothing as he left to retrieve meds capable of knocking her out and keeping her asleep until the light of dawn. Instead she focused ahead, eyes transfixed on the tarot cards and the missing spots following victim three and victim nine. While absorbing the images portrayed in the designs and following the known crime scenes along the coastline it became clear, the asshole who stole the most cherished person out of Amy's life also possessed eleven others. If Kane was correct in his mapping, and he usually was, the bastard had amassed a dozen victims. If he hadn't killed them, what had he done? The indignity and violations Errie and the others were suffering was the stuff of nightmares.

Twenty minutes later, in the quiet of the guest room with hot tea on the nightstand and drifting away beneath a down comforter and the effects of Restoril, that was all Amy imagined. Errie and eleven other women trapped in some unholy place waiting for a rescue that hadn't come and wouldn't, at least not tonight.

FIVE

T he combination of drugs slipped into the evening meal ensured his acquisitions would all sleep soundly. All but the one prowling down dark tunnels in favor of the warm, safe bed he provided for her. This ballerina would be a problem but not one unexpected. She danced with a reckless abandon when commanding the stage. He assumed she'd show nothing less when challenged and she didn't disappoint. Still, inspecting the room he prepared for her, the wasted accommodation, his displeasure weighed heavy. He sat on the edge of the carefully selected bedding, organic bamboo sheets amenable for her allergy to lesser blends, tempted to rest his weary head on the pillow and spend the night in the comfort of the space. Melancholy was a costly luxury. A strict commitment to time management and discipline afforded him continued freedom and the execution thus far to his plan.

And that? That was everything.

He rose from the bed and crossed the threshold leaving the door ajar. No point in closing it. She'd be back soon. There was something beautiful in strutting down the center of the tunnel, rooms left then right drifting by in succession, each filled with a life he could strengthen, fortify, and preserve.

He couldn't do that for the woman he loved most. In the past, weak and ignorant, he couldn't save anyone. The tables had turned. It was different now. He was different now, and oh so much stronger, learned, and formidable.

He kicked debris, scattered rocks and dust plumes chasing each footfall, listening to the soft sound of breathing encircling him echoing off stonewalls. They slept, dreamed, and breathed under his watchful eye.

Comfort came with the awareness he provided a place for that and could end it all as easily.

Making a sharp right, down an access tunnel off the main and one barely able to contain his shoulder span, he inched to a wooden door installed when preparing the site for use. He pulled the iron key from his pocket, attached to a key ring with others required for internal and external locks on the property. The heavy locks he chose provided an extra measure of security though it was unlikely they were needed. The area, remote and reclaimed by the natural forest it was embedded in, was near impossible to reach and even more difficult to locate or glimpse from overhead. Many times he stood outside its entrance, aircraft flying above, with a sense of true accomplishment. His hidden tomb couldn't be matched. Time had wholly and completely forgotten this place and he made sure to collect and confiscate any and all historical documents capable of reminding his enemies of its existence. And then he studied. Every detail ranging from obvious to minuscule check and check again until he could redraw related maps by memory.

Unlocking the door, he pushed it aside and entered the limited space. Distinctly confining to most, he found the small area perfect for a command center housing the monitoring system, information on each acquisition in house, and records of police movements and ongoing investigations into their disappearances. Though other larger areas could've accommodated his purposes more comfortably, located on the west side of the tunnel system, the dry side was preferable. This hub, on site, allowed him to handle the business end of his plans encased beneath tons of rock to emerge into the world leaving all evidence guarded.

No one knew who he really was.

In a way he pitied their naïveté. He was like them once, blind to the truth of those with the power to alter his fate and cruelly disillusioned, but not anymore. Since his awakening he viewed everyone through a clear and penetrating lens of accuracy.

A visionary, he held much to be revealed.

But the truth would be painful. In his experience it always was.

Inspecting the images on the screen, number four was moaning, trapped inside in a fitful dream. Ever since he explained how no one would discover she was missing for months she wrestled through the night. Tomorrow he would try to calm her fears. After all she was no less his than the others. No less invisible to one who would seek her out. A planner by nature and in his profession, he mastered an eye for detail. He missed nothing. And they, the police detectives aiming to retrieve those he now possessed, would find nothing. Nothing capable of leading them here. A sweep of related news updates confirmed the FBI's lack of progress since assuming the case.

He read the most recent headline learning he had earned a title.

OCCULTUS TARGETING EAST COAST

Occultus? From the Latin word meaning hidden or secret. It fit. "Give the journalist a gold star." His raspy whisper echoed back at him. However catchy, the headline was wrong. He wasn't targeting the east. They were decidedly behind the times. He had everything he wanted and needed. Well, except for the ballerina.

He activated a sweep of the tunnels claiming his seat, a leather barstool he brought in several months earlier with wooden sides and a well-padded cushion to accommodate his frame and studied the feed. Linking from one track to another, he examined each for a sign of movement. Finding none, he ran it again. Lighting was limited and the cameras weren't equipped to capture every possible space. The tunnels' far edges or areas preceding sharp angle turns were left in shadow. After an hour of tracing the dim pathways reaching deep into the earth his eyes grew weary. He spun the stainless steel bracelet of the Omega Seamaster watch on his wrist. It said he'd manage eight hours sleep, given drive time, if he left immediately.

He shut down the tunnel feed. Gazed over each room on the simultaneous room monitors. His eyes arresting at the sole bedroom with the open door, he tapped the screen.

"Good night, my tiny dancer. I'll be seeing you."

SIX

Jade set up the Airstream in the dark on the opposite edge of the last rest area before the National Park veered away from highway access. She had driven hard terrain to a space surrounded by concealing brush but flat enough to use as a secure base camp. Though remote she was still able to receive cell service and computer connection via a booster the tech team installed for her and Kane thinking it intended for camping and not surveillance purposes. Using a subsidiary stream, branching off from the main, a brief stroll through the trees for water and the stocked trailer as a tactical site she'd spare wasted time driving back and forth from town. It provided an advantage she wasn't about to disclose to the feds. Her onboard meeting with them was set for seven the following morning and by her watch, eight hours away.

Finishing the unpacking of dry goods, bedding, advanced first aid kit, and climbing gear, Jade scanned the trailer for anything missed. Making a mental note to bring extra headlamps on her return, she stepped out into the fresh air, locked the trailer, and made for her vehicle. Unhitched and ready to roll out, she jumped inside the cab of her Denali letting its high beams lead her back to pavement.

Several minutes and turns from camp she opened the driver's window enabling cool air to whip through the truck's interior keeping her alert and aware. Watching forest scenery drift by illuminated by headlights, she couldn't help but recall the feeling of freedom and peace they all experienced in this place only a summer ago. Campfire pits and storytelling, drinking under moonlight and skinny dipping with Kane safe beneath the canopy of trees and miles from civilization and judgment.

This place they fought to reach, seeking a safe haven and escape from the world, now lay transformed by evil. Every aspect that drew her to it as a refuge became a treacherous maze hiding Errie and quite possibly eleven other kidnapped women from any hope of rescue. Tiny hairs on her arms bristled and her body shivered in the crisp air rushing inside the cab but she refused to close the window or turn on the heater knowing Errie might be out there, far beyond the reach of the lights, weathering the elements and an enemy. And she understood exactly the cost of that particular hell.

Without warning power lines hanging low at the highway's edge became twisted lengths of tubing, the skim of cooled humidity casting shadows across blacktop gained a tinge of crimson, and her body remembered the helpless drain of life flowing away while the warmth of the world was traded for an all-consuming icy prison.

Her right hand smacked the heater on with an electrocuted reflex, her left triggered the automatic window closure and she drank in the heat shedding bad memories before they devoured. Shaking loose of dangerous thoughts, she dropped her foot heavier on the accelerator pedal. The truck lurched forward with force and ate up the distance ahead, but every mile home was another separating her from Errie and adding opportunity for a criminal to wreck all that was pure in her. Jade adjusted the temperature to a lower setting, the rage inside warming her.

This bastard crossed lines taking one of their own and had no idea who he was coming up against. The last enemy to tread boldly into her life with bad intention killed many before coming face-to-face with her. And regardless of the scars etched deep into her soul, she was here, fighting, hunting, and he was confined to a hospital bed. Worse still, she controlled every aspect of his pathetic existence. This aberration, no matter the flavor of crazy, would be fortunate to come out of the battle alive. Jade admitted to herself, though she hadn't to any other, the saving grace for the Redeemer was having Kane's hand on the weapon that shot him and not her own.

If it had been hers, he would be dead.

And this time she'd decided.

Her back pushed up against the leather seat, her shoulders dropped the tension they held, and her eyes scanned the road. Wide awake and emboldened by determination, the six hours of sleep awaiting her at home would be more than enough. She was anxious to meet with the FBI boys and be unleashed on the case. Kane and her thoroughly tracked the abductions so any shared details from the feds would only serve to strengthen what she already knew. The boys currently in charge wouldn't expect her to be holding pertinent information to reciprocate and she wouldn't. She hoped a grounded reason for her avenue of pursuit would present itself. If it didn't, she wasn't certain how to justify heading deep into what was widely known as unforgivable and uninhabitable terrain. She viewed having the cousin of a cop who held nothing but disdain for her when they worked together as a measure of good luck. If she was preoccupied with a goose chase, he'd be thrilled to have her out of his hair and on a path leading to humiliation.

And he'd be wrong and discover it too late just like his deceased detective cousin, Wenzel.

God, how she didn't miss him. Being it is taboo to speak ill of the dead, she made a mental note not to speak of him at all. The idiot locked himself in a car with a killer on a dark night down an isolated stretch of road probably thinking he could talk his way out of it. He couldn't talk his way out of a paper bag. Everyone could attest by the splattered mess left behind from that encounter. No one would say the one good thing the Redeemer did, which was putting an end to Wenzel, Jade included, but she didn't mourn the loss.

From the time she was too young to be on the force, even before Captain Grey pulled strings to put her into training early, she was intrigued by how past cases informed future ones. The knowledge gained or the understanding of a certain type of criminal lead to the arrest of the next. It wasn't a body of work many could stomach. Most people going about their daily lives were happier oblivious to these truths. But those entrenched in fighting crime, being the wall criminals smashed up against, treated their hard lessons like gold knowing they may one day provide the insight to save a life.

Still, it never made for polite dinner conversation.

Jade never worried much in that regard, either eating alone, with Kane her partner in life and on the force or surrounded by other cops. This was her world and she was fine missing out on social functions she wouldn't have fit into. Missing out on dinner altogether was another thing.

Her stomach rumbled at the thought of Kane's chili and minutes later, truck parked and combat boots tossed astray in their foyer, she headed into the kitchen, jacket still on, to find a bowl set aside with a note attached.

Eat Love!

Her hands wrapped around the pottery bowl to find it still moderately warm. Placing it in the microwave, she used its heating time to disrobe and pull on more comfortable attire from the clean but unfolded laundry pile so as not to disturb Kane or Amy. Grabbing the chili before the microwave dinged, she drifted into Kane's office. Pushing a leather armchair around until at the perfect angle to absorb the evidence board, she dropped into it and studied while savoring the spicy soul food. Happy for no table and reason to hold the bowl and warm her hands while its contents warmed her insides, her eyes cast over information coming to rest on the two empty spaces in the row of tarot cards.

"Who else did you take?" she whispered.

"Exactly what I was wondering." Kane sauntered in sporting bed head hair and looking homebound beautiful. "Hey lovely, glad you made it back and found the grub."

"Thank you," she said, smiling up as he kissed her forehead and then flopped into the chair opposite hers. "It's delicious by the way."

"I thought you might be cold." He squinted at the board, adjusting his position to hang sideways across the chair to see it clearly. "I think we're missing one in Louisiana and possibly Virginia. I dug deep but there's nothing."

"You can't find anything if nothing has been reported yet." Jade stood, set her near empty bowl down, and walked close enough to the map on the board to read the tiny print. "I keep thinking if Errie lived alone how long it would be before anyone logged her missing? I mean, she has long stretches between shows and her parents don't live close."

Kane snuck up behind her staring at the same map over her shoulder. "Meaning it could be weeks."

Jade arched her head to stare up at him. "Months."

"Okay, I'll search back further, expand the timeline and let you know if I get a hit."

"Thanks," she said, her back still to him.

Wrapping her in his arms and stepping close enough for his body warmth to envelop, he smiled down and spun her to face him. "You're welcome. Now come to bed so you can steal five hours."

"Five? I have at least six before——"

"No you don't. Not for sleeping at least." He swept her easily off her feet and proceeded to carry her to their bed, careful to remain quiet.

"Did Amy get settled in? How's she holding up?" Jade's eyes drifted to the guest bedroom end of the hall.

"She said five-star hotel level of care and I gave her meds. She's okay so far."

"I thought you weren't supposed to be lifting anything heavy yet," she scolded, knowing she posed no risk to his trained physique.

"I'm not but just in case let's take my muscles for a test run and see how they perform."

Jade laughed, shook his juvenile joking aside, but didn't object. Forgetting how bad things could become, trading nightmares for new memories was survival. And she resented the hell out of the bastard forcing Amy to learn a tool her and Kane preferred not to share with those they loved. Disappearing into Kane's embrace she held a promise to the man who began Amy's worst nightmare.

She was about to become his and make him pay for it.

SEVEN

"You've got to be kidding?" FBI Agent, Drex Lafine stretched his full six foot three height blocking the door-frame. "She was instrumental in driving my cousin out of his mind, but you're forcing me to work with her when you know the family history?"

His director, Michael Washington hung up the phone after trading words with Captain Grey. Incredulous to his rant or suspicions regarding the sanity of extending an invitation to work the case to a homicide detective as tainted by the job as Jade Carmichael was rumored to be.

"If family history was a factor, *you* wouldn't be working this case," the director said staring him back into his seat. "Face facts, Drex. Out there..." He waved his mitt at the doorway. "...I won't speak a word but in here, your cousin was an idiot and you didn't even like the guy."

"Yeah, true. I still don't trust a cop with a past like hers." Drex ran a hand through the thick mass of black waves giving reason for hair envy and shook his head. "It's not a good idea. She may know the terrain out there but—"

"Look, this asshole ripped a string of women out of their lives.

The only hint of a lead we have is he was headed their direction and no one has been taken since the Shadow Hook abduction. Carmichael has insight on a starting point and they won't cough it up without her involvement. You work the case with her."

"I won't. You want to find them? I work it alone." After years with the bureau and being one of the few cherry-picked out of his former position in international threat assessment, he knew he had ground to stand on. "And it's *yet.* No one has been abducted since Shadow Hook, yet."

"What if Lexi was one of the women? Wouldn't you want every angle covered regardless of personal bias?"

"Bringing my sister into this won't endear you." Drex had heard enough. He stood again, this time beelining for the exit.

"Okay, stop with the theatrics. I'll meet you halfway."

Drex halted a stride from the threshold. Shifting back around he held out his hands in a 'lay it on me' gesture and waited.

"You're about as big a pain in my ass as there is, you know that?" The director shook his head, stared down at the open case file, its updated version too similar to the past one. "You work it alone. You both work it alone. Updates together and everything that can benefit nailing this asshole and bringing those women home shared with each other and me. And, if I find out anything short of that is happening, I'll have your ass or hers and your badges. Understood?"

"Yeah, Mike. I wanna find them too." Drex dropped the pose as his voice gained an edge of sincerity.

"Not as bad as she does. This guy has the fiancée of one her own. I'm betting she's more determined than anyone to crack this."

"I don't give a shit who catches him first. I don't want her adding to the body count. One member of my family taking a dirt nap after working with her is enough." Drex spun on his heels not leaving time for a rebuttal. He still hadn't packed and didn't need to be online for the seven a.m. zoom meeting with Carmichael. He preferred to meet her for the first time in person, in the field, where he was most comfortable and most intimidating. He had her out-ranked, out-sized, and outperformed but something nagged at him.

Something between the headlines of the last case she closed. There were questions avoided and being a master at such he recognized aversion too well.

Stomping across the parking lot to his worn-in Hummer, he didn't look the part of a typical fed. Carrying with him the training earned in hot zones the world over he appeared more ex-military than FBI. He knew it and refused to conform. Slamming the door with a metal-on-metal revolt, anyone within earshot could surmise he was mad. Though he wasn't certain which aspect pissed him off more. Forced to work with a detective responsible for a family member's downfall, one key to a recent case that cost so many lives, or sharing information, which he hated on any given day, with someone he didn't know and couldn't trust. It all sucked. And justified a detour to the gym on his way home.

Drex could work with damn near anyone for the good of solving a case, but this was one time he was glad the terrain in the area him and the Carmichael woman were heading into was regarded as uninhabitable. He was more than ready to climb mountains. He wondered, was she?

He read accounts of the heroics in her history in law enforcement and planned to spend the next few days examining every detail of her past when not in the field. She was as much an enigma as the animal they hunted.

And what was the driving motivation for stealing women across a coastal trail in large numbers? Was he dumping them? Disposing of them into the ocean along the route? Or were they housed somewhere still breathing? If so, where and how were they being kept under wraps? In all likelihood the criminal's prison for the abductees resided near the residence of the last woman taken for the simple fact that he had worked down the coast to that end and hadn't, by all accounts, been active since. Moving more than three victims posed serious logistical problems. Transporting ten or more was a feat few could achieve single-handedly without detection. And they were watching. Drex was watching. Odds were the perp transported the first to second last one by one from west to east before eyes were on him. Knowing the heat would be turned up as the women disappeared, he shortened the distance to his hidden domain suggesting a certain aptitude.

This collector was intelligent, a skilled planner, careful in his execution, and a worthy adversary. All traits threatening his victim's safe return and Drex a successful end to the case. In truth, the women may never be discovered or, at very least, come home breathing but Drex intended to push back hard against that outcome.

Assigned to the case only days earlier, brought on out of desperation by those above, he wasn't much more familiar with it than Detective Carmichael. In fact, she may be further ahead given the personal connection she harbored to the latest victim. From what he ascertained from research and his cousin's email chain rant, Carmichael spent more time in the field than any office. She lived and breathed her cases and held cards close. Her partner on the force, injured to the level of critical condition and off recovering still, made headlines and even challenged reporters in front of the cameras. Carmichael never did. Elusive, even her home address and most of her background was scrubbed or misrepresented in the bureau's file. Grey's doing no doubt. Having one like him pinch-hitting for her set her apart.

Made her almost intriguing but unquestionably shady.

Of all the details plaguing Drex the one bothering him most seemed the simplest. Where the hell had she disappeared to after the Redeemer case closed? She had all but died on the scene and required months of medical care due to injuries but wherever she received it she wasn't there alone. The location of her partner Detective Kane Kolton, Carmichael's father, and Grey was undisclosed on and off in the weeks following. Kane exited the hospital and wasn't heard from for months, until a teaching stint. Grey took leave with a no contact standing order and there was more. Carmichael's father signed a nondisclosure issued by Grey. What was in it couldn't be accessed without alerting Grey. Drex could smell a cover-up a mile out and this one reeked but it was associated with the aftermath of a closed case not the case itself. It facilitated a measure of protection over Carmichael and those closest, but why?

The Redeemer, obviously posing the greatest threat, was gunned down and turned vegetable.

Before he checked in with Detective Carmichael to lay down ground rules for co-working the case he had a stop to make. One he orchestrated be done without warning or permission. He evaluated his approach while throwing gear in his go bag. Having packed countless times under the restraints of emergency protocol, he could do it blind better than any ten soldiers in wartime. His hands grabbed, folded, and stored while his mind constructed the best tactic. Both tasks completed, he locked up his place, slid back into his fully loaded hummer, and headed down the highway twelve hours early with time to spare for an ambush.

EIGHT

Errie woke to the sound of rocks cascading from the
roofline. Startled into panic, she assumed they were scattered across the bedrock by the footfall of her captor fast
approaching. The truth held little comfort. Instead of walking the
same tunnel she'd collapsed in, he was treading one directly overhead, casting debris in a drop trail from above. One that drizzled
dirt onto her body and into her eyes. Reminding of the instability of
the long-abandoned dwelling that trapped her. Shielding her face
from the fall off, she waited until it ceased directly overhead
springing from within the sandbags to inspect his movement.

Only strides ahead, an oxygen hole illuminated the tunnel and
amplified his heavy gate. And if she could hear him, he could hear
her. Quietly gathering her supplies onto the ground, she slid the
sandbags around to conceal her alcove. She couldn't come back to
this spot but didn't want to advertise she'd been there in the first
place. Lantern in hand she tiptoed beneath falling pebbles until
coming to a divide in the tunnel. With no recollection of its exterior
either option was as good a guess. Watching the roof until rockfall
indicated he was preceding left, she broke right picking up her
pace. She hadn't gone far when an indent in the wall caught her

attention. Stumbling and cursing the sound it made under her breath, she paused long enough to see a door embedded into the rock.

Escape. The thought of it washed over all others in her mind drowning them. A door meant access to another place, perhaps the surface. Without pause she threw it open, stepped inside and was drenched in blackness when it closed behind her. Only then did the thought hit.

If the staircase went up, and it did, she was mere feet from her captor and she'd probably made enough noise to announce that fact.

Errie froze, straining to hear sound from beyond the bottom step. Met with silence, she backed away from the stairs intending to exit, but the door that had opened so easily from the other side resisted. Heavy hardwood against hardwood combined with the dampness of the underground space made for a tight seal she couldn't break without notifying, with whining defiance, her presence to one she'd fought so desperately to avoid.

"No. Most victims react out of sheer panic giving the criminal the upper hand." It was Amy's voice in her head. Memory of her wisdom. Analyzing a documentary they watched retracing the actions of a stalker and his victim's failed efforts to survive his attack. "Patience, using intellect over fear, that's how you escape."

Errie's breath shuddered out in broken waves. The frigid air in the stairway drained any warmth her body held. Shaking, she clutched the door pull in her right hand, the unlit lantern in the other and waited. Counting seconds in her head by the thousand method anticipating distance made away from the stairwell access, she waited. Her mind contemplated. He could walk so far down the tunnel and return to this very spot above.

Wrapping her left hand over the right, lantern hung from her wrist, she yanked the door open with an unforgiving wail and bound out and down the dark tunnel she'd abandoned. The door reclaimed its position with a thud. Her heartbeat and labored breathing masked the rhythm of her feet and any sound of his pursuit. She drew little comfort knowing he would suffer the same indignity if he chose to use the staircase but if there was one, there were others.

Her eyes swept side to side as she ran. Now aware attack could come from all directions not just front or back. *Brilliant*. Minutes passed, long enough to assume she had somehow escaped detection. She broke stride slowing to a jog, a walk, then a hunched over stop gulping stale air.

And that's when she heard him. Footfall.

Not a full-out run but fast approaching and on the same level, no longer echoing from above. Straightening upright, she realized, unless she could stay ahead and outrun him, he had her. The tunnel proceeded endlessly ahead and behind, no way not to be seen. Swiveling to be sure he was approaching from dead ahead she spotted it. A now familiar indent in the wall a few strides ahead. Closing the distance to the enemy and out of options, she threw the door open expecting it to herald her position but it made no sound. As if used frequently or ill fit loose within the outer casing it swung open and closed behind her silently. Her glee for that allowance ended abruptly realizing this set of stairs also flowed one direction, down.

Accessing the same level housing rooms glimpsed through the airshaft and where she'd observed the man that stole her from her home mulling about without a care in the world. His lair.

Descending the winding stone stairs she kept one hand against the rock wall to steady her. Broken rocks littered the shallow steps and she feared injuring the two feet she relied on for escape. Catching herself when the steps ceased, she felt for the pull and opened the door anticipating more of the same, tunnels of endless dark. Instead she was met with blinding light. Any light was blinding to someone confined to blackness and she had been for two days. Squinting, her heart rattling echoes into her ears, she glimpsed a trail of exposed bulbs flanking the right side of the cavern wall just above head level. Studying the distance ahead and behind, she chose ahead knowing the entrance she'd been brought through origi-nally held no viable exit. Scanning the space, she ran for a way off this cursed level.

It wasn't long before the tunnel split. Knowing she'd encountered stairs leading up on the right and him to the left, she ran right away from the light. Shadows consumed the space and with it came the onset of exhaustion, the aftermath of panic and days without food. She ran as quickly as sure footing allowed until there was no hint of light or sound beyond the scattered air holes filtering from above. The tunnel branched again and she slowed to pause at the intersection wondering where to go and how to reach the surface out of this godforsaken hole. Heading left, as if this random choice could save her from discovery, she walked down the center at an even pace until a halo of light emerged ahead. It crossed her mind that in the disorienting darkness she could've circled the whole damn mine to come back into her kidnapper's domain from the opposite side.

Too tired to run and not certain retreating posed less risk, she gingerly approached until able to peek around a new corner. The tunnel closed inward to another doorway, this one much larger than the previous staircase access door. And it had been left slightly open. Within sightline from the threshold her eyes locked on a small nook with a sink, water tap, and food supplies. Mouth dry, head dizzy with hungry, she scanned the surroundings for any sign of life or cameras.

She couldn't risk being caught but wouldn't continue to evade detection by starving. Drifting into the space she seized a bottle of water from a grouping on the same shelf as protein bars and packets of something soft she afforded no time to inspect. Close by, a stash of plastic bags sat stuffed in a bunch. She grabbed two, doubling them for strength, swept an armful of supplies into them, spun on her heels, and was crossing the exit when another door drew her attention. This one mimicked an antique door to a wine cellar or a monk's living quarters. Beautiful, her hand smoothed across its aged surface realizing it had to have been brought into this space. A marvel of reclaimed or perhaps original time-tested wood, it was special. It stood to reason what was held behind it must be as well. A way out?

She couldn't turn away. Scanning the vicinity to ensure she

remained, for a time, alone, she unlatched the heavy door. Without a creak, it opened to a soft slide and suction sound. Inside, muted lighting popped on triggered by entry. Careful to close the door as she found it, she strode ten paces down a wide corridor to discover a bank of other, smaller, heavy wooden doors in succession left then right. At the end waited a door similar to the first, larger than the side doors. Cameras littered the hallway but all pointed into open spaces at the top of each door away from the hall capturing instead whatever lay enclosed within. She counted as she walked, twelve in total, and only the last sat opened. Before reaching it, she came by a door with a split of wood missing, enough to peek through and see behind. Veins pulsing with adrenaline laced blood she pushed her face close to the wood, breathing in its musty scent, tipped her head to align her left eye with the crack absorbing the image within.

Stumbling back, losing control of her footing, tangled in opposing directions, she fell onto the floor. Noticing for the first time the rock had been carefully covered with a straw surface. As if it was suddenly lit on fire she sprang up and bolted forward passing the last open doorway. A glimpse inside fueled rising terror. Sleeping quarters carefully tailored for a female prisoner, complete with extra blankets in a wicker bin by the door. Blood like ice, Errie grabbed the top one and flew for the doorway out, but something heavy slowed her approach. Her legs weren't complying with orders from her brain. The more it screamed for them to hurry the slower they plodded. Searching the area her nostrils, always sensitive, picked up the whiff of a scent reminiscent of her sorority sister's felt-tip pen collection. The source of the aroma poured down from a vent overhead. Dizzying. It explained the reason no one but her stirred or made a sound including the woman sleeping behind door number ten.

Not only had she entered the exact place her captor intended her to be housed, she'd delivered herself drunk with sedative. Rage swelled energy back into her legs. The drug stretched farther the distance to the entrance. In a last-ditch effort to survive, she spun to the similar back doorway, threw it open in one fluid motion, and exploded beyond it into the comparable safety of a darkened tunnel.

Swallowing oxygen with an open mouth, she ran ragged until a side door appeared. Exiting into it she climbed the stairs, legs leaden, thanking the Almighty when they rose two then three levels up. At the top she practically fell out the opening and onto the path of an almost collapsed offshoot of the mine. Clearly no one, including her enemy, had accessed this dilapidated space for decades. Breaking free of spider webs and disturbed dirt loosed by the mere vibration of her pace, she kept moving until it branched. Heading left to what appeared a safer track she didn't get far before a sea of rock collapsed behind her. Trapped in the darkness, drinking in dust with the air, she stopped running, dropped to the cave floor, deposited the supplies hanging from her arms, and fought with the lantern until it burst to life.

One semicircle later, seeing for the first time her fate, she cursed it, gathering her survival tools. "I fucking hate mines." She stared at her torn, makeshift shoes and then the endless tunnel out before them. "Don't collapse on me." She spoke into swirling dust. "I'm one you want to spit out. Swallow me with this bastard and I'll make you pay."

NINE

Kane woke before Amy, brewed coffee, and sauntered down the hall to his office to study a monster. The printer was heavy with pages sent overnight or before the break of dawn from contacts he sourced to round out information on all known victims. He hated seeing Errie among the photos and amassed evidence on the board. He'd printed out a second set of headshots for each victim and now used a separate sideboard to pin them up one to twelve, leaving two spaces open for the women currently unidentified. Deliberately he'd transposed the photos into black and white, forgoing the distraction of color.

His pale-green eyes set on each image, cataloging age, size, shared and isolated traits until arriving at his initial conclusion with new certainty.

"Nothing. These women have nothing in common." He spoke it to the empty room to find he wasn't alone.

"And how does that help us find him if no pattern exists?" Amy asked from the threshold.

Kane waved her in. "One exists. Not an obvious one."

"Great, so we're heading down the rabbit hole of possibilities—"

"We're narrowing our focus off the usual which may have us figure this guy out faster." Kane corrected. Taking the habit from Jade, Kane shoved the wingbacks closer to the sideboard and offered one to Amy. Still sporting PJs, she fell more than sat in the one to his left. "Look at them." He stared at the photos from first taken to Errie's placed last. "None of them are the same age so no shared experiences to back check, schooling or training. Different professions, if they have one. And they span the status from single to dating, married to divorced, children to none—"

"Or almost married," Amy interjected under her breath.

Kane flashed her a compassionate half smile and continued. "So when we eliminate these aspects what we're left with is a singular trigger for the Occultus. And, you know Errie better than anyone. We may not have the why but if we land on the what—"

"We're closer to the who," Amy finished his thought.

"Exactly. So we use the Jade method. Break down any identifier that sets Errie apart and then we search for a match in the others."

"It's a place to start. Thanks. Didn't have that yesterday." Amy twisted in her chair, scanning the room behind them. "Speaking of Jade, where's she at?"

"Oh. She headed out before the crack of dawn. Had an onboard meeting with the feds at seven and hit the road. She wanted to drop off extra gear at the trailer before meeting them at their high hide."

"Their what?"

"It's what Jade is calling their vantage staging area on the edge of the forest. Their guy is setting up on the opposite side to Jade, high on a ridgeline."

Amy chuckled. "Figures the feds are topside while Jade is literally at the bottom of the basin in the real muck."

"Yeah. She's familiar with the terrain so it gives her an advantage. It'll take their guy days to get far enough in to locate anything viable to house that number of victims. And she has a theory."

"Okay?"

"The guy exploited the river system deep in The Divide. He could transport by vehicle from the west to access the water, but hiking victims from the other way in? It'd be impossible to travel far enough to avoid detection. And their ranger is about to learn that the hard way."

Pride beamed from his smile and he couldn't help it.

"The downside is the west is the most unstable, cave-ins, rock slides, patches of shale and steep inclines," Amy warned.

"Yeah. That part, I'm not lovin' so to keep my mind off my partner tumbling off the side of a mountain with no backup, I'm sorting through this mess of paperwork and you're composing a list. Tell me about Errie."

Drex hated hospitals but not for the reason most in law enforcement avoided them. He lost more than one buddy to injuries overseas and the smell of sanitizer was enough to transport him back into blood-soaked ER operating rooms. He'd been shoved out of more than one and every time he left it was over for a brother on the table. His heroics in delivering them breathing to a place arguably equipped to save them guaranteed nothing. He couldn't avoid inhaling this hospital's filtered medicine scented air but wished he could. Scouring the entrance and halls for signs, he made it to the long-term care ward. A nurse's station sat adjacent to a set of double doors. No way would he be missed skirting by and landing a heavy hand on the access pad.

Pulling his badge, he held it out for inspection. The young nurse on duty examined it before turning her attention to him. "I'm here to see—"

"I know. We only have one resident here the FBI would be inter-ested in," she said, moving around the desk and casting the doors open. "Sanitizer, please." She pointed to a wall-mounted device. Closing his eyes against the harsh aroma he doused his large mitts. "I'll take you down. It's a bit of a maze with tons of machinery," she warned.

"Thanks," he said, following her in. If he hated hospitals, he friggin' detested this place. *Sweet Mother of God.* It literally housed every outcome men like him feared more than death. Two minutes down the hall, passing several versions of affliction, she heard him under his breath. "Jesus, put a bullet in me."

She spun his direction and he braced for an onslaught of criticism. "Right? If I could still hold a syringe, they'd never get me through the doors," she promised.

Relaxing in common company, he smiled. "Poor unfortunate bastards."

"Yeah, they have my sympathy. Well, all but the one you're here to see."

"Can he speak? What's his medical prognosis? If you don't mind me asking."

The nurse closed the distance between them slightly and lowered her already quiet voice to a whisper. "He can. Doesn't mean he will. And no one knows his prognosis except his medical team. We had to devise a whole new system after the murder attempt."

"Really? And how does that work?" As the hallway shortened and with it the option of rooms, he wished he had more time with the frank nurse. Drex paused in the empty hall and she stopped beside him.

"Honestly? It doesn't. We follow directed healing protocols so hard to hide much from the nursing staff. I know he gained consciousness months ago when they presumed that outcome all but impossible. And, they predicted he would never walk again but... you'll see. Don't be shocked when you see him."

"He's not the first man I've seen deteriorated and bedridden." Drex scanned the few doors ahead noticing the one with a camera outside it. Last on the left.

"No. That's what you would expect. He is on a cycle of muscle therapy paid for by a relative that I wish I could get in on. It stimulates each muscle like an intense gym workout so there is no deterioration. Heck, he may be in better shape now than before he was shot."

"Who in their right mind would pay for that?" Drex interest turned to infuriation.

"I know, right? There're rumors he comes from serious money and my guess is they're correct. He's ahead on the left. You can't miss the machinery. I have to get back."

"Thank you…" Drex waited for her name.

"Mell," she offered with a smile.

"Thank you, Mell." Drex gave her an all-knowing nod and strode off ready to meet the one who nearly killed his new partner. The curiosity that drew him to make the unauthorized stop in the first place solidified into a need-to-know. As he suspected there was far more at play with the past Redeemer case and its fallout than any news organization caught wind of. The course Jade and her partners walked to land this prolific killer a room in this hell house didn't matter a damn to him. Its lasting effect on someone he was about to work a case with did. Especially when so many victims' lives hung in the balance.

When entering a minefield, you want to know if the one walking beside you isn't prone to flinching.

A foot inside the space he was met by a bank of machines, some unplugged and stored for later use and others monitoring varying aspects of Nickolas Leigh the second. Drex knew who was paying for the impeccable care he received. Why? That was a question only the man on the bed could answer.

Across from him on the outer wall sat three half-length windows overlooking a park area below this fourth floor of the building. Though none opened, they weren't exactly bulletproof. Drex expected intense security measures and discovered there were none. He studied the room from left to right, stopping his inspection abruptly when Nickolas's eyes met his.

A vibrant deep forest green, they wouldn't be missed.

For the few seconds taken to close the distance to the end of the bed their eyes held, neither man breaking the stare. Then, Nickolas the junior dropped his to his hands crossed over his stomach. The top of the bed was elevated so he sat upright appearing no more ill than Drex and no less formidable.

"You're a big boy. The file said as much but I never trust another's interpretation." Drex watched for a reaction. Nothing.

"Thought I'd pay you a visit. I have a few questions." Still, nothing. "I'm working a huge case. Almost as big as yours but this guy isn't a killer like you. At least, not yet." Nothing but steady breath. "And I'm working with someone you know." This part Drex knew he was taking a huge gamble offering up. "Detective Jade Carmichael."

"You're not one of hers and you're not a cop, not from around here so who are you?" Nickolas employed an even, slow tone, low and strong, without a hitch or hesitation. Confident. His eyes drifted up, boring into Drex, revealing little, demanding much.

"And they said you couldn't talk," Drex said, deliberately relaxing his stance.

"They said I wouldn't." The control this man wielded was palpable.

"Nick. Can I call you Nick? I'll be honest with you; I am not well read on all the details of your case. In your current condition aren't you close to qualifying for transfer into Supermax? I mean—"

"It's not happening…" Nick waited.

"Oh, my bad. Special Agent Drex Lafine." Drex swung a chair from the corner and dropped into it at a distance but close enough their conversation couldn't be easily overheard outside the doorway.

"It's not happening…Drex." Nickolas offered nothing more but sat head up, undeterred by the unknown FBI man across from him suggesting a move to lock down. "Even you don't have that authority."

Nick was correct in guessing Drex couldn't force a move from his current posh private recovery but the certainty in his voice gave more away than the words.

"Back to the purpose of my visit. You almost killed Detective Carmichael—"

"If you had been there you would swear she'd come back from the dead."

Nick's choice of words registered for review later as Drex continued. "She survived but I'm wondering, and I don't know that you'll feel comfortable saying, did you want her dead?"

"You drove all the way to the outskirts of my small town to ask me what I wanted?" Nick's head tilted ever so slightly and Drex logged that as movement he wasn't predicted to ever employ again.

"I want to know how motivated you are to see my new partner dead." Drex didn't have time to tap dance.

"She has a partner. Did you ask Kane's permission first?" Nick retained a history on Jade and those associated with her and he wasn't willing to share.

"Actually...she asked to come onboard. It's my case." Drex prompted.

"She'd only do that if it involved someone she considers family and you...are not." Nick's voice faltered for the first time but Drex was betting the break was a result of his medical condition and not emotion.

"Right. Yes, she knows one of the kidnapped victims." Drex was treading on classified ground.

"One of? How many are there?"

"You answer my question and I may tell you," Drex offered knowing time alone had to be at risk of ending unexpectedly with the entrance of a nurse or doctor on patient rounds.

"I don't want her dead." Nick's expression added nothing but Drex caught the slightest glimpse of sincerity behind his eyes.

And there it was. Five words that altered the perspective on whatever went down between this killer and the homicide detective who came up against him. Drex had digging to do but anymore with this criminal and he could jeopardize more than his own future. Nick was smarter than average by leaps and bounds and surely not opposed to using the entire conversation against Drex. Before he could respond a doctor entered, head down preoccupied with the tablet chart in front of him.

"These numbers are promising, Nickolas. Yes...but I think we should increase mobility training—" He dropped his sentence with immediacy, recognizing his patient had a visitor. "I'm sorry, who are you and—"

"It's fine, Doc." Nickolas derailed his objection. "Drex is a friend of the family. He was on his way out."

Taking his queue to leave without incident, Drex stood, slid the chair back to its former place, and passed by the doctor smiling in response to his uncertain stare. At the threshold he paused, leaning back to make eye contact with Nickolas. "Ten," he said. "The number of weeks I anticipate being in the area. I'll reach out if it changes."

"You do that," Nickolas said. "I look forward to our next visit. And, Drex, let me know if you need my help with that problem we discussed."

A hundred questions swarmed Drex's mind as he strutted back to civilization. He had an avenue of inquiry nonexistent on the drive in. He started reading people as a kid, a mechanism of survival. As an adult there were few better. This killer was connected to the Carmichael woman more intimately than the ink on the case files admitted. And he intended to find out how right after he mapped a search grid for the Occultus with her.

He considered returning once he narrowed a deeper avenue of inquiry, but it'd be a cold day in hell before he relied on a killer for help to apprehend another criminal. He couldn't help speculating if the other detective on the Occultus case shared his sentiment.

TEN

T he collapse of the upper tunnel echoed through the mine system and drew him to Errie's exact location prior to the cave-in. The difficulty would be accessing the west side of that level. Rockfall sealed the tunnel and pinned the stairwell door shut. This confined damage to the upper passage but also prevented easy entry. Limiting his occupation to stable sectors, he hadn't spent a great deal of time surveying this partial floor system. Referencing the only maps in existence didn't offer much direction. Of the three in his possession, only two denoted the upper tunnel and indicated conflicting information. One revealed markings interpreted as surface access points. The other, an updated version, distinctly showed no outer access from the west side. Boring into the outer mountainside didn't coincide with his intention to remain elusive and hidden from the authorities that, by now, had begun hunting him. This left one option. Digging into an already dilapidated roof and running the risk of a catastrophic collapse that threatened not only him but all eleven of his guests housed below.

As for the twelfth, he prayed she was safe on the secure side of the upper tunnel, awaiting rescue. After days in the dark endless mine, he was certain she would happily retreat into the space he designed especially for her. A couple more days in the dark and she may return on her own accord. Hopefully she was fit to find a path back and hadn't sustained serious injury. Either way a nurse was on hand if she required care. He fought the urge to give into a swelling rage over the disruption she caused. Cautioning that he knew to expect nothing less from this little warrior. In fairness, preoccupied preparing for the approaching days, he'd allowed her to scurry about for too long. Years in the making he couldn't permit distractions to interfere. He had time to bring Errie back into the fold. After all, she was twelve, the last and most sacred of the chosen.

A few deep breaths later, he gathered supplies, a burlap bag containing water, food, a protective mask, and first aid items. Confident the eleven women who hadn't escaped him were resting comfortably, he locked the outer door to the sleeping quarters and made out into the mine. Twenty minutes later he climbed a short iron ladder attached to an outer stonewall and opened a hatch to the upper mine. The air above, thick with years of dust brought to life in the collapse, was thin of oxygen and smelled of earth, oil, and moss. Too small to fit through, he used his flashlight to scan the immediate area surrounding the opening where his head and one hand fit. The hatch was originally installed for the very purpose of passing needed equipment between levels. Seeing nothing unusual, he pulled back pushing the bag over his shoulders and through the space. Setting it as far right of the hole as reach would allow, he secured a tiny camera pointed the direction of the bag at the edge of the hatch, ran its cord down at a corner, pulled its door closed, and lowered back down to ground level. The ladder creaked and moaned against his weight on its iron with every step and grasp of his hands. Feet firmly planted on solid ground he inhaled deeply filling his lungs against the depleted oxygen knowing Errie could not do the same.

If his tiny dancer was not injured, she may stumble upon the supplies and learn there was no reason to fear for her life. The same could not be said for number one. A gamer and gambler rich on the manipulation of others, she was accustomed to winning. But being first had its pitfalls. A lesson she was soon to learn.

Returning to the sleeping chambers, he peaked inside each door, quietly closing and relocking them. All but the one designated for Errie. It he'd left ajar anticipating her return. Though the dancer didn't occupy the space, he stood inside the doorframe imagining her there. The room held the essence of her for him. It smelled faintly of her favorite perfume, was adorned with accents of the sage color she wore most often and was the only one fitted with the necessary ensemble for a stage performance hanging inside a standing wardrobe in the far corner. Locked, he considered opening it to caress the silk of her tiny shoes or the soft chiffon of her gowns. No time to envision, he backed out tipping the wicker basket and the blankets held within onto the floor. Quickly righting the mess, he made for the viewing room.

On a rotating sleep cycle, each given their hour of attention, exercise, and nourishment, they wouldn't hear the others sedated in slumber or him knocking about. And thankfully at this early hour none were awake.

Number one had been with him the longest. The scratches in her quarters counted months not days or weeks. And, in thirty-six hours the clock would start. Her time of preparation was limited. As pleased as he was with her weight gain and improved endurance, her habits made her particularly fragile and she'd fought every effort to reform. Too familiar, he predicted the outcome while shuffling the cards set before him on the small desk in front of the bank of monitors.

Splitting his focus between the motionless figure in room one and the deck, he laid cards down. They confirmed the story he expected. One of refusal to surrender and release and a warning of treachery and resulting consequence. Staring at his findings, he sighed. First the possible burying of a delicate ballerina and now a dire outcome awaiting one he worked so hard to heal. These were heavy crosses he carried, but he prepared for this.

They were mere scratches in his heart. Nothing close to the deep cut grooves he endured from the first woman he loved. Frailty posed the greatest risk to life, love, and peace. And the woman on the screen basking in the protection of slumber was sure to discover it too late. He wondered, shuffling his next set of readings, would they all end in disappointment? To date, his cards were never wrong.

———————

Watching rain teem down, drenching the asphalt and dispelling a sinister mist hovering low enough to impede a clear sightline to the private hospital's underground parking garage, Amy wondered if it was an ominous sign of things to come. Everyone involved in the Redeemer case had moved on. A few by force of rebuilding new lives, some with the help of their esteemed head shrink, Max, and others with fallout to repair demanding all their energies. Amy was the lone wolf, abandoned by the pack, forgotten at the kill sight, entranced by its aftermath. Or, just the unfortunate detective still standing and therefore assigned the newest case. The attempted murder of the most diabolical killer Shadow Hook had ever seen, the Redeemer or Nickolas Leigh the Second, as she now knew him.

For a first case one could assume her superiors held high regard for her abilities given the profile of the intended victim. Amy knew better. Captain Grey was as wasted as the rest of them by the toll of denying Nickolas any remaining freedom and placing him here, under physician's care and watchful eyes. Though masked in a vow of silence, two of the hospital's senior staff members were reporting regularly to Grey on any changes to his medical state. Especially those integral to enable him to become the slightest risk. There was much Amy didn't know, much she hadn't been entrusted with. Grey said it was for her own protection but she knew it was Jade who he protected and she understood why. In fact, it was the reason she was about to check in on a man she expected to only see again on an ME's table being fitted for a coffin. Unfortunately he lived.

All she could hope for now was that he didn't remember her.

Cozying up to a killer while Errie was in the hands of a man like him was about as fucked a position as she could enlist. But it got worse. In truth, she was investigating leads, interviewing staff, fitting puzzle pieces into place fully aware that no conclusion would be reached. No suspect apprehended. No charges ever laid.

Because if they were, she'd be behind bars. She alone disabled his breathing equipment, left no trace, and rode the elevator to the floor of her wounded team without a single person suspecting. And, yes, he'd been transferred to a far more secure location and remained safely tucked away and healing too well ever since. No one anticipated him regaining consciousness. He woke up. They said his brain was deprived long enough for irreparable damage to impede his cognitive abilities. He was lucid. The bullet Kane fired into his neck months back lodged at a location capable of triggering full-body permanent paralysis. His upper body functioned. And now his private medical team worked against all odds to help him walk out of this place one day.

And right into a cage serving consecutive life sentences with no chance of parole but even that wasn't guaranteed. He had been unable to stand trial for so long. The case kept being pushed for one reason or another. Amy knew the volley of his lawyers was fueled by his biological family's stronghold in judicial circles. Even his mother who specialized in bringing his kind into the harsh light of justice, bent and fractured by the path she set him on, worked to support his recovery. The world had twisted like vines weaving up the side of an abandoned castle until the origin of the root of truth disappeared in the mess.

She still wanted him dead. And hiding that fact was not only integral to doing her job. It was a matter of survival for her and, quite possibly, Errie. She couldn't help rescue her from behind bars. So sauntering down the hallway of the fourth floor, she cemented that fact in her mind.

"How's the patient today?" Amy asked the duty nurse before heading inside the unit to finish her follow-up with his doctor.

"Doing better than expected." The nurse tipped her head in the direction of his room. "He has had visitors. Family, I think but I didn't recognize him. Big guy. I came on shift as he was leaving."

"Who was on before you?" Amy asked, intrigued.

"Not sure but I could check the schedule," she offered.

"Thank you, Lyse. I'll check with you on my way out. I shouldn't be too long." Amy waited for the double doors to open.

"No problem. I'm here until midnight." Lyse dropped her head back into the documents on the desk before her as Amy crossed the threshold and vanished behind the closing doors.

Striding down the long hall, following it to the furthest side where the patient in question was housed, Amy wondered who had made the trip to see Nickolas and why. If it had been his mother or grandfather, Lyse would've said as she knew both. Outside of them, Amy wasn't aware of connected family. Perhaps Lyse was wrong and it was another member of his vast legal team. Stopping short of his room, she broke left and sought a door labeled, Dr. Emile Nnadi, Chief of Extended Recovery.

Tapping twice with the back of her knuckles on its plaque, she waited pushing thoughts of Errie down deep, trusting Jade and Kane were fighting for her, and knowing she had to do her part.

"Come on in, Detective," Dr. Nnadi said.

Amy opened the door, shook hands with the decorated specialist, and claimed a seat opposite his in front of his illustrious desk. "Thank you for fitting me in today," she said. "I imagine you're extremely busy."

"The timing was good. I had a review cancel due to the bad weather. What can I do for you?" The doctor folded shut an open file on his desk, sliding it to the side revealing a polished wooden surface outstretched before him to rest his crossed arms on. He settled in but his relaxed demeanor didn't fool Amy.

"I realize you are in a unique position, doctor. You have a patient whose recovery under your care has been nothing short of miraculous. And yet, it's not easily celebrated given who he is and his past crimes."

"Alleged crimes," he clarified. "We should navigate political correctness with caution."

"I can understand the difficult complexities this poses. Being tasked with finding out the exact details of the near termination—"

"You mean the attempted murder of my patient?" The doctor's stance didn't shift, but his tone warned her to tread lightly.

"As you said, politically correct. Deemed unfit to stand trial in the weeks and months following his capture and his punishment not yet fully decided, we're far from drawing conclusions on what exactly occurred to endanger his life following his initial placement in recovery at the general. And this is why your assessment or findings are so valuable to my case. Please." Amy offered the opening for him to reveal the conclusions she requested he gather the last time they met.

"It was all but impossible for the machine to falter in the way it did without human intervention. The room he was in was not guarded effectively—"

"To be fair, he nearly killed three detectives and they were all fighting for survival at the anticipated time of the incident," Amy pushed, expecting him to push back and giving no room in which to do so. "A killer confirmed to have obliterated many exceptional women, thus laying waste to a number of families and destroying a vast array of lives, well...one could rightly assume he amassed countless enemies. And the public at large was terrorized while he ran free deciding the fate of so many. Any number of people could take offense. And if you had beared witness to the horror left in his wake perhaps you would realize what a travesty it is for your exceptional skills to be used to prolong his existence."

The doctor studied her, dropped his eyes to his desk for a beat, and then locked his with hers, unflinching. "Detective, I save and restore lives. I am not in the business of judging or deciding their worth. I would think this was a mindset you understood but I'm not convinced. Perhaps you are not the ideal candidate for this investigation? Though I'm not about telling you your job, I won't allow you to tell me mine."

Amy didn't look away. "Your expertise involves compassion. So does mine. Unfortunately I see both sides of victimology while you are afforded only one. I am glad a man of your integrity is in charge of Nickolas Leigh's recovery. I just wish your talents could've been better served saving the lives of his victims."

The doctor said nothing more. Sliding the file he closed earlier across the desk at her, he nodded for her to take it. "Everything you asked is answered inside. I have patients to check on." His voice said the message she sent had been received. Not arrogant or combative,

Dr. Nnadi was a good man providing exceptional care to a monster he couldn't possibly know in the way she did.

Intimately.

"Thank you for this." Amy stood, collected the file, and shook his hand. "I have a couple questions for Mr. Leigh before I leave. Nothing in depth just housekeeping."

"Keep it brief," he cautioned. "I will be in with him in a half hour to check his physical and emotional state."

On the way out Amy casually nodded, deliberately nonchalant though they both knew she didn't give a rat's ass about either. "Enjoy your day."

A few doors down, she entered the room holding the Redeemer. Nickolas Leigh had been called many names before being discovered but she felt the one the media labeled him with, though in complete contrast to his nature, suited best. She found it odd in an era of mass social media how easily interest in him faded after capture. She chalked it up to the reports of him being shot and mortally wounded, transported to hospital unconscious, and not expected to live let alone wake, followed by the attempt on his life sealing the deal on his comatose state. The public washed their hands of him figuring him for a vegetable. Vegetables weren't cool coffee conversation. After his legal care was returned to his biological family injunctions were put in place locking out continued coverage and with them public knowledge of his existence.

Most assumed he was dead. Or, no longer a threat. As he raised his eyes from the book in his lap to meet hers, Amy knew better.

"Detective, what brings you by?" Nickolas carefully closed the novel, marking the page with an engraved gold placeholder. Sitting upright, as was the case whenever she came by, his upper body seemed stronger than it had on her last visit weeks earlier. He was gaining muscle mass.

"I have a detailed breakdown of your medical progress from Dr. Nnadi but wanted to hear from you if you recall anything of your time at the general hospital. Now that your memory is returning, as fractured as it may be. Do you remember any of the staff or anyone unknown to you entering your room?"

A smile escaped only the left side of his mouth. Nickolas was unfortunately striking. The nurses were enamored despite his history and watching him now she knew why. "I remember Max coming in while I was being transferred, Jade and Kane sometime after I arrived here, but none of the hospital staff there. Unconscious so…"

"Okay. Has anyone been by unexpectedly?" Amy wasn't getting anything worth writing down but she appeared to be doing her job. With him on full display the irony of his current condition and afforded protections while Errie had none forced her to swallow down bile rising from her gut.

"Are you feeling well, Detective? You're a bit pale."

Fuck, he was reading her. "I hate hospitals, we all do. So, anyone?"

"No. No one."

"And there's been no other disruption to your quality of care?" She scribbled in her notepad as if writing the secret of mortality though the words repeating down the page remained the same.

Bring Errie home and let the past go.

If guilt held the dark cloud she couldn't escape overhead, it originated from failing her pledge to be a great cop, an honest detective, an honorable person, and not an attempted killer. It wasn't caused by inconveniencing, if only physically, this man. And she came up short on successfully ending his life. In all likelihood the homicide attempt landed him here, in the lap of luxury medical care. Maybe that was where the guilt stemmed from.

"Do I seem the slightest bit concerned for my safety or wellbeing? Obviously, I am receiving exceptional care." He flexed his arms modestly. It was enough.

"The care here is next level. I'm interested in any glimpse, any flash of memory that can lead us to clarity on how your lifesustaining machine quit working."

"Amy? It is Amy, correct?"

Amy nodded and waited.

"Although the company responsible for the machine would wildly refute it, machines fail. Mine, a perfect storm of mishaps.

Low batteries, old batteries mistaken for new, an accumulation of moisture on its sensitive surface. I've heard the atmosphere in the hospital that evening was chaos. I believe searching for a villain in this circumstance is a waste of your precious time. If someone diabolical entered my space, I of all people would recognize them as such. Don't you think? And I have an incredible memory still, according to my doctor. Childhood memories have faded, but that's a gift. More recent ones are becoming crystal clear."

"Are you requesting we close the case?" The ground beneath Amy tilted.

"I am." Dropping his attention back to the book, he reopened it to the last page read. "If there's nothing else."

"Thank you for your time. Advise me if your decision changes." She made for the door watching as Dr. Nnadi entered.

"Amy?" he waited for her to again make eye contact. "It won't change. And I believe you have more important issues to focus on."

Why? Why let a potential crime against him go and why did he suspect she had more important issues?

It wasn't the tone or the delivery. Something sinister behind those electric green eyes sent shivers down Amy's spine lasting the distance to her car. Stepping inside it and slamming the door to the outside world, she scanned the vicinity for onlookers though they wouldn't read much through the downpour. Satisfied she was alone, she folded her arms around her waist and sobbed. Tears rolled like raindrops for Errie, for the trap her actions ensnared her in, and for what lay ahead.

A torrent to drown in.

ELEVEN

Of course it had to rain. Climbing steep terrain cast in sharp rocks and unstable earth wasn't enough. Mother Nature had to throw her two cents down on Jade's already difficult path. Trudging into a tent set up by the FBI agent's team, Jade knew she'd be unwelcome and outnumbered, but it didn't matter. Whatever direction they embarked on she would head down one of her own. The one Errie advised she take.

The crime scene flashed in memory as Jade's waterproof and fur lined, Timberland combats sunk into the muddied trail from the parking area to the tent. Outside of the clue Errie left behind, local cops were tracking leads in each respective town where a victim was previously abducted. A vehicle was captured leaving the scene of the third taken by a security camera on an adjacent building. The company once leasing it was foreclosed on, leaving it empty for months. With nothing inside to steal and appearing formidable from the exterior, their suspect could've easily imagined it was lacking surveillance, if he considered it at all. That abduction occurred more than nine weeks back, and the van spotted was abandoned two towns away on the side of a country road four days later. Wiped clean. Locals knew with relative certainty their citizen was transported inside but it gave up not so much as a hair or correlating fiber.

The Occultus was thorough.

There existed only so many viable structures to house the women. In the weeks since the feds assumed the case they hadn't stood sentinel. They actively sifted through every relic airline hanger, warehouse, railcar field, building, barn, and shipyard. Their efforts had been meticulous, exhaustive, costly, and futile. While watching the case before being drawn into it, Jade sympathized with their plight.

Now, no sympathy left, she yanked back the canvas doorway with singular focus—to save Errie before any of them. It was not a goal of pride. If a rescuer other than Jade stumbled upon and rescued Errie, Jade would celebrate her homecoming the same. The clock ticking down Errie's chance of survival was her driving force.

She was personally invested and willing to risk far more than the military top dog smacking orders down on the area map pinned to a back board in front of the team she was about to become a part of.

"I don't give a damn what you were told, French. I want a seasoned ranger in here. Someone who knows this area blindfold-ed." Agent Drex Lafine wasn't difficult to identify. He held command of everyone's attention and the intimidation was both subtle and fierce. "Oh, Detective Carmichael, perfect timing. Can you get in touch with a ranger who knows the lay of the land out here?"

"I'll put in a call. The problem your agents are struggling with isn't reaching a ranger. It's finding one who has actually been in this sector. It's deemed impassable and warded with signs saying as much for hectares in every direction from this point." Jade paused, brushing the dripping hair off her face. "The section where the drop to the river is steepest on both sides is known as The Divide but local kids call it Dead Man's Drop for a reason. Venture too far in and you're damn likely to never come out."

All eyes were on her and his response would tell her everything about what the next days or weeks held.

"So what would you recommend?" Drex asked. His tone was respectful and non-combative but she didn't expect it to last.

"There's a local tracker who retrieved a kid lost a couple years ago. I don't know if he's available or even—"

"Find him. Bring him here. I want him drinking hot cocoa in this tent by nightfall tomorrow if he's within driving distance. Can you handle that?" Drex was testing.

"If he's local, he'll be here," Jade promised, wondering if what was masked as an easy task was designed to be her first failure. Her new superior nodded and continued outlining their united mission without pause. She liked his no-nonsense approach. This guy couldn't have been further down the opposing scale of his cousin's incompetence if he worked at it. How the late not great Wenzel and Drex were related, Jade wasn't sure, but the fact they'd swam down completely contrasting DNA chains was glaringly obvious.

"I trust all of you brought the right gear for this cascading mud hole we've been thrown into. You have your sectors and unfortunately the weather has decided to weigh in on our timeline. So at the crack of dawn, weather permitting, we meet back here to brief, then into the forest. Be rested and ready. And remember those women are spending another long night in the hands of evil while you're cozy in your bunks." Drex eyed each of the four agents assigned under him, dropped his head to the door side, and they all disbursed without a word. Swiveling, more to watch them disband than to angle for the exit, Jade waited. Two sidestepped by her on the way out, issuing faint acknowledgment of her existence before she was summoned. "Detective, can you hang back a minute?"

After the last agent to leave dropped the tarp and entered the downpour, Drex spoke again. This time his voice held a casual tone. "Can I call you Jade?" he asked.

"Of course." She waited.

"I'm sure this is about as uncomfortable for you as can get. You're personally motivated and invested in catching this one and rescuing a friend. Despite this, from here out I will expect you to follow my lead. Will this be a problem?" he asked, locking eyes, not allowing deception.

"We both have the same goal, so no. I don't think so." Jade's honesty drew the slightest smile. "I plan to approach from the west covering this zone." Jade tapped the map, circling the corresponding space. "You okay with that?"

Drex eyed the area of interest, then her. "You know you're choosing the worst land to navigate?"

"Better one who has trudged it before than risk losing an agent down a slide to the gullet." Jade expected Drex to jump at the opportunity to force the cop in their midst out of the grid they allocated but he didn't.

"I don't plan on losing any member of our team and that includes you." Drex surveyed the map. His eyes remained focused on it, save for a beat when they glanced at hers. "I'll agree if you commit to checking in with me directly every hour."

"Every hour from daybreak to nightfall, you'll hear from me."

"Okay then, I'll see you bright and early tomorrow." Drex stood back and began gathering up maps and documents from the staging table.

"Are you heading back to town? I can recommend—"

"Nope. I'm here for the duration. Have a trailer and my Humvee at the back of the ridgeline. Get some rest tonight. You'll need it." Drex never glanced from his task as she exited. Like her, he made camp already and had no intention of leaving it until doing so with twelve victims and one perpetrator in cuffs or a body bag.

So far, she and the agent had a lot in common.

The thought crossed her mind she may not be the only law enforcer angling to spend the night drenched and alone in a search grid. Then she remembered he had no history in her neck of the woods, wouldn't even recognize the trail symbols or what they warned of until studying the maps he was busy sorting through.

No. She would be alone this night, on the other side of the bluff, aiming to come face-to-face with the Occultus in the most dangerous territory their fine state had. Not the best course of action for self-preservation, but the only one to fight the clock ticking down Errie's chances of a safe return.

On the drive to the opposite side of The Divide and the one

Kane, Amy, Errie, and her entered the forest from on their last trip, she couldn't help running down possibilities of how Errie directed her to this forsaken place. Her captor had to have said something about no one ever finding her where he was taking her. Did he hint at Dead Man's Drop as a threat thinking it'd be unfamiliar to Errie? After all, did professional ballerinas generally frequent impassable warded hiking trails? He would never suspect the scope of who Errie actually was. Her drive. Her fortitude. Jade prayed she held those traits close until she reached her.

The notion that Errie was already dead or beyond saving was not welcome in Jade's perspective. She simply would not allow Amy's worst fears a shred of life.

Back at her base camp inside the warmth of the trailer, she dried off, changed for the weather and trek ahead, and reviewed information her and Kane amassed. She made a point to read a little about each of the families left behind and terrorized by the unknown fate of the loved ones taken. Aware damage compiled in weeks or months in the hands of an abductor, personal insight may be required to garner the victims' trust to pilot them home.

Scanning the rough territory beyond the Airstream's windows she wasn't certain how she could usher several women, potentially harmed and compromised, back to safety. And she damn sure wasn't planning on leaving them behind. Packing a high-powered Tac light and colored filters to screw on over its lens, she thought at worst she could send a clear beacon Agent Lafine, Drex, could lead a rescue team to. And then the sickening wave of instinct washed in. The gut feeling every great detective relied on and suffered with. There was no easy way to bring the victims back out if this was where the Occultus housed them because they weren't meant to ever leave. At least not all of them.

But Errie… she had to leave.

No matter how she came at it the situation sucked. This was when she, and those with her calling, ran toward danger instead of away. Only this time, she was doing it alone. And not running but trekking through the worst damn unstable ground she'd ever been dared to cross. The last time she entered the area her boots had been new, dry, and unlined. The sun had shone and the weather was perfect. Staring by flashlight at the cold mud sucking her soles in with each step, the task she'd taken on weighed heavy. Amy's closeness to the case barred her from it. Kane, as rehabilitated as he appeared, was still under doctor's orders and couldn't risk another setback. And Tex, who owned the supporting role for all of the homicide unit's first ringers, hadn't recovered enough to use a weapon. Though she and Kane knew the man had all but become ambidextrous and was actually mastering the task of retesting at the firing range with his opposite hand.

Somehow it fit. She didn't want any of them out here in the dark with her. Finding Errie might provide the only opportunity affording Jade the space to process their last case and its fallout. Fallout that altered none of them as it had her.

Exploiting a natural animal trail, long-eared bats swooped at her head protesting her intrusion. Despite the beanie pulled tight over her ears, the thought of a landing prompt her to switch on her headlamp fending off the flying rodents of the night. At a break in the thick foliage, she reassessed options. If the criminal she sought used the waterway to get his victims into the deep of the forest, there were hundreds of acres he could access but a limited area with the prospect of caves. This was the grid her and Kane designated before she left town.

Entering at the far west quadrant, the grid overlapped the woodlands ahead in her mind. With no other way in, outside of a helicopter rappel line, she'd descend over the west shoulder from high ground to the lower riverbed, cross at an available natural bridge, and climb the east wall of the canon to the caves, working her way from south to north for signs of habitation. With limited time before daybreak and her requested presence at Agent Lafine's morning briefing, this first foray served to lay the groundwork and scan for obvious areas of interest capitalizing on the black night to hide her from view.

An hour in, her legs and feet ached from gripping their way to solid ground with every slick step forward. The animal trail disappeared beneath a heavy blanket of foliage. Unable to duck low enough to escape it she veered off the path seeking a break from the trees. Watery runoff forged its own river snaking toward The Divide. Jade followed, it being the path of least resistance.

Ahead, cast in the glow of moonlight, a clearing emerged. Wanting to run for it breaking free, if only momentarily, from fighting off branches and dodging and weaving the forest's forces working against her incursion, her pace quickened. Clinging to its edge may allow her an open view of the caves on the adjacent eastern wall. Short of picking her toque clean off, branches smacking into and over her head soaked it through. It released cascading droplets into her eyes and down her cheeks. She chose the left side of the clearing, angling her approach she glanced down to assess footing, realizing the once timid runoff was asserting itself. Her stride gained rhythm and when the rocks beneath her boots disappeared, replaced by mud, she lost the ability to slow down. A single misstep and she became one with the dark water surging toward the ridge.

In a crash and flurry of twisting arms and legs she had seconds to process the danger of the mudslide and how close it was to the edge. In a blinding break into moonlight she sought a branch, any branch, to impede her trajectory. Wrestling damn limbs for hours, when she desperately needed one, none existed. Catching sight of the outcrop where water launched off, falling to meet the torrent of the river far below, her hands grappled for anything solid to clench. Heaving in gulped breath as if it would inflate her chest sufficiently to float her body safely to the cavern floor, Jade's left hand made contact with something. Gripping harder than she had ever held a weapon, she braced for the echo of the small branch snapping under the weight of her and the rush of mud and debris. Instead, her body whipped left with such force her stomach impacted a tree trunk exploding all the breath held in her chest. Swallowing, desperate for oxygen while spitting mud, seconds passed before she absorbed that what remained pressed into her ravaged hand was not a branch but the time-tested root of the tree that winded her. Thrown clear of the mudslide she was slow to pull off the forest floor. Sore and unclear of the scope of damage inflicted, she tested her legs and arms before rising to full height. Careful to stay back from the path of the diminishing mudslide, she reached into a pocket for a balaclava she'd brought for concealment. Now used as a towel, she mopped off enough to see the eastern cavern wall clearly and an open gash in her left palm.

"Brilliant," she cursed. "Fuck. How the hell do I explain carving a hole in my hand before the first day of the rescue?"

A branch snapped. Then another. Something or someone was traversing an area below. Listening with more intent, she followed the sound hoping to identify if it was heading her direction or farther down the embankment. As the echoes grew distant, she inched closer to the cliff edge, careful to keep one hand gripped on a branch for security. Wrapping the rappel line she brought around a thick trunk and clipping in, she kneeled then crawled to peer over a stone outcrop not far from the one she could've catapulted over in the slide.

With headlamp and Tac light long since extinguished, she scanned by moonlight for the slightest movement. Taking in the expanse, she memorized markers then, drifting left to right, swept the wall visually. On the third pass her eyes locked on a flash of light. Visible for mere seconds, she couldn't determine from the distance whether it was a reflection cast by the moon or manmade. Either way she noted to inspect it closer in daylight on her return.

Aching as she backed away and gathered gear to retreat into the forest brush, her mind replayed the long trek in. She'd mapped the distance and roughly the trail taken on an app used by area rescue rangers. Expecting the long hike out to be more daunting than the one in, she found her footing and centered her thoughts on the evidence of the case.

Barring she survived the night and made it to the morning meeting, before she embarked on a return, she planned on giving Max a call from the Airstream. If her instincts were correct and the perpetrator that kidnapped the victims didn't intend on returning them to society then what was he planning? Pooling resources she'd get her trusted shrink to weigh in. Any bit of information leading to understanding the man she was up against was of value. And she knew it was a man. Despite every known aspect pointed that direction, a child witness claimed to have seen a man loading a heavy parcel into the back of a van near the abduction site of victim seven. Local police paid the tip due diligence but with no supporting visuals it meant little. For Jade it added clarity to the profile her and Kane were building.

Certain a man had taken the women, Jade had no idea why.

The victomology didn't match. Not even a little. Age, build, hair color, occupation, social class, backgrounds, marital status, sexual preference, financial standing, and all other obvious traits varied. Almost all of the women were of a slight build, not really accounting for anything significant to target. So how did he choose them? Jade mulled this over ignoring the throbbing in her left wrist, the occasional stabs of pain shooting across her palm, and the dull ache stretching out from the point of impact with the tree trunk across her abdomen.

The rain petered out to a drizzle blanketing the forest in heavy mist. Electing to trust her feet to feel their way to stable turf, Jade kept her head up maintaining course. Not far from the break way between the tree canopy and lower brush leading to the landing where the Airstream was tucked in, she caught sound of motion running parallel to her. Pausing, she held her breath sensing what-ever walked there knew to mask its movements. Without a howl to identify it as coyote, she guessed it was either a fox concealing itself out of fear of her or a bobcat. In the event of the later she had no interest in fighting off a feline and its razor-sharp claws. Snapping on her Tac light she swept it across in front as she ran for the trailer.

Nothing followed. But scrambling inside she couldn't close and lock the door fast enough. For one who pleaded for a key place on the hunt, there was no denying she felt more like prey tonight. The clock over the kitchen stove said it was nearing two. With a much needed shower and wounds to bandage, she'd be lucky to grab three hours sleep. Lining a chair nearest the door with gear for the next day, she dropped her soaked and torn clothing on the floor outside the shower and waited for its steam to fill the space before stepping inside. Dirt and blood swirled down the drain as she assessed the outing. It wasn't a complete loss. She determined how to get to The Divide hours sooner than the feds coming in from the east. Better prepared for the trek in and with a tested trail, she could focus on the area of interest longer in daylight.

And there was the flash of light off the eastern bank.

Dried and warm, she swallowed down hot tea, texted Kane her signal for *home safe*, and crawled into bed grateful the morning commute was short giving her a full three and a half hours of shut-eye. Drifting off on a cloud of exhaustion and ibuprofen, it was difficult to discern if the source of the scratching noise drifting between her ears was coming from outside or the start of a dream. If outside in the night, she thought fading out, chances were the animal tracking her had broke from the cover of the forest and followed her scent. And if that were true, her mind churned with the thought, it wasn't afraid of her and...she should fear it.

TWELVE

She called him Animal and the name fit. No self-control, he acted out of primal rage and instinct. Hungry, he demanded to feed deaf to her pleas to stop. She swore if she survived him and escaped this hedonistic trap no one would ever hear what she endured in captivity. If they did, she would lose her identity entirely and that she wouldn't allow. If she made it to freedom, the words would not leave her lips though the scars inflicted would remain forever. She understood now why so many women brought through the emergency room doors for care following a rape or assault refused to testify. Here, in the aftermath, clarity said to speak it gave it life, allowed it a place card in the path of truth, and she flatly rejected lending any energy to the violation of violence visited on her. A nurse, trained in the profession of healing, she didn't see a benefit to reliving what was already barely endurable.

Waking heavily laden despite throwing up most of the food she was certain was laced in sedatives; she fought the urge to submit again to sleep. The camera hovering over the top of the cell door blinked, in need of a battery change. She'd paid close attention to the last time it signaled this and listened intently, pretending to sleep, as he entered and swapped them out. Without a gauge for time, she devised her own and began counting down how long she'd be free of him before his next rounds. Her hand smoothed across the divots she etched into the stone wall by the bed, counting as if reading Braille, the number of days and weeks she'd fought through to earn the information needed for a chance at escape.

Wrapping the torn piece of fabric she'd ripped from the inside bottom edge of the sweatpants he provided over her mouth and nose, she carried the wooden side table close to the door. Ensuring its stability on the uneven ground, packing hay on either side, she stepped up, peering down the hall. Counting the doors from most distant to closest then beyond, hers was the ninth in a line of twelve. She'd known this for weeks, but her brain was starved to collect every detail precisely for record. The last door before what she presumed was the larger exit door, number twelve, had always remained open. The two others beyond hers did as well until filled by another victim. Watching his rate of capture, she was surprised the cell still waited for an occupant and feared for the woman meant for it. Had she escaped him or died trying? She couldn't focus on those thoughts now.

Scanning the upper roofline, her eyes locked on the exterior vent apparatus. It pumped a mist into the hall regularly unless he was making rounds. During his time inside this captive dungeon it switched off, by design no doubt. Clever, she used it against him as an indicator of his approach.

He wasn't coming.

The airborne drug activated to control the women through sedation dispersed at the farthest distance to these final rooms. Accounting, she gathered, for why its effect faded becoming less potent as it neared her cell. Still, she devised the makeshift mask to hold on to consciousness and her ability to fight back on days when she wasn't weakened by his ravages. Seeing the many doors leading to hers she forced her mind not to contemplate how long those taken before her remained in his clutches, though she mapped his movements enough to fear the answer.

With rock above, beneath, and at all sides, it was safe to assume they were housed underground. She hadn't glimpsed sunlight since she woke the first day, not even when he opened the outer door entering their space. False, manufactured light told her volumes about what lay beyond. And she tried to prepare. Every day, under the cover of darkness, she pillowed her blankets into the shape of her sleeping, slipped from the covers down the backside of the bed between it and the wall, crawled under and out of the camera's reach to the space directly below it, and worked her muscles. Training for freedom.

The Animal couldn't know. She was sure his research on her didn't extend that far back, but while living in the dorms, she roomed with a triathlete. She remembered the leg lifts, push-ups, wall Pilates repeated ad nauseum and was grateful for them now. In his presence she remained weak and prayed he didn't recognize the change in her physique. With so many to juggle and a twisted mind could he possess the clarity to notice and log every detail? Perhaps not. For he hadn't shown any indication of knowing she wasn't sleeping through captivity. Instead, she was learning.

Having watched a documentary on the lone survivor of a killer who dug a room below ground, concealed by overgrowth in a nearby park to house his victims, she wondered if the Animal who had taken her and the occupants of the neighboring cells have dug out this cage of savagery near civilization? Where she was, she decided, didn't matter only escaping it for anywhere but. The woman nearer the front of the hall moaned in her sleep, breaking into the nurse's debate. Not the utterance of a confused subconscious mind, but in resistance to accepting past horrors inflicted while awake. She did it every night now. Cried out in the dark for a rescue that, as of yet, hadn't come.

Believing it may never the nurse chose to hammer out one of her own making.

After all, it couldn't be worse than the abuse sustained from the moment he entered her life to when she'd exit his. There were so many thoughts she wouldn't allow to take form. From the torment her family and boyfriend of four years were enduring and the horror her best friend faced finding their shared home painted in bloody markers of a violent abduction scene to every second he laid hands on her. Instead, she chose to compile the pieces to build a ladder out of hell.

Stepping down from the table, she returned it left of its spot beside the bed and searched the hay for the shard of rock she'd spent days sharpening to a weapon. Using it to break into the wardrobe in the corner of the room, she left the sleazy renditions of nurses' uniforms and snatched the blue hospital booties from its shelf. Doubling then tripling them up, she slid her feet inside and headed for the door. The lower left section had been worked over for weeks. By the grace of God, he hadn't noticed the split board, or it was much thicker than she determined and would never pry entirely loose. Fear of calling attention by sound at this hour ended when one of the others had woken sick and vomited for three hours without response. Hands protected by layers of fabric torn and twisted into a brace fit for any wrist fracture, she hammered on the board with everything in her. Three hits in it broke out. Wide planked, almost enough for her small frame to fit through, she worked the edge of the sideboards until one gave way. Scurrying sideways in the hay like a rodent eluding a farm cat she was on the other side seconds later. And the Animal left so much in the open.

In a dead run she snagged an unopened bottle of water, gloves, a lantern, and a mess of supplies off a counter on the way to the exit door. Using part of the blanket she wore to form a sling, she filled it in a sweep and hit the doorway praying it wasn't locked from the outside.

Freedom from even this first layer of confinement shot a rush of adrenaline through her veins. The exit door flew open too easily forcing her to grab its edge to halt it from slamming against the rock wall. And then she ran. Blind at first, sheer desperation driving her feet flying down the perceived center of an outer hallway. No. Slowing enough to glance behind and confirm no one followed, she registered her surroundings. This was no underground dwelling constructed in a backyard by one Animal. This was a labyrinth assembled by countless crews a distant time ago.

This was a mine.

For what or how deep, she didn't know. Diminishing her gate to a walk she turned on the lantern. It blasted blinding illumination bouncing it from all sides back at her. Toying with the knob, she found a lower setting but still the light gave clarity to colored veins cascading through the stone walls encasing her. Swiveling back again, she noticed the camera mounted in an upper corner. Her feet flew newly fueled. Not knowing where an exit lay, she knew where one did not. Anywhere the cameras existed. So this became her goal. Run until there are no more eyes for him to see you with. Run until he is blind to your movements and do it fast. No matter what lay ahead this was a trial she welcomed given the alternative.

Sprinting forward from curve to curve, fork to fork, she imagined herself a mouse in a maze, certain death behind and faint hope of escape ahead. When her legs ached, she ignored them. Her throat dried and she drank from the water bottle without stopping, the splash hitting more than her mouth. When the pounding of her head and her heart competed for volume, she didn't lurch to a standstill. It wasn't until her lungs shot pangs through her chest that she slowed and stopped. Heaving in a hunch she fought to control her breathing. Eyes cast down to her feet she caught a glimpse that rose her head up and drew her.

There, along the midway point of the right wall, broken out rock framed the opening to a secondary tunnel, one that appeared to angle up. And out? If she'd been a larger size, she couldn't have squeezed in. Even her tiny form would require effort to sneak through and the risk of falling rock and debris was great. She secured the blanket sling tighter, set the lantern ahead inside the hole, and placed a hand on either side. Inhaling, relief shuddered through her as she climbed in knowing whatever happened from here, the Animal couldn't fit.

THIRTEEN

From deep inside the protected zone he watched a lone light bounce through the upper ridgeline of trees, quite concerning. In past years there had been, on occasion, a soul brave ranger, a hiker having veered wildly off course, or the rare case of someone like him venturing in with no intention of coming back out. This was different. Whoever walked there did so methodically, clinging to the western wall, deliberate in their concealment. And that approach had the earmarking of a cop infiltrating the area and hunting a perpetrator.

He didn't like the idea of anyone, law enforcement or otherwise, creeping into his isolated neck of the woods. He couldn't prevent it either so, concerning.

Following signs of their movement from the disruption of the long-eared bats on the north animal trail to the flash of lights and the bobcat tracking them, he watched. Waiting for silence, and the heavy downpour to shift to drizzle. Then, and only then, did he risk drawing near. Not so close as to place himself at a detectable distance from the Airstream unlawfully parked miles inside the restricted access markers. But near enough to know his unwelcome visitor planned to stay for longer than a night.

The west ridge bobcat left her prints in the wet ground stalking the newcomer. Cats were curious by nature and this person's presence suggested a definite departure from the norm. He shadowed its movements and hung back, monitoring the interaction from a safe, natural, high hide up a forked tree. The daring feline encroached into the vicinity to scratch at rope looped under a tarp. He waited for the Airstream's occupant to fling open the door, investigating the sound but no one appeared. The cat lost interest, at least for tonight, and retreated for drier ground under the forest canopy. He chose, like the wild animal, to return home and wait in comfort until dawn with intentions to make a closer inspection once the owner of the mobile home left it empty. If a guard dog existed, it would've shown itself at the bobcat's advance into its territory. He thanked the cat for this bit of knowledge, making a mental note to leave a carcass out and save her from hunting in the mud and rain.

The cabin was a short distance as the eagle flies, but a good couple hours or more if you didn't know the terrain like the back of your hand and he did. No one else. Normally he hated days like this past one, where the forest was blanketed by perpetual fog, rain, and overcast clouds sending it into a seemingly endless night. But this time the dark shadow highlighted the stranger's light, alerting of the intrusion, and allowing him to prepare. He walked carefully to keep his footfall on the vegetation rim of the animal trail, never leaving telltale prints behind. His moccasins were designed to cast nothing but depth impressions easily missed in the uneven underbrush but still.

Pausing at a division of the trail, he kneeled to inspect a boot print. Clearly discernible now, it would be gone before the first trace of day, washed away by nature's eraser. Grateful the forest aligned with his desire to disappear within it, this time it worked to hide more than his presence alone. Tracing the outline of the impression with a gloved finger he spoke to the wilderness, "A woman hunter." The knowledge of the intruder being female had no effect on his approach to navigating the dilemma. In his experience, women could be far more lethal than men and entirely unpredictable.

He used the light of the moon and memory to retrace the route back to his cabin, though accessing it was no easy feat. It required years of effort to complete and masterful stealth to acquire untraceable supplies to do so. Located on a rock shelf right of a steep drop off to the riverbed, the only way in was by scaling down a mountain climber's rope, concealed by color and vegetation, to the plateau. One misstep meant certain death but he sat protected by the natural stone embedded and serving as walls on three sides and a ravine allowing a wide span view of approach by any other means. His home for nearly two decades quelled all fears of infiltration without warning. In itself, its design posed a strategic defense against enemies, animal and human. A testimony to his choice of site, it made the enormous efforts imposed on him to hoist every element in worthwhile and worth defending. Inside, he closed the door grateful for the propane radiant heater and its warmth without the complication of smoke. He wasn't opposed to using the wood-burning stove and was well stocked in dry timber. Altering anyone to his location, however? That, he had a problem with. More so knowing his space was being encroached upon. For what reason he wasn't sure.

He checked the calendar noting the exact date. For years he lived season to season paying no mind to numbers or days. Now he marked it to track when the stranger arrived. He'd quit marking it when they departed. Stripping off his rain gear, he donned more comfortable attire and nestled in front of the fireplace, stretching his feet from chair to stool. Though no wood crackled before him, the heater more than made up for it, dispelling the inner chill and drawing the one friend he allowed to share this space.

Scythe, a rare mammoth black version of a Forest cat, leaped up, taking his place extending across the full length of his owner's outstretched legs and, being he stood six foot three at full height and was more leg than torso, that was saying something. He had no scale to measure Scythe's exact weight but in their time together, he'd warded off more than one wild animal including a coyote, gray fox, bobcat, and even a black bear the past spring. He guessed Scythe was pushing easily outside twenty-five pounds and what he didn't have in size he made up for in intimidation. He'd often pondered what he was crossed with, if there existed more than an oversized breed of domestic feline in his bloodline. His thick dark mane presented him as a rare but deadly dwarf loin that, as of yet, no animal elected to tangle with. Stroking down the silky fur on his back, he was grateful he counted him a member of the pride, if not always agreeing on who held the position of leader.

He reached into a small drawer inside the table where his coffee cup and a battery-reliant lamp stole center stage. Riffling around in an uncomfortable reach Scythe was unwilling to accommodate, he eventually grabbed hold of his laptop and pulled it to his abdomen. Scythe cast a warning stare adjusting his position to allow space for the device. A directional high gain antenna pointed to connect a usable signal for moments such as this, though he never stayed on it long and installed programs to scatter his IP address years before, updating them as needed. This was necessity only. In mere moments of sweeping headlines and news bulletins related to the area, his moderate concern for the unwanted tailgater morphed into a contemplation of panic. If he read correctly, their isolated hideaway was about to be flooded by the enemy.

Sliding the closed computer to the plank floor, he patted the cat's ears. "It's been too many years to care too deeply, buddy." The cat turned his head, staring as if questioning the logic behind the words. "Don't worry. If they come for me, I'll get you outta here first." To this, the cat bounded to the ground, clearing several feet soundlessly making for the only door leading to the outside world. Meowing with a primal depth he paced across the wooden floorboards. Raised in the mini fortress, Scythe bounced up the protective tree sheltering any view of the cabin's exterior, leaped over to the remaining unstable rock, and into the forest effortlessly where even its occupants refrained from treading making him free to roam as desired most days. But not now and perhaps not for a while.

"Not tonight, buddy. We have unwanted predators."

FOURTEEN

"What happens when comms are impacted? The deeper we travel into The Divide, the worse it'll be until we'll be lucky to hear static. Inside, on average of eight to ten miles from road access and civilization, even good radios lose signal and that's our target." Jade warned her new lead, Agent Lafine, that requesting check-ins, though reasonable to ensure the safety of team members, wasn't exactly viable. Two of the other agents assigned glanced her way, then back to the senior in charge. Lafine held up one of six walkie-talkies on the table in front of him. They appeared new and unlike anything Jade witnessed or had reason to use.

"Each of you will be given one of these. I found they work best in remote combat zones for establishing comms. They stay on your person from here out until this search is complete. You lose it to the forest or drop it in the river, dive into search and rescue mode. It doesn't come back; you owe me personally over four grand. Click three times every hour at your designated time. Regardless of signal strength, I'll know you're alive. Something goes wrong? Hold down on the button. You'll block out other signals and we'll all know to head into your sector. Got it?" Lafine searched the faces before him, coming to rest last on Jade's.

Combat zones. Jade couldn't help but wonder how many he'd been in and what fallout he endured during his time behind enemy lines. It explained a great deal of the intensity and confidence he commanded with. They were engaging, presumably, one adversary. In his past he'd have fought through far more in situations far worse. For the first time she was glad Wenzel's distant and contrasting cousin was at the helm of the investigation. She nodded her agreement with a respect that said so.

"You all have clearly outlined sectors. Remain vigilant about staying within them. You veer into another's without warning and you're liable to attract friendly fire. Detective Carmichael is taking the west flank. She'll be covering this ground alone unless a discovery requires our presence. Don't traverse the river without backup." Lafine referenced the area on the map for all to see. "She a beast when the weather hasn't dumped twenty hours of fresh water into her. You cross at the wrong place and we'll find your body downstream in the next state. Understood?"

The agents around Jade were stoic in their focus, their attention trained dead ahead. Her mind wandered, stretching its proverbial legs, vindicated to have claimed the grid most likely to house the Occultus, his victims, and Errie. It wasn't long after gathering gear that they disbanded to respective areas to dig in, literally. The past deluge transformed the forest floor into a sledge capable of unleashing a mudslide at every turn. The trek would be brutal, giving their suspect an added advantage he hadn't earned and damn sure didn't deserve.

"Sir, half my zone is down the side of a rock ravine," the youngest of the three male agents said. "Scouring the terrain leading in will take at least the next couple days but when I reach—"

"Any of you hit the cliffs, call in and I'll come or send reinforcements. The rangers' office and search and rescue are ready to bring in chopper support and climb teams. The SAR Officer, the vet with the most hours logged, will be at our end-of-day debrief thanks to

Carmichael, so we can review difficult terrain access then and prep additional officers. Trouble is they won't come in quiet so, until we're sure we have our guy cornered, we stay in stealth mode. No use of Tac flashlight beams cutting through the forest; no stomping in, announcing our existence. This guy doesn't deserve a warning and those women are counting on us surprising the hell out of him if they're here. Careful and silent, we're smarter than this guy, and now is the time to prove it."

"Are we?" Jade let the question slip under her breath, but they all caught it. "Sorry, sir. I've come across astute criminals with IQs far exceeding average. We don't know who we're up against but he managed to outsmart the law in at least ten states, this one included."

Drex held his stare on her for a beat, then said, "She's right. We don't know how cagey this bastard is, so don't risk being outplayed. Okay, you have your orders."

This time Jade didn't wait for the agents; she cut for the door and left the tent pulling away before they made it to their vehicles. Halfway through the briefing, her phone vibrated, in silent mode, alerting of incoming messages. One from Dr. Abraham Maxwell. She instructed Kane to forward Max a full dossier on the missing women and the case history requesting he weigh in, particularly on the potential profile of their suspect. Following eyewitness testimony their hunt trained on a single perpetrator though they weren't disregarding the possibility of secondary involvement. As of yet they ruled nothing out. Jade didn't trust the feds to share their intel and even if they did, she wouldn't rely on it alone. Drawing on her own sources kept her grounded and, with any luck, a step ahead.

Jade was anxious to return quickly to the Airstream to take the call with Max in private and touch base with Kane before heading into her sector. No one back home liked her going in alone. Not Captain Grey, not Amy or Tex, and definitely not Kane. Still, she believed it best. Her and Kane established a search pattern so he knew roughly where she would be from day one on. There was no timeline handed down on how long the team had to apprehend the criminal or bring those taken home, but one would come. One always did. Agent Lafiné encouraged her and the agents to think outside the box so when Jade suggested using LiDAR scans by remote drone he made calls. Individual sectors were being mapped in the morning and would identify areas of interest at the next briefing. Meantime, Jade would use the cave maps from archives to guide her.

No more than two hours passed from when she departed the trailer but it was a welcome sight. The comforts of home, the little things like the weighted blanket Kane packed her or the new survival equipment Tex hid in the main cabin cupboard said their energy of protection wouldn't leave her. Before unloading the truck, she sprang out and strolled to the edge of the embankment to the left, the bluff overlooking a wide expanse revealing uninhabited wilderness for as far as the eye could see. She wasn't a fool. There were a million ways to die out here not including the hands of the criminal who had to know they'd come for him. Yet, here she stood in awe of the breathtaking, untouched, natural beauty of this place. It spoke volumes about how much better off the planet was before being infested by over eight billion humans. She drank in the fresh air, crisp after the rain, before returning to the trailer and the dire business at hand.

Gear transferred inside, she sat with the extravagant walkie-talkie, rolling it over in her hands, inspecting the device while waiting for Max to answer her call. Checking the clock she clicked the radio three times, a return clicked back. Simple enough. Latching onto her belt, she snapped it in as her cell connected.

"Jade. Time is a currency, so I'll jump in." The tone of Max's voice announced his full analytical download mode. "I've sent both you and Kane my analysis for review, but he said you're headed into the field so I'm giving you a snapshot of the highlights."

"Thanks, Max. First, is it your opinion we're on the right track thinking these victims are still alive?" Jade wanted to believe a chance existed for the team to bring the women home to their families. Hearing confirmation from Max would fortify her on the path into the unknown.

"Yes. He's a collector, as you expected. But there's a timeline on your attempts at retrieval." His voice dropped to a somber register she learned to heed.

"Yeah. For now the search is open but we all anticipate the hammer falling if progress isn't eventful." The view of the vast forest flashed in her mind. So much ground to cover, so many caverns, valleys, caves, and sink holes with limited time, resources, and access.

"Not the timeline I'm referencing. Did neither of you notice the estimated time of Errie's abduction?" Max's voice held an unsettling urgency. "From what I read it was exactly noon when the attack took place. Is that accurate?"

Jade retraced the details of the scene mentally. "Yes. There was more than one reason to believe that."

"And I am almost certain of it." He continued with vigor. "I checked through and at least three others were taken at a time corroborated by key witnesses, camera footage, or other means. One had a laptop smashed during the attack. Number two, I think."

"Yes. The athlete from Arizona." She waited.

"Its clock stopped at precisely two a.m.; the time frozen by its destruction." His tone held punctuation but she wasn't following.

"Okay. Max—"

"Jade, Errie is his number twelve. The Arizona woman, number two. He abducted each victim at the time signifying their place within the collection."

Jade's mind looped around his words, landing hard. "Jesus. How did we miss it?"

"Easy to do when you're absorbing all the details of an active investigation with a potential site inside The Divide. My focus is his mental state. It's why you called me in. Point is this criminal has twelve victims and I believe the significance of the number doesn't end there."

"How so?" Jade's wheels turned down a new road of inquiry. "And why would he alert us by allowing the timeline to verify the count?"

Max inhaled deeply, exhaling before launching into a viable explanation. "He didn't have a choice. That's why. The number has incredible significance both biblically and universally. Twelve hours in a day, months in a year, it's the number of apostles chosen by Jesus, the number of the tribes of Israel, and it represents cosmic order or perfection. It isn't random and lends to the theory that he has clear intentions for them based somehow on that number." Max paused. "You have to find these women before they fail his idea of perfection, cause we both know at least one of them will."

"You sent all of this to Kane?" she asked while absorbing his perspective.

"I did."

"Max, if Errie is the last taken—"

"Yes. I thought of that too. You may have more time to rescue her but that's barring she doesn't break his rules. I'm betting he has a treasure trove of them."

"If his plan centers on the number it's fair to say it wouldn't activate until all were taken and—"

"And with Errie in his possession we're behind the clock."

Jade didn't speak, she didn't hang up, she held the phone in silence, worry and fear passing between them down the line. "I'll keep in touch. And if you have any other insights…reach out."

"Jade? Stay on stable ground, okay?"

"I'll try. Thanks, Max." Placing the cell phone on the table, she walked to the window facing the bluff and peered out. The expanse of forest, daunting before, held a new ominous aura. One familiar and unwelcome. One she knew Errie wanted the hell out of. "I'm coming girl." She spoke to the glass clouding the clarity of the world outside.

Strapping on the last of her gear she dropped the metal security blinds for the windows, sent Kane her exit time and love, locked the door on her way out, and began her trek into the wild never glancing back.

Three good hours from the bluff and ten miles from any road in, Jade's appreciation for SAR officers and rangers rose to new heights.

Fitter than ever, training with Kane and Tex, her muscles screamed in defiance in spite. Scaling up and down rock breaks with her feet on a constant diet of unstable ground demanded her whole body stay in sync, more rigid with every advance. The sun shone brightly when the trek began but now, due to the impenetrable tree canopy, there were minimal clearings where light arrived on the forest floor with its strength intact. Making gauging solid ground between the rock bed from slippery sludge created by previous rainfall much more difficult.

She passed the region where she'd glimpsed the light across The Divide on the eastern wall a couple hours in. Assessing the terrain in daylight, she realized reaching it required a long trek down the western ridgeline, across the engorged river, and up a rock embankment extending on the east slope for a mile or more. Noticing her time slot for check-in approaching at a quarter past the hour she paused for a breath, hoisting up on a bolder to let her tired lower limbs dangle from its edge. Guzzling from her canteen she surveyed her progress. The next flank being the river crossing, she decided to refuel and pulled food from her pack, careful to store remnants in sealed bags to avoid alerting hungry predators. The rocky stretch being prone to bobcats far more nimble than her on this Devonian crag. Sending her three clicks through on the walkie, she registered a return signal while taking in the view.

Not far from her, tree fall forged a natural bridge. From her position she couldn't determine the safety of crossing but thoughts of Errie dictated incentive. Back on her feet she wondered, closing the distance, if the feds had come across any evidence or breaks in their search. Discovering nothing, though methodical in her advance, she concluded the perpetrator used the river to gain access leaving no scent or sign of his incursion into the hidden realm.

He was smart, resourceful, and proving a worthy adversary.

Max's profile of their target swam laps in her mind while testing the logs and establishing the least adverse path over the weathered bark. A plethora of branches spanning the largest and sturdiest of the fallen trees prevented the option of roping across it. On the opposite side no trees stood near enough to toss a secure line to.

Spotting two boulders pushing in on each other, she inched carefully forward, securing her feet between two thick branches before throwing the rope. Three attempts in it caught and snagged, wedged between the rocks. If it would remain so if she slipped off into the river below she didn't know, but it was something. Strapping in and snapping the line onto her belt she stared at the ancient log below her feet. Moisture from past days billowed the scent of moss and musk up from ground level filling her nostrils. She'd grown up in this state; she knew its woods, escaping into them countless times. Wet logs meant the trunk could shed its bark, sloughing it off in large patches on contact with little or no warning. Not a comforting prospect given she was about to walk thirty feet across one in that very condition.

Errie. Jade averted her eyes from the drop below and focused on the exit to the eastern side and Errie. Her laugh. Her delicate physique bounding across a stage with such strength and grace it caused patrons to gasp and silenced Amy with awe. Her trailer-trash jargon delivered from such a pretty mouth. Errie was a compelling contradiction and one none who loved her were willing to lose. Jade found her footing and started across.

Reaching from branch to available branch, garnering every opportunity for stability, she traversed a third of the way before the water hit. From the bank there was no indication of the cast off but over its raging whitewater it was suddenly palatable. In seconds her hair hung heavy with moisture, her hands fought harder to find a solid grip, and her feet...she dared not glance down.

Systematic. This was her approach. One that served her in every previous case.

Left hand to next branch. Secure grip. Right foot to next space. Find balance. Right hand to new branch. Advance forward. And never take your eyes off the next target.

Halfway across? She had to be but couldn't stop or avert her focus to check. The wind, light and varying from breeze to gusts, quieted. Ferocious water below echoed up drowning out all other sound. Moisture, draining from her hair, dripped mercilessly into her eyes impeding vision. With no free hand to wipe it away she blinked repeatedly for a second, refocused, and plodded onward. What were the chances of her making it to the other bank without injury?

Why did she ask? The moment the thought floated to the surface the bark beneath her left foot slipped free before she found solid contact with the right. The branch she held gingerly, like a trapeze artist weighing a balance beam, resisted her instant clench, snapping off and sending her into a chaotic pirouette grasping at air, feet flailing for solid surface. She possessed none of Errie's grace. Speed of motion had her hydroplaning in no certain direction until her right hand locked onto a thick, solid branch. Her right foot caught between the main trunk and an angled knot pinning her solidly in place. Before her eyes regained clear vision, she spotted something on the shore. Gulping breath, safe but angled peering down at the violent water crashing into a rocky outcrop, she checked her grip before again glancing up. There, not far from her intended landing, she thought she glimpsed a man disappearing into the forest. With her left hand free she pushed the hair and water off her face. Peering through the haze she couldn't locate him and wasn't certain he'd existed at all. Hell, in the trajectory of survival, she could've humanized a damn tree.

Her eyes traveled the remaining distance to the east bank, shorter than anticipated, mapping steps before rising to resume the trek across. Nearing the end, she was tempted to jump and skip the last few footholds but the unstable earth beyond the tree bridge couldn't be gambled on. Easing off the trunk for broken rock, she adjusted her movements to prevent slipping, testing for solid ground before committing. A lone eagle screeched overhead marking its territory with an echoed warning. The boulder-blanketed ledge on the eastern side narrowed then blended with forest underbrush and trees. Feet worn from the lack of flat surface were anxious for the padding of the understory but she paused to ensure the weak connection of the security rope was reinforced. She could end up heading back in less light. At least the rope provided a secondary measure on her return. Trading hard stone for soft mossy earth inspired a notch up in speed. Dodging through the woods, she regretted thoughts of returning the way she'd come. Knowledge of the crossing didn't serve to make it less dangerous. And her new boss would never have approved. Far less if he witnessed her battered corpse drifting past him downstream.

The earth beneath her feet rose in sections, high over ancient roots, pushed up from beneath to expose cave height natural habitats. In other spaces it fell, dropping out of sight into thick understory so even a basketball star could stand completely concealed to eyes peering across the forest floor. Engaged in her approach for the eastern slope where the light flashed, she registered the reverberation of two or three broken branches before recognizing her feet were not the cause of the breaks. Pausing with her back against a cottonwood, she held her breath to listen. Minutes passed without sound other than the angry river. About to resume at a slower pace, she stalled as a branch snapped from behind on the animal trail to her immediate left.

A part of her hoped it was a black bear, the lesser of two evils, but the instinctive part knew better. She wasn't there alone. Advancing with more caution, she checked her weapon glancing back in a scattered rhythm hoping to catch the stalker. In just one of those moments when her head was turned, the forest floor gave way, rock, roots, and dirt flashed by as her body hurled down a collapse into the earth.

So sudden was her fall her mind couldn't process if it was over a cliff or into a sinkhole. What hit like a ledge, but may have been a thick stray branch, caught and tore at her thigh. It tossed her body altering its trajectory. Her eyes caught glimpses of dirt and tangled wood ropes burrowed through earth walls, then sky and back again before she slammed into a solid surface with force enough to explode the air from her lungs. Pain shot across her back; she'd landed face up. The scent of dirt engulfed as debris rained down. She gulped soiled air desperate for breath. Sheltering her vision from the cascade of loosed soil and vegetation she was grateful her arms and eyes were free of damage. Clearing her face of dirt she fought to capture her surroundings and see the high place she'd fallen from. The descent had taken a few seconds at most but as her vision blurred, she knew it had done damage, perhaps a concussion.

Fighting to stay awake, she focused on the sky above, clouds rolling over a blanket of blue. Her right hands smoothed over the back of her head, the source of radiating pain. It came back bloody. Then the shadow of something black crept into the periphery of the scene overhead, standing sentinel at the edge of the chasm, staring down. It wasn't a bear. A wolf? The expanse of her view reduced, giving way to an enclosing blackness but not before the man, the one she spotted at the river crossing, peered down on her next to the fur covered beast. Fading out, his image high above granted no comfort. Whoever stood there wasn't a ranger, an agent, or a cop and he didn't appear pleased.

FIFTEEN

"We're analyzing the Alabama abduction and enough markers are shared to be fairly confident we're at eleven. She'd be number six." Kane stood frozen in front of the evidence board in his home office watching his phone for the full weather report on The Divide. Knowing Jade was searching an already drenched forest, he hoped for clear skies. She didn't need anything more against her. "We've missed another one. It could be she hasn't been reported missing yet or someone isn't doing their job."

"Why twelve? You're pretty certain?" Amy asked from the chair she claimed days earlier, eyes fixed on the evidence. Keeping her engaged working the case served to preserve her sanity a little longer. Kane knew she'd break eventually. With luck it'd hit when Errie was home safe.

"We're sure. Max too," Grey bellowed, entering with renewed coffee for all after riffling around in Kane's kitchen for twenty minutes. Removing his clay chalice from the tight grip of Grey's forearm, Kane was grateful he hadn't offered paper cups.

Kane called over his head, "Max, anything to add on this number? Did you hear back from our contact at the church?"

"I did. Him and the Latin professor at NYU sent context." Following in closely behind Grey, Max carried his own mug. "I was telling the captain in the kitchen, there are so many variances, without more facts, narrowing in on any one may be unwise."

Kane slapped his phone on the table nearest; relieved the weather improved he rested on the arm of his chair. "We'll start by dissecting any version where twelve are required to elect a change. Twelve apostles, for instance."

"Twelve followers but these women were taken against their will," Max noted.

"Yeah, but he's kept them," Grey added. "Long enough to convert?"

"There's no way in hell Errie will ever be won over by a lunatic," Amy said, more to herself than the men.

"That may be true for more than just her so…if we remove this, what's left?" Kane studied Max, whose hands explored a mountain of paperwork in a downward tilt threatening to end up scattered across the floor.

"Here! This one has potential." Max smacked a folder down in front of them all on a central coffee table. Amy and Grey simultaneously rescued their coffees from likely spillage. "I haven't read through it all but it's an ancient Latin ritual that involves the sacrifice of twelve to 'bring back' one."

Kane fingered through the information, perusing integral bits before facing the group. "Is this suggesting a path for resurrection?"

"Do I look Catholic to you?" Max clearly thought the discovery granted him a pass on a deeper dive.

"Not to me," Grey teased. "Though you do tend to seek confession from us all."

"Seriously?" Max eyed Grey whose taut face creased as a smile spread.

"Okay, you two, cut it out. Focus," Amy demanded.

"Max, give me a rundown on this," Kane said, handing the file back. "Talk to the priest and prof. We need perspective on how this applies to our guy. Then we'll pitch it against what we know and see where we land." Kane brushed a hand through his blond waves and paced the board. "His motive may help Jade know what she's walking into and..." He faced Amy, promise mixed with temperance in his gaze. "... how to get Errie out."

"Cap, you sure you're okay with this? We're using Kane and Jade's home as base camp. If the feds caught wind of—" Amy's exterior showed fractures of worry.

"They're not catching wind of a thing we don't want them to. She's one of us. I'm good." Grey squeezed Amy's shoulder and walked closer to the board. Kane studied his face as he drank in case details. "The motives of this lunatic may offer guidance, but whatever he's preaching, he's bound to fight back if we try removing his pulpit."

"Agreed." Kane turned, locking eyes with each of them before speaking again. "What worries me more than the why is the when. How long has he been at this? The planning of one successful abduction is difficult. A succession of twelve, spanning twelve states, moving east to west without detection is damn near impossible. This opponent is brilliant, cunning, and confident."

"I'm not liking the sound of this, Sugarcane." Amy's complexion transformed, trading its usual dewy brightness for diluted gray.

"Detailed planning leaves traces," he reminded. "And we'll find them. He can only bury them so deep."

"Can we avoid that word moving forward?" Amy shook free of her seated position and headed out of the room.

Concern etched across Grey's face. "She'll only handle so much of this before—"

"She breaks," Kane finished the thought. "I know but she knows Errie better than anyone. That insight may help us take her back."

"That's barring that we can find her at all." Max said what they all feared.

Kane glanced at him, shook his head, and turned his back to him to face the board. "Yeah. We know but maybe don't voice it again." Staring at a copy of the same map Jade was referencing for the search grid, Kane's finger traced staggered marks snaking along the edge of the eastern ridgeline. "What is this?" He checked the table of contents and returned to the broken line.

Grey peered at the area and said, "Caves or tunnels?"

"Exactly." Kane stepped back noticing the vast coverage of the underground system. Grey glimpsed his way, at the map, and back again. When next they spoke it was in unison.

"Buried."

Spitting dirt across the metal track she collided with, Errie fought the urge to swallow. Diving free of dangerous rockfall, she landed close enough to absorb the aftermath in a blanket of soot and soil wafting overhead. Searching the tunnel floor she located her pack and dug for the water bottle. Rinsing her mouth out, she spat mud beside her and swallowed back a few gulps to clear her throat. On hands and knees she crawled to where she'd thrown the lantern before the collapse. Minutes passed until her palm pressed onto broken glass, not hard enough to cut but enough to know the lantern hadn't been spared. Cursing and growling in the dark, she lit it on the fourth attempt. The light flickered unstable, threatening to extinguish. She'd managed to acquire a flashlight but didn't want to waste its batteries not knowing what lay ahead. With a low light established she turned to see, for the first time, the newly formed wall of rock. With a tunnel remaining ahead, her choice of direction narrowed to one. The rock cave-in squashed, quite literally, any chance of her abductor following her from the former tunnel connecting to lower levels of the mine. The path forward uncertain, posed far better options than the one shared with the bastard who brought her here.

"Try to reach me now, motherfucker." Her harsh words echoed out ahead of her. She could only hope the access obstructed by fallen rock offered his only easy way to the level she now inhabited. And, she'd discover a way out long before he found a new one in.

Brushing free of debris, she vanquished thoughts of a hot shower or anything comforting that arose in her mind. Focusing instead on the task at hand. Aching and depleted, she plodded ahead at more than a walk, less than a run. Distance brought oxygen filled air and the promise, even if false, of escape. She paused near a shelf of rocky outcrop, sitting to check her water reserves and supplies. Both said she had limited time before lack of nourishment would usher in new levels of weakness. Contemplating next moves, moments passed before she realized the air her lungs drank in was fresh.

Fresh like outside. Fresh like freedom.

Gathering gear, she let her nose lead the way. The cave-in made the noticeable difference between the dank oxygen starved mine air and clean, rich air obvious. Without thought her feet gained momentum and before long she was jogging the tunnel. She assumed it was far left of where she started but gauging direction was near impossible. The further she ventured the more hopeful she became. Her thoughts turned to Amy and home. As much as she fought them, they swelled in her chest with every clean breath. She imagined turning a corner to an opening in the rock, a way out led by sunlight. But as she made a sharp right, what lay in wait way anything but.

Her feet stalled so abruptly she almost tumbled to the mine floor. A light shone, but not from any natural source. Beside a hole, a designed opening to the level below and one emitting oxygen pumped in by her captor, laid a pack, a flashlight, and...a camera? He was watching and waiting for her to reach this spot. Unable to access the level through fallen rock, he engineered another way to insert his presence, to continue his fucked-up game.

Careful to shift her supplies to her back in such a way that the camera would remain blind to them, she snatched the bag off the ground, grabbed the flashlight in her left hand, and flipped the bird with her right before kicking the camera to shit.

"Nice try, asshole, but I'm not done yet." She spat through the hole and wished his head would pop up so she could take it off his shoulders.

Not wasting time, she scanned the area. Same tunnel advancing dead ahead or a narrow one just right.

"Try and fit you piece of shit. I'm guessing you didn't anticipate one of us slipping through your meaty fingers and..." She checked the close rock walls entering the new path, placing her hand on the cold surface. "You didn't measure."

Snaking down the narrow divide she could only hope the rocks above her head wouldn't share the same fate as those that fell the day before. Either way she believed Amy would rather find her crushed beneath a pile of stone in an escape attempt than dead at the hands of this monster. She hadn't given up hope. She vowed to fight until she couldn't. And when her new tunnel closed in tight enough to trap her, she kept moving, inching, straining until it opened up wide to a space she could walk freely in.

Stretching, and determining it safe to steal time to rest, she opened the pack he left by the hole. Inspecting provisions for seals on the water bottles, tampered packages of protein bars, and any sign of interference. With the contents out before her it hit. What he offered was survival. He didn't want her to escape but he also didn't want her dead, at least not yet.

Swiveling to face the impossible passage she emerged from, she exhaled a sigh of relief, cracked open a new water bottle, and guzzled it. He couldn't know this space existed by means of the narrow way into it so perhaps there was another way out. One he wasn't aware of. One she could access before the new provisions ran out. Unwrapping the blanket turned sarong, she turned the clean side up, curled on top of it draping it over her. What she'd do for a couple sand sandbags. Snuffing out the new flashlight she placed it by the old and decided to leave the lantern on low. Its dim light cast away some of the demons, not all. When she woke again, she'd search for a new path out. For now, she'd sleep believing there was one.

SIXTEEN

Studying, from a distance, the intricate layout of his adaptation of Hebert's *pacours de combatant*, pleasure etched a rare smile across his face. The maze of challenges rose to test the level of warrior required for the sacred feat they were painstakingly selected for. Beyond the best and brightest, the obstacle course was designed to tear free fragility like husk from the ear exposing pure strength and determination only revealed when life hung in the balance.

And it did.

Each rope walkway, scattered foothold on the rock wall face, securely tethered rope or inserted pitfall, snare or landmine was set precisely to carve from the pawn that entered a worthy queen. Their presence on the sacrificial stone, as the last of them joined, would grant him the greatest gift mankind had ever experienced.

Almost a shame the world above would be blind to it all, at least for a time.

All that mattered was to see this journey through so he could wake her. He dreamed of those first words he'd say to reassure her. He promised she would be free of what threatened to destroy her when she woke again. And to speak those words...

It had to be perfect. So he broke from his musing and followed the delicate path to retest each section before number one was given the blessing of entering the course first. Yanking hard on a chain link his watch sounded a reminder. So engulfed with the beauty of the final details on the course, time escaped him and he failed to check on the women at the regular interval. They were all adequately sedated and he established reliable wake cycles, allowed him a little wiggle room, but he couldn't become sloppy so close to the end.

And there was the elusive number twelve causing havoc in the execution of his plan. The tiny ballerina posed challenges, but the alert when she disabled the camera he planted announced she was, in fact, alive. He found a measure of relief knowing the provisions he supplied would keep her safe until he chose to reclaim her. By the time he did she'd likely be grateful given the harsh alternative. He created a bond, even from a distance, by protecting her welfare though she defied him.

Thoughts of her resting tranquil in the room he prepared for her quietly thrilled him on the long walk back to the sleeping quarters. Soon, like all the other important women in his life, she would slumber under his protection.

Unfortunately the ballerina would have to wait alone in the dark of the upper tunnels. As unstable as they were and despite his desire to have her safely back, the woman he was about to wake demanded all his attention.

Number one.

A wave of sentimentality washed over him reflecting on the one he honed the longest. For months she recovered under his watchful care. When he rescued her in California, where their journey began, she was near death. Bankrupt, alone, and in complete despair she set down a path of self-destruction sure to end in overdose. In a month she was clean and healthier than in previous years. It required gentle coaxing but eventually she admitted the truth. From the moment he scooped her off the tile floor of the dingy apartment he vowed she would never again lack protection, nourishment, shelter, and the dedication required to restore her health. Turning down the long left bank, slightly narrower than more common well-preserved stretches, he found it amusing a location such as this presented a far superior existence to the one she endured before. And to think her family gave up on her, wrote her off. That was no family at all in his view.

Family never abandoned. And they never gave up.

Unaware, number one slept peacefully. Not knowing she had less than forty-eight hours before facing the greatest feat of her life. The cards said she would not meet it. He braced for defeat, though watching it play out in living color would be painful, nonetheless. A small part of him wished he could offer her more time to prepare. He pushed the thought away. Futile. The date had to be the date. Time stood for no man.

Or did it? He found a way but only for one. The one most sacred.

The dominoes stood in place. No stopping after the first had fallen. He paused two tunnels away to repair a lantern. It's light fading out due to a depletion of oil ignition. He sighed wishing human beings could be restored as easily. A quick top up from the supply closet, one for every leg of the journey, and it burned so bright he was forced to adjust its output. He stood in center of the pathway, curving rock walls on either side stretching to meet overhead in and unnatural, jagged web of smashed and exploded hard edges. This was life.

Exhaling the melancholy, his feet found rhythm lumbering across age-old railway ties used by track cars to ferry out spoils. Once a hub of treasure and hope, the stone held only empty dismay until he made use of it again. Now it housed a miracle in the waiting. Following the main track right again, his mood shifted like the tracks beneath his feet once did, unceremoniously but definite in the new lane.

"What is this?" he asked the foreboding space first in a breathless whisper. "What is this?" The question gained volume the nearer he came to the violated entrance, the splintered wooden door, the shambled length of hall from number eleven's room to the chamber's rear exit.

"What is this?" He was screaming but hardly registered the sound of his own voice. The oxygen pumping in overhead failed to quench the thirst of his lungs. "You daft bitch!" His father used the word decades earlier and launched a further indignity by defining the term for his mother saying it encompassed perfectly her ridiculous and absurd stupidity. Currently it fit. "What have you done?" Being a large man the low octave of his voice bellowed back at him within the confined space heralding the risk of waking the occupants from room one to the exit. Donning a mask, he cranked up the sedative release to ensure no extra complications while dealing with a second, and far less expected escape.

His quiet night of reflection was, quite literally, derailed for an all out war of will and retrieval. The nurse broke out of her space, somehow impervious to the sedative, hours before number one's scheduled freedom.

This would not do. The clock was ticking.

First, he inspected the space with the brightest flashlight he owned, damning the subtle hints of lavender, jasmine, sandalwood, and vanilla from the diffuser he gifted her. Examining every detail of how the escape happened and what she managed to take with her, a blanket, a waft of supplies, enough to hold her for some time, perhaps days. Thundering out, his size twelve boot kicked free the compromised board of number nine's door sending it in shards littered across the inner hallway. Inside his office space he rewound the camera tape watching for what was missed as much as what was visible. After several views he jotted down her provisions, time of escape, and pertinent details. He set his AI system to track her form through all available avenues within the mine system with alerts directed to his linked wristwatch and waited for results while formulating an approach to reclaim her.

He paced the hall, glancing into what was her sanctuary with every lap, pulled to the breach of rage he hovered at the entrance wanting to destroy every comfort afforded. Huffing he cycled the hall again, this time peering in at the remaining women, oblivious and dreaming. Ten. Ten plus the ballerina he was certain to reclaim.

Even Jesus was betrayed by one of his twelve. Perhaps this was ordained. It must be.

He stopped pacing. A wash of acceptance flowing in as his computer announced the AI mapping complete. Instructing it to print out findings, highlighting number nine's movements following her escape, he prepared for the night ahead. She had no clue what was coming her way and the exhaustion generated by defying the structure he provided her would work in his favor. As she slept, at what was sure to be the far end of the last tunnel mapped, he would infiltrate her new domain.

When she woke, he would be there, waiting. And his timeline would remain unaffected by her transgression.

With printout in hand his finger traced the route she followed to the far end. On the computer he clicked to enlarge this section. A cold draft crawled up his back seeing the area in sharper detail. From the information on the screen he couldn't be certain but it appeared a cross section had existed at one time. A crawlway, fit for the transfer of tools or provisions to be passed by pulley system from one larger tunnel to another, side to side or vertically, joined this original tunnel. Inaccessible to the average person, if fear drove her stupidity to risk escape, it may prod her small frame into a space where he could not follow.

Damn near impossible to coax a gopher out of its hole. Worse with its known predator awaiting it outside. And this one he couldn't drown with a garden hose. Like any animal he simple had to find the right bait. To do this you had to know the animal. What it most desired.

Number nine was a nurse and her bait was about to be woken up and dragged to the mouth of her hideaway.

SEVENTEEN

What Jade breathed in was not the expected scent of dirt and moss but warm notes cast off by a low burning open-wood fire and undertones of herbs. Recognizing her body was no longer jettisoned across the cold forest floor of a sinkhole didn't spur her eyes open. Instead, she held them shut, evaluating damage one muscle at a time. Allowing consciousness to flow in discreetly, she identified her horizontal position, the freedom of her hands and feet, and an overpowering pounding in her head. Risking it, her eyelids lifted to be met by the wise, discerning glare of a predator guarding its territory-one she had without doubt infringed upon.

"Scythe. Quit intimidating the poor thing. You can see she's wounded. She's no threat big guy." The low, calm voice came from somewhere beyond the space the large cat stood on a chair directly across from where she lay. Beautiful, the damn feline put the average bobcat to shame. "Don't try lifting your head just yet." It warned. "You dropped quite a ways down. I can't be sure of the severity of the concussion but we should take it slow."

Tempted to rise up to peer around the fur guard, Jade's head pounded sufficiently to delay her long enough for the owner of the voice to brush the animal from his spot and sit beside her. He offered her a wooden cup with a steel straw inside it. Accepting, certain she'd find no voice without it, she sipped the water until the dryness of her throat receded.

"I'm guessing it was you at the edge. Not sure how you pulled me out but I'm grateful…" She waited, taking in the rough edges of the woodsman before her.

"You can call me John," he said. "And the beast here is Scythe. He found you, though he's not exactly offering a warm welcome."

On hearing his name the cat bound from some place deep in the distance over the shoulder of the woodsman and onto the bed near Jade's legs reasserting territory. Reflex made her flinch. The movement triggered courses of pain across her shoulder blades and temples simultaneously. Unsure which hurt worse, Jade knew neither was good when miles deep inside The Divide.

"Where am I, John? I know where I was roughly when I fell through the earth but I'm with a team of investigators and if I've missed check-in, they'll descend on this area with dire consequences." Jade braced against the pain, pushing up from the mattress.

Staring down at the walkie in his hand for a moment, he said, "Well we don't want that if it can be avoided. You haven't been out long. We're not far from the collapse, inside—"

"Inside The Divide? But no one lives…" Jade let her voice trail reading the expression on the man's face.

"No ma'am. No one does. And I'd prefer we leave it that way."

Shocked and fully aware, she read a deep sadness in the older man's faded blue eyes. Something about his expression made her regret invading his small piece of the world. He clearly didn't fit in the one beyond the restricted forest. Eyeing the cat, who gave her permission to swivel her legs over the edge of the bed and sit upright by bounding back onto the wooden floor ahead, Jade breathed in slow gauging her pain. It lessened with deliberate relaxation. She'd be sore but wasn't seriously wounded, the mossy ground absorbing graver damage. The woodsman stayed a few feet away allowing her space. This was not the criminal she sought. Too on in years, too respectful in nature, and too broken to have assaulted, abducted, and detained a dozen women.

Though man enough to save one.

"John, I could've starved to death or died a hundred other ways if left at the bottom of that hole." Jade purposefully locked eyes. "I don't know where I am and I'm betting if you could get me close to the water, I would never stumble on this..." She glanced around the room. "... cabin again."

"Well, if you feel up to a walk, I know a river close by." The woodsman held out a hand to help Jade to her feet, then relinquished the walkie and backed up. "You should take this." He offered her a Pendleton blanket, not as heavy as the one covering the bed or those folded in a wooden bin near its foot but warm and dry.

"I'd hate to take it from you," Jade said, a grin coursing across her lips. "I'll never have a way to give it back."

The woodsman smiled, handed it over, and waved a hand at the beast lounging over several planks in front of a stone fireplace. "Come on you lazy rug. Time to put those paws to use."

Without thought Jade stepped toward what appeared to be the front door of the cabin. The cat leaped in front pushing her back. The woodsman gestured the opposite direction, pausing in front of her to light a lantern hanging from a hallway wall. "You go that way you'll be in for a fall worse than the last one," he said, a chuckle escaping him. She glanced back at the entryway, through the window there appeared to be a porch but beyond it the scenery melted into an uncertain blur.

Pain shot daggers landing under her shoulder blades. She surmised that the fall set her ribs out of alignment and with a little uncomfortable work, she could reset them on her own. Until then, the muscles screamed in defiance with each step. Checking an old mantel clock for time, she asked, "Is that right?"

"Never been a minute off in forty years," he said.

"Shit." Jade brought up the walkie, clicked the button and waited for a click back. When it came, real or perceived, the acknowledgment sounded louder, angry. She was ten minutes late and dangerously encroaching on the next agent's check-in time slot.

"Everything okay?" he asked.

"Tough boss," she whispered, to which he chuckled.

"I've forgotten more than I remember," he said. "But those still haunt me on occasion."

"Haunt us all on occasion," Jade agreed.

Though having vowed to forget the cabin, a detective's eyes couldn't help drinking in every detail from the tight, formidable log construction to the transfer into solid rock tunneled out God only knew how. Questions riddled her mind following the pair into the cabin hallway's darkness that soon became only cave. Wooden crossbeams interspersed with cemented rock transformed into solid stone, raw and broken. Evenly space wall lights gave way to iron hooked miner's lanterns. Beyond a thick wood-plank door set ajar, the minimal comforts of home vanished, replaced by survival tools, grappling hooks, rope, and hanging skins not quiet scrapped free of the animal flesh they once clung to. No weapons though, not so much as a knife in sight. She held her tongue and watched as light broke through ahead.

"Careful at the break here," the woodsman said, pointing to an opening back into the forest disguised by overgrown nature. "It's a bit of a rock maze descending down. Keeps the predators away. Not meant to be easy to traverse. Scythe dives over it with air under his feet but missing a step isn't recommended."

Jade focused on her footing heeding the warning, placing her steps inside his, one over the other, noting pitfalls between capable of catapulting travelers down a shale rock embankment to a violent end, mindful of the danger until reaching solid ground. By the time she glanced back up pinpointing where they emerged from the black void was all but a bad guess. Studying the gray-haired man before her, putting his age at late sixties, though his form said he'd outmuscle the boys back at the tent, she had no desire to memorize her surroundings just then. Drawing up beside him when the forest permitted, she was struck by how at peace he was with the treacherous terrain, no more bothered by it than the feline racing and leaping effortlessly along his side. He cut a path of ease for her making the long trek back almost pleasant.

"I never finished saying it earlier, thank you for saving me," Jade said as he held a branch back for her to pass under.

"You're welcome," the woodsman claiming the name of John said. "I'm glad Scythe spotted you before you disappeared and it's lucky you weren't on the animal trail just west." He motioned to a shallow break of greenery running parallel to the trail Jade originally followed in. "Old bear trap at the far end, ancient really, but the spears slammed into the ground below would still serve serious damage."

Jade stopped trudging through the thickening low brush and stared the direction of the trap. "Straight out from here?" she questioned.

"Another hundred yards or so near the tree line," he clarified. "The animals have escape it for decades, sense it's there. Humans not so easily."

"You know, John, I could really use the wisdom of a man like you while I'm covering this land." Regaining her bearings she registered that the direction they started from was far left of the search grid. He must have carried her more than a mile over perilous unstable ground.

"Good luck finding one," he said, not slowing. "I dare say one doesn't exist and you should be glad of that fact." The man's deep voice grew quiet on his last words. "You said you were with a group of investigators?"

"Yes. I'm afraid it's an ongoing investigation so details—"

"I understand. Don't want to be brought in on it just hoping you'll clear out soon." He paused waiting for her to close the distance that had grown between them. "Hate to be handing out more blankets."

Jade laughed as he smiled offering his hand to assist her navigating a steep rocky incline. The pain in her shoulders and head became more evident with every step. "The bulk of our crew is on the other side and will likely remain there. And, if you ever venture far enough out to the plateau beyond the river you'll see my trailer. I can leave it outside the door."

"No ma'am, it's yours for the keeping," he said. "Take it as a reminder to stay safe out here and steer clear of Divide drops. None of them are fun and most are deadly."

"So it would seem. Unfortunately I'll be searching through any and all big enough to fit me until I find what I was sent here to locate." Back on even land, the river close enough to echo a rush of rapids through the trees, Jade established an even pace. Anxious thoughts of Errie and a stream of other victims flooded in like the water in the gorge soon within view. The memory of crossing over the fallen tree and its slippery bark drove a wave of nausea through her gut. It showed on her face.

"You all right? Sickness can signal a serious concussion and—"

"It's not my head," she reassured. "Not looking forward to strad-dling the fallen tree I crossed over."

"Well it's a good thing you won't have to." His weathered hand pointed to a succession of three large boulders angling into the water at a tight curve in the stream. "The water's low here and the rocks are dry, well above the break. Jump from one to the next, aim at their center and you'll be across in no time."

Jade stared at the river. The rock bridge disappeared behind a chaparral of pine trees. "That's not even halfway across," she said, grateful for the low section but dreading dropping into it.

"Oh, come up here with me." He motioned. "The path isn't fully visible from either side. Once you've committed, you'll find it as easy as skipping stones."

Closer to the bank, the smell of the wet forest floor reminded Jade of her fall and somehow of Errie and what she might be facing for another long night if she didn't get fixed up and back into the search. Peering down the track of the river she was astounded how nature hid this clear crossing in plain sight. She would never have found it without John. Staring at the cold rushing water, mesmerized by its raw speed and beauty, she startled when the cat dove in mere feet from her with no warning.

"Oh for Pete's sake. You'll be drying out all night, you crazy beast," John chastised and the animal understood, springing back out and shaking water from its fur as if in defiance. "Sorry 'bout that, he's hungry."

"He's fearless." Jade admired the cat and its bravery, loyalty too. "I'll be coming back across as soon as...I can't afford to waste time. Need to be in the caves before nightfall."

"I don't recommend it, but you have a job to do."

"One lives depend on I'm afraid," Jade said, nearing the first boulder and preparing to cross.

"In that case..." The woodsman hesitated, as if deep in thought, but only for a breath. "Go east after you see the break in that tree line. The cave entrance you seek you won't get to heading on your original trail. It's before you think, right in the middle of the forest, long before you reach sight of the far wall. Look for clover."

Jade was studying the rocks ahead of her, grateful the sun remained bright in the sky, choosing invisible targets dead center of each rock, knowing once her feet left the bank there would be no turning back or hesitation permitted. "Clover," she repeated. "East after the tree line break and..." She turned to face her forest adviser but he had vanished. No sign of him or the cat. Scanning the area before her it was as if he never existed. The blanket draped tight around her aching shoulders said he had. With that she spun back to face the river and leaped.

———————

"Why all the old maps?" Nurse Lyse asked as Nickolas shifted the aged paper carefully across his legs in bed. "I think it's great how active you keep your mind. I don't think I'd be near as smart about that if I was in here."

"Thank you, Lyse." He cast a smile at her then dropped his focus back to the documents laid before him knowing the effect it had. "I appreciate your help. I was always interested in cartography growing up but it was never supported. I thought getting back into it now might..."

"Might be healing," she finished it for him, drawn into his trap.

"Precisely," he said, glancing her direction again. "I wish I had the tools to draw one of my own making. I've been testing my memory, doc says it's good to practice, on the symbols of rivers, caves, all of the forest markings."

The coaxable nurse reacted as predicted. "Write down what you need," she said, offering him a pad and pen from her sweater pocket. "I'm running out to pick up dinner for the nurses tonight. I'll make a stop. It's healthy to test your memory especially those relating to childhood."

Nickolas accepted the pen and pad brushing a warm hand gently over hers. "Thank you for this. If it wasn't for all of you here, well…"

"It's no trouble," Lyse said, beaming with a satisfaction that said she believed herself integral to his recovery in a small way.

He jotted down supplies, smiled up at her, and handed the note and pen back. Collecting them into her pocket, she grinned, the secret safe between them, and left. He knew she'd keep the note long after delivering his mapping supplies. He signed it *with deep gratitude for your impeccable care aiding my recovery, Nickolas*. He all but drew a heart with words, meaning none of it. But he needed to draw a map and fast. Time was ticking on Jade's missing friend and aiding in her recovery was crucial.

A forty-five-minute window existed before Dr. Nnadi would reach him making rounds. Time enough to search the web on the tablet he confiscated from an orderly during a routine scan two floors down. The private hospital provided him with a computer and limited access locked to a swivel TV tray. The information he desired to retrieve was such that he preferred no trace. In fact, every touch of the keys on the monitored device was orchestrated to sway intended perceptions his way. The state, still highly motivated to prosecute him into oblivion, would garner no help from him or his medical team. He hung his violent past on an orbitofrontal injury and, so far, the specialists were buying in, though none admitted this directly.

He had his ways.

And for something as important as this he needed outside help only one man could and would give.

> Dearest Grandfather,
>
> My sister is in trouble, against a criminal adversary I fear she is unequipped to defeat. Many lives hang in the balance and I am compelled to help in the way only I can. To do this I need access to maps marking everything time has forgotten about The Divide, particularly the area nearest the river.
>
> Ever grateful for your continued love and discretion,
> yours,
> Nick

He tapped send and waited for the acknowledgment. He knew The Divide. Considered escaping there countless times but his path was set in another direction until now. With Kane and Tex still in recovery, Jade faced this criminal with strangers she couldn't trust. Agent Drex was interesting, capable but not devoted to Jade or necessarily the outcome she desired. Only he understood the depth her commitment would take her to. And this time, he was certain, she'd sink further than six feet under.

EIGHTEEN

The nurse woke to the faint echo of scratching and a morbid realization she wasn't alone in the tiny tunnel she elected to crawl up hours earlier. Passing out under the weight of deep exhaustion from her escape and what she presumed was hundreds of tons of rock, she prayed for anyone but her captor to find her. This was not what she had in mind.

Unable to stretch freely, she slowly extended her arms out ahead of her body and turned to face the source of the disturbance. This was a moment to be grateful she was not claustrophobic. Shoved by her own force into a less than two-by-two-foot tunnel, not smooth but jagged with broken rock jutting out at the most inopportune places, all she could do was hope whatever creature shared the space was friendly. There would be no escaping it.

Inches above her hips, at a deliberate break in the rock wall on her right sat a small meadow vole, cleaning his whiskers and watching her intently as if in deep consideration of the new stranger invading its home.

"Sorry little fella, didn't mean to crash in but the options out there weren't conducive to survival, if you get what I mean." Her voice, a mere whisper, sounded as scratchy as it felt. The mouse-like creature responded by dipping its little nose and wiping its face as if conceding in understanding their mutual plight. She heard a faint giggle before recognizing it as her own. "Well staying here isn't really viable so any input you have on the best routes is appreciated." She shifted slightly to open the supplies she pushed in ahead of her and locate water and perhaps a crumb for her new friend. The creature studied the movement, then darted upward, disappearing overhead.

Overhead?

In the blackness of the tunnel she couldn't identify much other than the same stone the larger tunnels were formed in. But now she could see. Light was filtering in from where her furry friend appeared and vanished into. Scuttling her hips back she shuffled until her head was in line with the rodent's shelf. Pushing up on arms folded tightly at her sides, her eye met with the hole, seeing it was much more.

From this position she angled her head to glimpse straight up the opening. Aside from tributaries branching off its sides, the one left housing her new friend, a main tunnel stretched out of sight into the welcome light of the sun.

Drinking in the fresh air drifting down to her a wave of pain and sorrow hit with the force of every violation served on her from the second the Animal entered her home to steal her away from her world and her life. She swallowed it down. "No. Not yet," she promised. "When we're safe."

Blinking newly formed moisture back to clear her vision, she stared carefully up to the opening gauging distance. Though not as far as she feared, mere feet, the path to reach it was no less elusive than before. The difference being she knew it existed.

A way out. A way home.

Collapsing back to the tunnel floor, noticing as if for the first time the impossible cage of broken mountain surrounding her and the limiting position she welcomed in the heat of the evening before, she smacked the earth. Anger releasing the energy she required to move on. Wiping tears and dirt from her face she pushed her supplies forward and started the trek ahead taking solace in the fact the tunnel encasing her was angled upward.

Using her arm as a marker, she managed to clear all of five feet or so before spotting another opening like the previous one housing her vole. Excelling her crawl, fueled by hope, she met it in moments anxious to investigate. This hole was slightly larger, revealing a clear view of open air and sun above. It also confirmed that although she was moving forward, she wasn't ascending more than inches. At this rate she'd still be climbing to the surface the same time next year. Defeat made for a dangerous bedfellow and she fought too hard for freedom to allow it to tempt her to quit.

The memory of running, escaping to the exit, the women she left behind, this was her anti-venom against self-doubt. As the inner conflict mounted a visitor popped his head out of a hole on the left ahead, one she hadn't yet reached or noticed. Crawling in a now familiar ranger advance, gaining speed with each new leg, she pushed up expecting to find a similar air tunnel to the surface but this was different. Double the breadth and descending much farther below than above, this appeared more for the purpose of accessibility for the transfer of something other than air or sunlight. This time her furry companion didn't scurry away. He remained there watching her inspection long enough for her to observe the tiny white markings of his front feet and nowhere else.

"Hi, Socks. Thanks for staying with me. If you haven't sensed it, I'm not at my best. If you lead me out to the open I promise there'll be a reward in it for you."

The little rodent twitched its nose and jumped up the small tunnel to an opening in its sidewall above. This wasn't one tunnel; it was maze of them and she hoped they continued to increase in size as she ascended. She had become so entranced with the cycle of crawling, identifying air holes, inspecting them, usually with the encouragement of a small companion, that she didn't notice the opening below her space until she found herself falling into it.

Her supplies clinked and thumped down even as her crawl stance had her tumbling face first out of the tunnel and into a mess that caught her breath. Sunlight beamed through multiple holes in the granite roofline, refracting off the sparkle covering the floor. With nothing but stone surrounding her for weeks, the nurse suspected the mine was once used to source limestone, possibly quartz, fluorite and salt but this was none of those. Raised with holidays spent climbing mountains with her grandfather in search of natural gemstones, she learned to track veins in rock deposits, sift rivers high in regions others dare not hike, and identify fools gold from the real thing. Tears flowed freely as the light, so bright, hit her eyes, but not for the gems at her feet or the axe and other possessions left abandoned in this carved-out space. Wisdom said whoever stored their spoils in this safe room so many years ago did so with the intention of taking them out, which meant a way out existed close by. She curled around the realization that her escape was not only possible but eminent and, in the fetal position exhaling waves of relief, the now familiar sound drew her attention. When her supplies catapulted out ahead of her one of the protein bars bounced against a far wall where her furry buddy felt safe enough to indulge. Laughing gently as she watched him across the cave floor munching contently, she whispered, "Definitely time to celebrate, Socks. I'm about to join you. Give me a second to find the door for us to get the hell out of here."

———————

Consciousness didn't rush in even when survival demanded. Years of addiction reined down countless helpings of pain but even as her body registered its current threat her mind failed to clear, fighting the sedative. Her captor cursed her with the worst detox imaginable and then celebrated her survival in this, his private hell. He had lamented over lost years to her habit all the while drugging her daily. Managing the throes of reactions she knew something bad was afoot. Damn if she could get her eyes to open and see clearly or control over her hands to fight back. As vision, coming in blurred, distorted smears, began to capture some truth, she wished it hadn't.

The bastard that kidnapped her so many days ago, perhaps a season, had her under the shoulders, restrained by the armpits with one of his arms, and was scraping her body over the rough rocks, dragging her where? She wasn't sure. He had never done this before.

A whole lot of other things, but not this.

With each second, her situation became clearer but made absolutely no sense. She had not betrayed his rules, done anything to anger him, but she was clearly in the throes of being punished. In an effort to protest she screamed but heard only a muted rendition of her intention, muffled by a thick cloth stuffed into her mouth. The severity of the circumstance glared beneath the false light of lanterns lining a tunnel foreign to her. Her eyes cast from side to side, roof to ground seeing nothing routine within the space. And the smell, a strong, dank mixture, said they were deeper into the belly of the cave than they had ventured before. This was a space he knew well, navigating it in a rage but surefooted in his approach.

At a cross section, as he dragged her body behind him, she caught a glimpse of an immense metal box at the back of a large room. She didn't know what it was for, perhaps the generator used to power his underground lair. Many cords extended from it. She didn't care. What she sought was anything useful to save her life before he claimed it. The brutality in his actions said that was his goal.

Her legs ached but having worn thick tights he permitted to stay warm as her weight loss made her susceptible to the cold, she avoided certain cuts the rock floor would've otherwise inflicted. And as he turned yet another corner and slammed a pad activating more lights than her eyes had seen in months, she knew why having strong legs was vital to survival.

In front of her, dropping down beyond a steel guardrail, was an underground gauntlet the likes of which she had only seen in bad pulp horror movies. Rock caverns, steel grates, sharp blades, rope ladders and walkways over an endless black abyss, and all of it wet with moisture from some underground waterway sure to drowned you if the fall to it didn't kill you first, and it would.

What in the mother of Christ? Was this what he had taken them all for? To play satanic survival games leagues beneath the surface?

She wished the gag were out of her mouth so she could unleash every profanity ever uttered at him but that wouldn't aid in staying alive. The thought barely landed when he yanked the muffle out.

Why? She didn't know but the glint in his dark eyes said it was for no good reason.

She stared past him to study the cave roof, appearing a football field above where she was thrown to its floor. Stalactite forms scattered about the edges of this great opening confirming ever-present water flow from above while an active rush echoing up said an underground river existed below. How bad could it be? Washed away out of this place, out of his hands. Better to die that way, she thought. Fighting to stay awake and absorb as much of the surroundings a possible, she startled when he began yelling. Maybe more when it wasn't at her.

"See what you've forced me to do!" He was screaming, his head tilted back, focused somewhere above and completely disregarding her. "Number one will pay for your transgressions and on the most important day of her life!"

Number one? First taken, right, that was her. In this place where she lost so much, where they all lost so much, her identity was the first sacrificed. She was a number and…

"My name is Lauren Hamilton," she yelled it with the strength of defiance knowing she would pay. "I am Lauren!"

The blow landed before his head swiveled to face hers. It crumpled her to the dirt surface and had her spitting blood. "I am Lauren," she said, this time a mere whisper in the large cavern, drifting up from bloodied lips.

"I know you can hear me!" He continued bellowing upward, distracted by someone or something other than her. She wished she had strength to crawl or run away but the sedatives hadn't yet left her body. Lifting off the cave floor was akin to propping up a mountain with a twig. She slumped back to the ground but this time with her face turned to peer again at the hedonistic maze waiting below. "I will give you this option only once!" he continued. "You return on your own and I will spare her life. If you don't…if you don't you will be responsible for ending it in the most tragic way."

That didn't sound good. Lauren analyzed the words beneath the haze of drugs. She developed this ability over years of dependency. One benefit, she guessed. *If you return on your own?* He was missing someone. Someone escaped. And, she'd be damned if the last act she performed on this planet would be to help this monster coax a victim back into his clutches. She'd wait. And then, if it were the only thing she could do, she'd make sure he didn't get his way this time.

"I know you hear me!" he taunted. Lauren stared at the ceiling following the angle their captor's head was in line with and she saw it, a circle carved out of the stone not more than the size of a melon. Its circumference perfect and manmade, he must believe it capable of carrying his screams to the woman who escaped him. Setting his diaphragm fully behind his voice, he obviously didn't fear his threats reaching outside the area in his control. Sweeping her eyes over the expanse of this underground grotto, she became increasingly aware of the scope of his control and resolve in his planning.

Years in the making, but to what end? Hers, most certainly, others likely too, but something unimaginable was responsible for lighting the vast fire that drove him underground to these heinous lengths.

"What happened?" The words fell from her without volition. He stopped his screaming and focused back down on her. Strangely, regret softened his eyes.

"Number nine disobeyed the rules," he said, panting from rage, exertion, and raw emotion. "She jeopardized everything for the rest of you. I was never going to kill you."

He read her bewildered expression.

"I built this to show you the strength you possess. Freedom waits on the other side, as does the best version of you. One of confidence, free of weakness and the dangers of insecurity. I did this for all of you." Tears coated a resin over his eyes and Lauren fought to grasp what he was saying.

"Why?" It was all that fell from her lips though so much more waited to be asked.

"Because succumbing to your fears breeds evil and I want it to stop." With this, his pupils expanded, eating the color encasing them until only black remained.

"Okay," she agreed, knowing now was not her moment of defiance. It was destined to arrive, just not yet.

The aged paper was too decayed to be read in its entirety but the nurse deciphered a partial date in the lower right corner, 1825. That couldn't be right, could it? There was such history and mystery in the six by six-by-six-foot safe room where her and Socks ate and prepared for the journey ahead it was almost a shame she'd never be back to investigate it further. But she wouldn't ever be back. She located leather moccasins several sized too large and crusty with age but managed to tie them over her booties well enough to feel protected with whatever awaited her outside the mine. An old satchel, once housing random tools, was repurposed with supplies for survival. A large outer pouch held her flashlight for easy access. A miner's axe slid into a loop near it, handy for protection. In the end it was quite heavy but easily strapped cross-body. When she arrived home, she was keeping the satchel and what she filled it with. Closing the flap she threw a half eaten protein bar inside the outer pocket with the flashlight, glanced around one last time, and was about to finish prying open the heavy door she prayed lead outside when a sound stopped her.

Not so much as sound as a darkened demand.

Filtering up from the depths below her captor was threatening her to return. "Another reason to celebrate, Socks. Socks?" The voice was so ominous it had sent her furry friend into hiding. Where? She wasn't certain. Either way if the Animal was demanding she return it meant two things, one he couldn't get to her easily, and two, he feared her escape.

She set the satchel by the wooden door, which was more of a barrier than a true door, to leave both hands free to work the crowbar to pry it open. Thus far she was making progress, enough to grant her a peek beyond it to a crawlway filled with sunlight but she wasn't free of it yet. She left both to lean over the larger air tunnel and wished she hadn't.

Lauren.

The nurse heard the desperate scream of a woman named Lauren. One who shared her hell and her fate until yesterday. She strained to hear more from the woman praying she had escaped somewhere within and apart from the Animal. No luck.

He promised to kill Lauren if she didn't come back. That she heard clearly. The words rose up as if from the bowels of Hell, losing none of their venom along the way. "I'm so sorry, Lauren," the nurse whispered, glancing around the brightly illuminated space for her furry friend, dreading making the decision alone.

Then she remembered she wasn't making it alone. She wasn't making it at all. When she left home for college, her mother, her best friend, made her promise only one thing. *If danger comes, put my daughter's welfare first.* Those were the words she lived by, putting herself and her wellbeing first when push came to shove. It resulted in placement in the university study project of her choice, landing a safe apartment on the third not first floor of her building, the hospital employment she deserved, and her boyfriend. The last on the list hurt most remembering so she forced it down.

Not my choice, my promise, she thought.

Didn't make it any easier, but being as smart as she was, she knew her survival may hold the only hope for the others that remained. Lauren, she couldn't save.

"I hate you!" she screamed back down the pipe-like tunnel. "I hate you." This time she whisper-cried the words to herself. Knowing her decision didn't stop the pain. She thought of what to say next. Were there words to lead him away from killing Lauren? Nothing that wouldn't also put her in greater danger, give him more information than the bastard deserved. Knowing this she backed away from the crude game of telephone and stood center of the room, desperate to leave but not wanting to do so without Lauren.

Frozen. Unable to move though freedom was within reach. Paralyzed with dread and drained by remorse for punishment served on one who could never deserve it. Then it came, the demand of an angel, not one now but one soon to be. "Run! Run and don't look back!"

Screams followed. The screams of brutality. The nurse was no longer frozen in the room's center. She smashed the crowbar under the makeshift door with a might born of sheer outrage. The door broke free. She threw the satchel over her neck crossbody in one fluid motion and crawled ranger-style up to a surface she couldn't have been happier to meet if it was the pearly gates.

That place Lauren was in.

NINETEEN

Kane sat on Jackson's front porch waiting for the Texas ranger's son to tell him he was on the right track. Too many years spent relying on each other and battling together against evil to what they both anticipated would be the death of one or both of them cemented a bond, unbreakable. If Kane or, this time, Jade needed backup there was only one call to be made and that was to Jackson's phone. It didn't matter what his official position was. Days away from qualifying to be cleared back into service, he was never one to sit on the sidelines. And though a married man now, his commitment and loyalties never changed. When he exited the house, cold beer in hand, his smile said none of the connections he forged over time were weakened by his rehab away from the force.

"You got it?" Kane smiled.

"You had doubts?" Jackson handed a cold bottle to Kane and dropped into the deck chair beside him. "He's on standby. Fueled and ready to go. Just say the word."

"Thanks, Tex. I owe you." Kane clinked bottle necks with his best friend feeling relief wash over him.

"Yeah, well I'm hoping we don't need to send a chopper in after her, but if we do…" Tex, as his partners labeled him, stared out over his land, then turned back to Kane. "We'll be ready for anything she needs. Why can't there ever be an easy case?"

"No such thing, my friend." Kane swallowed back the cold drink, grateful for the time here. If nothing else visiting Tex guaranteed a beautiful view and a sense of peace, if only fleeting.

"I supposed not." Tex set his beer on the arm of his chair and wrung his hands, smoothing out the aches. "The likelihood of bringing Errie home is narrowing with every day that passes. I'm hoping Jade catches a break soon. If it were up to Amy, we'd unleash a retrieval team a hundred loose on that broken rock and scour it till there was nowhere left to hide."

"Yeah, I can't blame her but any of us set a foot out there and that'll be the end of our involvement. Grey stuck his neck out locking Jade onto the case but fed's jurisdiction so…" Kane stood, walked over to the porch rail, and drank in the view of the property. "It's so damn nice here."

"A world away, right?" Tex said. "You guys should spend more time up here. We have a guest cabin."

"When this is over, I'm taking you up on that offer. She'll need it." Leaning back against the railing, Kane turned his attention to the case. "I dug up everything I could find on Wenzel's cousin, Drex. By all accounts they were nothing alike, the guy appears solid."

"Good. He better be." Tex stared at the deck boards, washed a hand over his face, and then, as he always did, gave voice to what they both were thinking. "I hate that we're not there with her. Hate that she's on her own. And I'm not sure if it's too soon after—"

"I know. Me too but she needs it. Honestly, I was worried I was losing her. The ambition that is her. She's determined to bring Errie home. Just not sure where we'll be if she can't." It was Kane's turn to wring his hands.

"We work it," Tex said. "We work it from home but we're with her even if we're not allowed on the same stomping ground. I'll let you know what I find on the vehicle front. The perp had access to multiple trucks and vans and I have ideas on how. You stay focused on the profile and keeping Amy in check. Speaking of, did you hear the meat sac suggested closing the attempted murder case?"

"What? No." Kane bounced off the railing and sat back down beside Tex. "Why the hell would Nickolas Leigh do that when it makes him the victim?"

"Only one reason," Tex said.

"Yeah, it serves him but how?" Tension made its way across Kane's forehead leaving creases in its wake.

"That's a question we better solve before Amy puts it to bed. She's anxious to do just that, more given her current worries. My guess?" Tex faced Kane head on. "He doesn't need the attempted murder case solved because he already knows who was responsible and if that's true? Well, I want to know why he does when we still don't."

"What I'd give to march up to that private hotel he's in and beat it out of him," Kane stood and paced the length of the porch.

"Isn't happening and I can give you a list of reasons why." Tex stood, leaned against a support post, and watched patiently as Kane cut an invisible grove in his deck boards.

"When did Amy know?" Kane asked.

"The last time she checked in so…"

"Never mind, I'll ask her myself." Kane threw back the last of his beer and made for the steps down to his waiting truck.

"Tread easy on her partner," Tex warned from the top step. "She's where we were not so long ago. The middle of her worst nightmare on the edge of hopeless self-destruction."

Kane paused, strides before reaching his driver's door. "I know. I will."

Driving out the winding road skirting Tex's property, he couldn't help notice panic gaining strength the nearer he was to the exit gates. Errie was the one at risk but an uneasiness rose from the initial call when Jade discovered her abduction. He hadn't yet put his finger on it to either dismiss it as remnants from the past haunting him or identify it as a current viable threat.

Gut instinct, it couldn't be ignored.

He sifted details of the case through his mind. "Twelve to save the one." This biblical reference stayed with him long after Max stumbled onto it. If correct, the criminal who snatched Errie wasn't alone, perhaps in conducting the crimes, but there was another connected to him he intended to save. So thirteen victims? Great number, he thought, hitting the open road for home.

The precise time of the abductions was announced at more than one sight. Enough so that Kane read the case files Jade shared with him with fresh perspective, identifying three more time stamps covertly added but undeniably deliberate. One hidden in a lawn timer for watering cycles, another set to turn on a reading lamp midmorning when it would compete poorly against natural sunlight and was clearly unwarranted. The lamp details he heard from a local officer who was clearly committed to the case. So much so he contacted the abducted woman's sister and best friend to confirm if the lamp ever lit up early and hit pay dirt. The timer was a gift from her sister who preset it for an hour after sundown. No mistake. The criminal paused during a heated, even violent assault to alter its setting. Again this new perpetrator put careful consideration and planning into every detail and accepted risks to do it.

With every hunt for a new demon among millions of regular folks detectives were issued the impossible task of identifying the monster most likely, but with so many to choose from...where to look first? And, in this case, the *where* was as dangerous as the *who*. The Divide possessed the perfect elusive hideaway and had the topography to hide bodies never to be found.

Perhaps this was why his foot rested heavily on the accelerator and his heartbeat was set to remain elevated until he heard Jade's voice. Hunting to end the reign of an evil man is what they did and they were the best at it. Investigating side by side just made much more sense and he was anxious for those days to return. Too anxious.

Jade was meant to call in three hours and he aimed to strip away all the distracting noise leaving only solid leads to guide her. It wasn't everything he wanted to do. What he really wanted was to find the bastard she hunted for her, take her back home where he knew she was safe, and make a quick stop between to kill Nickolas

Leigh. Damn shame whoever tried last didn't succeed. All he could hope was that they learned from their mistakes and…

If at first you don't succeed, try, try again.

The day was a shit show. Nothing else to call it and Drex pitied the poor bastard who made the next mistake or asked him another stupid question. How the bureau kept turning out agents who, when dropped into the field, left their exceptional standings back at Quantico to transform into instant asshats he wasn't sure but they never failed to disappoint.

The youngest agent was hanging in, finding nothing in the way of results but still working his section. Two others located and investigated a bear den and a cave-in respectively finding nothing but pissed off animals to run from. At this point he was ready to tie them to a tree and yell "dinner." The one he deemed most likely to fail slipped down a shale rock embankment, landed lopsided between boulders and fractured his leg. Damn near had to airlift him out and by doing so would've announced their presence to not only the criminal they were supposed to be covertly seeking but also every media outlet within a fifty-mile radius. And this was only day one. God help us all.

Profanities fell from his lips in a steady stream under his breath while he trudged up the incline back to the tent after throwing the lackey into a disguised medical transport vehicle. He left before EMTs closed the door so he didn't risk succumbing to frustration and leaning back in to break his other leg. He threw back the canvas tent door to find two of his four agents, ashen from their near-death bear encounters, deep in life contemplation.

"Sir, I speak for the both of us when I say I don't think we were trained for bear attacks and—"

"No shit, French. That I got." Drex threw his walkie on the table and patrolled the map board gathering tolerance that wouldn't come.

"I know time is the enemy——" French didn't know when to shut the hell up.

"You think?" He couldn't stand it. If he left the fate of the victims up to these city agents they were as good as dead. "You two stay here. Wait for the ranger to come back. Go over all the possible sites with room to house ten or more victims, then map with him a way in. And don't miss a single site."

"Sir, I don't recommend you go back out to our grids so close to sundown," the other agent finally found her voice and he wished she hadn't.

"I don't think either of you are in the position to offer strategy. Stay here. Work the information we have. Block out all the areas previously covered and those with the most potential for us to review when I get back. And for Christ's sake, don't venture back out without my say so. Understood?"

The pair nodded in unison, relief emanating from them. Half a day on their grids and they were ready to put in for desk jobs. They had his vote.

Although meant to command and direct them, his participation had quickly become useless without being first in the field. He set parameters, divided grids, mapped known locations of interest, laid all the evidence to date out in a neat timeline and none of it seemed to matter a damn.

The only way the criminal he sought was coming out of this godforsaken forest was in handcuffs he slapped on the bastard himself. He studied the map intently for a few seconds, focusing on deep breaths and a new plan of attack.

This time, his way.

He could apologize to the bureau after he saved everyone and made the arrest. The one he hadn't yet factored in was the homicide detective who had come as close to death as he had in the line of duty. She constituted unchartered territory a dangerous as the region he was entering alone with useless backup and an outdated map. Battling unforeseen equipment failures the LiDAR scan would download digitally when complete and give him a three-dimensional scan of the grid search area. Until then he was headed in frustrated and virtually blind.

TWENTY

Amy sensed her resolve inaudibly fracturing at the core like the silence of a hurricane stealing strength off the coastline, drawing its power in the absence of sound, no wind, or birds, so still you strained to hear your own breath. The quieter it became the more violence would be unleashed. And inside, she could hear a pin drop.

Her, Kane, Jackson, hell even Max, had layered the evidence board at Kane's place to a degree seldom seen back at the shop still it wasn't enough. No breaks and the clock ticking down, regardless of the reassurances they all issued, grew in contrast to an unbearable volume. She hadn't returned to the house she shared with Errie. She couldn't. Not without her. Kane and Jackson scoured it over twice, initially and then when leads demanded new perspective. She longed to go home, but not alone.

And now this shit with Nickolas Leigh. She didn't know why he would encourage her to close the case that labeled him the victim of an attempted murder plot but wisdom said any reason he had wouldn't serve anyone but him in the end. Still, the monkey on her back was itching to be shed. And, in the wake of devastation and determination to solve Errie's abduction, she was too weak to carry it or fight him coaxing it off.

Amassing corroboration of the events leading up to the life-sustaining equipment malfunction amounted to a whole lot of nothing in the way of hard evidence. So, even in theory, she didn't have reason to stop looking. Driving back to the private hospital, she ran probabilities in her head, reasons why Nickolas requested to see her. The timeframe was also odd, an hour after his doctor left for the day. Usually visits were scheduled deliberately while his lead and other medical staff of authority was present to provide a buffer and watchdog their interactions.

Too sad, angry, and terrified to face a world without Errie, Amy knew meeting him, the Redeemer, in this state was a mistake. In the moment it didn't matter. She just couldn't give a shit even with her badge and freedom on the line. Slamming the car into Park, she snatched the file off the passenger seat, flung her door shut, and strode across the parking lot, unconscious of her surroundings. The pictures in her mind of evidence gathered in Errie's case and conflicting nightmarish outcomes hit so vividly the outer world competed poorly for her attention. It wasn't until she hit the entrance to his wing and realized no one manned it that her focus shifted to the present tense.

Brushing her hand under the wall sanitizer dispenser, she coated both then hammered the automatic open button waiting for access. The double doors spanned back smoothly to reveal an empty hallway stretched before her, stranger still not to see at least a few staff members milling about. The echo of her boots rang back louder than she recalled from previous visits and no one seemed to be listening but her.

Passing the rooms to reach Nickolas Leigh's, she witnessed the same rehabilitation apparatus and patients she had come to recognize asleep in their beds or living quietly from them. Reaching the room on the left where he waited brought a wave of uncertainty and trepidation unfamiliar to the experience. She rounded the corner to find him alert and sitting with two substantial files close on his lap. His hands lay folded over the separated documents and the glint in his deep green eyes when they met hers said he was holding all the cards and knew it.

"Detective, and right on time. Wonderful. Please have a seat." Nickolas gestured to a chair already moved at a comfortable angle close to his bed. Curious? Who moved it or was it left there by a visitor who came before her?

"What can I do for you, Mr. Leigh?" Amy asked with her best effort to appear nonchalant. She casually approached, setting a hand on the back of the chair but not sitting.

"Interesting. You know placing a barrier between us of any kind is behavior indicative of one whose intention is to deceive."

"You have a lot of time to read here, don't you?" Amy asked. "I myself am a busy law enforcement officer and am tired at the end of the day, hence leaning on the closest comfortable object without infringing on your personal space."

"I see. Well I appreciate the kindness but really do invite you to sit down." He spoke with his customary even, deep tone but the glimmer hadn't left his eyes. If anything, it shone brighter the closer she came. "We have quite a lot to cover before next rounds so I'll get right to it."

Amy skirted the chair and sat, pushing it back a few inches before settling. "I see you have paperwork. Do you have further claims to file?"

"Just the opposite," he said, a faint grin raising the left side of his mouth in what any women who didn't know him would equate to a sexy grin. "You appeared unconvinced when last we spoke about my theory on faulty machinery being to blame for my near-death at the general. So, given the legal team at my disposal, I requested a search be done, and you wouldn't believe what they unearthed."

Selecting the thick file on his left, he clutched the bound papers in his hand and extended it out to where she sat. The distance his long reach covered was surprising, the ease with which he presented it, alarming. Hard to accept this healthy, strong man was bedridden. Worrisome given *what* he was.

"Please," he offered. She kept his arm waiting just long enough to gauge its strength. No tremors, not a flinch.

Amy accepted the file, sat back in her chair, and opened it to peruse the papers within. A cover breakdown of the research sat at the front of the pile and showed with irrefutable verification that the company responsible for manufacturing the particular piece of equipment that failed him was not as reliable as they professed. Captivated by the proof in her hands, Amy half-convinced herself she may not have been wholly responsible for its malfunction. Outside of completely pulling the plug on the machine, fail-safes were in place for every worst-case scenario and even with her handi-work, should have kicked in to counter the effect but didn't. Moments passed before she sensed the sting of his eyes watching and measuring her reaction to the information. She steadied with a few slow breaths before meeting his gaze.

Amy closed the file and addressed him. "As informative as this appears at first glance I couldn't say for certain—"

"What is enclosed within that folder has been vetted extensively and, when read in its entirety, provides eyewitness contacts for verifi-cation, ones who never came forward to police," he said. "My point being, they lied about the reliability of their machine. The proof within would've remained hidden if not for an insider informant. Four others, manufactured around the same time and from the same plant, also failed costing the lives of three patients and harming a fourth. I was number five."

Amy turned her attention back to the documents she held, thumbing through while he spoke not giving him the satisfaction of her shock.

"The would-be killer is a faulty quality control process, not a person. I hope this helps you to close the case and free your focus onto much more pressing matters."

This caught her attention and her head snapped up, locking eyes with the monster in his glory. "Pressing matters?"

"Yes. That brings me to file number two." Though appearing ready to hand it over, he stalled keeping it close. "I'm aware Detec-tive Carmichael is working a case with the FBI involving a string of missing persons and I'd like to help if I can. As I mentioned, my resources are vast."

"So it would seem." The calm left Amy's voice and despite her best effort to hide it, resentment seeped from her pores casting a palatable bitterness into the air between them. "How the hell did you find out—"

"Agent Drex Lafine paid me a visit recently and I fear, without all of you supporting her efforts, Jade may not be as successful on this hunt as I'm sure you would all like."

He knew. He fucking knew. She didn't know why the FBI had stopped in to question a killer they previously arrested or how Nickolas made the connection to Errie and Jade but he had. The moment left her raging and speechless.

"He said she's after a collector and ten victims but he's wrong. The count, I suspect is twelve or more." He was talking fast and Amy's brain was recording every word, every pause. "There are few ways to transport so many and evade detection. I know someone who has access to CCTV footage for the major roadways. Matching the footage with the time stamps for abduction sites and the avenues less traveled…the ones I would've taken, well you'll see."

He handed her the folder and reaching for it Amy saw it was her hands shaking. His remained steady and calm. She snatched it away, slapped it on her lap, and opened it finding it difficult to breathe. Forcing a return to calm too late.

"Are you okay?" he asked. "It is a great deal to digest, I know. And the thought of Jade, Detective Carmichael out there in such treacherous terrain without all of you is, well, unsettling."

"No. I'm far from okay. I'll close the damn case as you've suggested, but…" Amy collected the files, stood kicking the chair back out of her way and knocking it over in the process. "… if you are attempting to interfere with a federal investigation this summer camp you're running will end in a damn quick hurry. Even your grandfather won't shield you from them."

"I am not leading you or her astray. This is an opportunity to help. One you and her both need. So take it before Lafine comes back. I'm guessing his next visit won't be so cordial."

Amy exhaled the hatred welling up inside her. Kane, Jade, and Grey all taught her to trust her emotional instincts in the wake of conflicting information. He meant what he was saying. For reasons she couldn't decipher he wanted to give them the upper hand and had gathered information capable of doing just that. She didn't have the luxury of time to weigh the pros and cons of taking him at his word. Errie didn't have time to wait. As if reading her thoughts, he spoke again.

"Go, Detective. You have eleven minutes by my count to walk out of here with those files and no questions asked. None of the evidence will trace back to me. The only one who will know where the leads came from is you. So leave. Leave now and go save your fiancée and Jade's reputation. Why, doesn't matter."

He was right, why didn't matter to her a good goddamn. She studied his face for a second, read his expression and all the things his eyes said that he didn't put voice to. He was scared but not for himself. He was genuinely worried for Jade and by default Errie.

Walking the hallway back to her car, much faster than she had come in, Amy knew she crossed a line. She wasn't sure if it occurred when she messed with the equipment and almost killed Nickolas Leigh, if it was coming here to see him secretly hoping for a way to close the case that threatened her or accepting files from him basically intent on doing his biding but it was crossed. And she realized with every fiber of her being, as she closed her car door, rolled the engine over, and exited the parking lot with new files on the passenger seat, she had passed the point of no return.

For Errie.

TWENTY-ONE

Two ropes hung at even heights off trees parallel from each other a few yards from the Airstream. Anyone watching could've assumed Jade was setting up a hammock until she wrapped her wrists in the ropes, suspended forward, and waited for the crack of her ribs.

"Mother of..." It was a muffled wail more than an outcry but she earned it. Her ribs popped back into alignment, relieving the pain from when they were knocked out in the fall to the forest floor. It wasn't the first time she reset them; it wouldn't be the last but damn did it hurt.

She checked the wound to her head when she first reached the trailer, slapped ointment on the scratches, and geared back up to find the entrance to the cave before she lost her bearings to nightfall. Any cave would descend into total blackness within a matter of feet so she didn't see the point of waiting until sun up. Whoever held Errie and the others wouldn't be waiting. Dropping the ropes to the ground she threw her pack over her pulsating shoulder muscles and was about to make for the tree line when her walkie erupted. The low voice of Agent Lafine echoed up from where the device hooked onto her belt.

"Jade, need to update you. Do you have comms?" he asked.

"I'm here. Reading you clear," she said, surprised at the clarity of the high-end walkie.

"Look, we've suffered some…setbacks on our side. A near bear attack and one on route to hospital due to a fall. I'm heading in to work French and Taylor's grids so we don't lose time. Are you on your way out of your grid?" he asked.

"No, sir. I located a possible cave entrance, came back to the truck to replenish before going in. If it's shallow, I'll cross it off the list tonight. If it shows potential, I'll reach out." Jade hoped by downplaying the lead she would be left to search it alone. There was something out there, she could feel it and the woodsman, being intent on having them exit the area, had been highly motivated to guide her in the right direction.

He knew the land better than anyone, including the ranger, she was certain of it.

"You sure you're good without backup? I could send Zac but I don't know how much help he'd be or how long it would take for him to reach you. Once we're underground comms will be useless so don't venture too far without me."

"No, sir. I won't. I'm good. Not sure it is anything yet. No leads on your side?" she asked, steering the focus away from her next moves.

"Not a damn one." His irritation was evident.

"Did the ranger show up? Anything on LiDAR we should be focusing in on?"

She heard Drex exhale heavily. "Ranger is supposed to arrive shortly; two agents are back at base waiting for him to review maps. The LiDAR scan was delayed but should be complete tonight barring any other fucking unforeseen problems. Let me know what you find and for Christ's sake, don't try fighting a bear or scaling a shale rock slide."

Jade laughed before touching the button to open the microphone. "Okay. Can we reset our check-in for a two-hour window? Don't think I'll make it inside and out in time and don't want you thinking I've been mauled."

Static colored the line for a few seconds. "Okay, set it for three hours to give us both time to search but if I don't hear from you then I'm sending choppers and blowing this whole spy game wide open."

"Yes, sir. On the hour, you'll hear from me," Jade promised, wondering just how bad Drex's day had been. And then she had a thought. "I think I may have something for you by then. Stay safe, sir."

She could hear the relief in his tone when he answered wishing her the same. He was nothing like his cousin. Instead of being an embarrassment to law enforcement like Wenzel had been, Drex appeared to match her drive and commitment. Pitted against the feds trust was difficult but if they had served the same team he would've fit in just fine. Thoughts of her own team, the one back home, and the capabilities of each of them made her hope by the time she returned to the trailer new leads would be waiting. Breeching the brush, she was grateful for a direction to head.

Every time she cycled back to the trailer, before it was in clear view, images of Errie guzzling from her black skull water bottle, waiting for them, ballerina limbs stretched out like a cowboy after a long ride, filled her mind. What she would do to see that again. To see Amy beaming with pride every time Errie out ran, out climbed, or outsmarted the rest of them. They were family. Jade could ignore the pain in her shoulders, the pounding of her head, the cuts, scrapes, bruises and discomfort for family. And the other victims, they were someone's family.

Anger filtering out from her center strengthened her arms as she pushed foliage aside. Its energy offered accuracy to her scans of the forest and resilience to her stride. In half the time expected she was ankle deep in a sea of clover staring at a hole in a rock wall. Overgrown and claimed by nature it was invisible, hidden in plain sight. If not for the woodsman's clover clue, she could've trudged by it a hundred times never recognizing it as an entrance.

"Thanks, John." Pushing vines aside, struggling beneath intertwined branches, Jade entered a new underground world. As streams of sunlight gave way to utter blackness, she switched on her headlamp hoping a hungry predator didn't vehemently guard the domain she invaded. At least, not the kind she couldn't slap cuffs on.

Not more than twenty minutes in Jade was glad her combat boots of choice had elevated soles and were waterproof. Moisture trickled in at all sides forming a narrow but slippery trail down the center of the cave. For the first leg, though low enough to cause her to hunch and wonder what might decide to hitch a ride on her back as she scraped by, the cave was a couple yards across. Rounding a corner, or more a natural deviation jutting left, the height improved but she was fighting for footing between broken rock.

Where the hell was the LiDAR scan? Would it even help in this situation? Perhaps to rule out surface structures not conducive to the space required to conceal multiple victims but below ground it was as useless as the agents Lafine condemned to tent duty.

The ground leveled out again and ahead she thought she glimpsed a pinhole of light. Pausing, she switched her headlamp off and focused on the farthest point of reference. Natural light was breaking through a distance away. Scanning from side to side with the light back on, she was grateful not to be sharing the tunnel with an animal, not that one couldn't enter behind her and make exiting back out a problem.

At their morning base camp briefing Lafine had laid out the evidence from individual local police working singular abduction sites and correlating federal involvement. All of it pointed the perpetrator away from where the victims originated. He wasn't remaining in the area. Mirroring every adept kidnapper, he fled the scene, driving away from possible discovery into the anonymity of a highway, country road, or mesh of streets to vanish from. Locals managed to swarm a couple of abandoned vehicle matches but to no avail. He left little to go on. Tire treads from a van said he switched vehicles, leaving in a Ford F-450 Super Duty pickup truck. The extended crew cab was easily capable of holding a sedated woman in the back. And with dark-ened windows, no one would be the wiser. Or, an innocent truck owner had the misfortune of pulling over near the space where the criminal previously switched vehicles having nothing whatsoever to do with the crime. Dead ends at the sites, leads pointing this direction, and empty searches of would-be places along the way said he was here.

Slipping over a branch hidden in the water, losing her footing, and meeting the wet ground with a thud, Jade cursed the one she hunted. "Damn you, asshole, for choosing this place."

And why did he? She opened thoughts to a flood of reasoning while trudging through the space. Did he grow up in the area and know it from childhood? Was he a park ranger, a hunter, a wilderness enthusiast of some kind? Did his background give him access to maps of the region and, if so, what career fields could narrow their search? Questions intended to identify the enemy sat among a steady stream plaguing her as they did all detectives worth their salt during a case. Working them, a possibility gnawed at her. It had been floating in her mind since discovering Errie missing. If the perpetrator stole women in a sequence along the coastline from west to east, he was obviously comfortable driving it, confident even. So who did that?

A transport trucker was too clear an option. The glaring flaw being pulling a semi-trailer into abduction sites wasn't ideal and shifting through a dozen gears didn't make for a viable getaway vehicle. This criminal had access to many means of transport, none of those spotted larger than a van. Her mind wheeled around prospects while she closed the distance to what appeared to be the cave's end.

The rock, broken free and dilapidated by time and weather, left a hole large enough for her to escape out of. Wind whistled in as if doing so with great force. Poking her head through she was grateful she hadn't anxiously dove out.

It would've been to her death.

Suspended several feet below the upper land shelf, the cave extended out flush within The Divide's highest rock wall on the western side. Dropping some hundred feet below, the river raged, funneled into the tightest point between the sides of the cavern. Nothing but a painful end would be met by anyone without wings from where Jade stood, boots planted securely behind a boulder, peering across what might be the most breathtaking and dangerous view of the warded forest.

Her walkie squawked, not meant for her, but she heard the voice of the junior agent, Zac, updating Drex on his findings. Unable to obtain a clear signal, she wasn't about to step outside or dangle the expensive device out the opening. Instead she left it clipped to her belt, catching intermittent words or phrases. By all accounts the younger agent was competent and, though sundown was creeping in, hadn't abandoned his efforts in his grid search.

Extinguishing her headlamp and setting her pack down she rifled through its contents until locating her water bottle and binoculars. From this vantage point she had clear, direct access to openings in the rock face on the opposing side. From the upper land shelf she would be staring at a downward angle, limiting view. Gulping down a quarter of her bottle in the stillness of nature, she listened as the voices over the walkie signed off and silenced. Her watch said she had a little less than and an hour and a half before check-in. Allowing forty-five minutes to stumble back and exit the cave, she had enough time for a thorough survey of the east wall starting from the area just below her to the surface level of the eastern ridge moving left to right.

The forest was losing sunlight but she hoped enough prevailed to allow her to search unhampered by the dark or the animals that would soon claim it. Despite the urgency vibrating from every cell of her being, there existed something tranquil in staring at the magnified images of geological fissures. She identified veins of varying sediment cascading across the stone. Although the area had been mined in the past for gravel, sand and salt, she visited jewelry stores carrying garnet stones and Herkimer diamonds sourced within the state and couldn't help wondering what remained hidden in this untraveled sector.

Despite the natural beauty filtering through the lens, frustration mounted. None of the openings offered a possible option for investigation. All were overgrown with vegetation, didn't appear deep enough to lead into a larger space, or we're clearly occupied by birds who wouldn't be present if a human invaded the space beyond them.

On her third pass from left to right the stillness captured by the binoculars was broken by scattered rockfall. The sudden movement was jarring and she readjusted the glasses over her eyes. Searching through the lens she couldn't locate the source of the disturbance so she dropped them to hang from the strap around her neck to examine the broader picture. Receding sunlight cast the lower portion of the rock face in shadows now and was quickly devouring upward. Her eyes ached, laser focused and fitfully sweeping as to not miss a stray stone falling. Tracing the trajectory the pebbles could have come from she thought she glimpsed movement but couldn't be certain. Grabbing the binoculars again she followed the same path and hit pay dirt.

Very near the top of the east bank, maybe a few feet below the land shelf, an opening existed but not like those she had ruled out. This one, enclosed tightly within a buildup of fractured surrounding rock, was clearly manmade and not Mother Nature's doing. The angle of the opening prevented her from viewing more than its outer edge. What she was witnessing, given the volume of debris being forced out of the hole, was something making its way out. An animal perhaps but whatever it was had better have wings. The hole suspended upward by the buildup beneath had no ledge, only a straight drop to the riverbed. Any creature forcing gravel out of its burrow had to be aware of what waited on the other side.

"What the hell am I doing?" Jade cursed the air never removing the binoculars from her eyes. "Errie could be fighting for her life or buried beneath a metric ton of rock and I'm glued to the fucking animal channel."

Realizing the futility in her current course of action she was about to pack up when something unexpected emerged from the hole across The Divide's cavern.

A foot. Then, the unmistakable calf of a very slight woman. Crawling out of the hole backward. "Oh fuck." Jade breathed it into the air while possibilities hit her from every direction. If this was one of the victims, was she being pushed out to her death where

Jade would have no option but to watch her fall? What the hell made the tunnel or hole she was backing out of? And how had she gotten in there in the first place? She damn sure didn't enter it from where she was about to exit it. Knowing if she screamed a warning and the captor was with the woman she would reveal police presence she weighed options in record time.

"Stop!" She screamed and heard her voice echo back to her, bouncing off the distant wall. Louder. "Stop! It's a straight drop off! You'll die!" She watched through the binoculars wishing they came with a microphone. "This is Detective Jade Carmichael! I am speaking to the woman exiting the cave! There is no ledge! If you are moving of your own free will, stop!" Her voice cracked and broke against the rock facing her but the leg kept coming, then two feet and a second calf.

The whole of the woman's right flank was loose and about to counterweigh the rest of her to certain death. The female was several football fields across the river break hundreds of feet up the cavern wall there was no way for Jade to reach her. The only chance available was to get her to stop moving.

Grabbing her water and chugging a swallow down, she dropped the binoculars, leaned further out her own cave than was safe to do so, and put every ounce of force God gave her behind her voice. "Stop! Straight drop! You will die!"

Scooping up the binoculars, still hanging over the boulder, she found the feet and the leg, not advancing out but searching as if seeking confirmation of somewhere to land. Jade couldn't be sure if the owner of the leg heard her or was seeking ground on her own accord. Not wasting time, she yelled again. "Not safe to exit! Turn around! Turn around now!"

The only command Jade could issue that afforded potential visual confirmation she was being heard. She studied the image and waited. Seconds passed with Jade hearing her own ragged breath, her chest pressed uncomfortably against the boulder as she hung just beyond safety of the cave. "God dammit," she whispered. "Turn around."

As if hearing her the leg slowly pulled back out of sight,

vanishing into the hole in the earth it originally appeared from. Good. This was good or damn sure better than the alternative. Not wanting to lose visual on the woman, Jade couldn't risk dropping the binoculars to try her walkie for Drex until certain the woman was safe from backing into oblivion. This was where she wished she could split into two and double her efforts. Glued to the woman's progress, she watched until even the feet were no longer visible.

Then she waited. Was there space for the woman to turn around and pop her head beyond the hole? This was not a fun game of gopher. If she could make eye contact, even for a few seconds, she may be able to identify her among the victims taken. Confirming their suspicions accurate and the search on target. Although her unreasonable heart longed to see Errie's head rise over the rubble, Jade knew her athletic legs and the one she saw did not belong to Errie, paler skin tone lacking the carved muscle of her ballerina friend. Still, if this was a survivor there was ample reason to celebrate. Jade wanted desperately for the woman to do that safely in her custody not a mile across a shale rock death pit.

Time crawled as Jade froze suspended over the stone watching until gravel trickling out of the hole said her attention was about to be rewarded. First white-blonde hair, a mound of it contrasting against the gray stone, then the head of a woman rose above the edge. Carefully the woman swiveled until Jade could see her face. The nurse, no mistaking it, the ninth victim taken. Her Nordic hair and angular features made her unique, and easily recognizable. Snapping her flashlight off her belt she flicked it on, waving it across horizontally with one hand while locked on the reaction through the lens held by the other. The woman's neck and shoulders were out of the opening enough for the nurse to assess her situation and realize exiting any further would lead to her death.

"I'm Detective Jade Carmichael!" Jade bellowed across the cavern. "Is he with you? Nod your head! I can see you!" Jade watched as the woman nodded that she had currently escaped her captor's clutches. "Good! Is there another exit? A way to reach the surface level above?"

"Where am I?" the nurse yelled out.

"A prohibited forest region in Upstate New York!" With this, Jade read the women's shock even from a distance through the lens. "We will get to you! I am not alone! Stay where you are! Nod if you understand! I will send agents to you!"

Jade registered the nod of confirmation before dropping the binoculars, shuffling back to solid ground, and snatching her walkie off her belt. "Drex are you on comms? Drex, can you read me?" She checked her watch realizing he could be out of reach for almost another hour, too long. Time enough for the bastard that stole these women to locate the one who escaped. Worse still, Jade feared the nurse, if forced to choose between dropping to her death or meeting it with her captor, may lose faith and leap.

Static. "Give me a fucking break," she whispered between depressing the switch-to-talk button. "Drex, I have a visual of a victim, do you read?"

Fearing the frailty of the nurse's mental state Jade crawled back out over the boulder and screamed, "We will not let him win! Stay here until I reach you! I will reach you! Confirm!"

"Okay!" The word echoed up like a small victory as darkness descended on the space between them and Jade no longer had the light to see the nurse across The Divide. Shuffling back fully inside the cave, she held the expensive walkie out the hole depressing the STT and barking into it. "Drex, Agent Lafine! I have eyes on a victim. Do you read me?"

His voice came back in choppy burst, thundering over the line as she turned the volume to its highest setting. "Detective…say you… victim. Confirm."

"I repeat, I have a victim, ninth taken in clear sight. She's on the eastern shelf, your side. Can't reach her. I'm inside a cave opening across at a hundred plus feet in the air. Do you read?"

Static answered then more broken speech. She cut back in. "Victim in sight. Your side…eastern shelf. Unreachable."

Jade spun the walkie in frustration nearly losing her grip but the act cleared comms momentarily. "Jade. I read you. Victim confirmed. Eyes on. Can you engage?"

"Negative. I'm directly across on the rock wall, western side of river. No access."

"I'm in a mine three miles from the river. Should we send rescue in flight?"

"No, sir. No perpetrator with her. May alert him. I'll get to ground in thirty minutes. Contact again then. Meet me at access point Kilo Alpha."

"Kilo Alpha. Run, Detective!" Drex's response said he read the urgency in her voice despite the interruption in comms. And would have a search party waiting for her at the mile marker. Until then, she prayed the nurse would hold to her resolve. Gathering her gear, headlamp, and flashlight on, and walkie back in place on her belt she ran the cave. Water splashing from every footfall slammed to the earth told any animal at the other end they dare not block her pursuit of justice.

TWENTY-TWO

"**R**un and don't look back!" Errie didn't catch all of the words echoing up from the vent tunnel but she heard the command issued by a woman not as fortunate as her. One suffering at their captor's hands for what followed was devastating. A sound not unlike the tortured cry of a forest animal brutalized and about to succumb to the violence of a stronger predator, quick and distinctly disturbing, but unmistakably a last plea for help.

One unanswered. And, one too close.

She didn't know how the woman below discovered she was missing to then inspire her to flee for her life. Perhaps she tried the same and failed. But if Errie had any doubts about her next moves the anguish of her fellow captive ended the debate and solidified an aggressive course of action.

After collapsing under a blanket of exhaustion beyond his reach through a narrow horizontal tunnel barely accommodating her small frame, she faced the challenge of traversing a vertical one it broke out into. The new space afforded her the height to stand fully upright, within walls tapering in so tight as to brush against her skin or returning back down the previous tunnel to search for other options. The tight fit seemed a blessing. Knowing what waited behind her, she chose to gamble on what lay ahead.

Before entering she paused in the broken space where the two intersected. Staring down to assess her body she was grateful the limited light cast the damage in shadow. So much of her was badly bruised, bleeding, scratched and scarred and painted in an array of dried mud and blood. Ballerina no more. The tattoo on her outer left ankle, a captivating artistic rendering of her in full Fouetté, had been cut through between legs and torso. She didn't care what condition she escaped in and knew Amy wouldn't. She was so much more than a stage presence, a title, a body, to those who loved her. They would celebrate all those things only because they served her in outsmarting and outlasting the beast that snatched her away from them.

Inhaling with lungs desperately in need of oxygen replenishment and met by a shallow musty return that proved the attempt futile, she gathered her resolve to push on. Crumbling in this dark divide ensured no one would ever know what became of her sentencing all those she loved to remain haunted forever by nightmarish probabilities and no closure. She wouldn't do that.

Wrapping survival essentials as compact as possible she pushed them in ahead of her, securing them over her wrist. Twisting a flashlight through her left bra strap she fashioned a shoulder lamp and slid in inching forward and praying the upright break she squeezed through would widen. If forced to back out she'd be doing it blind, unable to turn around. The smell of rock, so near her face, reminded her of the concrete parging her and Amy used to repair the lower skirting of their home. Damp yet dusty. Mere feet within the space a section of raw rock jutted out at face level causing her to arch and duck for clear passage. Another caught her knee and scraped but she didn't stop. For Amy, she promised not to. Minutes passed like hours with the memory of the woman's tragic screams playing over in her mind. She didn't want to know what fate she suffered but with a homicide detective fiancée Errie could imagine far too well.

A noise filtered down from above. Unexpected, it caught her off guard and she fought to contort her head for a possible visual of what created it. The beam from her flashlight reflected above offered no comfort. Broken rock, dirt, pebbles, and a crack towered over her caged space threatening to fill it and bury her within. "Head down and go," she whispered. A phrase Amy repeated when entering a dangerous call. Errie adapted it like life partners do and there was no better time.

Shuffling forward, water seeped through her blanket sarong at her sides explaining the unwelcome crack above. And to think she had been pissy with Amy when asked to crawl into their attic space to run an electrical cord when they were renovating. What she would give to be back home crawling safely through new nontoxic insulation. The changes they decided on to make the new home their own all resulted in a beautiful, blended space that truly reflected their lives. A training room incorporating heavy weights and a ballet bar, an outdoor space for cookouts accommodating friends and family, a target practice version of a dartboard to pay homage to Amy's shooting accuracy, and a kitchen with all the trimmings for...

The man who stole her from her life ruined it all. She was about to fill the limited air with profanity when she popped into a section where she could move her arms. Soon she was able to stretch out her kinks and walk freely. As this tunnel expanded it offered three tributaries to follow. The fact that two were limiting in size gave her relief. He couldn't fit to follow down them to intersect her. The last one offered the most promising way out but also was easily accessible in size for her captor. With no way to gauge where it would lead and him busy with other vicious endeavors below, Errie figured it was now or never. She turned into tunnel number three, secured her belongings, and bruised, battered, and almost broken took off like a track star. Her finish line, freedom.

John stood across from the fireplace of his rock-sheltered cabin where his cat flopped down waiting to be dried. He stared at the bin of blankets, housing one less than had existed there for so many years.

Scythe stretched out, rolled onto his back, and gazed up critically. "I'm just deciding which one to use next, that was the only light one," John defended. The cat glared out into the hallway beyond the room. "Oh, right, right." John disappeared, reemerging with a light blanket from a storage wardrobe he built a decade earlier. "Forgot about this one," he said, taking his place in the wingback and draping the backup over his legs. "It's actually nicer than the tan one I gave her. The blue is…refreshing."

To this the cat rolled back upright, sprang to its feet, approaching to sniff the rare oddity in their space. After deciding the blanket strangely new but still smelling of home, he tired of his inspection and returned to lie at John's feet.

"No offense, buddy but it was nice to hear my name out loud for a change," he said, leaning forward to pat the back of the feline's head. The cat turned and adjusted out of reach as if protesting. "Yeah, I know, not my real name. Never said I planned on getting used to it, you oaf." The cat eyed him disapprovingly and elected to move closer to the warmth of the fire. "Fine, be that way. I do think we may be crossing paths again and not by any doing of ours."

Pulling out folded papers from the side table drawer he opened the map and scanned the area just right of where he had chosen to live, hide, and survive undetected until now. "If she's working the area with the feds and they're on the west bank we may be okay," he spoke as if the sleepy cat was hanging on every word, knowing the truth but ignoring it. "They may not come out this far. That'll depend on what or whom they're searching for. That…I fear may become a serious problem."

With chalk, also from the drawer, he marked up the map identifying where he discovered Jade, the location of the feds and her trailer, and then he circled three distinct areas. Next, he pulled out his computer, hit a timer and began searching the web for possible reasons for their investigation. It wasn't long before he ruled out escaped prisoners, terrorists on the run, or a singular missing persons case.

The picture coming into view was far worse than any he antici-pated since catching sight of the lone detective encroaching on his land.

"This might require intervention, Scythe," he whispered to the sleeping animal. "We have to be careful again, buddy. Maybe just this one last time."

Shutting down the computer with information yet to probe but out of time before exposing his IP address, he turned to pen and paper connecting all the notes he jotted down during his search. Despite his reclusive existence he was well versed on advanced search and rescue protocols and the laws that framed them when crossing state lines. If the case he suspected brought federal involve-ment to his doorstep the detective he saved truly was on her own and out on a limb. She would require more than directional guid-ance from him to keep the feds on the west bank and blind to his existence. She promised to forget him, Scythe, and their home but now he would make her remember. Having visited her Airstream long before she alluded to it, he didn't see any signs that camping out on the edge of The Divide's restricted zone was anything but her idea.

The feds and her were keeping secrets from each other. He hoped that could continue until both left their current posts. It wouldn't though, not unless the case that brought them was closed quickly leaving him no choice but to help.

He put his head up to see his furry beast basking in the heat of the extinguishing fire. Instead of placing a nearby log on to stoke the flames, as was his tradition this time of night given the cold breeze, he quietly snuffed it out and turned on the heater. The cat lifted his head to object, then repositioned nearer the heater.

"Sorry, buddy. Can't risk the smoke for a while. Not until I help the detective find her man and leave our forest."

Walking to the rough kitchen area he skirted the fish cleaning table, the hanging herbs, and shelved dry goods for a wooden door leading to a food storage room secured from animals should one invade their space. Locked inside, behind a sliding bar system too difficult to be opened by chance, at the very back, pinned to the wall was the first calendar he brought with him when he made the deci-sion to stay.

The date on it was faded but even if it was completely lost to time he would've read it in memory.

April 1996

His weathered and wrinkled hand smoothed over the yellowed paper. So much time gone and yet the strength of what brought him here hadn't dimmed in the slightest. He stared at scribbled writing covering the first seventeen days and then the blanks following and occupying the remaining thirteen. He could still see the words though the bright pink ink they were originally penned with faded to a pale hue. His eyes coated in a familiar resin but no tears fell. With each year narrowing the time between life and death fewer did. "See you soon, kid," he whispered. "Dad has to save someone here. I think he'll let me come home then."

TWENTY-THREE

Lauren woke to the taste of blood in her mouth and a chill cascading through her body, unsure if the cold seeped in from the stone she laid on or from the knowing deep inside of what was to come. Her eyes adjusted slowly to the light, her left not completely as swelling prevented a clear view. All she allowed in those first seconds was gratitude, for she saw him hovering above on the ledge where he knocked her unconscious so far from where he dumped her beaten body. He couldn't get to her from where he stood without great effort and too much time. Time enough for her to pitch off the rock formation she identified as the one furthest from where she screamed and was punished. She knew where he left her.

At the gateway of the gauntlet with no way out save through it. Even that was an illusion. Witnessing the impossible trial he prepared while he berated the victim who defied him and escaped, she knew her weak arms and legs, her exhausted and ravaged body was no match for one, let alone all, of its pitfalls and challenges. And wasn't that the point? To toss her here and watch her fail so he could validate her worthlessness.

She wouldn't play nice.

Though the vehicle she was given to ride out this life was, in fact, weak and easily tempted to ruin, her mind learned over the last few brutal months how to find peace and she wouldn't let it go for him. If it were the end she faced, she would dictate it not him.

Lifting her throbbing skull off the ground she checked her arms and legs for breaks and found none though pain was a constant with every movement. *Not for long.* If her cracked cheek would've allowed, laughter may have erupted for he left her with gloves, water, and had poured her into a climbing harness of some sort while unconscious. Why bother? She supposed he was living for the delusion he orchestrated. Aware the moment she opened her mouth the agony inflicted on her cheek would be searing, she opened the water and drank clearing her throat, glad she still had a voice and intent on using it.

"Is the metal box a generator for all this?" she asked, yelling upward, staring into the dark void and the sick bastard at its core. "It really is a remarkable space. This must have taken years."

She waited. He watched but didn't speak.

"You have me here for a reason. The least you can do is given me a hint at how it all works. We both know I won't be telling anyone," she tempted. He bit.

"There's no reason for you to believe you won't reach freedom beyond the gauntlet," he offered, leaning against the railing far overhead.

She watched him, wishing it would break free and she could witness his body plummeting past her to its grizzly end. No such luck. "But how is all this lit up, powered so deep inside a mountain or cavern, wherever the hell we are? I assume the metal box is the generator. I just can't imagine how you dragged it in here without help."

"I didn't drag it in," he said. "It was constructed on site. No one helped me. Ever."

"That's amazing." She rode on his emotion. "And it powers all of this? Man, could we use your talents back home. The town generator failed with every storm that moved through. Blackouts for days."

"It's not a generator—"

"Then how in the hell did you—"

"Water power converted into energy. It doesn't matter!" He was yelling.

"It matters to me!" she yelled back. "If I am destined to die in this place you created to kill us all, I'm asking a few questions!"

"The longer you wait to enter, the more risk you face," he warned. She wasn't certain but it appeared as if he had checked his watch.

Time, she thought. He kept her for so long because this, whatever it was to him, had to occur at a certain time and that time was now.

"So what would happen if I never woke up? Then what would you have done? Gone to get one of the others?" she asked, baiting him again.

"No," the word slipped from him without volition.

"Oh, I see. So this time it had to be me." She adjusted painfully to near the edge of the isolated ledge she occupied. The only way off or onto it was by leaping to another behind or in front of it or coming from within the gauntlet. "Did you jump onto here carrying me? Damn."

With her vision adapting to the space she could see, following three similar ledges, she would slip out of range of his view. From where he safely stood there would be no continued line of sight if she could make the first three. It appeared as though he intended her not to proceed that way, to instead descend onto a rope bridge extending into the first leg of the course. Closer and equipped with rope handrails, it was the obvious choice but what lay beyond it? From what she glimpsed in the select darkness a climbing wall with scattered footholds and random ropes anchored to something or possibly meant to appear a safeguard but truly a pitfall once grabbed, waited at the rope bridge's end. Oh how he'd love to watch that.

"So I follow this flimsy bridge into the dark? Is that what you've planned?" she asked, not moving to assess it.

"The bridge is quite secure," he said. "It leads to the first opportunity to reach the higher levels, and by doing so freedom."

"And what happens at the end?" she asked, a plan formulating in her mind. "I have no idea where you brought me months ago or what lies above this place you reign, so what's at the end?"

His answer wasn't forthcoming. She guessed he hadn't expected grounded questions from a captive waking in a pit of hell. So she prodded, not for herself but for the one who escaped and the other women held in rooms beyond hers. Time. The longer he stayed focused on her, engaged in her helping of frustration, the more time the escapee had to put distance between her and this bastard.

"So I make it through and…what? Do you have a medical team on the other side? A chopper to airlift me to a hospital where I can recover and tell them all about my time with you? Recant every detail of this sick game you stole us to play?"

"It is not a game! I saved your life! You were overdosing when I found you!"

"And the others? They were all in need of saving?" Lauren had enough. Her body wasn't doing well. She knew what almost death was like having driven herself to the end a time or two. Though still stable on the ledge, the inertia of falling was growing in intensity inside her. The pounding in her head gaining volume and the icy chill descending down her limbs said death clutched her in its grip.

"Only one needs to be saved and she will be." He spoke the words as if aware Lauren's window of objection was closing.

Pulling herself off the cold stone, wondering if this was a bit of what Jesus experienced, dragging his body on a trail knowing the path lead to death and further pain, she stood, shaking, but staring up at her captor. "Your escapee, she's long gone. And if I'm granted one last prayer, she'll be the end of you!"

Her feet launched off the ledge with the grace of an Olympic pole-vaulter. In succession, without pause, she cleared the second and third of the ledges beyond the first where she was placed. Only after landing, with all the momentum behind her, could she see there was no fourth. She leaped into the dark void as soundlessly as she sprung out of his view. Not knowing what would hit first, what existed beneath where she lost ground, how she would suffer before dying, she left on her own terms knowing every brave second she stole from him was one she granted the escaped woman. He was right; she found freedom from him in the gauntlet and a last hope of giving it to those who shared her confinement.

TWENTY-FOUR

Drex scanned the skyline exiting the empty cave he wasted two useless hours on before receiving the alert from Detective Carmichael. All the training and money spent leading his team into this godforsaken area and it was the cop who broke the first lead in the case. Strapping the walkie back into his shoulder belt he read the clouds.

"Figures more damn rain," he murmured, stomping down a descending section of trail back to base camp. He called in for a drone to survey the location where Jade said she identified the victim crawling out of a small cave hole. Time moved backward when lives hung in the balance and returning to level ground, he physically shook off its grip and ran the remainder of the way back as droplets formed and hit his face announcing plenty more were sure to follow.

Agents French and Taylor were right where he left them inside the main tent at base camp but now a ranger, drone and LiDAR team worked alongside them. Information surrounded on visual screens linked to the drone and one connected to the upload of the LiDAR scan. Not terrific in the field, the two had amassed more than he expected before his return and were sifting through the information most crucial.

"We located two possible entrances in the area Detective Carmichael indicated she first witnessed the nurse," Agent French said, walking with Drex to the screen following the drone sweep. "It's unfortunately on the outer ridge at the edge of the drone range."

"Of course it is," Drex murmured. "So what can we see? Anything?"

"Yes. There's no heat signature in the surrounding area currently, but we caught a weak indication here." French waved at Taylor as she carried a complex map over and slapped it down in front of Drex.

"This is where we received the signal," Taylor said, circling the eastern ridgeline just before the cavern fell to the riverbed below. "We caught it here and when the drone finished its loop it was gone. If that was in fact one of the missing…"

Drex studied the map, and both screens, then back to the area of interest. "Let me see if I'm reading this right. The victim is spotted here, actually hanging off the fucking cliff wall, and you leave visual of her to circled back to nothing?" His voice, devoid of all humor and tolerance, said it best they jump direct to hard facts.

"The drone is designed to survey in circular sweeps to allow for more time in the air and coverage of a larger area before battery loss," French explained. "The second we identified a hit we had them circle back. Meaning, if she was there…" French pointed to the screen at the upper few feet of the cliff drop off. "… she wasn't within mere seconds."

"Are you telling me we just lost the only witness and victim in a slew of abductions to a damn fall from the virtual top of the cliff on our side to the worst section of river?" Drex felt the vein in his neck pulsating as his blood pressure skyrocketed.

"I'm, we're…" French waved to his fellow agent and the operators manning both the drone survey and the LiDAR equipment. "… saying it's a possibility. If the captor was there with a rope, snatched her back inside the tunnel, or threw her off the cliff it's unclear. We won't know until we can get there and investigate and with the weather moving in and loss of daylight, well sir, we're blind."

Drex turned to the drone operator. "What conditions compromise its use?"

"Nightfall we can handle after we switch out batteries, but wind and weather can ground us."

"Can you put her back in the air until the last moment possible?" Drex asked.

"Yes, sir," the eager young operator offered.

"Then do that now. You can set up in the smaller tent to keep your gear dry. Get her back up and work the grid from where you lost the signature outward with a focus on the river." Drex waved him back outside to do his job hoping to capture movement before the weather grounded their eyes in the sky. The operator carried his drone case to the tent flap, throwing it open on his way out. Rain and wind swept inside confirming, though motivated, he wouldn't be working late.

Drex exhaled and moved on. "Zac is hiking to the eastern cliff wall. From his location he'll beat me to it. We have to be careful here. If, for whatever reason, Detective Carmichael's identification was mistaken and we throw everything at this...we can't risk the lives of ten women on a maybe so until I have confirmation we stay under this perp's radar, understood?"

Everyone under the tent nodded. He read suspicion in their eyes and rightly so. Monitoring on multi-levels for countless hours and discovering nothing, the heat signature blip didn't amount to much. For all they knew it could've been caused by malfunction.

Locking eyes with the LiDAR operator, knowing she also worked the newest versions of high-tech search drones, he asked, "Did you see anything on there to confirm, without question, a female human was perched at the top of that cliff wall?"

"I'm sorry, sir. I couldn't be certain with the limited visual."

"Okay. We approach this as a possible, probable, sighting until we have concrete evidence. And, we do it quietly, nothing to compromise the lives of the other victims. We move in when we have a hope of rescuing them out of this hellhole." Drex watched as the heads of each man and woman nodded in agreement then he pulled out his walkie.

Knowing Zac was in camouflage, well concealed navigating the topography, he reached out to hand down a stronger warning than he delivered inside the tent. Zac could well be first on scene and what he did could tip the scales either way.

"I'm less than a half mile from the marker, approaching from due south, and have detected zero movement, even the animals scattered to hunker down for the incoming rain," Zac responded. "I'll approach in stealth but I've seen nothing yet. You'd think any victim fleeing would create considerable noise out here."

"Not if she's smart," Drex warned. "If our guy hasn't alerted to her escape, she may be in stealth mode right along with you. Eyes up. I'll notify when I'm close to your location and approach from the south."

Turning his attention back to French and the others, he marked areas onto the grid map. "French have them ready a second drone to approach on my line if the weather breaks. Mark every potential area on the digital LiDAR map and link it so we all have updated information on the land. It'll be a dangerous night search at best for this survivor and I can't risk any more of us out there so keep check-in tabs on our locations."

French was taking notes and following orders with a precision that said it was his calling. Anxious to leave them to it, Drex grabbed rain gear, checked his comms and climbing equipment, and readied to head back out.

"Sir, head office called twice while you were out. Media pressure filtered down and…" French paused, his expression pleaded for Drex not to kill the messenger.

"For Christ's sake, what?" Drex barked, glad comms hadn't allowed his boss to berate the situation with him while out in the field.

"We may make the late-night news. They don't know our exact location. Right now they're targeting Beaver River area," French said.

"Terrific. Next, they'll be fanning the flames internationally highlighting all the way to escaped into Canada. Put a call in to head office. Give them all our updates but leave out the details of the sighting. Tell them I'll reach out when I get back, after I confirm the validity of our new lead."

"Sir, it was Director Washington who called the last time." French warned.

With this Drex dropped his gear, requested the SAT phone, and walked out into the rain. Drops were now banding together and threatening to become sheets. He strode over to the parking area and jumped into the quiet protection of his truck. He dialed and waited to be patched through frustrated the call was digging into precious time but glad urgency would keep it short.

"Drex," Washington's authoritative voice echoed down the line. "We can't hold the media at bay much longer. Some asshole cop at the seventh abduction site wants his seven seconds and contacted a journalist with too much determination."

"Well, fuck, sir," Drex said, not taming his mood. "I'm out here knee deep in mud and shale rock, one agent down, and two bear attacks later, not really giving a damn about the eleven o'clock sound bite, surprisingly."

"I'm with you but give me something to shut them up."

"Okay. We had a heat signature blip on a possible, and previously unknown, cave entrance. I'm heading out in shit weather with Carmichael and the kid to confirm but with our eyes knocked out I'm not expecting it to be a fabulous night for any of us, if you get my drift."

The line held mild static interference but no voice for a beat, then Washington asked, "Is he there?"

"Yes. I believe so and if he finds out we are he could kill them all."

"Good luck tonight. Call me with an update when you get back. Reinforcements are standing by." Washington signed off and Drex brushed a hand over his face thinking it'd be great to retrieve a live victim who could nail down a precise location for the rest but knowing it was too much to hope for. Operations with this vast an area and too many dangerous variables tended to end badly.

Stepping into the downpour, he didn't make it three strides when the drone operator waved him inside the smaller of the two tents. "She's down," he said. "I'd like permission to retrieve her."

Drex eyed the digital camera capture and the mapped area of where the wind smashed the bird into a tree. The compromised expensive device was within a safe distance, not far from where they stood. "Sure, take agent French with you and hopefully she's in one piece."

"They're well built for this. She should be fine but I'd like to bring her back, ensure her condition, and prep her to fly again should this shit weather pass over."

"Sounds like a plan," Drex said, heading out. He wanted to scream "anything else" but knew better than to tempt fate. She was already well primed against them.

TWENTY-FIVE

In his flashlight's gleam a woman's body rerouted the river's flow exiting from an underground feeder stream at the east side of the mouth and John recognized, peering down at her fragile and brutalized frame, the time to help her passed hours earlier. He was left studying the damage as waves of fear washed over him in tandem with the water rippling over the still curves of a victim. If discovered there was no question what side of the law he would land on. Illegal inhabitant of a federally restricted forest, no chance he'd be seen as a concerned citizen. Still, tracing the flow over her small almost childlike frame, he couldn't leave her here to be claimed by the wild, torn into manageable bits by predators, and left undiscovered for all time.

Lifting her from the river and placing her somewhere the feds or, better still, Detective Carmichael was sure to discover her seemed his only option. Risk or not, she wasn't staying there, pinned waist deep at the creek's intersection.

Nightfall and rain plummeted the temperature well below average. The river would be icy cold but exiting it would be far worse. Miles now from his home, he faced hyperthermia trekking back after disposing of her. And any hungry animals along the trail would be certain to take scent of the body. Though for many, human decomposition would be a deterrent. For the worst it was akin to ringing a dinner bell.

A healthy distance from the cave wall of the canyon he hinted Detective Carmichael resume her search at, he was fairly certain he stood outside the current grid pattern. It didn't guarantee he'd stay that way but bad weather may force the search temporarily called off. He had to move fast for this nasty bit of assistance to work.

Stripping down to bare essentials he piled his clothes and boots inside his pack safely away from the rivers offspray. Scythe bound over almost knocking them curious about his master's sudden interest in a freezing plunge. "I don't recommend coming with but could you please keep your dripping fur off my pack?" John swept his hand and the cat shifted to the side, intent on watching. John carried the closed pack to a high ledge and heaved it across the water onto a dry shelf before journeying back down the bank for the water's edge.

"Really don't want an audience for this but if there has to be one it better be you."

Securing a rope tethered to a nearby fallen log, he made his way down the embankment glad it wasn't far at this juncture. Rocks dug into his bare weathered soles making him question his choice to remove the wool socks that would've provided some protection. The scrapes were quickly forgotten entering the water for his feet became numb once submerged.

With the sensation cascading up his ankles and calves he knew he had no time to waste. Moonlight shone down reflecting on the white flesh of the woman's shoulder and torso. Without another thought he scooped into the drink and under her.

Lifting her out proved considerably more difficult than her meager frame suggested. The cold water and onset of arthritis made forming a reliable grip almost impossible. The more he strug-gled with positioning, the more the body shifted awkwardly out of alignment. Risking losing it to the rapids, gaining strength with the current downpour, he tugged a third time dislodging it from what-ever held it there with such force it sprang up and met his shoulders in one fluid roll placing the dead woman's face too close to his own. Startled he lost his footing and fought the deluge to find stability with the added weight he carried. Electing to use the momentum, he scrambled left and right angling for land on the east side of the riverbank. Unable to halt, he tossed the body onto the bank with too much force and sent it rolling.

Jumping onto land before he was no longer capable, he met Scythe's wide-eyed stare of disapproval being that he remained on the west bank and expected him to return to that side. Making quick use of a half-fallen tree trunk the cat leaped and bound across the river until meeting the ground too close to the wet corpse. His reaction marked the first time in their years together when the cat backed away, low to the ground, in the grip of fear.

"It's bad, buddy," John whispered between gulps of oxygen and violent shaking. "We'll be okay. I just have to put her somewhere they can find her away from home and without leaving my DNA behind."

The feline crouched, stopped moving away, and then hissed. He clearly wasn't convinced and wanted no part of this plan.

Dressing from the pack, tossed nearby and dry, with hands refusing to function and legs that wouldn't stop vibrating was a difficult task. Once clothed, he pulled a large canvas cloth from the bottom. Usually used for foraging, he would manipulate it to drape the woman's body in. He located two similar sized branches and made a forest gurney with intertwined rope for transporting her. The intense ache in his hands called for him to stop. Ignoring the protest of his limbs and driving rain he forged ahead.

She came to rest along the bank with her face turned up to the stars. He identified multiple wounds on her though the limited light made them easier to digest.

"You stay focused on those stars from wherever you are now," he said, securing the cloth. "And I promise we'll get your body out of here, child."

Straining, frozen and aching, he tied the corpse to the gurney and began the hike to dangerous higher ground. Scythe kept his distance cutting a path ahead and swiveling back periodically to check John was following and hadn't succumbed to the cold. Twenty minutes later he located a fast-flowing secondary underground tributary nearest a natural creek created by the downpour and where they converged with the river on the east side of The Divide. This was most likely where the woman's corpse emerged from originally. John estimated it drifted four or five miles downstream before becoming lodged where he discovered her. Careful to avoid transfer, he unwrapped the victim and rolled her on her side, as she was at the underground river's mouth.

"Sorry to leave your body here," he said, gazing down at the sad and broken remains of a young woman who deserved better. He wished he could leave her beneath the cloth and sheltered from the rain but couldn't. "She'll find it and return it to your family so you can rest." He examined the exposed image against the one haunting his mind and, satisfied, packed his gear setting it under the protection of a tree, grabbed a nearby branch with a gloved hand, and swept any trace of them from the forest floor.

He broke the remnants of the gurney apart, tossing the branches into the river downstream, then returned to pack up the rope before selecting the fastest path back across and home. Scanning the area, he caught sight of a light cutting intermittently through the trees high above him on the west side. Panic riveted through him and he spun the opposite direction to survey the northeast. His chest heaved fighting both fear and the effects of cold but no lights emerged on this side. He waited for a few breaths, and seeing nothing, swiveled back.

It had to be Detective Carmichael searching in the cold dark night. He watched the rhythm of her movements descending south and waited until she swept the area below her with light.

Then, placing himself at considerable risk, he pulled his flashlight from his belt and made a distinct cross of light, one she would recognize as more than a chance sighting.

Switching it off and shifting as quickly as his frozen form would allow, he blended back into the trees. His hands were locking up. His legs grew heavier with every stride threatening to stop all together. As if sensing his distress, Scythe drew up alongside him, bumping into his legs sporadically for encouragement.

"They gonna oh owe me," he said, noting the broken words and slurred speech that didn't resemble his own. Traversing the river crossing a mile further south, where a natural land bridge connected to tree fall and remnants of a beaver damn, made it possible even with his body shutting down. He knew he didn't have far to go. When the dim light buried within their rock cabin hideout came into view he wanted to break into song, but his lips wouldn't work any better than his limbs. Plodding up the incline sapped every ounce of energy from him. He only made it three steps into the warmth of their home before collapsing to the hard wooden floor.

His last thoughts were a tortured mix of the young woman's death mask, the pretty detective's promise, and gratitude for having left the heater running.

***

Jade flew out of the back side of the cave pulling the walkie from her belt without breaking stride. Hitting the spongy texture of the wet forest floor after running over rock threw her rhythm out and almost catapulted her to the muck. Slowing up, she arrived under the shelter of tree branches and stopped to catch her breath. Time enough to notice the volume of rain soaking the area and recognize the newest in a long list of challenges impeding their rescue of the nurse.

Breath calming, she hit the STT button. "Agent Drex, sir, do you have a signal?" Knowing he was doing as she was, racing from underground exploring to reach the surface, she waited.

"Carmichael, I'm here. Approaching from the north, Zac from the south, can you come in from the west?"

"Negative. I spotted her at the highest point of the cliff wall. The only way from the west side is to drop down by heading south until I hit lower ground and can cross the river."

"There's no way I will risk you crossing an engorged river in the dark, miles in, with no way to reach you and a potential killer out here," Drex said, his tone firm.

Potential killer? The phrase interrupted her train of thought. The nurse was breathing last time she had eyes on her. "The victim was alive when I—"

"The drone captured the flash of a heat signature in the location you indicated. It circled back seconds later to find nothing. Weather has it grounded so we're blind but we may be out here for retrieval not rescue. Head back to base. I'll update you when we—"

"Sir, I'm the only one who saw her. I was raised in these woods; I'm good to go. Why don't I head down and call in before crossing? If it's dangerous, I wait until sun up but at least one of us will be in the vicinity if she heads this direction tonight. All our bases will be covered. I'm out here sir, use me."

The line was silent, not even static colored time while she waited, praying he saw merit in her course of action. She knew what she saw. The nurse was alive. She trusted her instincts and they said the woman fought like a warrior to escape. There was no world in which she would die easily so near freedom. The victim knew she wasn't fighting alone anymore. Jade promised her she'd return and she wasn't breaking it.

"Check in when you reach level ground. I'll decide then how we'll proceed. Zac and I may get lucky converging on the area. You start having trouble with comms or any other fucking minuscule thing you reach me!"

"Yes, sir. Of course. I'll make my way down now and will notify of any signs as I go." She offered more than he requested intent on forging a trust between them, one that would allow her to do her job and bring the nurse and Errie home. Even the smallest of details the nurse retained could lead them to rescuing the rest of the women and identifying the bastard that took them. That was information worth traversing the gorge alone in the dark during a rainstorm.

Signing out, she scanned the forest ahead striving to remember where the bear pit was in proximity to her current path. Making a point of steering clear of it, assuming whatever danger it posed in daylight would be exponentially worse under current conditions, she aimed to cling to the ridge line of the cliff. Not so close as to risk a sudden rockslide plummeting her to the bottom but allowing the chance to catch sight of anyone making their way down the opposite side or coming up the west bank.

Having committed the area map to memory, Jade knew the path out lead to confrontation with Drex or her. Heading further south on either side, east or west, sent the traveler deeper into unpassable terrain made worse by the storm. The Occultus's victims didn't know where they were, what part of the country, what state. It was the first question posed by the nurse so Jade felt safe in assuming none of the women, save for Errie, had any clue where The Divide was. The risk of heading the wrong direction, disoriented and scared, was great. From inside, where Jade slipped and trudged beneath heavy rain and sodden ground, visibility could reduce to mere feet with no clearing for miles.

She thought back to John. A few steps from what she experienced was a solid cabin with several rooms and a functioning fireplace, she lost complete sight of it. She vowed not to return, to leave the woodsman to his peace. In truth, relocating him amounted to that needle-in-a-haystack scenario.

Years earlier a local tracker saved the life of a kid who entered the restricted area on a dare, lost his bearings, and almost died of exposure before being found. Everyone who wore a badge and knew the difficulties of the territory offered to help. Jade had flown the area with Jackson and a friend of his who volunteered the use of his chopper. They lifted off in clear skies, low wind, and daylight conditions.

And couldn't see a damn thing.

Green. Loads of it for miles upon miles mixed with sections of rock in a variance of earth tones capable of concealing a lone person easily mistaken for a tree or deviation in color or formation. They remained airborne until he was rescued but after the first shift Jade and Tex agreed, outside of the kid being clothed in neon, searching from the air was useless.

The nurse was abducted from Southern Carolina, a stretch from the forest that now surrounded her. Jade imagined the state she was in, possibly deprived of food and water for a dangerous length of time and abused for weeks. Coming to a small clearing, an upper branch snapped back at her smacking into her headlamp. Its light flickered before stabilizing. She drew up her Tac light and blasted it across the cavern, down the river's edge, over the parallel ridgeline, and down the trail she walked. Nothing. Despite her personal investment she hoped the agents were having better luck.

After two hours of hunting for signs of life and making it halfway to level ground without a word of encouragement, hope was fading fast. Where the hell could the nurse have disappeared to so quickly? Like the relentless pressing of an elevator button, she knew asking Drex if they caught indication of the missing woman was pointless. He would light up the walkie if that were the case. Still, she fought the urge. Pausing to take a breath, shake off the deluge coating her hair and clothes, and put her head straight, she swept the area again with the powerful Tac light. Above. Ahead. Across. Behind. And below, on the east side of the river.

At the tail end of her sweep she thought she glimpsed movement but it didn't make any sense. Instead of occurring in any of the viable areas it was far southeast of her, too far for the nurse to have reached, deeper into the worst the forest had to offer, and nowhere resembling a place of help.

With her eyes locked on the area she watched as light drew a cross on the canvas of the black forest. A perfect, slowly painted cross, of vertical then horizontal light. The illumination disappeared before she could pinpoint exactly where it stemmed from or saw who was behind the dark artwork. The general area was very near the east bank of the river, lower and south of her current position. With clear instructions from Drex not to cross and a torrential downpour making it all but impossible there was no way for her to reach the area of interest until sun up. Selecting several visual markers to remind her, the curve of the river, distance from the base of the cliff descent at the junction from both sides, and a boulder a few strides from where the light broke the night, she memorized the location to investigate later.

Watching and waiting, studying the forest floor below for a

number of minutes, the light never made a second appearance nor did she detect other movement.

If anyone crossed the water from the east to make their way up and out, they would've been forced to walk right by her undetected. In the dark and noise of the storm it was possible but without light anyone unfamiliar had a slim chance of surviving the hurdles the forest handed out. Jade heard the tales of strange lights in the forest, unsettling sounds, and unexplained phenomena like fully formed stairs in the middle of nowhere with no foundation or remnants of a structure they could've belong to.

She heard the stories. She never once experienced any of it. Until now.

Protocol dictated she notify Drex but the thought of aiming efforts never to be rewarded over a single glimpse of light didn't strike her as rational. The signal wouldn't have been Zac. If the young agent traveled that far south and spotted her descending from the west, he could've called in over the walkie. Jade grabbed hers and opened comms. "Detective Carmichael here. Can I get a location check from you both?"

"Zac here. I'm closing in midway up to the marker on the upper east ridge." A couple seconds passed before Drex's voice colored the line. "A quarter click out. I'll be first on scene. Anything of interest out west Carmichael?"

"Negative. I'm about a mile from level ground near the river. No sign. Thanks for the check-in." As static reclaimed the channel, another possibility hit.

John.

The flash materialized on the east but very near the water and deeper south, almost south enough to invade the area concealing the woodsman from an intrusive world. Alerting Drex would have him expand the grid opening the federal search to land too close to where Jade's Airstream sat without permission and where John lived and rescued her from. One call threatened her authority over the west side. In addition, the chances of the cross of light having connection to the nurse or her captor were slim. No way would a perpetrator as orchestrated as this one risk death or exposure, announce his location, or venture out of hiding for one victim while abandoning and jeopardizing the rest. Nor would the nurse have traversed the distance without light to identify Jade's movements above and write a cross in the air only to disappear deeper into the forest.

John, however, could be in that area for a multitude of reasons, knew the land like the back of his hand, and would avoid extended use of a light source to remain hidden. If he wrote the cross in the air for her to see he had good cause.

Marking the sector in her mind for inspection, Jade refocused efforts on negotiating her way down the steep drop to the water in one piece. Coming to an enclosed space, escaping the constant wind and rain, she chose to break for a few minutes. Able to see over most of the lower canyon from this vantage point without fighting the downpour, she surveyed the distance not welcoming the next leg as hers were aching from the frigid air and endless strain of slopes and unstable footing.

She opened her pack, rehydrated, and decided to add an extra layer under her jacket. Waterproof, it stopped moisture from seeping inside but failed to do the same with the cold. Dressed and feeling warmth return, she tasted blood in her mouth and spat at the ground not realizing until then a stray branch catching her in the face a mile back had cut her lip open. By the time she made it out with Errie, Amy would owe her a spa date. And she hated them.

Jade smiled tearing the cut open again thinking of the last time she and Errie forced Amy into a rejuvenation day spa. Amy was the "fittest man there by far" as Jade saw it and anyone that straddled both sides of the fence was awestruck even in boxers and a gym shirt. Amy's ice-blue eyes against the dark backdrop of her olive skin and black lashes didn't help her escape stares of admiration. Jade always said she was the sexiest man she knew and Errie agreed. Amy didn't see her masculine beauty. Jade wondered if she saw her beauty at all until Errie showed her how lovable and amazing she really was. As tough as her best friend proved to be, Jade knew of no one who cared about everyone as much as Amy. When Jade's life was almost cut short and her injuries left her in a coma and Kane and Tex were in recovery from inflicted gunshot wounds, Amy split her time between hospital rooms while doing double duty at the shop to cover her missing comrades. The extreme exhaustion could've landed her in a bed alongside them, but Amy fought it all to stand vigilant until they were safe. She never once mentioned the sacrifices she made. Captain Grey, the only one who logged more time in the aftermath guarding his team, advised them without her knowledge. Amy's dedication and pain, and knowing it as Jade did, set a fire inside as she left the outcrop shelter.

Sliding and slipping, rain soaked and aching, Jade didn't give a damn what it would take from her. She wasn't leaving this treacherous place without Errie. And she'd risk the penalty from the feds if need be. In the dark and vast expanse of this forbidden forest she understood she was alone. She missed Kane, Tex, home and the life they all were rebuilding together. Here she saw and appreciate it in a powerful way. But along with that came the undeniable truth that none of them had another 'do over' in them. Healing required, no demanded, they do it together. And that meant Errie had to come home. Without her the puzzle that was them wasn't complete and Jade was certain, lost to the dark, they'd all fall to pieces.

TWENTY-SIX

W es Beaucamp parked on the edge of the Montgomery's property where the south and only road leading in met the intersection out of town watching the early morning sun turn the fields to gold. If he hadn't traded a pro football scholarship for law enforcement due to a late season knee injury in what seemed a lifetime ago, he expected he'd be sitting there just the same. He came up through junior and senior high school with Harper's older brother and wouldn't dream of abandoning the family at such a time as this. In the days following Harper's abduction he worried about her father's heart and her mother's resolve withstanding the torment they existed in. Matt was dealing with it better than his younger siblings and parents, on the surface at least. But with every day that passed, and many had, they broke a little more.

Today was the first day he gave them something to hope for and seeing how they clung to it on his way out of their kitchen, he damn sure didn't want to take it back.

The federal case hit the late-night news and everyone in town was watching. Though the information was minimal, they reported it likely Harper was one of ten or more women involved in similar abduction circumstances moving across the coast heading east. He and every officer involved with their jurisdiction's missing person was grateful to hand over case evidence and partner up with federal investigators. Not because they believed them more capable but because alone they had far too little to go on. Combined efforts increased the odds of success.

Wes was exceptional at what he did and he had unearthed next to nothing. When the local cop from New York called requesting information specific to the vehicle Wes identified leaving the area, he readily agreed to share everything he knew for a fact, and what he suspected, in trade for an update on what they were discovering. They believed, without question, the Occultus transported all the women to a singular location that FBI and one of their own was converging on, and the women were being kept alive.

Motivations for why the criminal did this or what they were enduring in captivity Wes could imagine. He left much out of the conversation with Harper's family shielding them from adding to the nightmare scenarios already plaguing them. Inspired to jump back on the road leading to the highway and drive down the coast to aid in the search, he knew the approach wouldn't be welcome or permitted. Forced to work the details he funneled all his energy on revisiting the vehicle he suspected was driven by the Occultus, with Harper incapacitated inside, to flee the district and eventually the state.

Wes rolled down the window, leaned an arm out enjoying the warm air. Sure to turn blistering hot but midday, flow in overshadowing his air conditioning. His eyes traced the towering Sugar Maple trees lining the property following them back to the family home of his good friend. Once a destination guaranteed to include laughs, comfort, and homemade lemon icebox pie, it now sat darkened by sadness under a cloud of misery. Not on his watch. Not for long.

Having spent his life in this charming hamlet of Harrison County he knew every place along the Gulfport-Biloxi area and spent summers at a family home in Long Beach. A target tourist destination where vehicles adorned with plates from as far away as

Canada and every state between weren't considered out of place. But this road, the one he pulled onto the side of to emotionally regroup, would only be familiar to locals unless …

Snatching his cell phone from the cup holder, he found the New York cop's number from the evening before and dialed anxious for an answer. When Detective Kane Kolton identified himself, he spit words out at him before realizing he hadn't reintroduced himself but it didn't matter. What he called to say did.

"He's a soft engineer! I'm sure of it. It's the only reason he'd have use of this road or even know it existed."

"Beaucamp, is that you?" Kane asked.

"Shit, yeah, sorry. You said to focus on transportation. I'm sitting on the only road leading into the Montgomery's land and there's no way in hell the average person outside this county would know to come here or how get back out unless…I think he's a soft engineer."

"Great," Kane encouraged. "But what the hell is that?"

"It's a coastal engineer. Someone involved in countering subsidence, reclaiming land, or sustainable natural management of coastal erosion. Christ, he'd have a choice of company vehicles and reason to run the coast, know all the roads including back ones, and have access to land maps and not just the obvious current ones."

"You're saying someone working as an engineer for coastal erosion would know how the land appeared prior to erosion?" Kane confirmed.

"Yes. So this guy would know hidden land features, caves, sinkholes, former structures that are now eroded." Wes could hardly catch air in his lungs, his pulse racing hand in hand with his mind. "If I'm right, we need access to the same maps they have."

"I'll reach out and see what I can find but I'll contact an engineer that's long retired and swear him to secrecy. If you're right, the last thing we want to do is alert the perpetrator by calling his company and giving him a heads up."

Wes checked his watch. On the roadside for half an hour, and not a single car had driven by.

"Wes, how the hell did you arrive at this?" Kane asked, appreciation lightening his tone. "None of us would've landed on it. I'm pretty certain no one out here even knows the term, soft engineer."

"My sister-in-law is a staunch advocate for sustainable beaches. I've seen them working in the area because a former storm drain was being converted and sustainable impact studies were conducted, blocking local traffic. Everyone was up in arms over the inconvenience while she barked back about the importance of soft engineers to protect our environment. I heard about it for weeks. I didn't put it together, well, I wouldn't have if it wasn't for your call last night."

"Hey, this is all you, brother," Kane said. "But it tracks. It gives our suspect access, prior knowledge, and an array of different vehicles to remain anonymous."

"And loads of time to plan at every site without suspicion." Wes couldn't wait to get off the phone and work this new angle. Finally he had something to hunt and he wouldn't stop until he nailed down the name of every soft engineer that worked the area over the last few months.

"Yeah, but it gives him something far more critical," Kane warned.

"What's that?"

"Hiding places."

Kane ended the call, tapped a message out, and dropped his cell phone to the table to meet Jackson's stare of inquiry as he sauntered in on the tail end of the call. "We've got a bead on our perp. A solid one," he said.

"Well don't stand on ceremony, spit it out," Jackson said, with a feisty Texas drawl.

"Don't get edgy on me, Tex," Kane joked, squeezing between scattered chairs in his home office turned "new investigative base" on route for the board with the abduction map. His finger followed the sites along the seaboard. "I need an erosion map."

"A what? Is that something we can print out here?" Jackson asked.

"Nah. I'll make a few calls, have a digital version sent, and a print couriered over. I want it the size of this map, to literally overlap it." Kane's focus never veered from the evidence in front of him.

Jackson left his chair and came up close to see for himself what had Kane's attention. He studied the coastline in silence, then faced Kane. "Erosion map," he repeated. "Our guy works the coast."

"Yep. And he knows everything about it, including all its secret hiding places," Kane said.

"Place enough to house multiple victims?" Jackson asked.

"Exactly," Kane confirmed, then sat down reclaiming his phone, searching for reliable map sources. "They're called soft engineers and they look for natural solutions to coastal erosion. It would provide legitimate reason for a stranger to enter residential areas without causing suspicion and give him access to an array of company vehicles."

"So never in the same one twice, no trace and an easy method of destroying evidence of transporting victims," Jackson offered, his wheels turning in rhythm with his partner's.

"How so?" Kane asked, distracted, connecting crime scenes with areas suffering from possible natural threat while narrowing down a safe government office to request maps from.

"Kane, if this guy works for a large environmental engineering firm those organizations have mass lots full of vehicles regularly and professionally maintained, cleaned, fueled up, and ready to go for employees. One professional scrub could lose any and all trace evidence but any vehicle could be cleaned and used multiple times by multiple workers before we ever narrowed it down. Evidence eradicated and the perp doesn't lift a finger."

Kane stopped searching his phone and locked eyes with Tex. "The more we find out the more—"

"I know. It doesn't look good but we may want to avoid mentioning the Occultus's talent for criminal masterminding from Amy. She's showing stress fractures as it is."

"Yeah, but she's the one who started me down this road," Kane said. "After she came back for dinner we were brainstorming in here before the eleven o'clock news kicked interest in the investigation into high gear. She suggested we focus on transport method to narrow our suspect pool and damn if she wasn't right. She left to check in with Grey at the shop, he was working late again, and I started calling local cops at each site. I hit pay dirt in Mississippi."

"What made her focus on vehicles? We only had two to track?" Jackson asked, creases across his forehead revealed concern more than confusion. "A van left on a country road where I'm betting he had his company truck waiting to flip into, and a car discarded unlocked in the worst part of coastal Cali. I think locals found a vagrant asleep inside."

"Don't know. Maybe one of her neighbors reached out?" Kane said, anxious to nail down a map provider.

"Did she say so?" Jackson asked. Kane recognized the under-tone of his voice signaling a point of clarity that required attention.

"Can't remember. Amid multiple calls to local law enforcement at each abduction site and the asshole reporter throwing Jade's search a serious curveball, I was…" Kane hesitated.

"Not listening? You? Never," Tex joked. "I'll ask her later. Maybe after we have a real name to attach to the Occultus and are closer to finding out where he has Errie held captive. So how is Jade doing out there? The weather has been shit. Damn good thing she's a decent outdoorsman."

"Yeah, I didn't hear from her until the middle of the night. She spent most of it in the rainstorm on the side of a cliff expecting sight of the possible victim she identified," Kane said. "She didn't sound good. The call was brief. She was exhausted. Defeated if I'm honest. Her and Agent Lafine were at odds but who wouldn't be under those conditions. She wanted to keep searching. He forced her out and shut it down. Said it was too dangerous to resume the investigation until the rain stopped. Can't say I disagree. She was planning on forwarding the LiDAR scan information when she arrived back at the trailer but I guess there were complications with it."

"When aren't there complications?" Jackson offered.

"The thing is, matching LiDAR data with the erosion information should trump the perp's intel on the land and give us something of value to pass on to Jade," Kane washed a hand through his waves and leaned into the back of his armchair. "I hate having her out there."

"Me too, buddy. We should update Amy and get her working the computer to mesh the details of our site chart, the LiDAR scan, and the erosion map once we have digital copies. You and I can work the live maps while she runs probabilities."

"Yeah, I sent her a message after I hung up with the cop in Hamilton County. I think the erosion map may help identify any other victims overlooked." Kane walked to the evidence board where a lineup of victims matched to the state they were taken from and read through it intently. "The one in Alabama is pretty much confirmed but…"

"You still think it's a baker's dozen?" Jackson asked, meeting him at the board and pinning evidence to the far side to make room for the arrival of additional charts.

"I do." Kane stood back, sauntered to a globe Jade kept on a shelf more for decoration than use. He tipped it so his eyes followed the seaboard. He paused in thought for a few seconds, Jackson knew better than to interrupt, then returned to stand assessing the board. "I'm thinking West Coast somewhere prior to Mississippi. The timeframe between the others doesn't allow space for an extra abduction."

Jackson gave the information a once-over, swiveled, putting his back to the evidence, and left to take a seat in the furthest chair. "So I'm guessing there'll be multiple locations he could take advantage of; these engineering firms will be numerous, and identifying one bad apple among thousands of potential employees could take years."

"Well you're a ray of sunshine," Kane said, coming to sit nearby. "Your point being?"

"How does this information change anything for us?" Jackson's eyes revealed deep critical thought. "Is it me or does this feel a little like a goose chase?"

"It would be without boots on the ground and the LiDAR scan, but in combination in may point Jade and the feds in the right direction. It's all we have." Kane cringed a little as the words fell from his lips. "And there's Wes, the cop in Hamilton. If he can track down anyone who saw the engineer's truck or even the guy up close by some miracle…"

"If only," Jackson said. "And have we heard anything from Max?"

"I'm expecting an update from him this afternoon so hopefully when we talk to Jade next, we'll have a lot to hand over. I know this only gets us so far. You and I need to dig into the why. It doesn't matter what this criminal does as a day job, if we don't know what motivates him…he won't lose his anonymity without both motive and opportunity."

"Agreed. So is that what you were working on before the call when I walked in? Victomology?" Jackson asked while staring down at the files Kane had amassed on each victim.

"Yeah, and I know we can gain insight to at least one," Kane said, shuffling Errie's file to the top of the pile.

"How is he choosing them? That's what I can't get a grip on. Errie has less than nothing in common with what we know about the prior abductees. It reminds me a little of—"

"No." Kane sat bolt upright. "Don't."

Jackson chewed his lower lip and then dove in. "Look, Nickolas is sitting there wasting away. Maybe we should use him before Cap agrees with him and Amy and closes the attempted murder case. When that door shuts, there'll be zero access to him."

"No." Kane made for the kitchen without glancing back, mumbling they needed coffee but they both knew better. Jackson didn't follow him out and he was glad. With every footfall, he seethed a little more. If Nickolas Leigh was to remain breathing, he had to do it outside Kane's reach. Any closer than far away was too close for his fragile existence. The attempted murder case remained unsolved and

Kane had been bedridden in the hospital when the attack occurred. Regardless, he believed there was still no one alive who wanted to see Leigh dead more than he did. And, if he ever found out who was responsible for sabotaging Nickolas Leigh's life-sustaining equipment, he'd be first in line to shake his hand. He couldn't help wondering why the criminal would suggest Amy drop the case. And that not knowing ate at him. Leigh had reason for every move he made and the Occultus was proving to be a similar aberration.

If it took one to know one Tex was right, Leigh, the Redeemer, would probably see right inside the mind of the Occultus. Kane knew, even if Tex and the rest of them didn't, the only thing Leigh would do with insight into a killer Jade hunted was weaponized the information against them. And Amy, Tex, and even Jade would be so laser focused on bringing Errie home they'd never see it coming so he…had to.

TWENTY-SEVEN

S tomping down the tunnel he half-convinced himself it didn't matter that number one never entered the trial as she was meant to, that she robbed him of watching her challenge, and fell to her death beyond his field of view. Alone in this consecrated responsibility urgency engulfed him. She hadn't escaped. Purified for the longest time of any of the women, she was the most flawed and defiant. Still, he spoke the blessing over her, placed her at the gates, and left her free will in her choice. She was where she needed to be. And he had a long hike back.

He noticed, for the first time, the shallow oxygen in the tunnels beyond the sleeping chambers. His lungs ached and a chill tingled down his arms, creeping across his shoulders and neck. Shaking it off he wasn't sure if the short-lived failure of this first sacrifice caused the distress, the unexpected escape of number nine, or doubt that all his efforts would be in vain. His meticulously choreographed plan left him unprepared for the sensation of chaos he experienced and striding down the dark hall he fought to regain composure. With every step forward the urge to turn back and recapture what he left behind tormented him.

By the time he reached the viewing room his unsettled emotion refocused into rage. They could never understand the unprecedented breakthrough he had given his whole life to bring to fruition. Few ever experienced the depth of dedication and love such an endeavor demanded. Expectation of them comprehending his level of clarity around what must happen was pointless. But to follow the rules, was it too much to ask?

Although their images filled the screens before him, he chose to venture down the corridor and experience the calm of the women in his care. With each door he opened he was replenished by their peaceful slumber. Forgoing adjustments to the sedative, perhaps its limited effect was warranted on a day like today. Things had not gone well but the cards predicted as much. And they were never wrong.

He paused, hovering over the sleeping form of number five, the one from the farm in Mississippi. She appeared so wholesome and tranquil, not tortured and tempted by drugs as number one had been. This sacrifice was further down the line with better odds of success. She wouldn't meet the gauntlet for days. He wanted to wake her, to be with her tonight and drink in the comforts of her. The date forbid those desires and the source of his rage gained clarity.

The nurse. He wished number nine was in her bed but it sat empty. There was nothing more to be done and a new day of demands awaited him. He spent nightfall in preparation for it and required a couple hours of sleep. Prescheduled to coincide with the slumber of the women. He walked on to the door of number twelve, left open and not yet inhabited. Circling back, he stood outside the first room he filled so many days and weeks before. From its threshold he smelled the scent of number one but refusing to enter, he could only draw what remained of her essence in with deep inhalations, not nearly as satisfying as when she was close. And she would never be again.

Sadness threatened to overtake him and he knew what he must do before retiring to rest. He permitted himself a limited number of visits as they distracted from the vital work at hand and obstructed his focus. More than once he came to sit with her and lost track of time, and mismanaging time under these conditions could prove fatal.

Checking that all doors were secure and solid, that monitors and ventilation were working optimally, he pried open a door set far back into the rock as to remain concealed when glancing down the short tunnel to the right off the main opening. It creaked and moaned as he pushed its heavy weight back revealing a short landing before a dual set of stairs leading up and down. A miner's lantern hung on the left. He lifted it from its hook, lit it illuminating both directions, and stood between the descending stairs to the left and the ascending on the right. He knew where both would arrive. The surface hadn't tempted him before and when it did, at such an important stage in his plan, it surprised him.

Sunlight. Maybe that was all it amounted to. Cold, dreary, and teeming rain on and off for days, his mind and body craved sunlight. Veering right didn't guarantee a reward; chances were the storm hadn't passed yet and the forest wasn't free of the darkness cast by heavy rain clouds. Still, he wanted to climb up and exit the top hatch. Three sets of stairs lead to sunlight. One he hadn't accessed since a collapse a month before he brought the first of the twelve here made it impassable. This one provided the most comfortable exit.

Glancing a last time, he shifted left and began the descent avoiding the long maze of tunnels back to the level where the natural cave met the mine. It was the reason the mine shut down so many decades ago. They dug until they broke through and then all digging ceased. Technology in the dark ages failed to provide the information required to see what was at risk and what was safe. Certain the levels above would collapse into the lake far below the surface, they feared the instability. And what repelled them drew him. He recognized what they were blind to. This oasis, below cubic tons of rock and mud, was a holy place. He worked on securing aspects of it for years before shifting his focus to perfect it as a home below the surface. And before this place chose him, before he committed to pour years of his life into making it theirs, he systematically eradicated it from every database of erosion risk in operation.

No one knew it existed and after transporting her here, no one knew they existed either.

He met the hard landing at the halfway point and pushed his weight against the outer access door feeling for a budge in its security. No movement. It clearly hadn't been opened since the last time he used it. He quit using it after the women arrived and had covered its outer side with rocks to conceal that a door was present. There was an upper access point as well but he didn't fear them reaching it as the outer tunnel was blocked by rockfall. In minutes he reached the last level and exited. The door protested loudly squeaking as he shoved it ajar. The noise didn't bother him. No one would hear it.

Fastening the lantern to a hook he installed right of the opening he reached for a metal switch dangling down from a suspended cord above and with a click the preceding hallway and bank of rooms were brought to light.

At the far end he installed a metal security railing, a safe space to view the ledges where he built the maze of challenges. This end had been constructed into rooms containing the ventilation and solar and water generated electrical system, his living quarters, and hers. Sleep called to him and his body recognizing it was within reach, lured him to head for the comforts of his dwelling. Pushing the thought aside he walked to the largest enclosed room before the ground dropped down to the open cave viewing area. Her room was very different from his.

No comforts lay within for she had no need of them. Not yet but soon. To the untrained eye there were walls, a rock floor like the others, a large singular metal box, and a multitude of wires. His eyes saw something amazing, a protection for the one most special to him.

Approaching quietly close enough to rest his folded arms on and peer through the glass top, he knew she couldn't hear him. The care he took when entering was a matter of respect. This place was sacred. As much to him as the tomb that once housed Jesus and gave him a place to exist in solitude until freed to rise again.

She would rise again. And he would be there waiting.

The glass only offered a clear view at its center, as if she was locked inside an oval photo with chemical damage creating a vignette of her image, its edges fogged. It was one of the flaws in creation he didn't anticipate but felt no need to rectify. He admired her more this way. Her dimensional reflection appearing lost to time, and she was. He estimated her age upon waking at twenty-six. It was exciting and sad for him knowing he had aged years beyond her both physically and mentally. There would be immense hurdles, but they discussed these before he put her under, slowed her breath to nothing, and suspended her safely with hope.

They tried everything to prevent arriving at this most extreme conclusion but, as if ordained, the world gave them no choice. And every year he watched and waited for an indication that the greatest minds put to the problem had finally solved it. Years turned to a decade and then, when he had all but given up, a documentary changed everything.

Still he couldn't chance waking her on a whim. So he prepared. Once the doctor was contacted, her revised medical information accepted, and he was assured the odds of success were all but guaranteed, he scheduled her for treatment and prepaid for her care. All that was left was ensuring God was on side and that required the offering of the twelve and personal surrender.

"Less than two weeks," he whispered. She appeared like fine china beautiful and yet fragile. "We're so close now. They will be waiting for you and ready to help and when it's complete I will be."

His thick hand, muscles formed from years of rockwork, traced her form on the glass as it had done countless times. He noticed the difference. Weathered by time and hard labor and so much larger than when he began, he wondered if she would recognize him, remember their life before, or would she fear him? That thought cut like a knife. He came to terms with the possibility as he did so many unpleasant others.

It didn't factor into the path he walked. Even if his life were damned, hers would be saved. And that, he decided long ago after her diagnosis, was enough.

The scent of mold and dust waft in disrupting the moment. He made a mental note to adjust the air filtration to compensate for the collapse where number twelve was trapped above. Another issue to be resolved but one with little cause for alarm. In his view the ballerina's escape efforts would only serve to wear her down making her more compliant when retrieved.

She didn't know where she was or where the tunnels on the level she occupied led. He did. And it was nowhere she would choose to stay.

TWENTY-EIGHT

J ade's fury drove her, slipping and careening in a twisted medley of gravel, mud, water, and brush, as if reaching the body five seconds sooner would save the woman in the water. And all she could think, between the stream of profanity coloring her thoughts, was this death was on Drex. If he hadn't shut them down prematurely, forcing her out of the forest by threat of banning her from further involvement in the case, maybe she would have found her alive. And being pressured off the grid because she couldn't risk abandoning Errie and her chances of survival to the feds, snapped the promise Jade made the desperate victim like the twigs beneath her feet as she ran the trail back to where the illuminated cross marked the night.

Even from twenty feet above Jade recognized the corpse, the white of its skin misplaced and foreign amid a sea of green and brown vegetation and the dark gray of the rock. Moving in what felt like slow motion but truly was dangerous momentum down the embankment, it hit her at the bottom of her slide with a similar abrupt impact as the boulder that caught her left ankle and threw her trajectory off in a burst of blinding pain; she couldn't save her from the river.

The cold air she gulped sent a dull ache through her lungs with every breath, the intense scent of wet pine became nauseating after countless hours smelling nothing else, and every part of her was either chilled to the bone or damaged and screaming in pain, but it all paled in comparison to the hostility surging in her veins. If only he had listened, if only he believed her, but he didn't.

When she returned with the others to base camp for what Agent Lafine said was to be "a sharing of situational intel," what confronted her was anything but. Arriving later than Drex and his newest agent, Zac, having traveled twice the distance, she was met by an array of expressions grimacing in preparation of what came next. Drex had reviewed the drone data himself, questioned its operator and the LiDAR scan operator, and combed through maps long before she made camp. The resulting evidence, in his senior opinion, pointed to one conclusion.

Jade's visual identification was unreliable and, according to every other fragment of information, flawed and mistaken. She misinterpreted what she saw. It likely was an animal.

"Seriously, what the fuck?" Her outburst wasn't expected and sure as hell wasn't welcome. The situation went downhill from there. Actually, it hurled downhill so fast neither of them realized the volume or intensity they gained until Zac threw his body between them forcing them to back up.

In all her years on the force, she had never been labeled incompetent. She didn't appreciate it. Or accept it. Having experienced it here, on her first case following the Redeemer's, without the backing or presence of her team, and in front of strangers caused a crack in her armor. She barely made it out of the tent with her position intact. If not for Errie she would've been happy to knock Drex flat on his ass and shoulder the fallout. Not an option, she fled back into the field with orders and a migraine.

Making him pay for his nearsighted approach she could live with. Having this victim pay for it with her life was another story. One with a devastating ending. Facing the cruel reality in front of her she vowed Errie would not be left to chance by ego. She refused to trust Drex with her survival and subject her to a fate governed by his dismissive arrogance.

The ankle support of her waterproof Dr. Martens allowed her to run not hobble to the river's edge to confirm, "with a close-up visual and or photographic evidence" as Drex had yelled, that a victim's body was positioned, badly beaten and brutalized, directly in front of her. She pulled her phone out and carefully snapped several photos of the corpse from all angles, zooming in on particular areas of damage. She isolated a grid using a hurried but mindful approach and stayed within it taking pictures of the area surrounding the dumpsite but quickly realized no evidence suggested the body was placed in the river at this location. Chances were it drifted downstream from where it entered.

Having cataloged as much as possible she reviewed the photographs. From the bank she couldn't see the woman's face or even her hair clearly. The storm turned up the river to fast-flowing muck-filled rapids full of dirt and debris. The woman's head, pinned lower than her torso, was barely visible. It didn't make the scene any less disturbing. Choosing a photograph that depicted the victim's demise with the most vile accuracy, she was about to forward it to the bastard in charge but stopped, her finger hovering over the send button.

John. She hadn't been completely alone in her hunt for this woman. The cross she suspected he made the night before gained much more meaning now. He didn't want to be discovered but he did want the victim to be. Jade estimated the time the corpse entered the water from the signal of the cross or close to. She was dead before Jade made it halfway to the river. This detail she would wait for the coroner to confirm and tell Drex. If she felt any pangs of guilt for standing on evidence out of protection of Errie they were erased by his one bad call. And now more than ever, she wanted him to stay on his side of The Divide. Thankfully this discovery fell just outside the grid on the east and nowhere near the woodsman's lair or her Airstream.

"Thank you, John," she whispered as waves of dirt violated the body washing away any hope of evidence. "I owe you, again."

She had trekked several clicks south across the ridgeline until it dropped low enough for a possible decent to this location. The river pitched right here before plummeting down another rocky incline. If the body hadn't been snagged by what appeared to be the force of an undercurrent from a feeder stream, it would've been shattered in the stronger white-water rapids and waterfalls. Regardless, her discovery felt nothing like a win. Surveying the far bank on the opposite side Jade couldn't see any noticeable areas of footsteps and though they would've been heavy, carrying dead weight, impressions could've easily been erased in the downpour of the previous night.

Standing vigil over the woman in the water, she opened comms. "Detective Carmichael here, who has comms?" She waited as the walkie burst to life.

"Zac here in grid one." He came through first and, reading disapproval of Drex's decision in his eyes when he broke up the argument between them, she was starting to like the kid.

"We're here, Detective," Taylor jumped on with an enthusiasm that spoke volumes about who he would've sided with had his opinion been allowed. "At base and reading you clear. Go ahead."

"Agent Drex?" she asked, knowing she had the attention of them all. "Do you read?"

"Yes, Carmichael, in grid two northeast of your location," Drex said, his voice mildly annoyed. "Wanna explain why you're coming in from miles beyond your grid?"

"I'm standing over the corpse of a victim and wondering how you'd like to recover it from the river?" Giving him nothing in her tone, no note of righteousness or vengeance, she kept the STT button depressed allowing no one to cut in and simply stated gruesome facts. "Appears to be a woman in her late twenties, early thirties, Caucasian, badly beaten. Could be the one I identified yesterday but until she's brought out, I won't know for sure."

Jade held the button for a second longer and then released it, reopening comms. "...is in the water? Is the body moving downstream?" Jade heard the first glimpse into how the agent's voice sounded when panicked. "How long—"

"The woman is pinned by rocks, it looks like the body was

snagged due to intersecting currents, hard to tell given the murky water but there may be an underground feeder stream. The water is coming in with considerable force at an angle but there's no upper tributary visible." Jade cut him off and kept speaking. "The body is submerged about three feet down. I'd like to have a second set of eyes on after—" Her thumb slipped and he jumped back on.

"I'll come in by chopper from the south and follow the river low to minimize detection but we're not waiting the three hours it'd take to hike in," Drex barked. "Wait there, secure the site, I'll be there soon," he said, pausing with the STT blocking a response. "Good work, Detective."

"I'm sending photos now," Jade said, refusing to acknowledge his compliment. "There's a pretty good wind coming from the west and no clearing close by." Pissed or not she needed this to go smoothly so she could get back to finding Errie.

"Don't need one." Drex signed off and Jade assumed the comms would fall silent but they didn't.

"Detective, I'll head to the east bank above you so I can keep eyes on until Agent Lafine arrives. I won't be much help from that high up but I'll watch over everything with my binoculars. Nice work, Detective, wish we'd found her sooner," Zac said, risking reprimand and standing his ground.

"Thanks, Zac. Flash a signal when you're in position. I don't think our guy expected her to be found but it's nice to know someone has my back."

Yep, she liked him.

Jade snapped the walkie back on her belt and, knowing there was little left for her to do, she surveyed the area wondering if somewhere, hidden in a web of trees and brush, John was looking on. If he was, she hoped he left long before the sound of chopper blades echoed through the canyon. It wouldn't be the first time a helicopter flew over or even the first time since the search began. Forest ranger sweeps of the area were routine, especially if weather threatened to down bridges they used further in. The bird's presence was a risk but she agreed, if only on this one point, with Drex. Time was their enemy.

Alone at the river's edge, before feds dropped from the sky onto her discovery she had a detail to work out and one she was grateful not to be confronted with over comms. She couldn't be honest about what drew her to the location of the body. And, as Drex pointed out, it was miles outside her designated search grid. Being that it sat very near the most viable location to descend off the cliff and down to level ground near the river, she planned to use that as reason enough to be at this junction. When she left their meeting, as heated as things were, she did mention her intention to come in from the southwest to east to cover the same territory the victim may have if she fled south from the location of the tunnel where Jade first saw her.

If the woman was able to find another way to access the surface, one that didn't involve dropping a hundred feet to her death, then how did she end up here? This body sustained considerable damage but nothing close to the condition it would be in if she had fallen and somehow bounced into the rush of the river. No way. This question was pivotal in narrowing the search for Errie. And with the ugly end of the victim caught in the rock bed there was a point of light.

If one victim made it out into the forest of The Divide so could another.

They had focused efforts on the right area and as vast and impenetrable as it was, they weren't there alone. Somewhere close the Occultus was hiding and it didn't appear things were going quite to plan for him. And that fact curled the corner of Jade's cut lip up a little for she hoped from here out it all fell to shit.

TWENTY-NINE

Before opening his eyes John considered that he had fallen too close to the heater and risked scalding his left side while unconscious, until the heater purred. Scythe, intent on doing his part, laid pressed up against him out of loyalty, concern or both. From this vantage point he couldn't comprehend how the furry animal made lounging across the hard wood appear so cozy and tranquil. In truth, it was uncomfortable as hell and he was quite convinced contributed to the protesting of every body part that met it. Dreading movement and knowing the alternative was worse, he slowly pried his face off the floor and shifted his weight to roll onto his side. The cat sprang to life and found a perch nearby to monitor his progress.

"Going to be a slow take off," he said, glad his words were no longer slurred and stammering out. "That was a close call, I'd say."

With consciousness came the memory of the dead woman, discarded in the river, her body wearing almost nothing but bruises, cuts, and signs of violation. There was no longer a question why the detective and her FBI counterparts were taking up temporary residence in his forest. And the reason, as serious as it was, put him at far greater risk then mere discovery of his vagrant lifestyle. It threat-

ened a link to a life that knew his real name and the sins that
followed.

"Been in these for more than one dance," he said, sitting up to
remove the crinkled clothing that clung to him. With hands aching
he undressed checking his body, specifically toes and fingers for signs
of frostbite leading to gangrene. The gamble of survival at his age
was all of fifty percent. "You better give me a bite if you find me
standing in the pantry too long staring at a shelf and forgetting why
I'm there. At least I didn't end up in a coma. Then what would you
do?" The cat came closer and bumped up against him. He gave him
a pat about the head and, using the wall, crawled to a standing position ambling for the shower. Accustomed to a quick cleanup in cold
water, this time he used the heat pump to warm the water and then
stepped in.

Bundled in warm clothes he wished he could light the wood fire
and shuffle his chair up close, but despite the waterfall shielding
them he couldn't risk it especially today. The detective would've
discovered the body after he left it the night before or early morning
when the rain stopped. Either way the forest was sure to be full of
activity he couldn't be a part of. Opening his computer he didn't set
the timer requiring only a short window to confirm his suspicions.
Minutes later he jotted down key highlights of the news coverage
and shut down the laptop.

Facing the worst-case scenario, multiple missing women in the
clutches of a killer who chose his forest retreat as a backdrop for his
sick murderous game, left much to consider. As it was the body
count was one but there was no certainty more wouldn't be added.
More deaths meant more boots on the ground. The media hadn't
yet nailed down the precise location of the search and it seemed the
detective and feds were keeping a low profile, which indicated one
thing.

The criminal didn't know they were there. It also pointed to the
team not identifying where the captor was holding his hostages.

The faster he was apprehended the sooner law enforcement
would vacate the area. Being restricted land it was not an ideal
destination for anyone but, apparently, this criminal. John already

risked his safety to aid in the first discovery but he would be forced to do more to protect his home and life. The detective was right to think having the help of a man who lived undetected within The Divide for decades on her side would be an asset. He was about to prove it.

Scythe leaped onto his lap, and he welcomed the living weighted blanket of fur. Stumbling inside the previous night, he doubted he would ever feel warm again. Stroking the cat's back while staring at the notes on the table beside him, he realized he had come to love the quiet existence they shared and wasn't ready to give it up easily. And it didn't feel like he was pitted against the detective or even the feds.

With pen still in hand, he wrote one word across the bottom of his bullet point list of notes, circling it several times as the cat, sensing him relax, started to hum.

Occultus.

The way to rid the forest of such a cancer was to find it and cut it out and that was exactly what he'd help the pretty detective do—even if she would remain unaware of it. When he was rested, he would pull out the oldest maps he owned, those he referenced to narrow down the safest sector to disappear from the world decades ago. There was no place this intruder could hide in his forest where he would stay undiscovered. There existed several locations below ground in the vast expanse of wilderness capable of being used to house victims and function free of discovery. The web of underground waterways was as endless as the natural cave system, not to mention the abandoned mines and railways. And John had visited most of them, investigating their security potential before deciding on his hidden cabin. He even converted a nearby cave to a storage space containing years of essentials so he could avoid resurfacing in civilization before time altered his natural appearance allowing him anonymity when he made one of the few runs in to replenish supplies. Thinking back to the days and weeks leading up to his exodus brought back a slew of unwanted and difficult memories, toxic memories.

Knowing it unwise but confronted by a moment of weakness he

pulled open the table drawer and, shuffling the contents inside, reached far back feeling for plastic. Removing the preserved newspaper clippings he was conflicted as always. They were a reminder of unbearable pain but yet he couldn't part with them for they also provided proof his child once existed and confirmed all she meant to him. The package emerged face down. He had forgotten the last time he brought them out, years perhaps. Flipping it over he wished, as he knew he would, that he had left them stored away. The first headline wasn't too bad. It simply said, "Investigation Far From Over." The one beneath it, that shifted inside the bag overpowering the others, caught his breath and loosened his grip sending the sealed package to the floor and spooking the cat. Landing face up, he read the bold letters.

"Sisters Dead by Unholy Hands."

Leaning to snag it from the wooden planks without tipping the cat off his outstretch legs, he flipped it over and shoved it inside returning it to the far back of the drawer, closing and placing both hands, now unsettled, on the cat. Scythe turned his attention to John almost chastising him.

"Bad idea, I know," he said, scratching between his shoulders. "I won't do it again."

The seriousness of the current problem gave him an instant path to refocus his mind on. Long past he'd read his daughter bedtime stories about the ogre in the woods. She giggled, swearing if she met one, she'd bring him to John's house to live so he could help with construction. John smiled but it faded as fast as it appeared. There was a very real threat in the woods tonight and he wondered what brought this monster here.

The location of the woman's body gave him insight as to where the Occultus was hiding. She had floated downstream, but John suspected that hadn't happened above ground. Where he found her and moved her from was an intersection between the main river running south and the fastest tributary from under the eastern ridge of The Divide. John had accessed three natural lakes hundreds of feet below the upper surface but two were several miles farther south beyond his home base. Only one sat far enough north to carry her remains to where they came to rest.

Knowing the general location wasn't like pinpointing the Occultus' lair on a map. The area John presumed the criminal could've disappeared into held the most elaborate cave system that connected to a substantial abandoned mine. Abandoned due to a dangerous lack of structural integrity. Anyone foolish enough to enter could be lost in a maze leading any direction to emerge miles from where they entered, if they survived long enough to resurface.

Although not surprising, it annoyed John that this criminal had been working, if the news coverage was accurate, for months inside The Divide and he hadn't a clue. A violation of a land that had become his, John sensed a rise of anger not experienced for many years. And then there were the haunting images of the dead woman.

Even in the dark of night he could see she hadn't been very old, maybe in her early thirties or younger. Her frame was so small he considered that maybe she had been starved before meeting her violent end. John understood the stealth approach of law enforcement. If the Occultus became aware of their presence, they may not find the captives before he killed them all. And, with so many access tunnels, he had plenty of opportunity to flee justice. John knew better than anyone how the woods could shield a lone man for miles. Long enough to escape into Canada if need be. If he thought of it, so had the Occultus.

What inspired such needless violence was a mystery for the detective to solve. One she couldn't apply her mind to fully without the apprehension of this monster that had taken up residence too close to John's sanctuary. Feeling circulation healing his body from the close call of hypothermia, he gently motioned for the cat to leave his warming pad position.

"We should grab some grub," he said, the cat prancing for the kitchen cut ahead of him. "Then I have work to do. Time to rid our land of the bad seed. He picked the wrong forest to hide in. This one is ours and he's about to be unceremoniously uprooted."

THIRTY

J ade caught sight of the chopper Drex commandeered before she heard it, white water rapids below drowning the sound by blending it into the fury of the water. It came in from the south low, snaking nearer, matching the curves of the river. Drex would've had to add extra miles to the trip to enter from this direction, it amounted to circling The Divide from northeast to south and back up the break between the east and west canyon. As mad as she was, she couldn't deny the move was smart, arrive fast and unnoticed from the northeast grid where they suspected their target was hiding. There was however one flaw in his plan.

She held the STT down and raised the volume of her voice knowing she had to compete with the noise in the cockpit. "I have eyes on you, Agent Lafine. You're about two clicks out, but there is no clearing in a one-mile radius of here. Is a landing site visible from your twenty?"

She waited, watching the chopper close the distance between them wondering what his next moves would be. "Take shelter from the west bank," Drex said. "I'll be down in a minute."

Take shelter? Jesus, he wasn't landing the chopper at all. With seconds to spare Jade found a secure break in the trees and charged up the slope to reach it. Wind lashed the surface around where she had been standing as the chopper lowered over top. A second later a fast rope dropped down from above and with it Agent Lafine rappelled, his tactical gloves working the line like he had done it a hundred times. And, by the looks of it, he had. Halfway to the ground a crosswind caught the propellers and dipped the bird right. The fast line pitched wildly and Drex clung in the wash until it steadied.

Hitting the ground on solid feet with a thud she felt emotionally if not physically, he signaled the chopper pilot who lifted higher to follow the river back the way he came. Jade's eyes darted from Drex to the bird and back again descending the slope to meet him at the water's edge.

"You could've said you weren't landing," Jade said, holding her hair back from the quake of wind.

Drex brushed a hand over his face clearing it of dust turned up by the blades. "I thought I did," he said, nearing the bank. "So what have we got?"

Jade motioned to the body. Dirty water washing over it seemed a further violation. "Doesn't appear she has been in long. I'm guessing anywhere from when we gave up the search to a few hours prior."

"You mean to say a timeframe close to when you spotted her exiting the cave or tunnel hole?" he asked, glancing at the victim and then upstream, north to their grid locations. "And how in the hell did she get from there to here?"

Jade agreed that was confusing given the timing and proximity. "As you saw from my photos, her head is at a strange angle and I can't see her face from here."

"Well there's no chance trace evidence would've survived in the force of this water. I'll pull her out and we'll send her to forensics and see if we get lucky."

Jade hadn't noticed the pack slung over his shoulder until now, watching him drop down he was facing her. He pulled out a body bag and laid it down near the edge of the bank.

"I'd like to confirm first and take a few close-up photos of her injuries," Jade said, helping arrange the protective plastic.

"Confirm? We know she is definitely deceased so…against the victim profile of the nurse?" he asked, locking eyes then returning to his task.

"No." She studied him for a beat. "If this *is* the nurse. Until I see her up close, I won't be sure this is the same woman I identified at the cliff wall."

"Christ," he said, shaking his head validating her suspicion his trust in her was fleeting. "What are the chances it's not?"

With this he walked into the river. The water waders he wore protected him from getting wet but did nothing to stave off the cold. "I'll carry her out with as little movement as possible," he said, the strong current breaking around his legs as they disappeared below the water's surface. "But I may need you to zip up the bag. My hands will be shot."

He frustrated her but it was difficult to stay mad at a guy who risked himself in cross winds to rappel from a chopper for this victim and was about to freeze pulling her body to safety. She nodded in agreement and shone her flashlight to the riverbed adding extra illumination for him to navigate the unstable ground.

Nearing the body, in three feet of icy water, Drex held his arms and hands above the waterline preserving their warmth until the last moment. "Looks like it's pinned between a boulder and a log," he yelled over the rushing current, his body swaying, fighting the water's force. "I may have to put her on this bank but I'll try to make it back."

"Don't lift her out," Jade shouted. He stared up, questioning her. "Leave it submerged, float it this way then we'll lift her together."

Drex nodded, his expression showed appreciation. She found this leader confusing but was grateful he cared enough to jump into the muck, literally, for a case if required. Overcast clouds darkened the area. Jade kept her Tac light trained on the section he occupied. Submerging his long arms, he grappled with the log that snagged the corpse, or the shirt it wore, freeing it. Turning slowly with the released body held at waist height under the surface, he followed a path Jade illuminated back to the bank. Kneeling to help with the dead weight, Jade reached for the upper torso of the corpse as he lifted her lower half from the drink. The cascade of rapids forced him to reposition and, in a split second during him heaving the body onto the shore, the log he messed with broke free of the rock bed, torpedoed straight at him, and hit the back of his legs. He lost balance and contact with the riverbed, sent the woman rolling toward Jade, and disappeared into the wash.

With a corpse between her and the river, Jade stabilized the body, jumped over it, and trained her light ahead in search of Drex. Seeing the light, he broke the dirty surface as she bound over rock and brush until meeting him at a curve in the river. She threw herself over the edge of the bank, lunging out to grab him. Being he was twice her size, she knew it'd take Herculean effort. Reaching out she clutched his weapon strap with both arms and swung him into the bank using the water's force. In one fluid motion they were soaked and piled in a heap on the gravel, Drex still half submerged but free of the danger of being swept away and over the waterfall drawing too near for comfort.

"Thanks," he said amid coughing water from his lungs.

"Yeah. Don't mention it," Jade replied, untangling her body from his. Pulling off the ground, she realized their condition wouldn't sustain them long. "How fast can the chopper swing around? We'll be too cold to hold the fast line to pull up and we aren't walking out of here easily."

"About fifteen minutes from when I notify him to circle back," he said, pulling his dripping walkie off his belt beneath his waders. "Shit."

"I'm glad it wasn't mine." Jade laughed. "The boss will make you pay for that you know?" She handed him her walkie as he dropped his waders, which became nothing but leg pools after the river flowed into the tops of them. He was soaked head to toe and starting to shiver.

Carrying his wet gear back to the area where the corpse waited, he set it all down in a folded wet pile several feet from the shoreline, reached into his waiting pack with hands shaking, and pulled a dry pair of pants and a hoodie from its bottom. Handing her the hoodie, which she accepted and held out expecting him to claim it back, he peeled out of his soaked jeans replacing them with the dry one inches from where she stood. She couldn't avert her eyes fast enough and he caught her staring. Smiling through clenched teeth, he said, "The top is for you. At least this way we'll both be half dry."

Jade threw off her wet jacket and shirt without hesitation and pulled his warm sweatshirt over her head instantly swimming in it. He laughed and reclaimed her walkie off the ground kneeling beside the pack. "Drex here. Mike, you got ears? We're wet fish and need a dry bed retrieval. Head to the drop now and tell Sam we need two beds. I repeat, two beds." His voice was as serious as ever but the expression on his cold face softened. "Mike here, sir. On the way to drop zone, two beds ready for deployment."

Drex handed the walkie back to her. "Better you keep this safe."

She clipped it to the dry side of her half-soaked pants and shaking, walked with him to properly store the woman's body in the bag for transport. They only made it a few strides when she stopped and swiveled to face him approaching from behind her.

"It's not her," she said, turning back and standing her ground until he came up alongside.

"It's not her?" he questioned, confusion mixed with tension from the cold in his expression.

"This isn't the nurse," Jade said, nearing the body and standing over it, inspecting the head area closely. "This woman has dark hair. The nurse by profile evidence and my identification is a platinum blonde. There's no way this is her."

"Hard to say how dark given the mud, but she's not a blonde," he agreed. "Are you one hundred percent certain this is not the woman you viewed through your binoculars?"

Jade couldn't keep from shivering, the more she fought it the more intense it became, and she was fairly certain it wasn't from Drex cornering her or making her nervous. "I am," she stuttered. "This is not the...the same woman but with...with the time in the water and decomp, I can't…can't be sure which victim, if any, this is."

"Okay, we'll figure it out back at base when we can think straight. We'll get her wrapped. Evidence collection will have to wait for steady hands." As he said it, she noticed he was focused on hers and they appeared to be turning a shade of cold blue so she pulled them into the sleeves of the hoodie for a few seconds while he rounded the other side of the corpse and folded the bag over. She reached to follow the zipper up her side but he skirted the body doing it up and nodded for her to tuck her hand back into the sweatshirt.

"That may explain why she came to rest here," he said, securing a strap over the bag, and closing his pack. "Chopper incoming." He pointed south as the black bird swung into view in the distance. "Not sure how you managed to grab me out of the river and prevent her from falling in after me but if you hadn't acted as fast as you did, we might both be lost," he said, watching the helicopter approach.

"Thh…thanks." Jade's words were slurring together and she wasn't sure how she would get from base camp back to her truck without revealing the location of the Airstream. The only thing she could focus on other than the ache of the cold was the face of the woman on the cliff. Whoever lay inside the body bag at their feet wasn't her.

Without a word, Drex marched over standing at Jade's back shielding her from the impact of the wind whipped up by the chopper's blades. Directly overhead, a stretcher emerged and was lowered to them. Drex locked eyes with her as if asking if she was good to brace on her own while he secured the body bag to the stretcher. His movements were so fluid and precise, she knew this was not a task he was unfamiliar with. Signaling the man leaning out the bird's door, the stretcher rose overhead. Drex threw his pack over his freezing shoulder and she could see him locking up against the cold like she was but fighting it harder. When the second stretcher lowered enough for them to board it, he guided her inside straddling her with arms beside her, placing himself at risk but ensuring she couldn't fall beyond his grasp. She wanted to grab the sides but knew her grip would prove faulty. Safe inside the bird, the man Drex identified as Sam locked the doors and threw blankets at the wet pair before swinging back into the co-pilot's seat and leaving them in the back alone. Jade sat beside Drex, unable to pull the half-mangled landing of her blanket loose to cover her properly. With shaking arms, he drew closer, fanned out both blankets over them, and let her fall back into a pocket between him and the chopper's wall.

"We're okay," he said. "You did good, Jade. We'll be back soon."

The noise of the bird was deafening without ear protection and she didn't care. The last thing she remembered was him pulling her walkie off her belt between them and hearing his low voice echoing beside her. She didn't regain consciousness until they were on the ground and the door slid open. Zac met them at a helipad and they transferred into a warm waiting truck. He drove them to base camp in relative silence, but his expression said he read the body retrieval was anything but routine.

As they came within minutes of base, Lafine spoke up. "You wait inside the truck," he cautioned Jade. "Kane will come and grab you when we pull up and take you home to recover. We can go over what she tells us in the morning."

The second the word left his lips, Jade's body tensed. Another night with Errie in the clutches of a criminal capable of inflicting the violence the woman in the bag wore. No was what she wanted to say but before her lips parted to speak, he leaned closer, as if deliberately excluding the conversation from Zac driving in the row ahead. "I know you want to get back out there. I do too. But if we are too wasted to handle this right, we hand all the power to this bastard. He doesn't know we're here. We have her and we're gaining ground. We'll get him, but not today."

Jade tried to stretch her hands out but couldn't get them to release. Every part of her hurt and she couldn't walk the space between two vehicles, let alone chase a killer down a cave tunnel. He was right. But how did Kane get involved? The thought hit and Drex read her expression. "Your partner called in with some good intel. We'll work through it before heading back out. Let me know when you're good to go tomorrow morning."

"Sun up." Was all she managed to say before the truck stopped, the door pried open, and she saw Kane's face plastered with concern before he scooped her up and carried her to his waiting truck.

Gathering Jade into his arms, Kane was shocked by the cold emanating off her body. Placing her into the passenger side of his truck, where he set the seat heater on high, he wished he didn't have to drive and could hold her on the trip back to the Airstream. He considered taking her into town, to the general for observation, fluids, and a watch on hypothermia damage, but knew if she was conscious, she'd be livid. Looking at her wrapped in a blanket from the chopper ride, he read she was about as close to the edge as one dare go but her extremities didn't show any signs of permanent damage. Belting her in and closing her door, he flew around the front of the truck, waved an appreciative acknowledgment at the agent who didn't appear much better off, and jumped in. Gravel flew as he left the lot anxious to drive her somewhere he could get both eyes on her.

"Thanks for…for coming," Jade whispered.

"Honey, wild horses couldn't keep me," he said, landing the truck's tires down hard onto the pavement of the main highway. "I have a mind to head to the hospital. I know you don't want that but if I don't see improvement at the trailer, you're going."

"Okay," she said, the warmth enveloping her from below was lulling her to sleep.

"I've got you. Rest, love." He wanted to slam his fist against the steering wheel or scream out the window in rage seeing the wreckage of her and knowing she deliberately avoided telling him how bad things were. Some part of him knew despite her silence. It was why he reached out to the feds before he heard back from her. Something felt off.

In truth, the agents and her were getting somewhere and when he returned home, he would tell Amy as much. Knowing sidestepping the dead body discovery wouldn't garner confidence in a positive outcome for Errie, he was intent on bringing information back that could.

After Jade was safe.

What the hell happened out there in the woods, in the overcast dark of the river? Having no right officially to ask those questions he could only wait for answers from Jade. And currently she was in no condition to give them. Down this road more than a few times, he had grown accustomed to detecting that stage in a case where it gained momentum that either carried you to resolution or mowed you down. Uncertain of which path Jade was on he could only hope and help ensure it was the former. But what did they really have so far?

If he and the Mississippi cop were correct and this criminal came from an engineering background, he needed more to narrow the search, find a name to go with their profile, and bridge it with area intel to unearth the location he was holding the captives in. All he knew for certain tonight was The Divide won and the agent and Jade lost today. Drex did admit that if not for Jade's quick actions he might not have made it back. That was a story he wanted the details of.

Checking on her as he drove nearer to the trailer, he could see her body shedding the cold in waves. How she would be in any condition to reenter the harsh forest he didn't know, and with all she endured in their previous case, he couldn't stop worrying. He decided to offer her support by staying on at the Airstream but knew it wouldn't be worth voicing. Interfering or inserting himself into a federal investigation as more than distant backup for information checks could mean his badge. She would never agree to risk that. And as sad as it made him, he was all too aware that she wanted and needed to tackle this case alone.

He left her sleeping in the warmth of the truck when he reached her camp. Electing to go in, deliver her gear and his for the night, turn up the heater and ready the shower. Minutes later, he returned to wake her and assist her inside. Desperate for rest, he knew returning her body temperature by removing the wet, cold clothing and applying external heat to her skin was paramount first. Sitting her on the edge of the bed outside the washroom, he stripped her clothes off, wrapped her in a fresh towel, and shuffled her into the shower. Throwing off his shirt and jeans to avoid off-spray soaking them, he stood shielding the door in boxers and steadying her until she could move on her own. Wrapping her in a warm blanket, determining a towel too small, he ushered her back to the bed, bundling her under the covers cradling her body with his.

"Well, if this is what it took to get you here for the night," she whispered before falling asleep.

Once her body quit shaking and he was confident she was out of danger he slipped out of bed intending to remove the wet clothes reeking of earth, moss, and decay from the river off the floor to discard them in the hamper where they wouldn't be tripped over. Grabbing his bathrobe off his hook, he carried them into the light and only then realized her clothes were soaked inside her daypack, she had been wearing Agent Lafine's hoodie. Knowing emergency situations called for safety-first protocol, he was also well aware how intense circumstances tended to bond people together.

Staying close somehow became an idea worth vetting.

Too early for him to sleep, he moved to the kitchen area where he wouldn't disturb Jade's rest and spread out the information they amassed together. It wasn't nothing. Among the documents in Jade's possession was a full criminal profile worked up by the folks in Quantico. It made for interesting reading and aligned with the suspicions of the team back home. The warning issued within hit with a familiar unpleasant potency. The federal agents had gone in with a guarded approach until they could be certain they were targeting the correct location. Now, Kane recognized it as a tactical move based on the profile. If this criminal knew his hidden fortress was under siege by law enforcement, they said, he may have no reason to keep the victims alive and decide killing them all in a spree was better than losing them.

The Occultus had gone to so much effort to select, kidnap, hide, and store the women. The motivation behind that far outweighed, in the expert's opinion, his own survival. Putting them and Errie in a perilous position if confronted and one they should make every effort to avoid. So going in guns blazing wasn't an option. Slow, steady, and stealth was the best line of attack.

It made sense now. Knowing the feds who were forced to bring her on would put Jade under a microscope, he did some digging of his own. Particularly on Wenzel's cousin, Drex, an international threat assessment specialist and ex-military wrecking ball. His background made him the perfect six-foot-three cutout for an operation such as this, in wild, dangerous terrain with an absolute necessity for ranger-style covert infiltration. The problem, which was becoming crystal clear, was the alternative outlined a close-in sneak attack that involved placing Drex, Jade, and the other agents in a direct line of fire somewhere underground, difficult to access or escape, and known far better by the perpetrator than them. An advantage that could prove deadly.

The information before him painted an ugly picture as disturbing as the worst of Francisco Goya. Kane jotted down notes to take with him when he left for home and information to follow up on and keep working when he was back with Tex, Grey, and Amy. It would be difficult, but they would have to steer Amy away from certain aspects of the case to keep her sane. Kane held copies of the tarot cards retrieved at the crime scenes in his hands, studying the style of art, colors, portrayal of each. This was what he would assign Amy to run down. It was not a fool's errand. He felt the key to unlocking the motivation behind the crimes and seeing into the mind of this predator lay within the cards. Why had he chosen the women he did and why ascribe the particular cards to each? They determined the cards came from an array of decks and no two cards from any one. There was meaning behind these choices and establishing it may be exactly what they needed to crack the Occultus case wide open.

As pieces fell into place, there would be no question they were up against a foe who dedicated years to seeing his plan play out in gory conclusions that none of them could bear Errie being a part of.

And worse for Kane, to save her he had to let Jade go and pray she'd make it back to him. If today was any indication, things didn't appear all that promising.

Sauntering down the hall, spent by a truth that threatened all he loved and aware he had no choice but to risk it, he collapsed beside Jade, curled around her, and fell asleep wishing they could wake somewhere, anywhere but The Divide.

THIRTY-ONE

Errie bent her head beneath the air tunnel inhaling deep breaths in gulps and straining her eyes to see sunlight, what she would do for it. There was none. The forest had to be overcast by clouds, perhaps a storm. It would account for why her feet were soaked and all the tunnels she ran were slippery with moisture and smelled of mold, moss, gravel mud that once was dust, and an earthy decay. She was grateful in all the scents assaulting her nostrils she didn't smell him. She hadn't allowed herself much time to think about the day he broke into their home, knocked her out, and stole her away. But standing, with her face pressed into the rock, drinking in oxygen from above, she remembered the smell of him.

It wasn't good.

He smelled of this place, the body odor of a man after a long day working outdoors, and something else, something unexpected. The musty undertone of dry ice. One of Errie's most humbling achievements in the world of dance was being chosen to perform for a famous artist on stage. The coveted singer was known in Europe more than America but the show was packed and appreciated by fans the world over. In that performance one of the challenges was the presence of fog on stage. An effect produced by the use of dry ice. Dancing in it for Errie was simple but the vague musty scent, night after night, became nauseating. She couldn't forget it and this man who had taken her against her will carried the scent. And though she ran possibilities through her mind, she couldn't envision why.

There were obvious details impossible to forget like his height and large build or the sound of his voice, but Amy always said it was the seemingly insignificant aspects that posed the greatest threat to most criminals. Errie tried to memorize those. If she made it back to freedom and Amy, she wanted to do everything to hand him over with evidence enough to put him away for life, if she didn't find a way to kill the motherfucker first.

As her breathing calmed, she pulled back from the rock wall to assess her surroundings. If she had to guess, she was fairly confident her current location was miles from where she started. Snaking through rock in the dark, she lost all sense of direction. The only thing she knew was this level sat above where he had been with the other captive. The distance, despite not knowing where it was lead-ing, gave her comfort. Anywhere was better than close to him. Why he hadn't yet come in search of her shifted from being a blessing to a concern. His failure to pursue her down the dark, cold mine tunnels could mean he was otherwise engaged with the other women, like the one who screamed out, or he didn't feel the need.

Errie prayed to stumble on a way out long before she was next on his list. She heard the tragic fate of the woman he was focused on earlier and had no interest in sharing it. With nowhere to sit she laid out her pack as a table on the hard ground at the far edge of the tunnel where no water seeped and sat cross-legged to eat and rehydrate. Scanning the distance, she noticed an odd formation not far ahead. With provisions restored, she made her way to it, her flashlight trained on the bulge of rock.

From her side, it appeared as a curvature protruding out of the wall but when she arrived, she realized the curve was part of a semi-circle cored out of the stone. Cautiously stepping into it and pointing the light up inside, her breath caught. She saw rungs. A circular tunnel extended high above and on its far side, metal rungs had been inserted to form a ladder. The fact that they began high overhead said whoever used them would've had an easier method of reaching them or was a literal giant. Perhaps a lower ladder intended to match up to the higher rungs existed at some point.

Casting light in every space surrounding her, she scoured the tunnel for something, anything to help her reach the higher steps. Rope, loose rocks she could build a pile to climb up, wood she could brace between the two walls or pin at an angle to tiptoe up, she saw nothing. Dumping her pack in the alcove, she set off further down the space, desperation driving her.

To miss a chance at freedom for the sake of three feet added an insurmountable insult to her situation. Soon, hopelessness transformed her steady gait into ragged running.

Expanding the distance between her and the rest of her supplies, those few things she gathered to fortify her survival, didn't sit well. With each step, the terror she pushed down fought harder to reach the surface until full-out panic consumed her.

Without warning, her legs buckled and she dropped to the wet rock foundation, tears streaming down her face. The truth of her wounds and exhaustion eclipsing the hope of escape, she anchored her mind on a single memory. It wasn't the night of Amy's proposal, the day they moved into their new home or the day they bought it, or even her most recent birthday celebration with all their friends and family. One day, months after their relationship began, a mutual friend was introducing them to her new husband. The expression on Amy's face, a simple glance in that moment, told Errie she intended to stay for life. Life.

Get up and fight.

Wiping her face, she stood center of the tunnel, waved the light back to where she had come from and then circled around to where she stood. Ahead, three feet to her right, sat a broken pickax. Grabbing it in both hands, she marched back to the ladder, slammed it against the rock wall at an angle, threw her pack over her shoulder with the flashlight protruding out its top, and proceeded to climb up far enough to clench the bottom rung. Kicking, scraping, and hoisting herself up she ascended until both feet were set firmly on the lower rungs and she could hold fast to rest before starting the climb.

With light dancing wildly ahead of her, she had only one thought. If a hatch existed at the top, she hoped the damn thing opened.

The cabin hummed with a palatable quiet absent of Kane, who left at the request of the feds, and Jackson, who swung back to his place to shower, check in on the livestock, and crash for a few hours. Amy dozed on the sofa listening to a blues track Kane deliberately set to play in the background to drown out her head noise. Knowing what they were facing she didn't fight the fatigue this time believing it wise to rest for a bit while Kane went to retrieve Jade and meet the federal agent at the helipad. He said he'd phone if Jade were in any danger so no news was good news. With all of them working different aspects of the case they arranged to reconvene the next morning at sunup and Amy wanted her wits about her, corralling them had become a full-time job of late. As "She's Crazy" by Cold-fire filled the space, she let go of the reins and drifted to sleep.

The smooth departure from consciousness failed terribly to prepare her for the violently abrupt return.

As though someone reached into her dream, rising up from the floor of that latent space to grab hold of her left leg, a nightmarish realization made her aware she was fighting a foe across The Divide between reality and dream state. In a fog too slow to lift, she struggled against the clench tugging her literally off the soft surface her body slept on. It wasn't until she hit the hardwood of Kane's living room her consciousness burst to life. Even in the darkness of night, she made out his form at her feet dragging her across the floor. There was no mistaking whom the outline belonged to though that fact couldn't possibly be accurate.

She twisted her foot free pausing the momentum of her aggressor. Instead of securing his grip on her ankle, he leaped the distance to her face seizing her neck with both hands. With their heads within inches, his voice carried into her ears with a hiss of breath. "Surprised to see me? I thought you might be. I came for Kane. My lucky day to find you lounging on his couch."

Her voice constricted by the crushing pressure of his grip crackled out, "It can't be. You…you're bedridden."

"Not anymore," the Redeemer said, laughing as the depletion of air in her lungs started a wave of dizzying confusion. She wondered why her hands couldn't fend his off and considered he had suspended them before she woke. The blackness in the room drew closer announcing the end of her resistance and then a flash of Errie colored her mind. Twisting and turning her body he lost contact for a second, long enough for her to scream out. "No. Errie needs me, you…"

His hands were back, compressing down harder, and his face was so close she felt the heat of his breath cross her neck. "Trust me, Killer, she doesn't need you…you can't save her now, she's already dead."

Whether fear, rage, or the torment of both, Amy gained strength anew, releasing her right arm from whatever held it, she threw a punch landing squarely at the side of his head, breaking his contact with her neck. Gulps of air replenished her lungs and with it she steeled her resolve to keep the hits coming until one of them was down, unable to resurface.

It was then Jackson's voice broke through the battle, disrupting the scene, and waking her to reality. "Jesus Murphy, kid, what in tarnation are you wrangling behind those closed eyes?"

"What? I…I thought he had a hold of my neck." The panic of constraint hadn't yet subsided. And a lack of oxygen had her drinking down deep inhalations. "I…I couldn't breathe and—"

"Yeah, you're wrapped up pretty good between the blanket, your hoodie, and what the heck?" Reaching between Amy's head and chest Jackson released the pull cords of the oversized hoodie she had borrowed. Somehow in the fit of restless sleep they looped the knob of the side table butting up to the armrest of the sofa. Twisting to free the restriction of the blanket wrapping her left ankle she catapulted to the floor weighing down and tightening the hood cords trapping her neck. "Glad I came back before you hogtied yourself." Jackson helped her sit upright on the floor, lifted her back up to sit on the sofa, and helped straighten up her disheveled attire.

"Who had you by the neck?" Jackson asked, handing her the mangled blanket off the hardwood once she was settled.

"Nickolas Leigh," Amy said, pulling the blanket in close feeling stupid and embarrassed.

"You're having nightmares about the Redeemer still." His compassionate tone underlying the acknowledgment.

"Not still," she corrected. "Never did before...before investigating—"

"The attempted murder case?" Jackson finished it for her.

"Yeah. And now with Errie...with everything, it's a nightly occurrence. That's why I was considering closing it," she admitted, though so many more reasons existed.

"Look, kid, I can't begin to imagine what you're going through—"

Amy locked eyes with him, their shared history written between them. "Yes, yes, you can."

"Nikki is at the ranch fast asleep, kid. I can't. And if all this is too much close the damn case." Jackson patted her on the shoulder. His support had never felt so pure. "If we find anything new, we reopen it. I was ready to tell you to pass it to me before I read the machine failure data. No one gives a damn what happened to Nickolas...well except his rich family but even they aren't pushing for answers. They have their hands full keeping him from lockup."

Amy sighed, shook the insanity of the moment off knowing she'd dreamed of him attempting to kill her in her sleep and that was exactly what she had done to him lacking a favorable result. Now her intention had become hazy and pointless. All that mattered was bringing Errie home safe. Whatever punishment she faced, if it hunted her down, couldn't match what she was living with every second knowing what Errie may be subjected to until they saved her.

"I'm telling Cap tomorrow," she said. "If he doesn't agree I'll—"

"He will," Jackson assured glancing at the table and noticing its compromised condition. "I think you cold-cocked the table, lucky it didn't take offense, I might've."

Amy ran a hand through her mess of waves, her eyes finally absorbing the comfort of the room. "What did you come back for? Besides uncanny radar for my self-strangulation attempt."

"Ha, ha, right. I think I found something and I couldn't wait till morning to match it against what we have. You up to working in the office with me?" he asked. "I'll make the coffee."

"Well how can I say no to that?" Amy tore the hoodie off over her head and dropped it to the floor. Jackson laughed as she stood up and kicked it up to her hand.

"I'm guessing you're not wearing that again."

"Hell no," she said. "I'll be back in a minute. Gonna find a button-down sweater."

Amy's boots echoed down the hallway of the private hospital with the potential to wake the residence of the rooms she passed. She didn't care. A skeleton staff left it open and unguarded for a couple more hours. When seven o'clock hit morning rounds, breakfast trays, and the day's new batch of medical tests would render the quiet unrecognizable. For now, she was on her own. Nickolas sent a text just before five a.m. and, reading it, she abandoned sleep and Kane's house and hit the open road with the petal down. Parking in the shadow of a grouping of trees she stomped across the lot wondering what game he was playing at and if it really posed an opportunity to aid in Errie's recovery.

As bad of an idea as it was, she didn't have a choice.

Rounding the threshold to his room, she grabbed the door, closing it on the way in. He appeared as he always did, upright in bed looking healthier than the rest of them. And, as last time they met, he held a file under his large, manicured hands. This one appeared thicker than the previous ones he prepared for her, the attempted murder case research uncovering the flawed life-sustaining equipment and the soft engineer data on the Occultus case.

"I see you have something for me," she said, lifting the chair from the corner and throwing it close to his bed without hesitation. "I have a couple housekeeping questions first, to ensure we're working on the same premise."

"Of course, Detective, please," he said, opening the floor for Amy to interrogate him.

"I won't waste my time or yours asking how you ended up with victim profiles, including my fiancée's, or what resources you employed to arrive at your conclusions, but what I do want to know is why. Why are you inserting yourself in the Occultus case?" Amy asked, locking eyes when he tipped his head up to analyze her.

"I suppose that's fair, Detective," he began. "I wouldn't disclose my methods or resources so that would be a waste of precious time. I'm not doing this for you, and I believe you know that. Not for your fiancée either. Jade is out there in rather inhospitable conditions without her crew, without backup, and facing an equally dangerous adversary-not like me mind you."

"Well I'm not sure there's another quite like you." Amy's voice belied the compliment as the worst of insults. Knowing she had to tread carefully she was having difficulty doing so.

Nickolas allowed a one-sided sly grin to escape then dropped his head down slightly addressing the file and continued. "I do not agree with Detective Carmichael failing or falling short against the FBI team who has jurisdiction over this multistate case. My motivations are simple as this goes. I want Jade to catch her man and save the victims before the feds." His head raised, his deep-green eyes not locking on hers but drilling through them to singe her very soul. "I will be the only one who ever gets the better of Jade."

Amy didn't know exactly how to process his omission. Was it as simple as no one but me is permitted to triumph against her? Or was there so much more her stressed out swirling in pain brain was failing miserably to land on. Guessing it was the later she pocketed the words in a review later memory file and kept listening intently.

"So what do you have?" she asked. "Your text said you identified who we need to look for. What do you mean?"

Nickolas leaned forward, his reach reminding her she sat far too close. He scooped the file off his lap in his left hand and offered it to her. In a flash her nightmare flooded back and his proximity made her wince though she shifted her weight to conceal the reaction. She accepted the file with calm steady hands and met his eyes without shrinking back.

He grinned. She hated it when he did. He was so handsome and calm it unnerved even her. *Monster.*

"I mean, I'm getting to know him, your Occultus. And when you're finished reading that you will too. So cliché to say it always points back to the mother, but in his case it's true. And let's face facts we can't become monsters without being raised in Hell. At the very least, an isolated aberration doesn't present as often. This criminal you seek forfeited years into his plan and selected carefully the captives he believes play into the story."

"Story? What story are you referring to?" Amy said, unable to swallow her patience much longer but knowing there was no other way to pry whatever clues the Redeemer may have garnered from his sick fascination with Jade's current case. Errie's survival may well hang in the balance. Amy inhaled deeply but quietly and forced restraint. "Give me your crib notes, who are we hunting?"

Nickolas bit his lower lip releasing it with a half chuckle he sent chills across the space between them as he studied her for a moment stretching it out far too long. "This one is using the women he collected to save one he couldn't save when he was young. His mother didn't save, I'd suspect because she herself was too weak or compromised. One failed, one faltered, and twelve will pay for a righting of a past a monster refuses to accept."

Amy recorded everything he said on her phone running its dictation program inside the pocket closest to him, but her mind memorized his words, nonetheless. She sensed something true in them. "And you decided this solely based on the information inside this file?" Amy asked, lifting the file off its resting place on her lap.

"Well not solely," he said. "I am an accomplished murderer with one hell of a twisted mother-son relationship history. I'm sure my background lends a unique perspective to such matters."

"I'm sure," was all that fell from Amy's lips. Whatever information he stored inside the file she held had to have some merit. How she would process it or hand it over to the team was a whole other hurdle.

"Whatever the Occultus has orchestrated he lined it up long before he began the abductions which means he's on a timeline. One launched the day he took his last captive, your fiancée." With this, Amy met his emerald gaze again. He read the panic in her eyes and answered it before she could tame it. "Yes, you should be scared for her but know this, she is the last. Be glad she was not his first."

THIRTY-TWO

D
r. Abraham Maxwell sat at his large mahogany desk after hours when the professional building was all but emptied with a heavy malaise shadowing him. The Occultus file was growing substantially at a rapid pace and Grey requested he quietly weigh in and get back to Kane and Jackson with his insights. He canceled his appointments upon receiving the information and after three hours of intense scrutiny didn't welcome the conclusions he arrived at. Sharing those with Kane presented a hard call among many the two were forced to participate in. He was tiring of them but knew this was why Kane had come to trust him. He wouldn't risk their bond, even for Amy.

With his notes arranged into the most digestible sounds bites and aware time was an enemy and Jade was once again placed in a high-risk position, he readied to deliver the news. Sending a text to Kane's cell phone, he warned him it was not a conversation either of them would benefit from if anyone else overheard the particulars. Kane text he was, for the time being, alone in his home office. He picked up on the first ring.

"Hey Max. So how bad is it?" Kane asked, his voice reflecting the mounting strain more than Max anticipated.

"Kane, I wish I had better news," Max said without hesitation. "The profile work up should provide Jade with the intel to aid in bringing the Occultus down and offer insight she can use against him if the worst happens. Being the most vital information to arm her with, you'll gain some concrete windows into his personality and mental constructs that should benefit. That, as it turns out, isn't the bad news."

"Okay. Look if you've outlined avenues to help Jade break this perp and protect herself from him, I'm a happy guy. I can't expect more than that," Kane said, his tone slightly more upbeat.

The inflection in Kane's voice made Max wish he could leave the conversation where it was and say nothing more but he couldn't. Instead he drew a long breath, eased farther back into the leather of his chair, and braced. "Kane, it's not the intel that poses my serious concern, it's how it was arrived at. I'm reading document after document typical to our work, but the victim profile section Amy added...well it's not from her."

"It is," Kane assured him, sounding distracted by the evidence he was viewing on his side of the call. "She worked it last night...or early this morning but I didn't get a chance to see it yet. She has it on her."

"Yeah...I guessed as much," Max said. "There's a reason for that."

"What?" Kane's focus narrowed back to the call. "There's a reason?"

"Kane, there's no way to say this without fallout, so I want to premise it by conceding the information has the potential to save lives." Max let that sink in for a breath. "I know the handwriting in the margins and it doesn't belong to Amy."

"Okay so she had someone she trusted review the victim profiles to strengthen her conclusions. Makes sense given what's at stake for her," Kane said, clearly not sharing Max's concern.

"That would pose problems if the person was outside the force or the legal community but this...this is worse," Max warned.

"How? How is it worse? You said whoever she shared this with has literally given us keys to what makes the Occultus tick, right?"

Kane asked. It was a fair enough question. One Max knew Kane wouldn't like the answer to.

"Yes. Yes, he did. But Kane, the man with the insight was Nickolas Leigh." The shock and impact of his words silenced the other end of the call. "I conducted many mental competency tests with him, all to combat his legal team's justification for special privileges. In fact, there have been so many filed I've lost count. I can read much more than the average person from an individual's handwriting, you know it's a hobby of mine. Amy sought help from the Redeemer or he offered it. Either way, this profile is formulated based on many of his direct conclusions."

"You're saying Amy employed the assistance of the most vile killer we've ever had the misfortune to come across? The one that almost cost us all our lives, Jade's life?" Kane's voice started low but gained volume and intensity as the realization landed. "You're telling me my friend, my trusted partner, one who calls me her brother in arms, handed over classified information about Jade's case, a federal case no less, details that compromise her, to a fucking monster?"

"Yes. I am." Max couldn't allow Kane to go over the edge. "Kane, Jade needs every advantage to stop this criminal and by the looks of what I'm seeing this helps her do that. I wish it wasn't under these circumstances and he had no involvement. We will track down the rabbit hole of his motivations for weighing in eventually. My guess is it was because he could. That fact alone keeps him attached to Jade in some way in his mind although we know that is a fantasy. I believe Amy is using him to protect Jade, solve this case, and bring Errie home alive. And now I'll ask you, would you do any less if it was Jade taken and Amy in the field? You don't need to answer that but you do need to admit it before Amy walks back in that door.

"Kane, you don't have the luxury of ego. I have read and reread the data. His conclusions are sound and right now that is all you should care about." Max listened to breathing over the line, first almost a panting then slowing to a steady rhythm.

"Well fuck," Kane said finally. "What the hell do I do with this?"

"Work the case and worry about this after Errie and Jade are home." As Max said it, he believed it. It couldn't matter how they caught this criminal or saved the lives of his victims and returned home safe. Not now and maybe not ever.

"Does Jackson know?" Kane asked, his voice held less ego and more...fear.

"I doubt anyone does," Max admitted.

"So Captain Grey's in the dark too?"

"Everyone, until or unless you tell them," Max said. "This is where I hand it over to you."

"So what's in the file, Max?" he asked, shelving Amy's betrayal until after he decided the worth of the information gleamed from the act.

"A full picture. And the one I'm looking at says Errie is alive and may make it out of this. Heck, they all could."

"No, they all can't," Kane corrected. "Jade and Drex discovered a body downstream from their grid search. That information wouldn't have made it into your package, it's still being processed."

"If the evidence is leading me in the right direction the body will belong to the first woman taken. And that determination couldn't have been made without Amy's section. I don't presume to know how he amassed such a complete overview but I suspect it has more to do with his personal history than his access to wealth and the connections it affords."

"Max, you're doing it," Kane said, his voice regained that "comfortable in the chaos" tone it usually held. "The abridged version. You're saying it takes one to know one?"

Max wanted to smack him when he dumbed down his vast analysis to a cliché and he did it a lot. The problem was he was always spot on. "Yes, damn it."

"And you trust this?" he asked.

"Not for a goddamn second if all the supporting hard fought investigative information didn't line up to meet it, but it does."

"Okay." Kane didn't speak for a moment and Max allowed the

silence to hold respecting him taking the time to process. "Send it all to me, including Nickolas Leigh's sidebar notes. I'll let it ride unless Amy opens the door until after it's solved, but I'm bringing Tex and Grey on board. And you know that'll have Grey at your door. I'll handle this side. You handle Grey. Oh, and Amy is seeking his approval to close the attempted murder case. Not sure how that'll go down after he hears about this."

"Maybe you should wait until he weighs in on that. Tell him after," Max suggested.

"I'll consider it. Truth is it may be the most pointless unwarranted case of all time but if there is a killer out there intent on taking him out and we let it slide…"

"Yeah, I know. It's the job no matter who or how justified," Max said, quoting Kane from a previous conversation.

"You do listen to me," he said, pride in his tone.

Max was glad they could still joke. "Yeah, yeah. I sent it all before you answered my call. How is Jade doing? This Occultus is a serious bad apple but she's been up against worse. I know she wanted to ease back in on her own but damn, couldn't it have been a simpler case?"

"No. Errie," Kane answered. "She's taking hits as expected but there's no one better."

"Yeah. Let me know if you need anything," Max said, wishing he could do more.

"I will, and thanks." Kane ended the call, Max knew, anxious to digest the findings he sent before dealing with Amy. And his next call, without doubt, would be to Jackson. Max was glad Kane had him to weigh in and give balance to his perspective.

Max sat in the silence of his empty office grateful the challenges of the past strengthened the bonds between them all. Even Amy drawing dangerously outside the lines didn't shake Kane the way it may have a year earlier. Yet something about the timing between her eliciting a criminal profile from one and the same and pushing for case closure on the attempted murder started to smell the second he dropped the call with Kane.

Unfortunately for Amy, after so many years analyzing monsters, Max was too familiar with the stench not to recognize the most marginal hints of it and knew it meant only one thing.

If left unchecked, it would wreak havoc.

THIRTY-THREE

J ade blasted the heater inside her Denali not appeased by the brewing warmth of the new day. Despite a vague memory of committing to a crack of dawn meeting with Drex and the team clarity of consciousness aimed for hours later when the intel from the body could be added to their collectively amassed evidence. And it allowed for both of them to recover a little from the ordeal of the previous night. She slept with visions of the dead woman telling her secrets interrupted by flashes of leaping over her corpse and bolting across loose gravel and unstable wet ground to snag Drex from the river. During a very hot morning shower, she fought the panic surging with urgency to locate Errie and the other victims. Seeing firsthand the gory aftermath of the Occultus removed any question about *what* he was, an accomplished abductor and a heartless murderer. With mounting gravity, they had to unearth *who* he was and she hoped Kane and her team's efforts would aid them in that endeavor.

Surprisingly Drex welcomed police collaboration, though he apparently made it clear it was to remain informative support from a distance. Before Kane left, they both reviewed all they knew to arm Jade with everything he gave Drex and more. Max was also weighing in and should've completed his review by the time she was finished at base camp. She breathed in deeply and gradually inched the heater off as she drove sensing them gaining ground on this criminal. It came at terrible cost as it always did and she hoped their efforts prevented additional losses. No guarantees.

The closer she came to the turn-off leading to base camp, the more focused her perspective on the case became. The missing piece she was most curious to see, though the new data Kane and Max committed to forwarding over would without question prove no less compelling, was the completed LiDAR scan. With the impossible challenges Mother Nature and technical issues presented it was all but amazing the team managed to finish it within the forty-eight-hour window they were given. Jade guessed the sheer intimidation of Drex influenced their determination and if it had, she was glad.

They knew the Occultus was hidden in the forest range of The Divide between their grids and they managed to stay invisible to him so far, but that was all about to change. This new piece would unmask the understory of its sheltering vegetation and expose its vulnerable places. If they could close in covertly, they may lower the risk of his escape and raise chances for victim retrieval.

Jade hoped for a way to keep John out of the equation and prayed his world sat out of reach as they peeled back layers of wilderness. Saving Errie and the other women was clearly first priority but she preferred not make John collateral damage. The thought was still swirling in her mind when she entered the tent, completely unprepared for what awaited her.

Coffee and sandwiches perched on a new table in the back left corner by the evidence board and Drex had brought in area heaters on either side of the computer screens pumping the tent with warmth. Jade would've laughed if not for the images that stole center stage. Wearing a cable-knit sweater, Drex had his rather large back to her, studying them. The room was devoid of the other agents.

A million questions circled Jade's brain but none of any intelligence made it to her lips. "What the hell?" Flew out without volition.

Drex spun to meet her astonished gaze. "I know, right?" he agreed. "This is what I downloaded from your partner and Dr. Maxwell. I sent the other agents out to patrol the grids this morning. They're sweeping the outer boundary and won't make it back for a bit. I thought it'd give you and me time to make sense of this. That shrink of yours must give a damn interesting psyche eval. Remind me to avoid the hell out of him."

"What am I looking at?" Jade asked, moving up to lean beside him on the edge of their draft table. "Are those cutouts of the victims?"

"Yep. And they added one potential victim to round us out at the suspected twelve. We're following up to confirm but it looks like a match so far," Drex said, not moving from his space next to her to take it all in.

"Is this how he sees them?" she asked, turning her attention from the board to Drex and giving him a quick once-over.

"Your doc thinks so. Not sure how they arrived at this but..." Drex met her stare. "How are you?"

"About as good as you," she said, turning back to the board and standing again to near it. Before her twelve outlines, black cutouts of the victims all in relatively the same pose, sat in a line from first to last taken. On the row beneath the women regained color, clouding what was remarkably visible when no features existed save for their shape. "They are identical."

"Without all the identifiers we as humans use to categorize individuals there's no mistaking it, add a single one and you lose the picture altogether," he said. "And they all appear—"

"Weak? Or at least vulnerable," she added. "Like the perfect women to be overpowered."

"Yes," he agreed and closed the distance to stand touching sides with her. "And the question left is who should be right here?" He tapped an open space he left in front of the first victim taken.

"They've been selected to mirror someone, girlfriend, wife,

mother, sister?" Jade pondered. "Well I didn't expect this, but it's good. It's a break in the motivation I don't think we would've seen if not for Max."

"Max?" Drex repeated, staring down at the evidence.

"Dr. Maxwell, he's Max to us," Jade explained. "I don't understand how he arrived at this. It's a methodology I've never seen employed before. You?"

"Nope. Working from scratch instead of using all the labels," Drex added. "Without family history, status, career path, ethnicity, religion, age, or detailed appearance, basically everything we normally rely on to connect a victim pool, the clarity of what the killer sees emerges."

"Well looking at this there's no question they are all linked in his eyes, but why did he take them? I mean, he could've killed them at the abduction sites. And I'm not sold on the death of the woman we discovered playing out to plan for him."

"How so? He certainly inflicted damage."

"Yes. Maybe too much damage. And there was no card."

"Card? Tarot card, like at the crime scenes?" Drex asked.

"Yes. He started all this relying on the symbolization of each victim represented by a ninth tarot card, different decks, but matching a depiction of that specific victim." Jade pointed to the victim headshots and the replica of the card found at their abduction sites attached at the lower right corner. "Errie's is the ballerina."

"Your friend," he said, studying the connections with a respect Jade appreciated.

"Most were isolated," she said. "And all were witness free so if murder is his end game why wait and go to the extreme difficulty of transporting them, housing, and hiding them here?"

"And," Drex added, transfixed. "Why here? How does this guy connect to The Divide? Being it's a forbidden forest, government restricted land, it's not like he would've trekked through it at any point. It's bugging me."

They sat in silence, side by side, mulling over the newfound perspective. When Drex's phone rang it startled them both. "The lab," he announced, staring at the caller ID. "Your team did excellent work here, Detective," he said before answering. "Drex here," he spoke into the phone. "Okay, can you run it down for me and did you type it against the information I sent?"

His voice though baritone became melodic background as Jade's brain assimilated the new information in combination with the evidence Kane brought on the perp's possible background in soft engineering and everything they knew from having boots on the ground. She couldn't see a full picture yet but she sensed it unfolding. Stepping back to grab a coffee from the table she noticed the computer screen set up to display the LiDAR mapping. She was interrupted before bending to inspect the first rendering.

"You were right," she heard Drex say. He was off the phone and grabbing coffee of his own. "Wasn't the nurse. Victim one. Lauren..." Drex approached the victim board set up when they first made camp.

"Hamilton," Jade said. "Lauren Hamilton from California."

"She was heavily into the drug scene. It took longer to identify her as a victim, let alone the first. There was a whole lot of noise around her abduction." He picked up a marker from the table and wrote above her picture.

First Identified. Discovered Deceased.

Jade shook her head, stomped over to a smaller evidence board isolated for building up the profile of the Occultus, and slammed one of the largest pins they had into the center of the area reserved for his picture. "We need to get back out there and find him." She slapped the space. "So I don't have to see you write that over another woman's head shot."

"We do but there's much more to review before you head out. I'll go over details with the agents when they arrived and won't keep you for that but you need to see this." Drex plucked a chair off the ground and carried it to sit in front of the LiDAR mapping screen, dropping it beside his. "Have a seat. This is next level."

Excited to see this particular part of their tech at work and equally anxious over what it would unveil, Jade shuffled her seat close for full inspection of the screen before he logged in. He chuckled and shifted his rather meaty shoulder aside as not to impede her view. "You've been waiting for this," he proclaimed, his voice lightened.

"Maybe a little," she joked.

"Okay so watch and be amazed." Drex ran the program first, revealing the three grids from far above the vast area, then removing vegetation to strip them back to ground or solid formations, and at last lowering to fly a virtual tour of the space washing over each in slow motion. It was an amazing search instrument. A game changer. "This is where you spotted the nurse, victim nine," Drex said as the camera flew down the river canyon between their respective grids.

"Wait, wait, there!" Jade hit the screen with her finger targeting an area. "Can you move in or expand—"

"Yeah. Here, let me zoom in and enlarge the cliff wall." With both of them glued to the image in such proximity no one entering would've caught a glimpse.

"There, right there," Jade erupted.

"The blackened area depicts a hole," Drex said. "We can't see below ground but we can identify openings just like that one. This is where she popped her head out?"

"Legs first, then she drew back in when I screamed across the canyon for her to stop, turned around, and stuck her head out," Jade said, glad he was taking her word at face value.

"Well, Detective, I'd say we have an entrance to investigate. A starting point at the very least and one we would've been hard pressed to locate without this," he admitted. "Check out the same location with vegetation." With a stroke of a key, the hole vanished behind rock formations and brush shielding it from above.

"Can we get much closer?" Jade asked, pointing to the upper region of the exterior surrounding the hole.

"Jesus, yeah. I see it," Drex said, zooming the lens in. "It looks like—"

"Mashed down brush. She crawled out of there. I don't have a clue how she could've reached the upper plateau without falling but our nurse escaped." Jade turned her attention to Drex. His face was so close, too close. She could smell his cologne and see behind black lashes the flecks of icy blue in his eyes staring right back. "You can't investigate the opening," she said, not breaking their stare.

"And why not?" he asked without blinking.

"You won't fit, send Zac," she said, turning and commandeering the keypad before he could stop her.

"What are you?" he asked.

"How many entrances are identified around this region?" she asked, zooming out to include the distance between where they discovered the body, the canyon dividing west and east grids, and past the section where the nurse made contact.

Drex reclaimed the computer, typed in a directive, and inadvertently expanded the terrain further than Jade wanted. Panic tightened her chest as she recognized the river crossing John brought her to, the space beyond it that they journeyed together, and the waterfall hiding...it couldn't be. But it was. Knowing what she was looking for Jade watched the LiDAR outline of a partial cabin. John's cabin, sitting on the outer southwestern edge of her grid. Stealing the computer back she zoomed in slightly, enough to remove his domain from their focus, and pointed to the body dump zone. John's was artfully concealed within the rock wall behind an active waterfall in such a way that no one ever suspect its existence but she wasn't taking any chances.

"There, that's where the Hamilton woman surfaced and where you were almost washed downstream and over a waterfall," Jade reminded. "So can we trace the river back from there closer to the nurse's location?"

"Okay, let's map out from the nurse and see how we can narrow this down." A grin escaped Drex and Jade couldn't help but smile back despite herself. "We're gaining ground on him."

"We are," she agreed. "Is this downloaded for us all?"

"No, but it will be before you make it back to your grid. I was actually waiting for this. To see if together we could narrow it to a vital focused position."

"I say we cut everything but the data within this region we've identified," she suggested.

With a few keystrokes, the LiDAR map dissolved the areas beyond including John's cabin. Though it disappeared from her vision Jade locked it into memory with one thought in mind. To reach him and used his combined knowledge of the area with her new high-tech map to find the Occultus and bring Errie home.

THIRTY-FOUR

This was easy relative to what she could be enduring. The mantra Errie repeated in her head moving from one rung to the next up the tunnel ladder as the tubular rock walls closed in tighter and the darkness blacker with each step higher. The rungs, cold and metal to the touch when she entered became dangerously slick with moisture and the previous damage to her ankle slowed her ascent. There was no break. No place to stop and rest save wrapping a worn arm through a rung awkwardly to lean against the damp rock for a breath. And breaking her rhythm risked developing a new one that may not be as steady or sound. One slip and …

She couldn't think like that. And was wise enough to avoid dwelling on opposite thoughts. Those ones where a hatch opened and Amy was waiting on the other side to lift her from the darkness and carry her home. Situations such as hers rarely ended so easily. Her brain found a middle ground being grateful she was not in a restricted captive state like the other women but that brought a deep sadness and regret. Errie knew there were other women. Her abductor, the monster, said as much when she was fighting the chloroform and he was slamming her body down in the back of a van.

She was the last.

She didn't want to think about how many waited between her and the first or how long he had them...worst still what he did to them. Amy worked homicide. Errie knew too much. Without consciously planning to, each rung she passed became a marker. One foot closer to saving the others. Her freedom meant theirs, she would make sure of it. The intention strengthened the grip of her hands on the wet metal and gave the placement of her feet an added certainty. Perhaps this was why she had escaped his table and fled when the others didn't have that option. It was hers to do so she would.

In her head for so long, careful and methodical to ensure safety, she was shocked when the bouncing light in her pack met a metal seal instead of more rungs. Pausing and securing herself to the wall, she leaned her head back to study the exit of her climb. A wave of terror seared through her. The hatch did in fact have a large lever securing its closure and the odds of it opening easily didn't appear likely. Evidently, even from ten rungs down, it was original to the mine, decades old. What were the chances of it not rusting permanently shut or being welded in that position from the outside once the mine closed? Casting these doubts aside, she resumed her climb to the top. Water ran freely down the rock wall.

"Thank Christ. I mean, thank you, Christ, for stopping it from soaking the ladder completely. If you could keep the water pinned to the rock, I'd be damn grateful," she said, her voice echoing back at her she realized her choice of words. "God damn. Fuck, I suck at praying but I was saying thank you. If you wouldn't mind opening this shitty hatch, I'd be forever grateful, please. I can't promise to clean up my mouth. Tried for years then said to hell with it."

Giving up on grace in recognition of her endless stream of profanity she tested her stance making sure both feet were secure, wrapped her arm tightly and uncomfortably around the second from the uppermost rung and heaved with her free hand on the lever. It popped the hatch open on her first try to reveal a space above but not without a jettison of water drenching Errie and everything below. Losing balance in the unexpected watershed, her left foot slipped free and chaos ensued while she struggled to clamor up through the opening. Grappling with loose rock and a pool of water to raise her upper body out of the hole, she splashed, twisted, clawed, and kicked until her legs made it through and she could land clear of the hole and risk of falling into the abyss she escaped.

Resting her head on an arm to rise off the pooled water but too exhausted to alter her collapsed position on the rock surface, she breathed and cried thinking it'd be okay to die right here. Out of her captor's reach and above rather than below. It took time, and she couldn't know how long, before she gained strength to shift up off the ground. Time became a useless determination when everything was cast in relative darkness for days. A lover of sun, she couldn't imagine how difficult it was for those he'd taken long before her and wondered if they saw any light since he shadowed them. The climb stole from her every ounce of energy she had. Even expecting her eyes to absorb a new surrounding or her mind to assess the new problem it may pose presented a challenge too great. With the last exertion she could manage she reached the hatch cover, flipped it closed, and secured its upper lever to a locked position. Knowing wherever she now laid it was far from the monster, she rolled, spent and cold, into a fetal position away from the water, pulled her pack off using it as a pillow and shivering fell asleep.

Drex sent out the focused LiDAR map in a group release so the agents in the field would have it the same time it downloaded to him and Jade. Zac suggested moving the border inside it to do a closer perimeter sweep before they came in and Drex agreed. Alone in the tent he was staring down the evidence and finally feeling there was a hope in hell of nailing this guy and saving lives, in no small part due to Detective Carmichael and her team. He understood the background file he had on her with new clarity. Her bravery caused problems, she drew outside the lines, and seeing her reasoning up close he decided he never really liked where they were set in the first place. Rare to meet someone as selfless as she was, most cops and feds would find it unnerving and it was.

She was.

Drex washed a hand over his tired eyes, taxed by studying maps and details on evidence boards for too long, remembering detective Kane's face at the helipad. Shadowed in fear, and not for the victims. Kane was terrified of losing Jade. He said nothing of the sort, may have been the calmest and coolest guy Drex witnessed in similar circumstances since returning home to the states from the last warzone. In another life, they would've been friends, but not this one. Drex recognized the cold undertone when Kane spoke. Like the low, almost inaudible, growl of a dog warding another off its turf. Drex heard it, understood it, even sympathized but there was something Kane didn't realize amid the chaos—Drex was the big dog, it was his territory, and he didn't scare.

The intel was solid though and for that he was grateful. Especially in light of the mounting demand for results. He knew Carmichael sensed it too. Whether desperation from the victims, their own expectations to deliver, or pressure from above, the timeline was inching into the red zone. Like the acknowledgment hit the ether and lit a fire under his superior's ass, FBI Director, Michael Washington's name magically appeared on the caller ID of his phone.

"Hey, boss," Drex said casually, knowing the call would be anything but. "How's everything back in civilization?"

"Not very fucking civil, I'll say that much. Where are you at with the case? I need a full update because you may be about to have a bomb dropped on it." Washington's tone said his anger was pointed at someone other than Drex but that seldom made a difference. The brewing shit storm would target Drex either way.

"Well of course 'cause it's the only thing that hasn't hit. I mean, storms, bears, I recently had my ass almost washed over a waterfall in white rapids but please bring it on," Drex said, not willing to bend to appease some bureaucratic bullshit, which he was certain caused Washington's panic.

"Waterfall? Are you serious? Well this just keeps getting better and better. Explain that and where we are on closing in?" Washington asked, his voice now carrying hints of concern intertwined with his frustration.

"Detective Carmichael and I trimmed the LiDAR map and have refocused to a refined search grid, identifying access points to the most viable hidden spaces potentially capable of accommodating multiple victims but covert investigations of each will take time. Oh, and the terrain is dangerous as shit, if I failed to mention that earlier," Drex replied, sparing no punches. "I had my knees knocked out by a tree floating downstream while carrying a corpse to shore and came as close to hyperthermia as is humanly possible bringing it back for forensics with Carmichael. Her too by the way, the hypothermia thing. The good news is our working relationship is gaining ground nicely, forged in fire so to speak."

"You really are an ass Drex, you know that?" Washington added.

"So I've been told," Drex said, getting comfortable in his chair awaiting the bad news. "What or who is the bomb?"

"Sam Harlow, the only damn news anchor in the country who had to have grown up a town over from Shadow Hook and happened to follow and report on the Redeemer case," Washington said without admiration.

"So this Sam, he's connecting dots and up in our business?" Drex asked.

"*She* definitely is. If she has it her way, your location will be smacked up behind her head on the six o'clock news in broadband from NY. I'm slapping threats down and dangling red herrings but I give us no more than two days before offers of an exclusive aren't enough. There are too many states affected and too many victims to keep her from altering the public."

"Have you tried telling her she will most definitely cost them all, and possibly law enforcement in the field, their lives if she doesn't shut the fuck up?" Drex could hear his heartbeat pounding in his ears. *Fucking media.*

"No. I haven't admitted a thing and I'm hoping to mislead long enough for you to bring them home before I have to."

"Well if push comes to shove, give her my number," Drex

offered, knowing any one-on-one with him would lead to unemployment for one or both of them.

"So, media ruination aside, you are locking in on this Occultus?" he asked, moderately calmer.

"Yeah. We know why the victims were chosen, we think we know how he was able to transport them undetected, but we are seeing with blinders on. He killed one but we think it may have been outside his end plan. I frankly don't give a damn what that is if we can shut him down first but spook this one and we'll have a mass grave on our hands not a cave system full of victims." As Drex explained, new ideas brewed. "The aspect driving me nuts currently is why he brought them here, why this place? I'm not from here and I don't get the appeal. There are countless abandoned sites across the seaboard. Will you put the best and brightest on it if I send relative data through?"

"Anything to help remove the monkey from our back," Washington said. "I'll get them on it and have results soon."

"Thanks. We need another piece of the puzzle to drop before he shreds mine. No surprise I hate the filthy little beasts." Drex ended the call, scanned the evidence, his eyes resting on the LiDAR map.

"Where are you hiding?" he said to the empty tent. His eyes bore into the space surrounding the area Jade witnessed the ninth victim emerge from. Tapping it with his finger, he circled it on a printed version, a format he preferred, folded it and shoved it in his pocket before throwing his pack on and heading back into the wild. Deciding, if this prep favored this uncharted forest so much, he would get well acquainted with his chosen empire, up close and personal knowing the clock was ticking and news waited for no man.

Worse things existed than being wet, cold, dirty, injured, and lost in a forest of predators and Errie tried not to think of those worse things peeling her bruised body off the floor of...she didn't remember where she was exactly in the mess of tunnels and then it flooded back, the ladder, the hatch, the water. Staring across the surface, she saw the pool of water that reformed from runoff over the closed and locked hatch to the ladder below.

Saw it because light, sunlight, was pouring in from above, not capable of exposing every recess but casting the ground recognizable. She woke with her back to the center of the room. Facing inward now she feared lifting her gaze to take in her surrounding. The last few times she woke it was to nothing pleasant. Forced to find her pack, her mouth dry and head pounding from lack of nutrition during constant exertion, she found the source of illumination. The same bore holes that existed on levels below fed light and air from the surface. Here they were simply filtering more closer to the top. Crawling over to peer up one to determine how close would wait until she gathered herself. Everything hurt, some areas competed louder than others for the attention of her pain receptors, her left ankle, hands, and shoulders stole first to third place. In the light, the gravity of her ordeal couldn't be minimized.

"What a fucking brutal mess," she said, rubbing the bruises coloring her arms and legs. "The only thing you're playing on stage is the elephant man and you could save on the costume budget." Tearing a small piece of cloth off the blanket turned sarong, she inched over to the pool of water, the rainwater was mountain clean. Starting at her face, she washed, rinsed, and repeated. Removing the dirt only made her injuries more evident but it felt better. Turning her face upward, she squinted tracing up the wall for where the runoff was coming from and locating it, stood with much effort and hobbled until underneath the crack in the upper wall soaking her long hair and rinsing the last three endless days out. Resembling a ravaged version of herself but at least recognizable, she carried her pack to the area most hospitable, drank half of the second last water bottle she had, and absorbed the space in the dim.

It wasn't like the spaces below. It appeared newer. The chisel marks were those of a modern-day concrete saw unlike the chipped and uneven markings left by earlier methods. Errie ran her hand across the stone, smooth. She walked the room from side to side judging it no more than ten feet by maybe eight or nine and whatever made it had been removed. There were no machines or tools inside unless …

In the far corner opposite her dry enclave an aged tarp was thrown in a heap next to a mound of rocks. Afraid to lift it for fear of what it hid, assuming the criminal she evaded was the same one who left it, she pulled out her flashlight to examine its outer edges. No signs of blood or carnage. As if worried someone was watching she backed up a few steps and inspected the room again sensing there may be more she missed on first assessment. The hatch remained locked so he couldn't get in…and she couldn't get out.

No exit. That's what didn't sink in at first glance. Was a door hidden behind it, another tunnel? With a compelling motivation, she moved in, clenched the dirty bottom edge of the tarp, shielded her face from the disruption of layers of filth, and yanked it off its crumpled folds. A swarm of dust engulfed her despite efforts to cover her eyes and mouth. In such a small, contained space there was nowhere for it to go. Swiping the air in front of her and forced to retreat back into her corner, she waited for it to clear and the ability to recognize detail again beyond the haze. Then she wished she hadn't.

Having neared the space where the heavy fabric had sat undisturbed, she stood, mouth open undeterred by the tacky dirt filtering inside it, eyes gaping at a methodically ordered array of more explosives than any one person, outside a demolition expert, should ever have reason to see this close up.

"Oh, you have got to be fucking kidding," she said, afraid to move but knowing she must. "So kidnapping us wasn't enough, you sick motherfucker. You plan to blow us all to kingdom come."

Tiptoeing in her makeshift worn moccasins suddenly grateful they had no heavy soles, she neared the stack, bending down to study it. Her flashlight's gleam looking specifically for wires. And after a few moments, still in awe, she found them. Attached to every bundle, and there were many, at the backside wires ran out in streams of five then combined eventually dropping through a smaller bore hole between the floor and wall.

"Fucking wonderful." She breathed the words.

The explosives were there, the connecting wires, so where was the detonator? She would've sliced through them all, hell chewed through them with her teeth if she knew a damn thing about explosives. She didn't and couldn't locate the trigger or...another way out? Standing, backing away from the avenue of mass of destruction, she forced her mind to find clarity. The tunnel ladder she came up was too small for the man she fought in her kitchen. Still semiconscious when he carried her out, the drop to the ground was a long way down and his shoulders were broad. His hands like catcher's mitts. No way. He had to have another path in to extend the original space that connected to the ladder from the rock for housing his unpleasant surprise and ushering in and arranging this pile of fiery hate. Errie's eyes drifted to the adjacent mound of rocks sitting right of the explosives.

"Okay so you set it up and buried the exit thinking none of us would ever make it this close to the surface alive through the ladder access. Bastard," she said, guessing removing the rock may lead to the surface but knowing she didn't have the days or weeks required.

There was no way out but back down the way she came unless she discovered a cement saw in the pile of boulders. Waiting it out wasn't a viable option. The taste of freedom from below made her a fiend for more. More than that, if she didn't make it to the surface and tell someone what the cops were truly up against the women below had no chance of survival and would never ...

The cops. Jade. *Oh dear God.* The thought stopped her breath.

If losing her fiancée wasn't bad enough now Amy could face having Errie and Jade taken from her, blown to literal smithereens. And she brought her into this, not that anyone could've stopped them. But, if she hadn't smeared the goofy rendering of The Divide, the one she teased Jade about during their last hiking trip, in the bastard's blood after she cut him and he smacked her to their kitchen tile, none of them would be out there in the forest closing in on a monster blind to the greater risk.

"You piece of shit." Errie's breath was hot and her voice sounded foreign. "I will get out of here but you...you won't if I have anything to say about it." She stomped back toward her pack and the farthest place from the dangerous cargo forgetting the stone under her feet, the water cascading from above, and how the combination of those elements reacted underfoot.

Slipping backward, with far more momentum than she realized she put into her stride, both feet flew out from under her launching her body, with a supersonic quality, airborne then impacting the wet stone ground with a massive splash sending waves quaking to every outer wall. If not for the buildup of water at that spot her head would be split open and gushing. As it was, she'd have a four-alarm headache and a damn sore ass to add to her long list of injuries. "Can't one fucking thing go right?" she cursed, slapping the pool of water returning in waves at her sides with her free hand while elevating the hand clenched tight around the flashlight. Submitting to her soaked and wounded position, she rubbed the back of her skull checking for damage and confirming, by the size of bump, a mild concussion at the very least. Her neck dispatched a web of pain in protest for having threatened to lift her head off the surface. She dropped it back deciding there was no need and it may stop the room from spinning. As her eyes focused and her hand holding the flashlight extended the beam dead ahead, she saw what her captor may have missed.

Directly overhead, sunk deeply into the rock and ancient support beams, a decrepit roof hatch left untried for decades waited to be opened. And Errie would be the one to do it, as soon as she could pry her battered body and pounding head off the floor. "Thanks," she whispered. "But next time you answer a prayer of mine could it come without the ass kicking?"

THIRTY-FIVE

S tating a lack of faith in technology and its reliability in the field, Jade requested a printed version of the LiDAR map targeting her quadrant of the focused area so she could secretly amend it. In the parking lot outside the tent she sat in her truck, grabbed a marker, and traced the section where John's cabin was before the details left her. The problem with the scan, the only one it would seem, was it didn't penetrate the rock surface of The Divide, leaving underground tunnels and caves hidden. Entrances to them were indicated as black spaces devoid of anything for the lasers to read. And the scan could map within the tunnels by flying its drone through any given one or sending in a robot mapping-dog. Drex was sure, and Jade agreed either option wouldn't be met favorably by the predator they pursued.

Jade had a better idea. One, regardless of the recent trust forming with Drex, she didn't feel the need to share.

If anyone knew the tunnel system of the caves in these parts it was John. Living in the region deliberate in his conviction to remain obscure he'd have more than one way to stay hidden. His firsthand knowledge tied to their updated map gave Jade the best chance to find Errie and not another broken victim's body.

Pulling into her camp, the absence of Kane hit. His presence while she recovered meant everything and more than that his dedication turned their home into a new homicide investigation pit with Jackson, Amy, Grey, and even Max breezing through a revolving door building the case in a way she couldn't from the field. Kane had leads to run down and he was hot on the trail of the transportation angle. All of it sounded reasonable and relevant when they dove into it at the crack of dawn. By the layout of evidence she woke to on the kitchen table of the Airstream he couldn't have slept more than a couple hours.

She asked about Amy before he pulled away and he sidestepped it gracefully guiding her focus back to the search. He was right. Jade didn't have the luxury of commiserating with or for Amy. Her job meant delivering Errie safely home to celebrate, it demanded the entirety of her brainpower.

Sitting at that same table now, restocking her pack, a sense of unease and excitement swirled in waves just below the surface. Not an unfamiliar sensation. It was one of many reasons she returned to homicide after…after the last case.

Staying on the force hadn't been her intention before she found herself in vengeful hands determined to end her life. It came later, when she was sleeping. That was how Kane preferred to describe her time in the coma, and her memories during it said he wasn't far off. More than sleeping or dreaming, she walked a path in a different world and saw everything she judged before from a new perspective. When she woke, he expected her to stay home and be done with homicide, pursue other directions. She set him up for that. But as soon as she was released and given the okay her new combat boots hit the ground running.

She was reinstated before Kane or Jackson. Oddly though her life came the closest to being snuffed out they carried injuries affecting their performance that held them back. Their respective disabilities served to transform Jackson into a cop who mastered a better shot with his nondominant hand than his go-to and Kane fought his way into the best physical shape of his life outside of organ damage that was still healing. Grey, overprotective given the cluster fuck the case ended on, pushed their reinstatement out until the docs confirmed them one hundred percent healed. Jade silently rejoiced.

She needed to walk alone for a bit.

Ducking under branches weighed by previous heavy rains, slipping on moss and broken tree limbs cast to the ground by high winds, and climbing over unstable rock, she thought, be careful what you wish for. Or be more detailed.

It wasn't long before she was tracing the path she became acquainted with at John's recommendation when they met, the one protecting her from hidden bear traps, sinkholes, and the quagmire root systems. Descending the ridgeline was almost pleasant in the calm of daylight and nice weather in comparison to her last venture this direction. Capitalizing on clear skies, she paused intermittently to survey the forest. The nurse, she believed, may be lost, disoriented, and fighting to survive somewhere inside it.

Noting game trails, matted surfaces, and telltale signs of movement, Jade watched for anything that said a larger human predator had traveled the restricted zone. Finding nothing she decided to walk the lower bank once she reached the river before making her way to John's cabin. With each footfall she welcomed the fresh forest air, the hints of new vegetation, and the peace of the uninhabited region to heal and calm her, more aware of why John chose to live out his days here.

Drex was approaching from the east and Zac from further south on the east side, pushing in they planned to converge on identified cave entrances nearest to the sighting of the nurse. Victim one's body drifted down river during torrential rains making it a poor indicator of where it came from or where the others were held. Using the LiDAR map they targeted three openings and would coordinate efforts before breaching the subterrain. Jade, being closer to the target by a solid hour of trekking had time to learn its secrets if John was willing to share them and happened to be home.

He truly was the least likely to expect or welcome visitors. She also hoped the cat was recently fed and feeling lazy, wary of the untamed house pet.

Following the river, diligent in where she stepped so as not to disturb any exit point in case the nurse or any other victim escaped by means of the river, her eyes washed the west bank and scoured the east. She stopped periodically using her binoculars to zoom in on areas of interest across the river. Nothing fostered results until she literally tripped over them.

Descending a shallow bank to near a site where a slight path appeared, her boots caught a web of rope. Dirty and obviously soaked by prior rain, it didn't belong there. No one was allowed to freely hike this sector well inside The Divide, so deep it lay outside their grids. Donning gloves, Jade traced the frazzled mess back to its source. Tethered to a nearby fallen log, the rope was used to secure entry into the river.

Entry made more difficult by a massive rainstorm?

Jade stood with the rope in her hands staring at the intricate knot fastening it to the bark. Someone had to be skilled to secure it in this way. Swiveling back to the river she sidestepped to the bank searching the distance around the rope's end, adrift in receding water. Kneeling, she brought the binoculars to her eyes and scanned the adjacent east bank looking for something that said she was perched at someone's crossing site. After three meticulous sweeps, she found it. Not one but two depression points. One showed rhythm of movement up the bank with deep possible footprint impressions and the other...the other was a singular sunken indentation like a heavy objected had been dropped onto the soft earth, perhaps made softer still by the rains.

"Oh Jesus," she said aloud, a wave of shock jolting her upright to view it again from a standing position. "A body."

Climbing the bank back to the log in haste, readying to bag the rope as evidence she leaned down low to undo the knot. The vantage point and bright sunlight free from days of overcast clouds gave her eyes a clear line of sight to a muddy area a couple feet away sheltered by tree limbs protecting unmistakable prints below. Cat prints, too small to be cougar.

"Oh John, what did you do?"

She was certain he drew her, with his illuminated cross, to

discover and claim Lauren's battered body, but she hadn't considered that he risked discovery, DNA transfer, or being caught transporting it to the location it came to rest at. "You moved her," she said, studying the surroundings as her mind formulated the picture before her. "Why? Why risk that? Unless…"

She dropped the rope and pulled her map out realizing she covered far more ground than she was consciously aware of and John's cabin wasn't far off. "That's it. You were giving her to me and keeping the feds from crossing the river."

Moving fast she untied the rope bagged it and placed it in her pack. She walked over the cat prints in the mud and toured the stretch on the bank scuffing potential impressions. John discovered Lauren here, it wasn't the kill site and the Occultus couldn't risk straying this far out with a victim or her corpse. The cover-up wasn't much but at least if Drex found the site, he wouldn't find anything of interest on this side.

Citing the map now anxious to make the cabin with time to question John first about the tunnels and then the body, she chose the fastest approach and picked up pace. If any evidence of a human predator existed in or outside her grid, she was fairly certain it didn't belong to the one she hunted. Leaving the cleaned site in her rearview, she was newly emboldened. The questions and persuasion she anticipated requiring to motivate John into compliance hit new levels all but guaranteeing her his help.

If the feds knew he tampered with a body amid a full-blown, multistate investigation his forest life would be obliterated, replaced by a confining box with bars for windows and no pets allowed. It wasn't the outcome Jade wanted and posed problems for her as he could expose her prior knowledge of his existence. It was becoming quickly complicated.

Her mind danced around possibilities right up until spotting the waterfall. His cabin, buried into the rock face behind it wasn't visible even close up. She remembered the treacherous stone hopscotch leading out of it and the only path accessible around the dangerous terrain right of the falls. She barely began the climb when a low growl and hiss froze her mid-step. *What had John called the cat?* She prayed as the word left her mouth she hadn't got it wrong. "Scythe, it's me Jade. It's okay, buddy. I'm not your enemy," she said softly, her voice blending into the melody of the waterfall. The cat sounded from behind her but she couldn't judge exactly where and turning suddenly didn't seem wise.

"Oh for Pete's sake. We have one nice visitor in twenty years and you want to scare her off?" John appeared in front of her and waved a hand dismissing the feline's near attack. "Didn't think I'd be seeing you again so soon. How did you find me?"

"Well if I'm allowed to come in for tea without being shredded in the process, I'll tell you. We have quite a lot to discuss." Reading his expression, though leery, she knew she was at least welcomed. Whether he'd answer all her questions was up for debate but she carried a trump card to negotiate with. Before she made it a step forward, her SAT phone rang. Drex and the team contacted using the walkie, so it meant one thing. Kane and her team were reaching out and they'd only do that if they had a solid lead.

"I'm sorry," she said, pulling the phone from her pocket and ensuring her location was off. "They won't see my exact position but I have to take this."

John backed up a step, nodding he understood but not appearing particularly happy about it.

"Hey," she spoke into the phone. Kane's voice was static filled at first and she couldn't make out what he was saying. "I'm not reading you clear."

"Back up," John instructed. "About ten feet."

Eyeing him with requisite suspicion, Jade backed away, the line clearing as she did. At the base of the climb, Kane's voice came in crystal clear.

"I think we have him," Kane said, *we got you bastard* enthusiasm coloring his tone. "I found out why he targeted the area, the soft engineering angle links up access to survey maps. I may be sitting on the company he worked for and I'm close to getting a name. I should have confirmation in an hour, maybe less. Hang in, girl."

"Terrific," she said. Hearing the excitement in his voice reminded her of earlier days. She wasn't really out there alone.

"Where are you and Drex at?" Kane asked.

Jade felt the power of John's stare. It was a gamble coming to him, and this was testing his patience. "We're trekking in from all sides to broach the subterrain and close in. He has three choppers on standby and alerted county to enforce road closures if needed. I'll lose comms once inside despite the repeater."

"Okay, I'll reach out to you both when I have it. Stay brilliant and I will see you on the other side of this."

His way of saying I love you and it fortified. The more knowledge arming her, the better the odds were for the desired outcome. Knowing *who* the Occultus was and having insight into his motivations was crucial but it wasn't tactile and didn't replace boots on the ground. Jade wanted hands on the creep or better yet cuffs and Errie, she needed to hold onto her and deliver her back to Amy. Dumping her phone back into her pocket, she looked up at John returning to the base of their climb.

"So that visit?" she said.

"I expected one, just didn't anticipate you'd have time for it given the high-stakes game you're closing out." John motioned to the first in the line of stones safely leading into his home and Scythe bounded up beside her, studying her but more out of curiosity than as a possible meal option.

"So you know why we're here?" she asked, allowing him to take her hand and steady her as she stepped. The information he held gained urgency.

"I think I have a pretty good idea. Hard not to given the media heat." John lifted aside a band of heavy greenery at the top of the climb to reveal the entrance.

Scythe pushed by Jade, almost toppling her over and down the rocky embankment. John snagged her arm, regaining her balance and held it, guiding her inside. Glancing into his eyes, Jade said, "I didn't think you'd keep up on current events."

He smiled, let her pass in front of him, and spoke from behind her. "Only when I have to."

THIRTY-SIX

Kane hung up and marched down the hall of the private hospital wishing it was not abuzz with activity, wishing he was armed and could make the corner, opening fire on Nickolas Leigh. No chance. The nurse who allowed him into the wing attempted to brag on the "tremendous rehabilitation strides" old Nick was making until she met his eyes. Kane was sure she was rethinking his admission after the doors shut behind him.

"Great, you're awake," Kane said, coming fast into the serial killer's cushy recovery room. His legs weighing heavy and boots landing hard. "I need a minute."

Leigh's doctor wore the same expression the learned nurse had, shock mixed with disapproval only, having far more authority, the doctor wouldn't be so easily sidestepped. Not willing to waste time Kane employed a different tactic.

"I'm sorry, Dr...." Kane said, waiting for a name.

"Dr. Emile Nnadi, Chief of Extended Recovery," the doc said, appearing anything but pleased.

Kane flashed his badge. "Doc, I'm afraid it's time for a coffee break. I'm involved in an active federal investigation and what's up for discussion is restricted information." Kane pushed by the doctor and pulled a chair close to Nickolas who said nothing but gave much away with his glare.

"I won't have my patient interrogated without proper—"

"Oh, you have this all wrong." Kane laughed. "Nickolas's insight is needed for a homicide investigation. Time is critical." On these last words Kane locked eyes with Leigh, difficult to do given the similarity of his and Jade's. In no other way did they appear related but in this one vibrant physical attribute it became undeniable.

"We won't need long, five minutes?" Nickolas suggested.

"Yes. Thank you, Doctor," Kane said while escorting the doctor out of the room and shutting the door behind him. Rushing back to Leigh's bedside, he moved so fast a wind followed him. "Who is he? Give me everything you have on him."

"And why should I do that?" Nickolas didn't sound smug just simply plying for more information.

"Jade is heading to Middle Earth to confront an Orc without comms or direct backup so you will help me defend her or—"

"Landslide Geo-surveillance Systems or LGS," Nickolas said without hesitation. "It's as far as I've got. Look for the engineer responsible for providing the government information relevant to the last time they expanded or altered the restricted zone. They paid him to survey and he rewrote The Divide's history. And wrote his target zone out of it. I'm sure it's how he knew he could house the victims without discovery."

Kane felt his eyes bulging out of his head. He hadn't expected Nickolas to be forthcoming or admit his involvement, let alone point down the path of the Occultus' destruction. "Would you care to tell me why you pushed to close the attempted murder case?"

"Amy told you, huh? It's a waste of time," he said nonchalantly. Kane hated how easy it all was for him. "Doesn't serve a purpose."

"And you trying to kill me, Jackson, and Jade, that had purpose?" Kane's heartbeat pounded in his ears, sending a tremor down his limbs.

"You were shooting at me. I shot back. And I didn't try to kill her. I tried to save her. I was going back to her when you shot me," he said, an undercurrent of venom in his tone.

Kane matched the venom and raised stakes. "And all the inno- cent women you murdered? Wait, no, not just murdered, but tortured and drained the fucking life out of? You haven't paid for what you did to them, their families."

"Not innocent. And you think I haven't paid? I've paid tenfold whatever punishment this world could hand down. You have no clue what you're saying."

Kane rushed him, stopping short of a cinching. "Whatever that sick fucker who fathered you may have done was not the fault of those women, not Jade's fault, and it didn't give you carte blanche freedom to pay your pain forward."

"Be careful Kane, you're talking about Jade's father too. And the blood coursing through our veins bonds us to a demon and it takes monumental extremes to break that connection. You could never understand. I am not a threat to Jade. In fact, I live to protect her." Nickolas delivered the words with such calm conviction anyone listening would have believed them gospel.

Anyone but Kane.

He wasn't about to be schooled by the lunatic they brought to justice. "You are fucking insane and this...this isn't over," Kane warned.

"No. It isn't but you have to go," Nickolas countered. "And, the Occultus has a sibling. If your name belongs to an only child, it's not your guy."

"How the hell do you figure?" As he said it, Kane saw the ribbon of truth in Nickolas's green eyes.

"He didn't do this for him. He did it for her. I would know. I—"

"Don't. Don't you fucking dare." Kane stared at the door and at the proximity of his hands to Nickolas's thick neck. He saw red, and the room filled with a static buzzing.

"Doc, perfect timing," Nickolas said, breaking the spell. "We just finished up. And detective, if you need help with any other aspect, please don't hesitate to reach out again."

Kane brushed by the doctor with enough momentum to leave him spinning in his wake unapologetically. He stomped rather than walked the hall and didn't realize he held his breath until gasping for air crossing the parking lot. Too intelligent to dismiss a single word out of the Redeemer's mouth, Kane knew his racing pulse was triggered by the truth within them. There was something deeper in whatever lingered between Nickolas and Jade after what happened. He held her so near death but didn't let go and she had done the same with his care following the shootout until his biological mother's family resumed authority over it.

It wasn't over. He could feel it and hated it, but he couldn't change it.

Driving the distance home, he threw the lights on and broke one hundred and twenty miles an hour on the highway. Using hands-free, he barked demands call after call until he cornered a manager of LGS by threat of criminal charges to forward him the contract employee list attached to government-requested surveys of The Divide dating back twenty years to present day. The printout was promised to be waiting for him when he slid into his driveway. And so was Amy.

Standing outside the house, she held her position until he shut the engine off, coming to lean on the hood of the car. Kane glanced out the windshield at her, then back to gathering his phone, keys, and notes from the passenger seat. He understood why she lingered here and didn't go inside. She assumed she may have lost the privilege.

Closing his door, he came to lean next to her, no direct eye contact. This would be difficult enough without that added pressure.

"You went to see him," she said, her head bowed and voice defeated.

"You went first," Kane replied, his keys and notes steady in his folded hands.

"I can't lose her," Amy said, her voice shook and Kane recognized the heartbreak causing it. "I didn't know what he was doing until I did and by then I didn't care if he cost me everything but I never wanted…"

Kane pushed off the car and came to stand in front of her. "He may have helped. We have a lead waiting inside because of him but there's no way he won't make us all pay for it."

"If he tries…if you or Jade, any of you. I'll finish what I started." With this, Amy locked eyes with him. Hers glistened in a coat of fresh pain awash because of Errie's abduction and presumed suffering, escalated by the admission of her betrayal opening their lives back up to the Redeemer's wrath to garner possible leads, and driven home by a truth Kane and Jackson suspected but didn't want to admit.

"It was you?" Kane asked without requiring confirmation. "Amy, why? You disabled his life-sustaining equipment after I shot him. Why would you throw everything away to end him?" He paced away from the car.

"Everything was already gone," she reasoned. "I walked operatory after operatory, you dying in one, Jackson losing use of his arm in another. He burned it all to the ground. I never saw Max or Grey devastated like that. And what he did to Jade…He won. I…I don't know. It was a second of rage and weakness and—"

"And that's all it took for him to own you and he does, make no mistake." Kane circled back to her kicking at the pavement. "I don't know how this ends, kid and I don't know how I can protect you from him."

"You can't and I wouldn't ask you to. It was my choice and I failed at it." Amy's voice gained a stronger vibration, one threatening to break her.

"Hey." Kane dumped his belongings on the hood, clasping her hands in his. "No. He doesn't get to win over any of us. Close the case. Tex and I will back you with Grey. We'll figure out his end game when Errie is back home safe. He's not going anywhere and either are you."

"Are you two done swooning over the damn sports car?" Jackson barked at them from the porch. "Can y'all get in the house? We have a case to solve and I'd like to introduce you to the Occultus by his given name before the media gets a hold of it."

"You've got him?" Kane grabbed Amy by the shoulders shoving her up the walkway. "Fan-fucking-tastic, Tex! We have to tell Jade before her comms go dark."

Entering the house, Kane read Jackson's face before he spoke.

"I tried, buddy. She's underground but Drex is calling back in." He checked the time. "Three minutes and we need our ducks in a row."

Amy came to life again when they gathered in front of the evidence. "Yeah. I think I have something for them too. Don't know what it'll mean in the field but..."

"Go," Kane encouraged, knowing they had zero time. "What is it?"

"The meaning of the tarot cards. I've done a major deep dive and the significance points to divine completion, like a spiritual transformation, and the reclaiming of one's power, authority through the fulfillment of elevation in the eyes of God. I don't know how this guy is doing it but he is using his victims to achieve trans-formation. For him or someone else? I don't know."

"I do," Kane said, casting a glance to Amy acknowledging the help he had getting to his revelation. "Our guy isn't doing this for himself. He's doing in honor of his sister. What we don't know is who stole his authority to begin with."

"Now how in the Sam hell did you figure it's for his sister before you even read the employee background?" Jackson blurted out, grabbing the paperwork he had been studying waiting for Kane to arrive and handing it over.

"Call it a lucky guess," Kane said, accepting the file and scan-ning with a fevered urgency. "Charles Silas, early twenties then, a kid really, contracted for an erosion study to guide a potential expansion of the restricted Divide Forest...Jesus, over a decade ago? This bastard has been planning this for ten plus years." Disbelief was shared by all three. "He grew up near the lost coast of Cali-fornia with his mother and sister until..."

"Yeah. There's the kicker," Jackson said. "His sister was diag-nosed with a rare form of childhood leukemia before she made it to her teens. Their mother failed to secure her a spot in the new drug trial that should've saved the girl, apparently fighting her own illness and drug dependency. No father in the picture. Don't think the sister made it. Nothing on her from six months after diagnosis."

"And now the captives pay for perceived sins from his child-hood?" Kane said.

"Maybe?" Tex shook his head. The insanity of criminality never failed to disappoint.

"This wouldn't happen today," Amy said, reading the information on the family history Kane passed over.

"Why not?" Tex asked.

"This illness is curable today." Amy glanced up as Kane's phone alerted to the incoming call from Drex.

All three checked in with each other, readying to download every detail to the head of the FBI team simultaneously praying the information would make it to Jade before she crossed paths under-ground with Silas, better known as the Occultus.

THIRTY-SEVEN

His head was fuzzy and clarity of thought was like speaking under water, diluted and distorted, he didn't register the alarm was a breach warning and not his sister's cryostasis failing. In a haze of panic, he seized the monitor allocated for reading her medical condition off his bedside table and met it with confusion when the nontoxic sugar trehalose cryoprotectants read optimal. Not until the alarm buzzed a second time did he realize what it was for. It had only sounded on one other occasion when a bear decided the south cave entrance a possible bedding down site. Out of bed, slippers on, he crossed the stone floor to a desk, flipped open a laptop, and activated a program to search through the six exterior access points for which one showed prohibited crossing. Only the three largest, those accommodating entry of an adult human, were fitted with camera surveillance and none of them triggered.

An upper hatch, one never used by him and surely too decrepit to be trusted had briefly alerted. Acknowledging the signal, it cleared from his screen and he waited for it to sound again. Searching its surrounding area and recognizing its close vicinity to the last collapse he could almost assume it compromised and faulty.

Still he made a mental note to check it when time allowed. It did present a risk. Not only by the potential breach, but because he would be forced above ground, out in the open to confirm its condition.

A place he swore not to go until the challenge was met and his sister set free. Oh to breathe clean fresh air again and no longer fear discovery.

He switched screens with new interests to scrutinize. Staring at the wire trace for the explosives planted throughout the mine he felt again the pangs of shame that no one would ever know the true history made below the broken rubble. The placement ensured the detonation would bury all evidence of those that gave their lives for the pursuit of glory and the method of achieving it. He couldn't lay bare the success of his venture. Doing so would also expose her to immeasurable scrutiny. After all the time robbed from her, she deserved the grace of anonymity while recovering.

Minutes passed and the alarm remained quiet. Awakened an hour prematurely, he considered returning to sleep but knew these twelve days of sacrifice stole slumber too easily. There was little point in fighting that fact. Instead he dressed, deciding to check again the challenge that lay mere hours away. For this next participant would prove quite the opposite to the last.

An athlete from Arizona, she would fight her way through, he was certain. But was he really? So much had transpired he hadn't had time to address the cards. At his table near a natural water runoff, he transformed into a mini indoor waterfall finding its fragrance and sound soothing, he lit a candle and shuffled the cards. Candlelight licked the rock wall and danced on the high ceiling as he readied to be shown a glimpse into the future.

The master who taught him to read tarot predicted his mother's downfall, her failure to protect him and his sister as children. She, a neighbor who watched them often when his mother was in the hospital, explained their security shouldn't have been her burden to bear alone. His father was the first to fail them, the first card to fall, abandoning his post as protector and provider when his mother's instability, her illness, and medication dependency became too much for him.

Miss Daisy predicted the coming night of horror and instructed him to hide his sister away. Even then she showed signs of frailty from the illness yet undetected. He heeded her warning and acted to protect Molly but forgot to hide himself. He never knew to fear doctors. In his experience they always acted to help his mother, sister, and him when illness threatened so he didn't understand when Miss Daisy said the man prescribing pills to his mother was dangerous. In his young mind he decided her mistaken. Then the man his mother bought her medication from followed her home one night and reclaimed what she owed him in pain, the second card to fall. Watching it play out as predicted he knew if he survived he would beg Miss Daisy to train him so his fate would never again be left to chance.

And here in the coldness of the cave he remembered the nights alone standing guard over his sister, left to wolves if they dared return. He got better at defending their place in the world. He grew older and stronger while Molly became weaker. When his mother failed to secure her a place in the medical trial that was sure to save her life, it was the last time he'd allowed anyone to fail them again. She dealt the third card, sealing his fate. By the time their mother drew her last breath, he guaranteed it'd benefit them. She didn't know he had taken out a life insurance policy forging her signature years earlier. The money transferred without question into an account he controlled and they vanished.

Flashes of that night when her medication provider invaded their home and the cruelty the wolf inflicted still haunted him, too young to understand any of it then it all made perfect sense now. Incoherent after swallowing her evening pills, his mother remained in a fog, not registering the shatter of broken glass downstairs or the heavy footsteps approaching. Shoving Molly into the crawl space where they often escaped to play and blocking it with a rocking chair to obscure it from view, she stayed safely stowed away. His mother, in the state his sister referred to as liquid, unconscious with movements resembling a Gumby doll and bones transformed to rubber, couldn't register fear or pain for that matter. So though he worked to inflict it, her lack of reaction failed to satisfy the wolf. He came searching for prey he could truly hurt and found him fleeing out a second-story window too slowly to avoid the merciless claws that dragged him back in.

Home was the very worst place to be when locked inside with a predator.

He couldn't understand rape, too young to know the word or its meaning, but he grasped that his mother had endured a terrible violation while he hid his sister. That the same fate could befall a boy was simply beyond his comprehension. He fought to maintain his silence so Molly would not risk her life coming to his rescue. What he endured stole from him his right of manhood and so much beyond it, but Molly never knew, no one did.

The women he selected were plagued by the same weakness that killed everything pure and good in his mother. He saw her in all of them, the drug addict from California, the pro athlete who broke the rules to win, the nurse accused of pocketing medications perhaps to ply them like the wolf, or the ballerina who melted down during a stage performance clearly out of her right mind and spewing defiance. He couldn't stop his mother's weakness but he could ensure theirs served a greater calling.

Splitting the deck and laying down the sequence, he didn't like what they revealed. Having no choice but acceptance he read each, committing them to memory. Leaving them open on the table he blew out the candle, turned on a lantern, opened his weapons safe and selected a fully loaded sidearm. He hadn't had to employ the use of one, not once during the acquisitions phase. But the cards said a lone wolf, one of equal power, would challenge him. He didn't know who would arrive to threaten all he built. He did know he was way better at fending off wolves than they could ever be at hunting him. A lifetime of surviving them crafted him into the alpha and the pack didn't scare him anymore. He learned the hard way how to lead them into the depths of hell and had become one with its darkness existing too long below the surface.

The weapon would complicate the approach he preferred to

take presenting the second woman to the challenge. She had been with him, complacent for the most part, for long enough to fear him but also recognize the secret to survival existed in acceptance of a stronger assailant's power over oneself. A truth he inherited so many years ago.

But acceptance to survive didn't make living worth the price. Walking the gauntlet's rope bridge he kneeled three-quarters of the distance across, removed a buck knife from his ankle holster, and sliced back and forth until a fraction of support was left on the final three rungs. He didn't see it as sabotage, more an exit strategy from a painful existence and a death designed to serve a higher purpose.

THIRTY-EIGHT

A few feet inside John's cabin, Jade paused and popped her ruggedized tablet out of her pack, comparing the digital version of the LiDAR map to the printed version she brought, ensuring Drex hadn't downloaded additional data. Seeing it was the same and studying it she recognized the brilliance of John's cabin's position within The Divide. The waterfall all but obscured it. She processed the new information from Kane and the team while stowing the computer away. It'd be all but useless to send or receive from as John erected a jammer around his site. Difficult to know how he managed it but she no longer worried about having her location identify it. He had already seen to it.

Watching her swing her closed pack back over her shoulder, John read her thoughts. "I became a master of water and solar energy after the first few years out here," he explained, guiding her ahead of him. "It can't guarantee invisibility but I've muddied the waters."

She chuckled, allowing the cat to lead her down the rock hall. As strange and unconventional as his existence was it held a calm presence Jade respected. She didn't mind being in the hidden space, in fact, kind of enjoyed it. Studying its walls and accommodations she viewed it as a marvel. From where she stood it resembled the coziest hunter's cabin imaginable, from beyond a secret forbidden hideaway. Perhaps it brought out her adventurous side or his presence there affording her a unique and exclusive glimpse meant more to her than it would most?

She offered her hand gently down to Scythe who brushed her leg, encircling her before locating a spot to flop across the heavy planks. He sniffed it while eyeing her intently. "Funny, I do the same thing," she said. The cat pushed his head up taller, reaching her hand permitting one brief contact before bounding to the far side of the open room to regard her from a distance.

John motioned to a seat at the table in the kitchen area. Pushed up near to the front window of the structure, it was bright and welcoming but standing in close proximity to the thick glass she realized why her vision beyond it had been blurred the last time she was there. Water. She was literally viewing the forest through a waterfall. The main pane was sealed completely but the upper coinciding windows had handles. He caught her studying his handiwork and joined her.

"They open," he said, reaching out and pulling a heavy lever. With a soft slide, the horizontal pane arced open and a rush of noise filled the space. Installed in such a way that the angle was tight at the bottom and wider at the top it prevented water spray but allowed the freshest drift of air inside. He adjusted it to leave the slightest opening and backed away.

"This place is impressive," she said, inspecting the glass, drifting a hand over it.

"It's hurricane glass, a combination of tempered and laminate and can withstand winds over three hundred and fifty miles an hour. Heavy as hell too," he said, leaving her to analyze it while he managed a kettle on the stove. "Tea?"

"Yes, please," she said, taking her seat at the table and noticing the workmanship of both. "You built all of this?"

"I did," he said, handing her a clay cup and sliding onto the seat across from her.

"That must've taken—"

"Years, yes. I'm grateful every day it's done. Too old to go through that again."

"Something tells me you could handle it if you had to," she said, leaning on the table. "John, why did you move her body?"

"I guess I shouldn't be surprised but I am. How did you know?" he asked.

Leaning down to the pack she set beside her chair, she opened it, removing the bagged rope, and pushed it across the table to him. "Found this by the river along with cat tracks in the mud." Jade smiled across at the cat sleeping stretched out on the floor in the next room. "Thought it wise to return it to you."

"I was so damn cold after carrying her out of the river and finding the right place to put her back in-felt awful about that, barely made it back. I forgot all about leaving the rope," he admitted. "I wanted to make sure you found her and not on the west side, our side of the river."

"I figured. That was a big gamble. If the feds caught you carrying a body…you could've been shot on sight," she warned.

"Wouldn't be the first time," he mumbled. "I'm sorry. I didn't know what else to do."

Jade studied his face for a beat, gulped her tea staring out at the waterfall, and then back to him. "I realized you were trying to help, even scuffed up all Scythe's tracks. I need your help again. If you're willing."

He drank his tea, the cup disappearing in his grasp. "What kind of help?"

"The tunnel system. I need to know what to expect underground." Jade pulled out her map, unfolding it and flattening it to the tabletop. "We have isolated a target zone for where this criminal may be holding the other victims but if we leave him a way out or alert him before we close in, we may lose him and all of them."

John studied the map and then her. "Why are you doing this?" he asked. "This is not the Great Smoky Mountains. This terrain is rugged, harsh, dangerous, and unforgiving. The feds I get. They have no choice given jurisdiction but you're a homicide detective, you said. So why is a cop like you out here risking her life on a federal case?"

"The killer has my friend." Jade said it, wondering why she wasn't more guarded. "There was a time not long ago I considered leaving law enforcement. Too much pain. But these victims, the women he has taken, deserve to be saved and I'm capable. And Errie, she's family to me, one of the best people I know and I promised my best friend, her fiancée, I'd bring her home."

To this John dropped his head and examined his cup. "Shouldn't make promises you can't keep," he said, his voice had an undercurrent she hadn't heard previously. Sadness? Before she could question him, he stood and retrieved papers from an open shelf. Returning, he laid them out beside her map. The paper smelled of age and was yellowed and made fragile by time. He studied her before sitting. "There's more though, isn't there?"

"I know how it feels to have the most important person in your life ripped away by the hands of a killer." She wasn't sure why she was telling him the truth; something in his eyes said he understood. "I won't stand by and let that happen to anyone I care about and do nothing."

"You can't," he whispered, then claimed his seat. "There's no way to block all the avenues for escape unless you throw a hundred officers down there, but it isn't a natural tunnel system you're up against. It's a mine." Jade's expression demanded more, and reading it, he shared his map. "This one has been abandoned for a good fifty years. How he stumbled onto it I don't know but it's the perfect location." John met her gaze. "Good for him, bad for you. There are natural tunnels here." He swept his hand over the central region on her LiDAR map. "Even cave systems that access the underground river but nothing like the mine. Though partially collapsed in places, when I toured it there are whole levels extending for miles still secure and no one would ever hear a sound beyond the cubic tons of rock overhead."

"This?" Jade pointed to a mass of snaking lines over a vast section of the forest that appeared to be drawn by a middle school drafting class. "This web is an accurate depiction of what's under us?" She couldn't believe it. If what he revealed was factual did the government that restricted the forest know?

"Yes. And more than that, it may be the only map of it left in existence."

"And how is that?" Jade asked.

"When I arrived here so many years ago, knowing what else was out here with me was essential for survival. I couldn't embark on building a place like this to live out my days to then find out years later the area was being annexed out to expand a major hiking trail or sold off to a recreational firm for a park lodge outfit, so I researched everything. And here is where it gets interesting. Deciding on this restricted zone." His hands indicated on one or both of the maps as he spoke and Jade's eyes followed. "I did it knowing the instability caused by past mining, weather events, and natural sink holes made it my own trap for anyone fool enough to cross the line."

Jade raised an eyebrow, receiving an apologetic shrug in return. She didn't interrupt; the information golden to her purpose.

"I considered making use of the mine. I investigated all the natural caves, took two years, but none of them presented without serious challenges. The mine had space to build a town but I couldn't get past the lack of daylight. I'm an outdoors guy and it's a subterranean world. After deciding against it I went back, four years or so later, to my information source—a data base for such things—to see if any smaller versions existed convenient for storage and..." John hesitated, then stood and grabbed the kettle and replenished their cups. "Point is, all the information was gone, wiped clean like it never existed."

"You're saying someone removed it?" Jade asked, realizing John wasn't just a reliable source of intel. The woodsman was a gold-mine. "Did you inquire with any authority as to why?"

John eyed her for a second from over the rim of his cup, then quit sipping and set it aside. "It wasn't really high on my agenda but yes, I asked. I did it carefully as so not to expose the truth. I kinda viewed it as a stroke of wild luck at the time. If no one knew about the mine it meant even less interest in my home base."

"And? What did you discover?" Jade sensed the urgency return to her gut, hitting hard and swirling the juices internally.

"It disappeared. Vanished digitally and in any available record I could find. Easy to do given anyone who would've worked the mine would be as buried as it was by then. So I brought my original in, made one extra copy, and locked it away here. If I ever needed to go underground, I had plenty of ways to move out undetected. And it's how I know where your victim most likely came from."

John switched papers bringing a new map to sit over the one of the mine. As his weathered hands smoothed the aged paper, Jade's mind overlapped Kane's information with John's. The Occultus had survey access, targeted the perfect underworld, and then erased it. John's next map had river and water source markings Jade recognized, the same currently being used on hiking trail maps. In three locations it appeared lakes existed though Jade hadn't tripped over one yet in her exploration.

"Are these ponds?" she asked. "I know all that runoff has to pool somewhere but I haven't seen one yet."

"They are but not above ground." John smiled as he answered and it hit her that he probably hadn't collaborated with another living soul in a very long time. "They exist deep below surface, lakes and tributaries from each link up to the main river. I think your victim came from the largest of them."

"You think she tried swimming out to escape him, and didn't make it?" she asked. The idea wasn't a bad one.

"Something like that. Where she ended up, she could only have originated from this one here," he said, finger circling the blue mass on the map. "The others wouldn't have the force or the space to accommodate a body passing from below to surface in the main river. It would've, she would've been stuck," he said confidently. "I swam them. This one accesses the main but you'd want to have an oxygen tank or lungs like a seal."

"Could she have made it? I mean was there a real chance?" Jade asked.

"Not without training and a whole lot of luck."

"So he killed her and she was washed out by the storm waters." Jade was speaking more to herself than him.

"Most likely," he agreed.

"This is vital information. Can I make some markings on my map? I want to have one clear reference going in." Jade glanced around in search of a pen and John caught on.

"There's one in the drawer," he said, motioning to a side table.

Jade leaped from her chair excited to organize relevant facts and head out fully armed. How she would explain stumbling on the perfect lair to the FBI, she'd tackle on the way in to catch a killer and save the victims. With that outcome she was certain the "what brought you to it" would fall into the "who cares" category for Drex. Throwing open the drawer harder than she intended, she disturbed the catnap, bringing the lighter contents of the drawer to the floor.

"I'm sorry." She apologized, returning items to their place, still in search of the promised pen. Finding it she picked up the last item strewn onto the floor, a plastic bag full of what appeared to be newspaper clippings. Without thought, she flipped it over and met the headlines. "I know this case," she said, staring at the articles. "I was too young to have even heard about it but my captain mentioned in many times to me. It was the one case he never solved on account of..."

She didn't hear John slip off his chair or cross the distance to where she kneeled on the hardwood cleaning up the mess she made. Nor did she see him, her eyes transfixed on the collection of articles related to the nun murders from some twenty years earlier. Three headlines and a few subtitles later she sensed him standing over her. The cat did too springing to its feet on guard a few lengths behind John. And when she turned her head up to meet his stare no words needed to be spoken.

John hadn't left the world because of mere tragedy and an inability to cope as she imagined. Like the suspect she hunted, he was a killer in hiding. This changed everything.

At a disadvantage, sitting awkwardly on his floor in the middle of The Divide Forest outside their search grid, with no one near for miles, all she could do was wonder if she'd be allowed a chance to make it out the door. Reading her eyes, he did exactly the opposite of what she expected. Backing away and signaling to the cat to disregard the energy of fear showering the room, he returned to his seat at the table and waited.

Jade stood, contemplated dashing for the exit, and then examined harder the man in front of her. "This is you," she said, nearing him and her pack.

"Many years ago," he said, but his voice didn't reflect the intention of a killer. She knew how they boasted, the defiance and justification coating the inflection in their voices. His held none.

"John, I'm a detective. You knew this before you helped us find the body," she said.

"I did. It's why I helped then, and why I'm helping you now." His eyes held hers. She read no betrayal in them, no pride.

"I'll ask this once and don't lie to me. Are you a killer like the one I'm hunting down?" She asked it, knowing to save Errie and the other women she needed his information and there was simply too much of it for her to retain sufficient details by memory alone. To save lives, she'd be forced to work with one killer to stop another and risk her career while putting her life and theirs in dangerous hands. All she had to go on in this moment was her instincts and a fleeting hope that the man who saved her from the pit she fell into was the same one seated across from her.

"No. I am not like him. You have nothing to fear from me," he said, and she believed him, not understanding why. "I want to help you, and I can only hope you'll allow me to remain undiscovered. In the end, that will be your decision to make. I will not leave here unless it's by death or handcuffs."

"I don't have the luxury of time. If I did, I'm not sure what I'd do with it. Lives hang in the balance. You help save them, and I'll consider that after you tell me the whole story. And I expect you to be here waiting when I'm done and the troops have cleared out," she said, her eyes narrowing in. Kane said they resembled green lasers cutting through the night when she did that, unavoidable.

"I will be here," he promised. "And I will tell you the whole story. You'll be the first and only one to hear it."

For twenty minutes the two worked revising her map to include the easiest points of access and lines of escape. John gave her warnings about collapsed sections and hidden ladders leading to the surface. She assumed one of those may have been how the nurse found her way to the cliff hole Jade spotted her at. He included river and lake depths so she knew what she could jump into and what had the potential to pull a person under never to resurface. Without all this there would've been no way to fight the Occultus and win. If John's dates were correct and her target had anything to do with wiping the mine off every available information source for such things, he had been planning this criminal action for over a decade. That kind of commitment was not to be underestimated.

Jade could only imagine what they were all about to crawl into. If it was anything as surprising as the day had proved to be thus far they were all in for a world of hurt.

"John, if I don't make it out," Jade spoke, pushing up from her chair while his focus locked onto her, "promise me you will try to find my friend and get her to safety. She's the prettiest ballerina you could ever imagine."

"My daughter was a ballerina." Jade read shock at his omission. He vocalized it without thinking. "I promise I will help if it comes to that, but you're really good. I mean one of the very best. You will find her and you will save their lives."

"How can you be so sure?" she asked, folding her precious map and swinging her backpack over her shoulder.

"You found me."

THIRTY-NINE

Drex would've preferred to be up against an idiot instead of a killer with an IQ over one hundred and forty. "The examiner noted on his employee record he wasn't even paying attention for a number of questions and still ranked well into the genius range, he never divulged that to our guy," he said, explaining his concerns to Captain Grey, who called after his detective's downloaded viable leads confirming the criminal's identity. "We're still pulling information but none of it will help our approach to the mine." Drex paused on the ridgeline to take the call before comms dropped.

"Have you confirmed it's a mine?" Grey asked, having been told agents were deep diving tracing family lineage and all connections to Charles Silas.

"Not on paper but it's most likely he followed family history underground," Drex said. "We'll know soon enough."

"I can send the other detectives in," Grey offered, his voice belied his fears remaining calm and steady.

"Appreciate it but, if anywhere, your people are needed outside the forest to prevent his escape if we force him out of The Divide. They've navigated the back roads. There are too many exit points from here for us to cover and locals know the lay of the land," Drex said. "By the time they got here, we'd be underground. There's no quick approach going in stealth."

"Hear you," Grey said. "We have hospital emergency staff on standby. What are the chances of him making it out of the woods? Or heading into town? I mean, giving his vast knowledge of the terrain—"

"And how long he's lived here...he could have a hundred avenues of escape that we're not privy to including river use and underground tunnel systems," Drex agreed. "Our best hope is to corner him below without jeopardizing the victims. Truth is we have no idea what we're walking into. Thanks for the medical standby I have a sinking feeling we'll need all the help we can get on the other side of this."

"Contact me when—"

"As soon as we resurface with this garbage I'll call," he promised. Having researched the relationship between Grey and Jade before meeting her he knew what she meant to Grey and understood it firsthand when she rescued him from the river. She was one of a kind and couldn't be replaced. It made him anxious. "I have eyes on the entrance. I'll be in touch soon."

Drex hung up with a tornado of emotion propelling him forward. Nowhere near his east side entrance, he cut the call in favor of time to process. Knowing *who* they were confronting, how long Charles Silas had to orchestrate his plan, and the dangers against them didn't present them with great odds. And all the back up in the world wouldn't improve them. One victim was dead. They'd locked on the location of the others, and there was no safe approach that involved a hundred boots ripping into treacherous lands alerting their target. Having broached enemy territory many times before, Drex knew the likelihood of it not being armed, moni- tored, or protected by some countermeasures was slim to none. He expected to meet with violent pushback and worried it might not be directed at him. His young rookie agent, Zac, or Jade could end up on the receiving end of nasty business and he'd be miles away down a different dark hole.

"This fucking sucks," he whispered it but caught the attention of a nearby grazing deer. She popped her head up and pounded the earth with hooves springing in the opposite direction, sensing a predator in the midst. "Sure make it look easy."

Drex's boots slipped in one step, were trapped in another by roots, and dropped inches lower than expected jarring his hip in the next forcing him to admit he loved nature but couldn't wait to be out of this particular section of it. Trekking in he reflected on the conversation with Kane. There was no arguing the validity of his research, findings in support of the case, or the motivation for it. And though not surprising, Drex knew Kane and Jade were partners outside the force as much as within it, it irritated. He cut Kane off abruptly shifting the narrative when it hinted at becoming personal. He could say, under pressure in the hunt, he didn't have time to hear Kane's concerns. He'd be lying. The more Kane inched closer into the case reconnecting with Jade the more Drex sensed an unwanted rival on his turf. Since holding her in the helicopter after she risked her life to save his, he hadn't viewed her the same way. He'd served in plenty of dangerous ops with countless fellow enforcers but couldn't recall meeting one as close in intention as her.

With walkie at the ready, he cleared his throat and refocused before opening comms. He'd downloaded relative intel sharing it with the team before the call with Grey. Despite this, the update came in after their descent on the mine and he couldn't be certain what was accessible to his team without confirmation. The repeater was providing extra reach but wouldn't guarantee reception after dropping underground. Zac, Taylor, and French were approaching position, acknowledged receipt of the new information, and would await instructions at their respective targets on arrival. Jade, closer to her entrance than the rest, had yet to check in.

"Carmichael, are you on comms?" Static filled the line, broken and crackling. He shook his head resisting the sign of what was to come. "Jade, you have ears?"

"I'm here, Drex," she said, her voice clear. "I lost comms for a second, but they've restored."

"Yeah, we've done work to boost the signal. Hoping it'll hold."

"I've dropped into the entrance. Will they read below the surface?"

"Depends how deep we descend. No way to be sure. Did you receive the latest intel?" he asked, wanting if nothing else to confirm that.

"I can't pull it up, can you summarize?" she asked, her voice echoing. She was in the tunnels.

"Our target's name is Charles Silas, he's had access to the mine for over a decade. The grandfather he was named after was a lead miner on the lost coast. He saw a string of success pulling gold out of Gold Bluffs Beach near Humboldt County. They reconnected after his mother's death and he paid for young Charles's engineering degree. His sister was diagnosed with a terminal illness in childhood, may have been the catalyst to his criminal disturbance. No read on her since shortly after their mother's death," Drex said, watching his entrance come into view. "Jade, he could have the place monitored and defended. He may already know you're there."

"I figured as much, so we go in fast and quiet," she said, undeterred. "What was her name?"

"The sister's name was Molly," Drex answered, but his tone questioned her focus.

"If I'm trapped down here with this deranged killer, I want something that will give him pause. Sometimes it's all we need."

"And the difference between survival and—"

"Yeah," she said it with her voice breaking between static interference. "Drex, I can hear water. What do we have for backup?"

"A full arsenal of choppers, road blockades, and check points as well as emergency medical standing at the ready," he said, knowing it wouldn't do a damn bit of good beneath the surface. "You said water, like the river?"

"Yes, or worse, maybe a waterfall? Good luck on your side, and even if I don't respond, send updates, it may come in sporadic, but I'll keep checking."

"I will, you too, and don't take unnecessary—" A screech of high-pitched interference forced Drex to rip the walkie from his ear.

"Fuck." He clipped it onto his belt and slid down a ridge of broken rubble into a shallow trench leading into the mine.

Trees grew interspersed with high bushes and webs of limbs on both sides. Stopping short of the level surface, he ducked behind a grouping to remain invisible to possible surveillance and brought up his day and night 7 Class binoculars off the top of his pack. Scanning his approach and the original mine entrance, he detected no obvious outer cameras but something more alarming.

Analyzing the half moon of protective cement and the iron door at its bottom left, all of it effectively concealed by natural plant growth, gave credence to the Occultus' commitment to his game. Whatever it was for him. What he couldn't anticipate was an FBI agent who survived war and broke into and out of bunkers to come knocking. Riffling through his pack, he pulled a package out. He requested access to explosives authorized for use within the forest to remove troublesome beaver dams before he arrived on site. Not exactly a match for the furry water inhabitant, the one he hunted fit the description of a varmint in desperate need of extraction far better.

A few quiet but difficult strides forward through the mess of vegetation and he kneeled before the door, inspected its seams locating its hinges, and packed key vulnerabilities with what he called "entry gum." Quieter than one would assume, the small explosion may go undetected if Silas was deep within the mine. The outcome would not, however, be the same if he was standing on the other side of the door. With Jade already trudging the tunnels he wasn't waiting for a welcome.

Retreating back into the blind he sent the signal for Zac to engage, reminded to put their comms on silent mode, and let them all know how he was getting in. Not allowing time for opinions on the matter, he blew the door, drew his weapon, and broke through the smoke with binoculars on into the lair of their killer.

The infrared mode gave him clarity the state of the cave would've robbed him of otherwise. Able to discern machinery and details of his surroundings, he spotted the entry into the deeper mine beyond this vast opening. A metal table, similar to an operating stretcher in med barracks, sat near the tunnel. He imagined it was used to transport the victims or…shutting the imagery down, he headed into the widest rock hallway hugging its side as he climbed lower.

His eyes cataloged every detail from the lanterns hanging every fifteen feet to electrical cords tracing along the ceiling stretching out before him. There were switches in a dugout the size of a London phone booth and a computer tablet on a rock shelf possibly used for monitoring as well as an open bottle of water. Drex tossed the bottle in his pack and opened the computer. The screen offered nothing of use, code protected. He scanned around him and headed back down the path knowing if a victim escaped the Occultus the utter blackness of the mine would render them all but blind.

Surveying the ground when its texture altered underfoot, he noticed straw or hay scattered as if fallen off a bale during transport. *So he started a farm or trained donkeys to tour the depths.* The ridiculous thought spun through serving to remind him the guy remained hidden and in control of the abandoned mine for long enough to do both. Light threw off his vision and he pushed the binocular up in time to see a roof mounted camera pointed oddly away from his approach and in the direction of a large wooden door. An open tunnel branched off heading left of it. Closing the distance Drex located the latch to open it and the bolt extending into the rock wall locking it from the outside. Reaching up he tipped the camera limiting its view to ceiling height. Sliding the bolt free, he dropped the binoculars down and braced knowing the one who locked it would come calling the second he pushed the heavy door open. What met him on the other side was nothing he expected, far better in that the Occultus was currently nowhere to be found and far worse in the state of women corralled in the stalls before him.

Leading injured and traumatized victims to safety through the rugged forest posed considerable dangers and he prepared for such adversity. Carrying each out, one by one knowing there were possibly eleven, before being discovered? Now that complicated the hell out of things.

With no time to debate options he remembered the metal

stretcher at the entrance and ran the tunnel to retrieve it. He couldn't save them all and odds were he'd be killed trying, but with each footfall he vowed the bastard wasn't keeping them all and with some well-earned good fortune he wouldn't get his hands back on a single one.

"Zac, pick up," Drex barked into the walkie pressed close to his mouth without slowing. "I've located the victims and Silas is not, I repeat, not at my location. I need you to create a diversion at your end to draw him your way. I have to carry the women out of the mine. They are all drugged unconscious. Do you read?"

"I read," Zac responded, his tone intense. "Distraction to draw him my way. You've got it. I'll come up with something."

"Make it something that doesn't get you killed," Drex said, reaching the stretcher. "Call for French to send medivac to base camp and have boots on the ground to deploy to my pinned location at the ready but not until I say so. If I don't get them all out before he notices we may lose them."

"I understand. I'll have it done," Zac promised. "Good luck, sir."

Drex ran, pushing the table ahead of him back to the stalls glad it was equipped with wheels designed to navigate the mine floors and wondering how many victims he could push uphill at one time while fighting not to dwell on the violence he just asked his youngest agent to invite his way.

FORTY

John watched Jade disappear into the forest seeming to respect her instruction he was not to follow her and fully intent on defying it. The crash course he delivered on the mine and its intersecting tunnels with the natural ones snaking deep beneath The Divide and corresponding waterways didn't scratch the surface on the world below the forest floor or the dangers therein. The criminal she sought had years to memorize and customize that domain to suit his needs. She was entering it, figuratively and literally, in the dark.

He knew what he risked and considered for a breath why he hadn't handed her a pen. Why did he direct her to the very drawer that held his darkest secrets? Maybe it had been too long, and he didn't want to live another year without telling the truth of why he left civilization and what really happened before he did. He'd square away with the danger he placed himself in after he did what was necessary to help the detective and the many victims held beneath the surface. What Detective Carmichael didn't suspect was the vendetta brewing against the man he held responsible for the whole mess of it, his discovery by the detective, the destroyed lives of the victims and those who loved them, and the converging of law enforcement on his woods.

Disconnected from society for so long he'd all but forgotten the sensation. But the criminal who chose the wrong forest for his dark deeds reignited a fire, dormant for decades, it resurfaced with vengeance bringing to light all the bad memories of a brutal past responsible for triggering it before.

John was angry and the last time that happened, people died.

Cutting a parallel path to the detective's chosen one, John hung back using forest coverage as camouflage. This was his world and he knew it so well. He left the cabin doing something he hadn't done for many years. He locked the inner cabin down preventing all access in or out and he did it with his feline friend inside. There'd be no following him today. Thinking of that turn of key, he touched his breast pocket, ensuring the two keys he carried remained safely stowed. One gained entry into the cabin, the other to the detective's Airstream.

After rescuing her from the pit when they met, a key ring fell from her pack. He inspected it noting no ATV key and finding a duplicate key for the trailer she'd parked on the outskirts of the western ridge. Removing one, he hoped she wouldn't notice. The second key sat three away from the first on the ring behind larger keys. He replaced it with an old one he had belonging to the trailer he first used during the building stage of the cabin. The door it opened long since crushed in a distant junkyard. He kept hers not to harm her or infringe on her personal space but for emergencies. In his experience, they happened frequently to those trekking beyond the warded forest boundaries. Safety vanished crossing onto the forbidden land and at no time more than today.

Unsure of how he could provide aid or the consequence he'd face for doing it, he found mild comfort in the fact that currently, no other law enforcement shared their west side. His plan was to hang back, come in behind Jade, and assist her exit if needed. That all went to hell when a terror-stricken scream broke the silence of the forest and sent its creatures stampeding from the sound. As they fled out, John ran in.

Breaking his protocol of covert advance, he charged forward with full abandon. The shriek echoed off the canyon walls projecting out from the bank left of the entrance to the mine. It didn't originate from inside. John watched Jade disappear within the rock opening several minutes earlier. Even at a slow pace, she'd be deep enough not to have heard the woman cry out. And if she was inside, who was outside screaming?

John couldn't pinpoint the sound while storming through the forest. When it erupted a second time he halted to listen. Certain it originated from the canyon, he dove past the course to the mine entrance breeching the left bank as a third and final holler stalled. Hitting a mix of shale rock and loose sediment, he half ran and half slid across the bank some thirty feet up from where it leveled off and twenty or so from its upper ridgeline. His eyes trained on the estimated location as his mind searched the map of the tunnel system. Remembering a hatch access occupying the region, he panned back and forth above, unable to lock on anything useful. Dropping his field slightly lower, he didn't catch view of the hatch but instead a vertical depression in the canyon side. It wasn't much, a path where erosion sent a section careening to the riverbed or...

A body fell.

Several dangerous feet across the steep incline, a girl's body lay snagged between loose rubble and a cluster of trees growing out of the canyon wall. To reach her, he risked losing stability and tumbling to his death. Worse, if he made it to her, he'd have to carry her back without toppling over and having her share that fate. Dropping his pack behind a boulder so it didn't slide away, he tore his rope from it, secured it to the nearest tree and then his waist, and prayed it long enough to provide a measure of safety for them both.

Digging in his right foot to counterbalance his weight, he moved as quickly as possible to the girl. Each step closer, his eyes examined her for signs of movement or consciousness. Part of him hoped she would not wake. Doing so may cause sudden panic and send her tumbling. Coming near, the possibility that she may not be alive and he could be risking his life for a body recovery came and went by force. This was someone's daughter, someone's friend. Two steps from her, he watched her tiny chest rise and fall. Alive.

Planting both boots wedged at the upper edge of the tree trunk closest, he tugged on his line checking its strength before inspecting the small frame at his feet. The girl's body was badly damaged. Bruised and battered, but he saw nothing to suggest neck or spinal injury. It appeared as if she'd fallen and rolled the length of the incline, meeting the tree grouping with a thud capable of knocking her unconscious but not deadly. Carefully, he plucked the girl off the ground and secured her over his left shoulder, keeping the added weight on the uphill side. With each step back to safety, he tugged on his line, wrapping it around his arm as he moved.

Passing the halfway point, he was thanking God there was no wind, knowing the updrafts throughout the canyon could be violent and he was already treading on shaky ground. But he spoke too soon as the girl woke fighting for her life and mistaking him for her captor.

"I'm not him! I'm not him!" John shouted but couldn't be heard over her protests. "Stop or you'll send us both to our death! Look down. Look down!"

The girl stopped yelling and grasped onto him with a death grip throwing out his balance. His foot lost grip, and they started to slide. Using the line, he forced stability back and froze, both of them instantly silent and still facing the riverbed below.

"Detective Carmichael sent me to save you," John said, hoping to calm the girl at the mention of law enforcement. "The criminal is still in the area and we are not anywhere close to safety." Her breathing relaxed from intense panting to slower deeper breaths. "I will get you out of here, but I need you to cooperate or neither of us will survive this. Do you understand?"

"I...I don't feel..." Her body compressed, limp over his shoulder again. Fighting injury and exhaustion, the sudden terror on waking drained her ability to remain conscious. Crossing the last treacherous steps to level ground, John didn't view it as the worst outcome. Her compliance allowed him to travel faster. And there was only one place he could go.

Unable and unwilling to send up a flare to the feds on the east side, he headed back along the game trail to Jade's Airstream. The only place, he thought, that could be reached by her partners and provide a quick escape for him back into the woods. If he got lucky, he might effectively sell the cops on the girl stumbling to the trailer unaided. Delusional, he doubted she'd be seen as a reliable witness.

The mine entrance Jade entered well behind him, he all but ran the distance to her camp with the girl unaware. It wasn't until he unlocked the trailer, set her on the closest flat surface, a sofa behind a table, making it appear she collapsed of her own freewill inside, that he registered the severity of her injuries. And if he addressed her wounds it'd amount to a temporary fix and there'd be no denying his involvement. She required immediate medical attention.

He found the fridge stocked with electrolyte and carbohydrate-rich drinks. Grabbing one with a gloved hand, he snapped the lid off, placed pillows behind the girl's head to elevate her, threw a blanket over her body, and poured the slightest amount of the replenishing liquid into her lips. She licked the moisture. He repeated the process three times before setting the bottle within her reach. A med kit sat on the counter. He moved it beside the drink, popped it open, removed Tylenol and set three pills on the table. He gave the girl more fluid, then left her briefly to search his surroundings.

Well versed in the wild, Jade positioned a CB in clear view on a shelf in the kitchen by the window. Still used by truckers, hunters and travelers, he pulled it forward, dialed it to Channel 9—reserved for emergencies—and prayed for the girl's sake someone was listening.

Opening and closing the talk button he produced a series of three short clicks followed by three long and three more short. His SOS was repeated five times before the girl began to regain consciousness. Abandoning the CB, he searched further into the sleeping quarters and located a long-range radio. The detective definitely came more prepared than most to his neck of the woods. Setting it to 168.55 MHz, he returned to the girl, placing it into her hand. One he knew she'd clenched him with and still had use of.

With this final act, he gave her the best odds of survival and was turning to leave when she spoke.

Not fully conscious but with fight left in her, he listened as her rambling gained coherence. Recognizing words, they made no sense with missing parts and no way to string them together. Placing the radio in her hand, he said, "Call for help."

Her eyes lifted for a few seconds. "Thank you for help…"

"Yes," he encouraged. "Press this and ask for help. I'm needed as backup for the detective."

At the mention of Jade, the girl launched up, her eyes springing open but not making contact. "Explosives," she breathed the word. "Rigged to blow. Save them."

The flush washing over John's face descended his spine landing like grenades at his feet. He spun out of the trailer, cleared the three steps to the ground, and slammed the door midstride back into the forest at a full speed run.

The criminal bastard trespassing on his land didn't just intend to use it to violate the victims he collected in secrecy; he planned to blow it to smithereens with them all inside it.

Including Detective Carmichael.

FORTY-ONE

Jade knew she was closing in on the natural underground lake and canal, the sound of its rushing water echoing all around her in the darkness of the tunnel. Knowing light would alert the Occultus to her approach, endangering the victims, she reduced her flashlight to a penlight, seeing enough not to slip or break an ankle on fallen rocks in her path but limiting any glimpse at the depths ahead. Lacking both field of view and sound, everything audible drowned out by the raging river, she crouched down, sliding along the inner wall avoiding the tunnel's center. The scent of the forest she'd become accustomed to transformed here, replaced by something oddly cleaner, quenching her lungs, oxygen rich. Trekking in thirteen minutes ago, she was deep enough for the opposite to be true. The Occultus devised a way to pump oxygen below. The thought confirmed everything they suspected.

He existed in this lower realm far too long, tailoring it to meet his every need.

Contemplating other possible ways he altered the space she followed a curve as dim light broke the blackness ahead. Her feet no longer brushed rubble, the surface below them becoming smooth. Reflecting light, it almost appeared polished. Pausing at a break between the tunnel she traversed and a larger opening, she vetted the expanse. A circular space fed by two other tunnels on the opposite side, there was no place to hide once she entered it. It dropped down a level beyond the light to her left. Listening intently, she registered this lower sector to be where the water noise was loudest. This passage, built into a livable space functioning with electricity, water, and clean air, was undoubtedly chosen by the criminal specifically for its access to the underground river.

Brilliant really, and terrifying.

Jade searched the domed zone from floor to etched roofline. Her eyes traced cables overhead coming from a tunnel right of hers, added to by others meeting them at the next tunnel and grouping to drop into a large room directly across from her position but at a natural elevation. Lit, the cables were not its only metal contents. She glimpsed a flat metal surface beyond the opening but couldn't discern it in detail enough to identify what she was seeing. With everything right of her illuminated she would drop lower shifting left into the darkness and climb upward from that side to remain hidden for as long as possible.

Trouble was expecting it to be solid ground. Focused on the modified inhabited space, with no way to know if the predator was moving inside it, she skirted the tunnel opening, descending onto broken rock, and almost off its edge before realizing she was on a natural shelf hovering over a violent drop to the rushing water below.

Panic set in while fighting to stop the momentum on the slick surface of the moss-covered stone from plummeting her off its edge. Every foot placement was met with a downhill trajectory greasier than the last. Requiring both hands free to grasp onto metal stakes driven deep into the rock providing the start of a constructed railing, her penlight flew free bouncing across the rocks and over the ledge. With no light to guide her, she couldn't return safely to level ground. Unable to trust footholds without confirming visually, darkness became the enemy. Wrapping her arm around one of the stakes, she accessed her Tac light knowing the second it turned on she'd become a beacon and an easy target for the Occultus. Struggling free of her jacket, she wrapped it over the light, dimming its reach, flicked it on, and muffled her own gasp.

Like a mini subterranean Grand Canyon, she sat compromised on the slippery edge of an open hole in the earth where a river raged far below in the vast blackness and the shiny cavern wall opposite her was a football field or two across. Never having seen anything like it, all she knew was she wanted to get the hell away from it and fast. The modified Tac light guided her up to the inside of the railing. She stumbled and slid, then ran it angling for level ground and the edge of the left side of the dome, concealed by shadow. If her adversary was present and caught sight of her it'd be over before she could ever pull her weapon.

Jade had been inside all of fifteen minutes and almost lost her life without having confronted the killer. The odds stacked against a successful outcome hit hard but her determination to find Errie was far stronger. Steadying her breathing, she reassessed the area, turning back to the location of the drop zone. Her eyes locked on a level previously hidden from her below the ledge she traversed. Seconds passed as her mind processed what was laid out before her. The criminal had erected a literal punishment course of challenges, a hell of his own making here in Middle Earth.

"This is how Lauren died," Jade whispered. "You bastard. You tortured her and she fell to her death." Shock stalled her breath, but passion reignited it. "You don't get to do it again."

Scouring the livable side, she watched for movement, sound being all but collapsed on beneath the heavy water. Seeing none she was about to begin searching from left to right for Errie, the other women, and the man she'd hold responsible for the violation of them. She didn't make it two steps when light ahead flickered, burst on, and then extinguished.

Cast back into darkness, Jade heard him coming, heavy, angry steps, and froze inside an alcove between the outcrop bridge and a hallway leading to what appeared to be a section of rooms. Standing inside a two-by-two-foot carved-out space with no coverage, she knew there'd be no hiding from him, no element of surprise, if the lights burst back on. All she could do was silently switch from holding the Tac light to her weapon and pray he didn't sense her when he breezed by.

Surfacing from the second room beyond where she stood, he'd been within moments of her the whole time and hadn't a clue. He marched past so swiftly she barely registered their close proximity when his shadow disappeared from view. One thing was certain. He cast an enormous shadow. If she didn't get the jump on him …

Errie, their ballerina, was so much smaller than Jade. She plucked her off the ground once to throw her into their pool. Like a child, she was so light. Her and anyone her stature would have zero chance defeating a man this size. Jade's blood boiled as her brain set to work on a way to incapacitate the beast. And evidence declared her description fit. The one advantage she had was that he was completely distracted by the power interference and indicated no awareness of her presence.

Not sure if the outage was a blessing or a curse, Jade crept down the hall after him praying he didn't solve the electrical problem before her plan was in place. She slinked to the edge of what appeared, in the dim light of a singular candle on a wall holder in one corner, to be a vast bedroom when the shadow of a second figure drifted over her. Spinning to greet it, she glimpsed a smaller form dash from the far side of the shared hall to the room where the electrical cords intersected. Whomever the shadow belonged to didn't acknowledge seeing her. She watched it vanish beyond the threshold and then, like a wolf entering the wrong den, stealthily back out. Silent in its retreat, Jade's eyes followed it.

Unfortunately hers weren't the only ones tracking its movements.

FORTY-TWO

In all his years of rescue ops and the countless crazy situations he'd fought his way out of or been dropped into Drex labeled this the absolute worst. The women, anesthetized and compromised, shared one indisputable, glaring trait. They were all tiny, childlike in size. Compared to Drex's rather large six foot three frame they appeared like fragile broken china dolls. Being forced to pile them two at a time onto a gurney in a race to save their lives made his stomach somersault in ways he knew he wouldn't soon forget.

Starting at the furthest end to work his way back out, he jammed the far exit door shut. Providing no protection against bullets, if the Occultus showed up unaware and unarmed, it would buy him precious minutes. The interior quarters, lit by overhead lights, held numbered rooms. The one labeled twelve was unoccupied and showed no signs of ever having been. Drex made a mental note and moved to the eleventh. Scanning quickly for injury, he wrapped the first woman in the bedding blanket and placed her sleeping form on the metal tray. He did the same with the occupant of the tenth stall. Ripping a repel belt off his pack, he secured them tightly to the table hoping neither woke, imagining the added terror that reality would cause. And, like a linebacker in the final countdown, he flew back through the tunnel he came down, pushing the dead weight uphill ahead of him leaving his sizable back an open target to the criminal who might interrupt his efforts.

Sweat dripped from his hairline snaking down his neck by the time he reached the entrance and level ground. Not pausing until the gurney met the opening lip where he blew the door off the entrance, he lifted the stretcher over the rubble, limbs aching against the strain, and propelled the women to a blind behind a grouping of trees protected from view and the elements. The sunlight beyond the darkness of the underground pierced his eyes forcing him to squint against its intrusion. Night would fall over the forest soon. For now, he was grateful he and his team weren't fighting that as well. He snapped the belt off and laid the women gently on the ground close together. Studying their faces, he confirmed Jade's friend was neither of them. Knowing the wild held its own predators and the injured, sleeping women were easy prey he wished he could do more. Shoving branches around their bodies, he built a makeshift deterrent, collected his belt, and ran back to repeat the process for the next two women.

Five trips. To secure and unload victims without their captor catching up with him. If he didn't, the outcome was clear, someone would die today. It required both hands free to steady the stretcher and navigate the tunnel and terrain to deliver them above ground. And, the considerable noise of traveling over stone with heavy weight echoed out in all directions of his efforts.

Covering the expanse between the women and the entrance, he pulled his walkie free calling out while comms were dependable. "Zac, two victims out, seven to go. Do you read?" The line filled with interference and Drex fought the urge to smash the expensive device on the nearest boulder. "Zac? Do you have visual on him?" He hadn't heard Zac signal back since receiving his orders to create a distraction. Jade had maintained radio silence too leaving Drex with nothing but a sliver of hope and a vast shitty imagination. Crossing back into darkness he fastened the walkie again on his belt, dropped his glasses, and blinked forcing his eyes to adjust faster to the change.

Halfway back to the women, the dim light cast by two wall-mounted lanterns remained but the overhead light that existed in the holding chambers sizzled and extinguished. "Fucking figures," he said under heavy breath. The urgency inside his chest clamped his muscles around his heart and lungs forcing him to gulp rather than breathe air. It felt heavy, weighing down worse with every movement. With eight and seven strapped in, he flicked on his head-lamp to avoid crashing into the sidewalls on his way back. The nurse Jade identified escaping into the forest would've occupied number nine. She remained unaccounted for.

Reaching the security of the blind and setting the fourth woman on the ground with the others, his lungs gasped for air. His shirt was soaked clean through and there wasn't a muscle on him not burning in protest. Swiveling back to face where he exited it hit him that he may not actually save them all. After fighting for endless days to locate them that reality wasn't acceptable but he was only one man. The thought landed as the first woman he placed on the ground moaned. The sound was sad, defiled, the final protest of a wounded animal blended with a mournful plea.

And it was fuel.

Spinning away from the trees he raced the length and flew into the darkness with defiant energy. The power outage could be Zac. If the victim's survival and the regulation of his underground lair depended on electricity it may warrant the criminal's attention long enough to …

"Keep moving," he breathed it cornering into the chamber. Passing the first open stall he thought of the condition of the victim he and Jade retrieved from the river. More fuel.

With victims from the sixth and fifth stall loaded and making the trip to the surface, he passed the three-quarter marker, now familiar with each leg of the journey. Unlevel surface demanded this section be navigated with eyes locked on the ground, drifting the gurney left and right to avoid larger rocks in its path. When he put his head back up, a man blocked him, standing dead center of the tunnel ahead, his shadow all but consuming the stretcher. Drex couldn't see detail, cast in total darkness blocking the dim from above, all he could discern at first was an outline. Rotating back and forth to night vision before exiting, he'd switched out too soon. His eyes adjusted and as the image cleared the shadow did something unexpected.

It raised a hand to its face and motioned with a finger for him to stay quiet. He recognized the frame more as it closed the distance. Agent French, having his location pinned had run the forest to meet him in his struggle. Drex exhaled, his breath heaving out with relief he almost didn't want to allow himself to feel. Without a sound, French grabbed hold of one side of the stretcher as Drex shifted position and they careened the rest of the way with ease.

It wasn't until they broke outside, with the first signs of dusk creeping over the trees, that French spoke. "Zac alerted us after your request. We have everyone on standby to airlift and close in on your word, sir. I just couldn't leave you out here—"

"Thanks, French. Perfect timing. Have you heard anything more from Zac or Carmichael?" Drex asked, unbelting the unconscious women and lowering them to the site with the others. Six. Too many and not enough, he thought.

"Zac reported he'd devised a way to draw Silas to his local. Haven't heard anything since." French spoke with eyes trained on the unconscious lineup of victims. "This is…"

"I know. Don't go there yet. We're not done," Drex warned as the two raced back inside the mine. "With any luck they're working together to keep him busy or bring him down. We have three more to bring up before shifting our objective."

"Three? I thought there were at least four left." French said it with his eyes locked dead ahead.

"So did I." Drex felt a pang of regret knowing the twelfth room was intended for the last victim taken. Errie. Jade's friend. So close to the final extraction, he checked the faces of those remaining below before they loaded them on the gurney. "Damn."

"Sir?" French asked, strapping the two women securely beneath the belt.

"Detective Carmichael's friend," he said. "She isn't here." The words barely left his lips when the report of gunfire echoed overhead. Distant, the threat posed hit both agents and they read each other's thoughts.

French grabbed hold of the gurney and bolted out ahead, pushing like he was made more of iron than muscle and sinew. Drex threw the last victim over his shoulder and followed, ducking and weaving in the dark, fighting to reach the last light of day and wondering the whole time if the next bullet's impact would hit a whole lot harder.

FORTY-THREE

Gunfire erupted from the next room, its reverberation echoing off every stone surface surrounding Jade and cascading down the tunnels. She dropped to the ground to minimize the chance of catching a bullet in the crossfire. Both men flew past her, one grazing her shoulder with their leg in a dead heat back to the darkest realm of the cavern. Not seeing clearly, Jade couldn't get a bead on either man without casting herself into the chase, and if she did, who would find Errie? Her mind whirled as her feet flew in pursuit with evasive action. The larger of the two she identified as the criminal she sought but the second man was inches shorter than Drex so who?

Charles Silas turned his back to her exposing the gun he'd shoved into his belt as he caught the smaller man, who disabled his electrical system, with both hands lifting him off the floor. When his head raised above the man's broad shoulders, Jade recognized Zac, struggling for freedom. He hadn't a chance but fired a single shot before releasing his weapon, grabbing at his pocket in search of something else. The Occultus, not breaking stride from the chase, used the momentum to catapult Zac over the railing Jade ran across earlier. Knowing what awaited him, the endless drop into the abyss, she knew better than to call out but regret expelled in a breath too loud. The Occultus swiveled and time stopped as they stood face-to-face.

"You take a step and I'll shoot you dead and you'll join him," she promised, her voice brimming with hatred. "Toss your weapon to me and fold your hands behind your head."

His face wore the purest expression of shock she'd ever witnessed. He truly didn't expect a single person to infringe on his domain let alone more than one and a female cop no less. He didn't comply but he didn't move either. He stared her down. Even in the dim remnants of light his eyes were haunting.

"Where are the women?" she asked, gun trained on him. "Where are you holding them?"

He cocked his head, studying her, sizing her up. "Safe," he said. She caught his eyes drifting directly behind her but couldn't risk glancing.

"Toss your gun and put your hands—" In a breath, he charged her lunging forward not to make contact but close enough to smack her weapon from her grasp. She pulled the trigger before it was sent flying across the smooth stone surface into the darkness beyond reach. She ran like hell in the direction of her weapon and away from the canyon. His stride was twice hers and he was highly motivated to end her interference. Catching the reflection off the black barrel, Jade dove landing with the gun at her side. Her only thought was to regain control and extract the location of Errie and the other women but any hope of that vanished as a report exploded off the tunnel's stone surfaces.

Her eyes darted to the gun not yet fully within her grasp, then to her body in a split-second sweep for an entrance wound, and finally at her attacker. Her nostrils picked up the unmistakable scent of burned nitrites as her eyes followed a curl of smoke off the body of Charles Silas. The big man staggered with arms clenching his midsection back over the unstable rock to the very ledge she climbed off of to apprehend him. Then he slid out of sight into the fall. Checking again, her eyes swept the scene registering that the trajectory of the bullet came from behind her where Zac discarded his gun before being tossed to his death. Turning her head, awaiting execution, she watched a shadowy figure advance quickly from the blackness.

John.

"Are you hit?" he asked, rushing to her. "Did he get a shot off?"

"What have you done?" she said, anger and fear brewing together. "You shot him and killed any chance of finding the women!" Her mind spun, enraged at the prospect of dealing with the murder of Silas amid the defeated rescue of his victims, clouding her focus until she realized John was yelling back.

"The walkie!" he said it multiple times before she connected him pointing at the light blinking to indicate incoming contact.

"Carmichael here," Jade said into its mic adjusting the volume but the voice on the other end spoke over her not registering.

"… if you read…found the women…taking them to safety… nine…repeat nine. Nine and twelve unaccounted for. Jade, Errie is not here. Do you…your friend is not here." Agent Drex, his voice desperate with a mix of fear and exhaustion had been trying to alert her to the discovery of the victims. For whatever reason Errie was not among those he was in contact with. A tormenting mix of relief for those rescued and fear for Errie's fate washed in.

Jade tried again to return comms, but John tore the device from her hand. "We have to go now!" He was screaming and she realized the violent altercation at the hands of a killer threw her back into her childhood home with the Redeemer, and for a second or two, interrupted reality.

"I am not leaving until I find her!" Jade sprang off the ground, stomped back deeper into the mine. John caught up to her as she entered the electrical room Zac had fled from. Inside she felt around an obvious electrical box until locating a lever. Pushing it a second set of overhead light burst on.

"No!" John shouted at her, grabbing her hand before she touched the panel again. "The entire place is rigged to blow! It's why I came and why we have to get the hell out now. Explosives!"

"Jesus Christ." Jade said it, reading the certainty in John's eyes.

"You go! I can't, Errie isn't with the others and I can't…how do you know? The explosives, how…"

"I found a victim; she escaped out of a hatch and fell down have the damn mountain. I brought her to your trailer to be rescued but as I was leaving—"

"The nurse," Jade said it without volition. "I identified her escaping from the west side and then we lost her."

"She saw them, the explosives," John said, his breathing ragged and eyes wild. "We are leaving together."

"John, I will not go without knowing she's…" Jade spoke, walking deeper into the room. The metal box ahead suddenly gained a possible purpose as a container full of explosives. Tipping her head to inspect it, Jade jumped at the face staring back at her blankly with frozen eyes. "What the actual fuck?"

"Now you sound like her," John said, staring at the popsicle girl behind the glass.

"What?" Jade asked, wondering how in the hell she was supposed to extract a frozen woman from a metal box and save Errie before explosives brought a city of rock down on them.

"The nurse I found," John said while putting his hand on her arm to guide her out. "You can't save this one, there's no way to restore human flesh once frozen. The lunatic was insane. I'm sorry for whoever she is but—"

"What about the nurse?" Jade asked, her instinct narrowing her focus to this one pivotal point.

"She was unconscious, mostly rambling but swore like a trucker. Little bit of a thing, I thought she was a child she was so small—"

"Like a ballerina?" Jade physically felt her eyes light from within. "John, is she okay?"

"She's in bad shape but they should have her by now. I left her to come get you. She said to tell you about the explosives and…"

"John, that's Errie. You said she swore half conscious?"

"Yes. The profanity made me realize she wasn't a child. She was so covered in dirt and…I thought…I saved a ballerina?"

Despite their dire predicament, if she blew with the mountainside, she'd die happy. Errie wasn't hidden somewhere in the rooms with the frozen girl. She was being rescued. "You did, John. I'll thank you when we're out of here."

John hesitated, casting his eyes over the cavern. "There," he said, pointing to a small depression in the rock wall of the tunnel they entered through. Jade missed it completely on her approach, her penlight limiting details on the opposite outer wall. "It should take us out closer to the bear pit."

"The bear pit?" Jade questioned him with strides becoming a full-out run. Being blown to bits was no longer on her docket for the day.

"By your trailer," John corrected. "Climb fast."

"No shit?" she said, casting a downward glance his way before disappearing inside a laddered shaft. With space to climb unimpeded, she still felt the stone closing in around her. If an explosion was imminent, the ladder out made for a perfect cannon and they its ammo. Her hands clenched every rung up a little hard, a little faster.

"No wonder you're friends; you sound just like her." John climbed with hands grabbing the rungs brushing her feet as they left them.

Jade never contemplated the hatch being closed until it came into view a few feet ahead. "What if it doesn't—"

"I pried them all open the day I knew what you were here for," he said from below.

Fresh air hit and was never as welcome as she unlatched and pushed the lid open. She climbed free and turned reaching to help John, knowing if the mine blew, they were in no way clear of risk. "Follow me," he said, racing, sliding, and floundering down an embankment. Jade was glad the shadow of dusk hid from clarity. Holding her hand, he guided her until the forest became familiar. Back on the western slope he stopped short on level ground, a distance from the mine and out of breath. "Go back to your trailer, the forest will flood with your people once they know he's no longer a threat. I'll take the bear pit game trail back to stay out of sight."

"John, you shot him and—" There was so much she hadn't

addressed, so much still threatening the future and a potential bomb ticking.

"Your agent shot him, his weapon." John handed over Zac's spent gun. "I know I'm not out of the woods." He said it exhausted but smiling. "You know where to find me and I'll be there, but go to your friend, get the hell out of here."

Jade glanced both directions and knowing all he'd done and risked, she nodded and took off racing for Errie and safety. John vanished as he did and she pulled her walkie. "Drex, it is rigged to blow!" she barked breathless between leaps over unstable earth. "Drex, I'm out, get away from the mine!"

"Jade, French and I have backup transporting them to be airlifted from base camp. What the hell do you…"

Drex's voice was the last thing she heard before a blast imploding from the mine's core shook the ground and altered the face of The Divide. Jade watched, thrown to the forest floor, as the east bank of the canyon crumbled in on itself. When the rock met the river below, the dust and debris cloud cast the forest into a blind fog. If not for Errie, she would've stayed there, collapsed on the moss watching the aftermath swirl over the treetops of the western ridgeline. Struggling to regain her footing, Jade focused on the path she knew and bolted for the Airstream and Errie hoping everyone else was free of the impact zone and wondering if more was to follow and how or what ignited the disaster.

With the Airstream in view, she replayed every moment since the Occultus cast his shadow in the hallway. Both he and Zac, poor Zac, aimed on the electrical room. Was Zac aware of the criminal's intention to blow the mine and tried to prevent it to buy his team time? Or did Zac's interference, the power outage, cause the explosion. Was that why the Occultus' last stare shot over Jade's shoulder to the same room, or was it the frozen girl drawing him? She didn't know and glancing at the newly formed rockslide on the eastern side she was sure they never would.

Jade's heart raced with fear and excitement to lay eyes on Errie, hands more, to make contact and know she was real and alive. It distorted her emotions and ability to process what waited inside the trailer.

Errie battered, blackened by mine dust, dirt, and blood, swollen and gaunt at the same time, lay barely recognizable on the sofa. A radio sat beside her, an empty bottle and an open med kit. Her eyes were closed, and Jade feared the worst sliding to her side. She didn't reach her when Errie opened her eyes and spoke.

"Lock it, please." Errie's eyes were on the door. "I've wanted to since I got here. Don't know how…I couldn't get up. I think my leg is broken. It's damn good to see you, sister."

Jade spun, locked the metal door, and rushed to Errie's side. "It is so damn good to see you."

"Even like this? Christ you are fucking desperate, aren't you?" Errie's dry lips cracked as she smiled, blood seeping down from the corner of her mouth.

"Jesus." Jade grasped her as gently as possible and held on for dear life.

"I knew…" Errie fought to breathe, to speak. "You'd come find me. Tell her he never touched me."

Jade pulled back from the embrace enough to be face-to-face with her friend. "How?"

"I ran before he came back that first day. I was in the depths of hell this whole time. I heard it blow."

"Yes. Christ. I have to get you outta here and to the hospital. We don't know if that's the last of it." Jade spoke coming back to the realization of their circumstance. She stood gathering the radio and locating her truck keys to drive Errie and her out of The Divide. Her friend was conscious but so damaged Jade feared internal bleeding along with a host of other similar critical risks.

"Is he dead?" Errie asked, pulling her swollen lip inside her mouth, smearing the blood like hellish lipstick unaware.

"Yes. I believe so he—" Jade never got to finish her sentence. A bullet aimed at her head detonated into the glass of the kitchen window, followed by two more. Absorbing its shock, Jade readied her gun. "Stay down. I'm done with this motherfucker."

Jade made herself an open target, counting shots as they

followed her across the trailer windows to the doorway. "That's five, asshole," she said, throwing open the trailer door. Half his size, disappearing into his shadow, she flew across the gravel, closing the distance between them in seconds, and as he rushed her, she planted a single round into the dead center of his forehead. Charles Silas fell face down, his head brushing her outstretched gun hand as he landed at her feet.

"My family built that trailer. Bulletproof, you sick fuck." Jade spoke as his body crumpled.

She didn't look down at the killer's end. Instead, her eyes were glued to John, running in behind Silas, carrying the nurse. When their eyes met, an understanding passed between them. Jade ran back to the trailer, grabbed her keys, and hit the fob unlocking her truck as John angled to place the dying woman in its back seat.

"Where?" Jade asked, racing back to carry Errie to the passenger side.

"The bear pit," John said, his eyes gleaming with moisture. "She doesn't have much time. Drive fast." After Jade loaded Errie, he slammed the doors while she leaped into the driver's seat and revved the engine. She sent gravel behind propelling a dust cloud around John, as he stood abandoned with the body of the Occultus at his feet.

FORTY-FOUR

Anticipating a longer drive to the general hospital with Errie and the nurse, Jade didn't travel five miles before meeting a highway blockade and a waiting ambulance. John's radio reach-out was received, and medical support dispatched. They awaited clearance to come closer when the explosives halted them at the police checkpoint. She was grateful Amy wasn't at this end of the area. Seeing Errie in her current state would burn the painful image into her brain, never to be erased and they'd all paid enough.

Jade helped transfer the two women and could only hope they both made it as the ambulance lights vanished into the distance. Medical staff demanded she accompany them back for care and it wasn't until they pointed it out that she realized a bullet grazed her sometime during the struggle soaking her side in blood. A flesh wound wasn't getting in her way. She didn't know how the rest of her new team fared before or after the explosion. She hadn't had contact with Drex since the detonation caused the rockslide.

Slamming the door of her truck with its engine still running, she sped past the flashing lights of the duty cars limiting highway access with her foot firmly positioned on the accelerator. She didn't let up until sliding too quickly to a stop at their base camp. Her boots hit the gravel the same time Drex burst from the tent closest, informed she was on route by officers at the last checkpoint. He didn't ask permission, nor did she take the time to grant it when he embraced her in a bear hug, neither releasing as they stood alone in the car park.

"I thought the worst after I couldn't reach you," he said, not letting go.

"Me too. It wasn't great. He escaped and I killed him at the site of my trailer on the western edge," she said, pulling away with a sheepish grin for having illegally inhabited the restricted forest.

Drex laughed, letting her go. "I knew it. I'll send the team in to recover the body."

"Send away, they'll be pulling slugs out of the side of my Airstream. There wouldn't be coverage for that, would there?"

"Funny," he said.

"The victims?" she asked, scared to hear the answer.

"All nine were transported to safety. I won't lie; they're in bad shape but they're alive."

"Errie and the nurse are on their way to the hospital too," she said, dragging a boot, cutting a hard line in the dirt. "Errie evaded him from the day she arrived, found her in the forest, and the mine beat her up pretty badly on its own. Odds aren't good on the nurse. She did escape and then fell into a deadfall bear trap. It was old enough not to impale her but…"

"I won't ask how you managed to get her out," he said, shaking his head at the irony. "And Zac?"

Jade dropped her head and inhaled a deep breath. "He fought Silas and if it wasn't for him, maybe none of us go home. Silas threw him into the underground lake. I don't know if anyone could survive the fall, let alone find a way out but I know there was one because Silas made it out injured. We need choppers scouring the river downstream, I'll take them if—"

"No, show me on the map. We can't put them up until it's safe to fly. They're not combat pilots." Drex reminded her the immediate access to helicopters meant local dispatch and no one experienced in flying over a possibly live threat of secondary explosions in a rock canyon known for wild updrafts. "He's my rookie. I'll find him and bring him home one way or another."

Jade pulled out her phone, brought up the map, and indicated where Drex should focus the search based on the information John gave her about the real point of departure from the underground river of the victim he moved. "I'm really hoping he's in one piece. He deserves to walk out of this and he's the only one who can corroborate what I saw down there." Jade watched as headlights approached from the highway.

"Which was?" Drex asked, eyes locked on the vehicle, his expression somber.

"Drex, Silas constructed a gauntlet, like a medieval challenge to torture his victims. I saw what the woman we found endured before plummeting to her death." Jade's stomach turned at the memory.

"It was likely a test to deem them worthy, that whole religious ritual thing not that any of it matters now buried under thousands of tons or rock," he said, more concerned with the outcome for all of them then the deranged motivations of Silas.

"That's not all," she continued as a truck pulled in behind hers. Its lights became a spotlight on the two of them. "I found...well Zac drew me in there...a woman, young, preserved, frozen in some type of cryostat container." Jade spoke with the vision of the girl's frozen stare haunting her thoughts.

"Jesus," he said, staring at her side. "You've been hit. You're bleeding. You need to go in and get that looked at tonight. That is an order."

"It's a flesh wound, I'm fine. I want to go over everything with you," she said.

"We'll regroup to review all the evidence after the explosive experts deem the area secure. It's fucking disaster and the media is closing in. Given the landslide, the preserved girl may never be found. Frozen, she was out of the equation a long time ago. Send me your notes. We'll trade and reconvene. Pretty sure your ride is here," Drex said it taking a step back from her as Kane ran the lot to reach her. Before he made it to her side, Drex smiled down at her, a defeated acceptance in his eyes. "If you need me...ever...you have my number." He turned his back and walked away before Kane threw his arms around her. Feeling the familiar warmth of his embrace, Jade relaxed for the first time in so many days, but her eyes followed the man leaving.

John didn't take a scenic route back to the cabin, instead he used a shortcut over a forgotten rail bridge to close the distance fast without being seen by any approaching choppers. He expected once the dust cloud dispersed, the feds would swarm the forest along with explosive experts. So much of their sacred evidence was sealed beneath metric tons on rock but if the victims survived, they carried the truth of the horrors below in their memories. And he knew memories like that didn't fade fast or easily.

With thick tree branches arching and blending overhead, the forest reclaimed the short bridge. Overgrowth transformed it indistinguishable from the natural foliage flanking it. Only the sound of his well-worn boots impacting the rail ties announced it as manmade. Halfway across, the valley beneath opened up to a vast view of the river from both north and south. One disappearing into a sea of endless green, the other into the now damaged eastern side of The Divide. He stopped here, protected, to breathe and reflect inside the woods he loved. They would not be his again for a while. He'd be forced to remain hidden until they completed their investigation of the aftermath. He could do that.

With every muscle aching in a cascade from one to another of pain, he would embrace quiet time inside the cabin with Scythe, who by now was very cross with him and would require devoted attention and treats. A far better outcome than the alternative.

Detective Carmichael would return for her answers. Oddly, he was almost looking forward to giving them. She was good and not just defender and protector good, but all in good. And there was something more.

The way she'd burst from her trailer, racing into a direct line of fire to take down a criminal diabolical and damn determined to say the least? He knew that kind of fearlessness. He once was it.

Despite everything that transpired, a new hope swelled in his chest. Relaxing before continuing the last leg home, his eyes examined the new landslide. It all but rerouted a section of the river. Not in a way that jeopardized the forest, just an additional elbow in the existing snake. The real violence all occurred beneath the picturesque expanse. John appreciated that the above-ground terrain remained unaffected by the criminal's intrusion.

His eyes swept the riverbed below as breath replenished him for the trek ahead. About to move on, he shook his head, defeated, swearing to the woods he loved. "Oh come on, for Christ's sake." Far below him on the shore, something didn't fit. On focused inspection, he realized begrudgingly why. The shape lying half in and half out of the water had two legs, two arms, and would've walked upright if it weren't dead or unconscious. Recognizing the flap jacket of the feds on its back, John knew he couldn't just leave the person there without consequence to both him and them.

Crossing back over the bridge with a regrettable purpose, John pushed back into high gear sliding and running to the body. The young man was unconscious, but didn't appear to be shot or beaten by anything other than the river. Sheer exhaustion knocked him out. He was alive and in relatively good condition. With no choice, John uploaded the kid over shoulders, not thanking him for the added weight. He plodded along the shoreline upstream until within proximity too close for comfort of the collapsed mine. Finding the familiar fork between the underground river dirty and turned up by the landslide, he placed the agent near its edge but out of harm's way hoping the kid regained consciousness after he was out of sight but before animals returned to the area.

With night descended and the forest cooling fast, he hiked at a pace less than a run but faster than a walk, focusing only on the next step to avoid any other possible distractions. Inside the cabin, met by vocal complaints from Scythe, he used his burner phone to contact Jade with one last message.

Your young agent made it out, at the fork. Get him before the animals do. Unconscious.

It wasn't a rescue, but that was never his job. He hit send stepping back into the shadows hoping they embraced him once again.

FORTY-FIVE

Kane didn't want to let Jade go, but he yearned more to get her the hell out of the reach of the forest and all she'd endured there and back to civilization. His eyes scanned her, registering damage on the way back to his truck. She offered to drive her Denali and follow him, insisting she was fine. He helped her into his passenger seat and closed the door, jogged to the driver's side, and leaped in.

"Tex is coming for it," he said, holding her hand while he reversed back onto the highway, relieved to be leaving the base camp in their rearview. "Got a ride from patrol. He'll bring it home and meet us at the hospital. Are you in pain?" he asked, motioning to the injury seeping blood at her side.

"Can't feel it," she said. "Adrenaline."

He nodded, watching the road. "So how bad is it? Errie?"

"I killed the Occultus outside our trailer," she said. He ignored the empty road and locked eyes, his demanding details. "He made it out after falling into the underground river. He was shot. I don't know how he survived, but he's done now. Drex is sending a team in. I'm not sure when we'll see our Airstream again, but I love that trailer."

Her voice faded, distant into bad memories. "I'll have Drex call me when they're done with it," he reassured her. "Tex and I will get it cleaned up and bring her home."

"Okay. I want it back," she said, shaking free of the spell. "Errie is in bad shape, Kane. The only grace is all the damage she endured came from the mine and her efforts to escape. He never laid a hand on her after that first day."

"Well that's a damn good thing because the others…I called Drex as they were being airlifted. The violation…it's really awful. And thanks to you, over."

"Not just me; I had help," she said and then hesitated. "He's nothing like Wenzel."

"Drex? Yeah, he handled it all, including our involvement like a pro." Kane didn't face her. He let silence drift between them. He had questions, an endless stream but tonight was not the time.

"Not only him," she added. "The others were great too. I just wish…his youngest agent, Zac—Kane, he risked everything to buy time to get the victims out and it cost him his life. Silas picked him off the ground like he was made of straw and tossed him into the abyss. I think Zac sent a round into Silas, and maybe I wouldn't have stood a chance if he hadn't wounded him."

"He fell in the same place Silas did?" Kane asked, his heart rate slowing finally as they talked. "Any chance he made it out before—"

"I don't know? And now the whole place is a landslide, and we can't even get in to search for him."

"Hang on," Kane pulled the truck off to the side of the road and grabbed his phone, looking up a number. "Send me the location where he'd most likely exit the mine." Seconds later, he was on with a friend of Jackson's. The owner of a chopper and former Air Force. "Do you think you could fly a couple passes over Divide coordinates if I send them your way? The regulars aren't schooled in updrafts and explosions." He listened for a few seconds and then added, "Can you do it using night vision and heat trace the ground? We have a friend who may have made it out past the explosion site, but he'll likely be injured and need air transport to medical."

Kane pulled back onto the road, Jade staring at him, grateful.

"Thanks, buddy, I owe you critical. Let me know when you find him." When he hung up and set his phone in its holder, Jade grabbed his hand back until her phone pinged. She read the incoming message and smiled. "If I fall asleep, wake me when they find him?" Holding tight, she allowed her head to drop back into the headrest, and they drove the rest of the way in silence.

Hospital staff raced in groups through its hallways attending to eleven of the twelve Occultus' victims, Jade, French, who sustained minor injuries, and a slew of regular patients contained in a separate wing. She laughed, walking in recognizing Errie's voice, a string of profanity coming from her, as medical staff set the injury to her leg and knowing she'd be fine. Perhaps more foul, if that was possible, but fine. As much as Jade didn't want to infringe on their precious time, knowing home waited on the other side of care she cooperated as they stitched and wrapped her wounds. French and her shared a room separated by a curtain she drew back from between them to compare notes.

"So he discovered the women in stalls on the north end before I even made it to the underground canyon?" she asked.

"Yeah, but they weren't at the entrance. It was a good ten-minute drop downhill through the tunnels when we were racing it," French explained.

"You said they were all drugged? How did you get them—"

"I only came in at the last minute, right before the shots rang out. Drex carried them all out, two at a time on a gurney—"

"Uphill through the tunnels, alone?" Jade asked with a dire picture forming in her mind.

"Yeah. I'm surprised we haven't seen him in here. The stall area had the drugs emitting overhead in the forced air system. He was subjected to them while rescuing the women. I've never seen anyone…"

"He needs to get checked out," she said, worried for Drex's welfare.

"Okay, you tell him," French said as a nurse returned to tend to a wound on his leg.

"How did you know...about the drugs?" she asked, fully wrapped and given the wave of release.

"Victim nine," French said. "The nurse, she was in the worst condition but stopped staff to give us the most detail. We found out just before you arrived. I think she was afraid she wouldn't make it. We'll go back to interview her more thoroughly when everyone is stable."

Jade nodded, exiting the room with the physician who sewed them up. "You wouldn't happen to know which room the nurse is in? I'd like to check on her...thank her before I go."

With directions to the allocated recovery room, Jade braced for the impact of seeing the extent of the nurse's injuries. The list was immense. Broken leg, compound fracture of her arm, extreme dehydration, and a myriad of serious injuries sustained before her initial escape or during it. If coherent, she didn't plan to ask her a single question, just thank her and try to provide some measure of comfort.

The image was as bad or worse than Jade imagined. Everywhere she looked, damage had been inflicted. Sad for her and not willing to add to her trauma, Jade turned to quietly leave, but the woman was awake and attempting to speak. Despite the litany of physical challenges, her mouth and voice remained unscathed.

"You're one of them, aren't you?" she asked, slowly and from a depth of great pain. Easy to guess, given her battered police attire and bandages.

"One of the detectives? Yes," Jade said, moving closer so her voice could be easily heard.

"They said you were out there the whole time...searching for us?" Her eyes were kind and bright. Jade didn't know how.

"Yes. I was out there from the day the last victim arrived. She's a dear friend of mine. I am so glad you're here now and safe."

"You're the one who warned me, the one who yelled across the canyon." She spoke, studying Jade's face.

"Yeah, that's me."

"Can I ask you...they wouldn't tell me...is he dead?" It was information she shouldn't be handing out, but Jade understood this assurance would allow her to heal.

"Yes. I killed him. He is gone. And all my team will be glad to hear the nurse is in safe hands now." Jade backed up readying to leave. The woman desperately needed rest.

"No," she said, her voice gaining a defiant strength. "Tell them Milan is safe. That's my name, Milan. I'm not the person he kidnapped from my home...I'm not the nurse anymore."

Jade understood, her lips pulled tight in agreement as she nodded. "I will tell them. Milan, it's a pleasure to meet you. You are incredible, fearless and strong, and you beat him. I'll be back when you're feeling better to answer any more questions you have."

The brave woman rolled her head to the side, exhaled deeply, and let her eyes rest on an old leather satchel hooked to the bed. Jade left, praying what she saw behind those closed lids was family, home, and nothing more.

FORTY-SIX

The Airstream never appeared more inviting illegally perched on a new plateau on the western ridge of The Divide with a new coat of paint and upgrades. And, given federal authority to be there for evidence collection, Jade chose to view the permission granted as a lifelong residency pass. After the dust settled literally and figuratively, Zac was air transported to the hospital helipad and given a positive prognosis, and they all recovered and reconvened to close the Occultus case, the forest called her back. And John.

Following a path she traveled once in fear and desperation, a sense of peace was born from the chaos. So much evidence was brought to light. They assumed the frozen girl was Charles Silas's sister, Molly. A brilliant engineer and scientist of sorts, he found a way to preserve her in cryostat form until a cure for her rare form of leukemia could be found. Achieving that, the evil that twisted him while she slept guaranteed her death and burial beneath tons of rock, never to share the genius that brought her that far.

Jade and Kane were set to meet out at Captain Grey's estate in a few days. Instructed to arrive hours before the others, Jade expected a rundown on her participation in the case and his course of action in fully reinstating Kane and Jackson. His voice, when she spoke with him being discharged from the hospital, said there was more underlying his urgency to meet. For now, she was happy to be walking the forest that helped her, and the recluse it housed, win against a madman.

No one knew about John. Not Kane or Drex, and certainly not Grey.

If he was responsible for the nun murders some three decades earlier, she required context before deciding how to proceed. His existence threatened trust she spent a lifetime forging with Grey and every other important relationship she had. So why risk it? Why not hand him over the moment she woke in his cabin? The answer was complicated and simple. He saved her life, the lives of victims and Zac, and did it all risking his. These were not the actions of a cold-blooded killer. She knew born killers, intimately, and he was not one.

Skirting the new river route and viewing the transformed eastern ridge, she couldn't help but think it appeared solid, less treacherous. It hid no criminal beneath its skin. Even the weight of her pack was welcome, it held replenishing supplies for John and toys for Scythe, not survival gear for battling monsters. Sun broken free, casting shards of light through the forest understory making it appear lit from within. And in the early days of summer set a perfect temperature. Jade breathed it in, relieved the case ended with Errie and her team safe. She would carry regret for not reaching Lauren soon enough but that was the trade-off for being in homicide. Regret came with the territory.

John didn't come out to greet her but the cabin coverage of greenery was pinned back with a walking stick and Scythe waited to lead her inside. John sat at his table watching water fall and the blurred forest expanse beyond it, tea and his same clay mugs out waiting. And something else she hadn't seen before.

In a large plastic zip-locked bag, an article of clothing rested under his hand.

His eyes lit when he turned her direction but they revealed a sadness she suspected existed but never witnessed so raw.

"John?" She slid onto the chair beside him as the cat brushed up against his leg, pushing into it and not breaking contact.

"She was my daughter," he said, traveling down a distant and horrible road in his memory. "No one knew. My best friend, really my brother, he made mistakes and broke Lace's heart and when he left, I feared she wouldn't recover. I was too close, too convenient. When he came back from the mission, changed and committed, I couldn't tell him. She begged me not to. When we found out she was expecting...I didn't know until the baby was two. By then I was her uncle, and we were a happy family. It was enough for me until the Catholic school."

Jade watched his face transform. The sadness replaced by sheer rage, his hand gripped down on the package on the table and Scythe backed away, lying out of reach, eyeing John.

"I dropped her off sometimes, picked her up when her mom and dad couldn't. She was good, not great, but okay. Then she switched sides at the campus to attend middle school. We all noticed changes in her behavior but no one, none of us imagined the brutality they inflicted. Her mother was set to pull her. She'd gone in several times, complaining to the head of school over the use of intimidation and ridicule to control the students. The Headmaster seemed oblivious, more interested in the school's perceived reputation and registration demand than what was happening under her nose."

Jade drank her tea, engaged but questioning how a strict education married into the case Grey couldn't solve and all he told her about it. Three nuns were found murdered. The cause of death, strangulation. And no witnesses came forward, no DNA or trace evidence left behind. Scrubbed clean. No motive came to light. The violence occurred in the home the nuns shared but security cameras on the street leading to it caught no one. And the strangulations were severe. A difficult way to kill another, strangulation demanded enormous effort from the perpetrator. For all three to be killed in this same manner, the same night, roughly minutes apart required inhuman strength or...incredible hatred. The kind Jade watched filter into John's eyes.

"I wasn't notified. I didn't know until her mother called me to the hospital. Everyone, the whole family gathered there praying. They said she'd fallen down a flight of stairs but the wounds...I returned to the school that same day inspected the staircase for myself. No blood, no telltale marks, there had to be for what occurred. Then there was her uniform. It didn't show evidence of impact. So many of her bones, broken..."

The picture forming said at very least John couldn't have been of sound mind when the attack happened. Not following a loss of this nature.

"There wasn't a scuff and the nuns had access to her clothing. Problem was I knew she wasn't wearing that uniform when she attended that day. It was a special celebration and students were permitted to wear appropriate clothes of their choice." John ran his hand through his gray hair and stared out the window seeing into the past.

When he lifted his palm off the bag, Jade recognized a girl's dress, ripped and bloodied but old, some thirty years old? "John where did you get the dress?" she asked.

"From the nun's closet, hanging with the others," he said, his trance not broken.

"Others?"

"Yes," he said, locking eyes. "They killed five girls before mine. I tracked the names, accident reports, and evidence until I was sure. It took months. Then I confronted them. The worst of them, Sister Magdalene, laughed...didn't even attempt to deny it. Her and her sisters thought I would leave. They believed themselves untouchable because they had been for so long."

He stared back down at the table. "Killing them was the second hardest thing I've ever done. Burying my little girl was the first. I couldn't let anyone else suffer that and no one, not the cops, the church, the administration of the school, would even consider their involvement."

"And the accidents? I'm guessing they stopped after the nuns were dead," Jade said, seeing the pieces of the picture come together.

"They did. No one suspected me because in their view, I didn't exist. I wasn't related. I was a family friend. And I'm sorry I had to do that. I know I couldn't do it again if I had to now but…"

Jade had no words until, "I'm so sorry for your loss," she said, placing a hand over his. "I could take the dress, have it tested and—"

"For what? It won't bring my daughter back and it doesn't excuse what I did in the eyes of the law. You know, she'd be about your age if she lived. If…I hadn't dropped her off for school that day. At least I lived long enough to save one ballerina. So now you know and you can decide what happens to me next."

"I'll take the dress into evidence and I will close this case, but not today. Maybe not while you're alive." Jade stared into his eyes, an understanding of two who faced the same type of evil and lived harboring its fallout passed between them. She stood and retrieved the bag from under John's hand. He let it slip free and watched as she crossed the room. He tilted his head left, and she followed the prompt to round the corner and see a hole in the floorboards, a chest exposed beneath. She placed the bag inside, closed the lid, replaced the boards, and returned to John.

Taking his hand in hers she led him to the front door of the cabin, the one leading to a stone outcrop and the backside of the waterfall. "Is it safe to go out?" she asked.

"Yes," he said. "It was built on the rock."

Jade unlocked and opened the door to the porch and a torrent of noise and off-spray. Together they stepped into its rain. He didn't let go of her hand standing beside her. She knew tears consumed them both. John cried for the loss of his child and the burden of taking lives in pursuit of sparing others. Hers were shed for the loss of all the victims she couldn't save beginning with her mother and the burden of tainted blood running through her veins, mixing with her mother's pure lineage. But neither would witness them, The Divide had a way of devouring the gravest secrets.

FORTY-SEVEN

Captain Grey stood with his back to Jade as she walked the expanse of yard to the patio where the scent of brisket filled the air encircling the cookout cove, lounge chairs, and pool deck. As a surrogate father of sorts she learned over the years he possessed many talents having nothing to do with his leadership in crime fighting. Successful investor and chef being two. Seeing him enjoying the day outside the shop and the seriousness of their profession warmed her heart. The secrets she kept from him could spoil that if allowed to but she knew him at the core and decided her choice to protect John aligned with it. Someday she'd find a way to bring the truth of the Nun Murders to light without moral penalty. Until then only The Divide and its sole tenant remained its keepers.

"You're here, good," he said, checking on the meat and sensing not seeing her approach. "I wanted time before the others arrive to discuss a few matters of concern."

"I figured as much," she said, coming to stand beside him, choosing the task of vegetable prep, and selecting her favorite knife from the block on the counter. "Did you hear from the feds yet, receive the case closure file?"

"I did," he said, closing the BBQ lid and turning to face her. "Pretty damn impressive if you ask me and also risky. By your own admission, you confronted the Occultus without backup, injured, at least twice. I'm not pleased about that fact."

"I knew you wouldn't be but trusting me and my independent judgment again, well it's one of the reasons I was so grateful to be assigned to this case."

Grey motioned for her to stop chopping and join him in the lounging chairs. "Kane parking the truck?"

"Yeah, and chatting with Tex," she said, taking the seat next to his. The yard was beautiful, vast, and a second home for her.

As she crossed her feet at the end of the lounger, he smiled. "Keds? Laces untied? Haven't seen your feet in shoes for a while," he said.

"Yeah. Time to remember what off duty feels like," she admitted. "I wasn't out there alone...the team, all they did back home for the investigation."

He nodded his approval. "They would've gone insane without being involved, some more than others. But you *were* alone out there and you did a damn fine job. It wasn't only me you impressed. The feds' assessment was gleaming and unexpected given your headstrong approach. Sounded like you and Agent Lafine became quite a team."

Jade didn't answer right away. She scanned the rolling landscape for a few moments. "Drex was nothing like his cousin, Wenzel, not what I expected."

"I have a strong suspicion he'd say the same about you. He basically did. And whatever relationship you forged will serve us moving forward. We can lean on his contact if needed so...well done."

"He said that?" she asked, her eyes watching Kane and Jackson enter the yard.

Grey waited until she faced him again. "He did. Said if you ever need him, he is a call away."

He read it in her eyes there were feelings there, a deep admiration and possibly something more. He confirmed it, switching subjects before Kane walked within earshot.

"Well here comes trouble," he said to the men, motioning to a cooler full of beer and summer beverages. "So what am I to do with you? 'Mutt 'n' Jeff.' Neither of you listen to a darn word of advice I give. I said two more weeks but you…" He pointed at Tex, waving an accusatory finger. "You go and qualify to be reinstated by mastering the firing range with your left hand. And your counterpart here passes his doctor's assessment at the end of this week. If you waited, you'd all have an extra week of holiday time in this fantastic weather, but no." Grey laughed as Kane snuck a peek at the brisket and gave him a nod of approval.

"So we're back?" Jackson asked, looking eager.

"You can all come back, full duty, a week from Monday," Grey confirmed. "Not sure what you all have against pool time?"

"Not a damn thing, Cap," Jackson said, hip checking Kane off the deck and into the pool fully clothed.

They all burst into laughter as Kane tossed out his soaked sandals and shirt and swam the pool in his khakis. "Tex, you're seriously an ass, you know that?" he yelled. "The least you could do is hand me a beer."

Jackson walked to the pool handing over Kane a drink and sitting on its edge with his pants rolled and legs in the water to join him. Kane's dark skin glistened in the sunlight. Jade mouthed the words 'boxers or jocks' to him. He flashed a mischievous grin and mouthed back 'neither.' Jade shook her head smiling and thanking God he was hers.

Watching her partners, she turned to Grey, keeping her voice low, she asked, "Amy closed Nickolas Leigh's attempted murder case and you let her?"

Grey's hands twisted around his beer bottle. "The evidence confirmed a history of malfunction with the life-sustaining equipment derived from the manufacturing plant and there was nothing tangible to suggest human involvement." Grey waited for a breath and then continued, his voice a whisper. "Even your half brother wanted it closed, Jade. I know there are concerns all around, hell, nothing with links to Nickolas doesn't cause concern, but I believe it's for the best."

She watched his eyes reading much more in them then what was contained in the words he spoke. "Okay," she said. "For now."

Jackson threw off his shirt, jeans, placing them beside his cowboy boots and dove in with Kane as Jade shook her head at them. Kane motioned to the yard behind her and she turned seeing Amy and Errie, moving slowly on crutches, coming to join them. She cast a glance at Grey reading his eyes. "It was bad but believe me, Errie escaped the worst of it." He nodded but she caught his eyes lingering on Amy for a second too long. More had transpired while she was in The Divide than she realized and, despite how often they warned her against it, she knew who she had to visit to make sense of it all.

———————

Jade stood at the nurses' desk outside the private recovery wing holding her badge for her name to be checked against allowance for access in the computer. A few keystrokes later the nurse stared up concerned. "I'm sorry, Detective, you don't appear on the permission list for law enforcement. I know it was recently modified, so maybe—"

"I'm not here in a professional capacity; I'm on the family list. Nickolas is my half brother, though that is to remain classified as noted in the file," Jade said, staring at the door ahead to avoid the nurse's stunned expression and deflect the typical additional questions.

"Of course," the nurse agreed, checking a different screen. "Please go ahead."

The automated doors opened and Jade crossed beyond them, her Ozzy combat boots with lug soles almost silent on the hard tile. She didn't intend to announce her presence today. She knew her way in. She walked the same hall to see him unconscious and paralyzed after she recovered from his attack on her. And many times since watching him transform through his biological family's efforts and manipulations of medical support and the courts.

Kane shot him in the neck at the conclusion to the Redeemer

case and medical staff all but wrote him off, but he survived. His life-sustaining equipment failure should've killed him. Still he lived. They said he'd never recover the ability to move but he was transferred here after his biological grandfather, a celebrated judge, was released from the hospital and awarded conservatorship. Intense therapy and a team of the best and brightest assigned to his case altered that outcome too. Given the uniquely tailored rehabilitation program he was in optimal condition from the waist up and, Jade suspected, more was possible. For reasons she couldn't yet comprehend, he wasn't allowed to leave this earth.

That was the concerning part Grey referred to. Nickolas Leigh, her half brother and the serial killer formerly known as the Redeemer, had power protecting him, and was gaining strength. His confidence was such that he encouraged the closing of the case investigating the medical breech that had threatened his life.

That was more concerning.

Jade rounded the corner expecting him to be sitting comfortably, gleaming from his bed, nurses swooning over him as was the case during most visits. Tempted to decorate his bright room with crime scene photos of his dark deeds, she feared it would only lose her access to him. The people surrounding and protecting his life didn't see him as she did. They never would. But his bed came into view without him in it.

It was empty.

Sticking her head into the hallway, she scanned for staff seeing none. Retracing her steps, resenting the crisp sanitary scent assaulting her nostrils, she ducked into rooms flanking the hall until halfway back to the exit. A nurse adjusting the IV of a sleeping patient was startled by her abrupt presence. She waved her back out into the hall and appeared, annoyed, seconds later. "Are you lost?" she asked, or more accurately demanded.

"No. I'm here to see Nickolas Leigh in room—"

"I know what room he's in, we all do. This is a private facility," the nurse criticized. "If you know his room, why were you poking your head into Mr. Davidson's?" She motioned to the doorway she'd come out.

"Nickolas isn't there," Jade said, recognizing a mild tremor in her voice. "Where is—"

"I'm sorry, miss, but only a select few family members are allowed personal information regarding his care and or his where-abouts including—"

"I know! I'm one of them! Now, where the hell is my brother?" Jade lost all patience. Panic rising to the surface, she forced calm back into her voice. "I'm Detective Jade Carmichael, and I want to know where Nickolas is."

"Okay. I'm sorry, we haven't met before. I didn't know you were…he is undergoing a new therapy off grounds."

"What?" Jade heard the words but was having trouble processing them.

"I said—"

"I heard you. Off grounds where and who issued the authority for him to move from…" Jade spun halfway around and back again, the hallway closing in on her.

"The courts granted it a while ago in the event it was deemed necessary by his team lead. It's a remarkable water therapy and if you haven't noticed, we don't have a pool equipped for it here."

Jade's patience was eroding as visions of Nickolas's last days of freedom bled across the backdrop of her mind. "Where is my brother?"

"You have to ask the physician on call for him today. The name and contact information will be listed on the protocol board in your brother's room." With this, the nurse put her back to Jade, disap-peared inside Davidson's room, and closed the door.

Jade returned to the room Nickolas should have occupied, eyes searching and landing on an information board right of his bed. Pulling her phone from her back pocket, she snapped a picture of the doctor's contact information. Expanding the photo to ensure it clear and readable, she saw something captured in it. Dropping her phone back into her pocket, she stared at a sealed envelope pinned to the bottom left corner of the corkboard. One word was written across its front in handwriting she recognized. She became familiar with it because she'd sent it for analysis during the

Redeemer case. It belonged to Nickolas Leigh. He'd written, **Sister**, in its center.

Jade snatched the letter, flipped it over, broke a wax seal on it, and read.

I knew you would come. Life will always bring us back together. I am healing. I know you wonder about my health and progress. This next leg I must do alone but don't fear, blood of my blood, we will reunite soon. Until then I've done what I could to keep you safe while we are apart. As for Charles and Molly, well, as we both know, some cannot be saved.

Your Loving Brother, Nickolas

A LOOK AT BOOK THREE:
DARK INTENT

COMING SOON

ABOUT THE AUTHOR

As a thriller author, owner of a successful developmental editing company for authors, a ghostwriter, and journalist, J.L. Hughes is grateful to be immersed in her respected field working with other accomplished writers. On the inside cover of dozens of novels, she contributes as editor or ghostwriter to both fiction and nonfiction in every genre from true crime to fantasy, sci-fi to horror—all for the love of story.

J.L. and her family enjoy city life against the adventurous backdrop of the Rocky Mountains.